RANDOM HOUSE

LARGE PRINT

Also by Carolyn Haines
available from Random House Large Print

Buried Bones

SPLINTERED BONES

Carolyn Haines

RANDOM HOUSE
LARGE PRINT

*The Library of Congress has established
a Cataloging-in-Publication record for
this title*

0-375-43248-5

www.randomlargeprint.com

FIRST LARGE PRINT EDITION

10   9   8   7   6   5   4   3   2   1

This Large Print edition published in
accord with the standards of the N.A.V.H.

For Jennifer Jones, Gloria Howard,
and Mitch Walch—true horsemen.

ACKNOWLEDGMENTS

The only two things I ever wanted in life were to ride horses and write books. I'm still working on both of them.

As a child, I often wished I'd been born in an earlier time, one when horses were a necessity instead of a luxury. Older, and wiser, I realize now that a human's relationship with a horse is a gift, and should be considered such.

No less a gift is the friendship of my fellow writers in the Deep South Writers Salon. They kept me on the trail of the story. Many thanks to Renee Paul, Stephanie Chisholm, Rebecca Barrett, Jan Zimlich, and Susan Tanner.

It would be impossible to thank Steve Greene for his help, especially his support and encouragement. His expertise in law enforcement and human nature was, and is, a tremendous resource. He asked the hard questions that made Sarah Booth a smarter gal.

My agent, Marian Young, was invaluable—as a reader, a negotiator, the voice of reason, and as a friend.

Kara Cesare and Kate Miciak at Bantam made the process of editing and creating a book as pleasurable as such a process can be. It's a better book because of their insight and skills.

Once again, the Bantam art department deserves much praise. Jamie Warren Youll—you have the touch.

A special thanks to Kinky Friedman, who generously allowed me the use of his character and himself.

And I must acknowledge my four-legged companions and my "perfect" horses, Miss ScrapIron, Mirage, and Cogar. The outside of a horse is, indeed, good for the inside of a person.

SPLINTERED
BONES

There is something about warm soil that
connects the past and future into the present.
The earth is female in the truest sense of the
word. Life springs from it. It is the power of the
feminine, the base of creation. For a Delaney,
land is the source of family and heritage. For
me, Sarah Booth Delaney, the last of this old
Southern family, the rich soil of the Mississippi
Delta holds the promise of seed and growth—
the fecundity that my own womb has been denied. Or at least denied for the moment.

The black soil was rich and damp beneath
my fingers as I turned the earth with the
trowel. Gardening isn't one of my passions. In
fact, this was my first attempt. But I had been
inspired by a master gardener's words, and the
pull of a hot March sun on this Monday
morning had been irresistible. Beneath my
gentle hands, the ten containers of various
herbs would sprout into lush health. I might

not be Mother Nature, but I was apprenticing as one of her daughters.

In this new venture, I was aided by my heritage. Dahlia House has some of the best topsoil in the world. Anything can grow here. And I had the books of the late Lawrence Ambrose to guide me.

I picked up a plastic container, checking to see that it was lemon basil. I held it aloft, asking the sun to power it to a huge shrub, a Godzilla lemon basil! Holding the basil and my trowel aloft, I felt the power of a gardening goddess. I would yield a crop! And I would never go hungry again!

"Girl, you holdin' that hand spade like Xena about to be struck by lightning. What's got you out here in the hot sun grubbin' around in the dirt like Mr. Green Jeans?"

I lowered the sacred vessel of basil and my trowel and looked into the dark-chocolate eyes of my nemesis and companion, Jitty. Lucky for the rest of the world, Jitty afflicts only me. She's a ghost. An old ghost with a streak of bossiness a mile wide.

"I'm planting an herb garden, if you must know." I knelt back in the earth, searching again for the sense of power and strength that had evaporated.

"Get you a sun hat. You thirty-three. Almost

thirty-four. If you let that sun beat down on you, your neck's gone go all crepey an' look just like puckered chicken skin. You ain't got but a few good years left. You better preserve what you can."

Jitty took a seat on an overturned bucket. Rocking back on my heels I looked at her. Her skin was a smooth milk-chocolate, and it covered a body that curved and swelled in all the right places. Death might not be a pleasant experience, but ghosthood had some definite advantages. She would never age, while I would plump and wither, depending on which stage of decline I happened to be in.

"Gardening is good for you," I said, knowing that logic would never work on Jitty. She was obsessed with one thing and one thing only—getting an heir for Dahlia House so she could continue to reside in the old plantation once I "passed." Prospects for continuing the line weren't looking encouraging.

"What would be good for you would be a little horizontal exercise." Jitty nodded knowingly.

"Lawrence said gardening relieves stress and gives a sense of satisfaction. We'll also have wonderful spices and seasonings to cook with."

Jitty raised one delicate eyebrow. "Cook? You good at fruitcakes—the kind you make and the kind you attract. Listen to me, Sarah Booth, time is runnin' out. Better you figure out how to sprout you a baby and leave the plants to someone else." She stood up and I was shocked to see that she was wearing baggy sweatpants and a sleeveless T-shirt. *My* pants and shirt. "I got us a plan."

"No!" Whatever it was, it was going to be humiliating for me.

"It's a good one."

"No!" She was scaring me.

"Just listen to it. I've got it all figured out. Right here from the safety of Dahlia House—" She suddenly turned her head. "We'll discuss this later. Company's comin'."

Before I could get off my knees to argue with her, I heard the sound of a car pulling into the drive. Instead of stopping at the front, the sleek brown patrol car pulled to the back-yard and Coleman Peters, Sunflower County sheriff, stepped into the March sun.

Tall and lanky, Coleman walked up and rested a booted foot on the landscape timber that marked one boundary of my herb garden. I noted that his boots were worn but polished. Coleman was like that. He took care of things. It was one of his nicest qualities.

"Well, well, Sarah Booth, I didn't know you were a gardener."

Brushing my dirty hands on my jeans, I slowly rose. "I read Lawrence Ambrose's herb book. I thought I'd give it a try. He claims herbs are easy to grow."

Coleman's doubtful expression made me survey the ground I'd trenched by hand. It was still a little weedy.

"I'm delivering a message," he said. His blue eyes were hidden by shades, but his mouth let me know that it was, indeed, bad news.

"I'm flattered. Personal delivery by the top law enforcement official of Sunflower County," I said. "I'm all ears." My attempt at lightheartedness fell flat.

"Lee McBride is down at the jail. She's asking for you." His delivery was completely without inflection.

I was struck by a vivid memory of Eulalee McBride astride a powerful gray stallion, her red hair flying out behind her. She reminded me of a Viking princess. We'd known each other since first grade.

"What's up with Lee?" I tried to keep it casual.

"She's confessed to the murder of her husband, Kemper Fuquar."

Coleman acted like he was on *Dragnet*. Just the facts, ma'am.

"She killed her husband?" Repeating bad

news is a Daddy's Girl tactic to elicit a response from the other party to see exactly what reaction is expected.

"She's confessed."

I sat down on the landscape timber by Coleman's leg and tried to think. Kemper Fuquar had never been on my list of favorite people. He was handsome and charming and entirely worthless. Sure, he looked like Zorro on a horse—dashing and stylish—but there had always been an edge to the man. I didn't run with the horsey set, so my exposure to Kemper had been limited. But the few times I'd been around him, he'd made me ill-at-ease.

"Did she say why she killed him?" I asked. The sun was hot on my back but I didn't want to move. Coleman faced the light, giving me the advantage. I felt I needed it. There was something distinctly odd in Coleman's stiff behavior.

"Lee needs a good lawyer. Maybe you can make her see that. She knows her rights, but she isn't paying much attention to them."

"Did she do it?" I asked him.

Coleman lifted his shades and finally looked at me. "It isn't my job to determine guilt or innocence. That's for a jury."

I knew then I was walking on delicate territory. I just didn't know why. Coleman was a professional, but he'd known Lee for as long as I had. Because of Lee's interest in horses and the outdoors, she'd been close friends with many of the boys, including Coleman.

"Lee confessed to the murder?" I asked, going back to a safe question to which I knew the answer.

"She came in this morning and turned herself in."

"How was he killed?"

Coleman cleared his throat. "It was a bad scene. She said she hit him in the head with something, but it's hard to tell."

"A head wound sounds pretty definite."

"Not after the body's been trampled by a fourteen-hundred-pound horse. There wasn't a solid bone left in him, Sarah Booth."

2

The Sunflower County jail jutted off the east side of the courthouse, an old wing of crumbling red bricks that was an architectural eyesore and looked incapable of holding any serious felons. I'd been inside once before, and I knew it wasn't a place of sunshine and light. Maybe that was what depressed me when I saw Lee sitting on the blue-ticked mattress. She'd always been a creature of the sun and of action, her red hair flaming and her green eyes burning. The woman in the cell had not heard us approach, and her posture registered defeat. Coleman hesitated a moment and then stepped back several feet.

"Eulalee," I said softly, wanting to alert her to my approach. She instantly straightened, once again becoming the undefeatable Viking princess, the slender girl who'd turned her back on inheriting a fortune to follow her dream.

"I knew you'd come, Sarah Booth. I don't have any money and I know a private investigator costs a good bit, but once I'm out of here, there's money coming down the road. By next year, Avenger will be bringing in the stud fees that will put Swift Level in the black." She hesitated a split second. "Can you wait?"

Her green eyes held worry and resignation. In the past few years I'd seen her only a handful of times, and I remembered that she'd been injured on almost every occasion. Horses were dangerous animals. Even when playing, they were capable of inflicting serious damage.

"Money isn't the issue," I lied. Money was always an issue with me as I hung on to Dahlia House by scheming plots and Irish luck. Still, I was more than a little surprised by Lee's blunt admission of financial straits. Lee ran a full-scale breeding and training operation at Swift Level, and it was the home of the very glamorous Chesterfield Hunt. The spit-and-polish, gleaming-white-fence elegance was splashed all over Cece Dee Falcon's society pages during hunt season. There were foxhunts, elaborate hunt breakfasts, hunt balls, hunt blessings—all requiring boodles of money.

"Money isn't the problem, here," Coleman said. He was at my side, and he spoke to me, not Lee. "The trouble is that Lee's confessed. You can't help her, Sarah Booth, as long as she insists that she killed him."

Lee looked at him, a long look that held regret and sorrow and sympathy. "I'd like to speak with Sarah Booth alone," she said.

"Talk to *her,* Lee, then shut up. And get a lawyer. A good one. Boyd Harkey might—"

"No lawyer! I can manage this myself. Sarah Booth is all I need. If she'll help me, I'll be okay."

Coleman's left eyebrow arched up half an inch and spoke volumes of his opinion on that. He said nothing, just turned and left the jail. Lee and I were alone.

"I've made a real mess of things," she said. With Coleman gone, she relaxed her shoulders and I saw how thin she'd become. She had always been lean, but her body was now so sharply defined that it looked as if her shoulder blades might cut through her blouse.

"You want to tell me about it?"

"There's not much to tell. Not much that will make a difference. Right now my concern is for Kip." She bit her lip hard enough to whiten it, and it was sheer willpower that dammed her tears. "I'm worried about her. Will you look out for her until I get out? It's a lot to ask, I know. She's a difficult child. She's smart. Sometimes I think she's too smart. And she's been through a lot. Way too much for a child her age. Could you take her, just for a while?"

"You want her to stay with me?" I wasn't known as the nurturing type.

"Just for a little while."

"Your folks—"

"I'm dead to them."

I'd heard that Lee was estranged from her parents. The gossip around town went that Lee had been disinherited shortly after she'd returned to Zinnia from Lafayette, Louisiana. She'd come home pregnant and married to Kemper. Shortly after Kip's birth, Auralee and Weston McBride had moved to Italy. They hadn't returned to Zinnia in fourteen years. Talk was that they'd never even seen their only granddaughter.

Lee's attention was focused on the jail floor, a dirty gray cement. "Kip needs someone to watch her. In many ways, she's a very special child. She's also angry, about a lot of things."

"I don't know anything about kids, Lee."

She finally looked at me. "With Kip, it wouldn't matter if you did. She's not exactly your average teenager." She paced to the end of the cell.

Baby-sitting a teenager wasn't exactly how I

saw my career as a private eye developing. I was about to decline when she spoke again.

"There's no one else I can trust to do this. Kip needs someone tough. Someone she can't manipulate or run over. You can manage her, Sarah Booth. Will you?"

"Okay. Now tell me what happened," I said, glad to shift the focus, at least for a while.

Lee shrugged. "Kemper and I got into it last night. He was drinking and he slapped me around." She began pacing the cell. "That was always the preliminary to a real beating. A few slaps. Then it could go either way. Sex or a beating. Lately Kemper seemed to favor beating me more than screwing me."

She swung around to face me, and I was stopped by the haunted aspect of her features. Shadows seemed to dance in her eyes. She shrugged. "I went down to the barn. Kip had told me that Avenger had a loose nail in a shoe. With Kemper drunk and mean, I decided to try to stay out of his way. He seldom went in the stallion barn. He hated Avenger, and the horse returned the sentiment."

Her voice was shaky, but she kept talking. "I had Avenger's front hoof in my hand. The nail was going to have to be snipped off and the shoe reset the next morning, when I could call the farrier. The nail was too dangerous to leave, so I had the nippers so I could cut the head off."

She wet her lips. "Avenger tensed, and I looked up. Kemper was standing in the barn aisle. He walked over to the wall and picked up a riding crop. Then that smile came over his face. The bastard looked right at me, smiling like he did when he was going to do something cruel, and he said, 'Come on out here. I'm going to beat you within an inch of your life, and then I'm going to work on that horse.'"

She turned away abruptly so that she spoke in profile to me. "Avenger was going crazy, so I stepped out into the aisle. He started hitting me across the back. During the past few weeks, he'd gotten meaner and meaner, but this time he acted like he meant to kill me." She rubbed her forehead with one hand, shielding her eyes. "I'm so ashamed for you to know how we lived. It was so sick."

"What happened, Lee? You have to tell me the truth, with as much detail as you remember."

"I ran into Avenger's stall, trying to get away from Kemper. He was afraid of Avenger. The horse hated him, and I thought if I could just get into the stall, Kemper would leave me alone. Avenger was rearing and pawing the air, kicking the walls. I remember that the hinges on the door gave this terrible shriek, and I wondered why Bud didn't hear the commotion and come down. I found out later he had a date."

"Bud?"

"He's the trainer." She looked up for a moment. "Sarah Booth, this has been going on for so long. You can't begin to imagine."

How true that was. I couldn't imagine the Eulalee McBride that I remembered from high school taking the first fingertip of abuse from any man. Lee had defied her parents, the school, and anyone else who tried to wrap her up in a neat little package. It was hard to believe that she'd lived with a man like Kemper for longer than five seconds.

"You went into Avenger's stall," I prompted.

She nodded and picked up the story. "Kemper was so angry that he came in after me. He was wild with rage. I'd never seen him so out of control. Anyway, Avenger lunged at him." She swallowed and took a deep breath.

"Go on," I urged her.

"Kemper grabbed my hair. He was slashing at me with the crop. I got free and he lunged at me again, but I was quicker. I stepped aside and tripped him. He crashed headfirst into the wall. He was drunk, and for a moment he just moaned and thrashed around in the shavings. Avenger was dancing and pawing." She finally looked into my eyes. "I tried to get out of the stall, to get away. Kemper grabbed my ankle. He jerked, and tried to pull my feet out from under me. It was all I could take. I had the nippers in my hand. I hit him. I brought the nippers down on his skull as hard as I could."

Up to the point of bashing his brains out, I'd held out a glimmer of hope for accidental death. I reached through the bars and touched Lee's arm. "Did you tell all of this to Coleman?"

"Every word of it."

"You need a lawyer, Lee. A good one."

She shook her head. "I don't want one. I'm going to represent myself."

Lee had always been headstrong. She refused to go to Ole Miss and pledge Phi Mu, the McBride heritage sorority. Her folks had withdrawn college money, so Lee had packed up her things and caught a bus to Lafayette, Louisiana. She got a scholarship and a job, and in three years earned a bachelor's degree in animal husbandry from Northwest Louisiana Tech.

Though the general consensus of our group was that Kemper was a charming scalawag and a scoundrel, he and Lee seemed happy. They had renovated the old Parker place, renaming it Swift Level, and Lee began breeding and training horses. "And they lived happily ever after" should have been the concluding line of their story, not "Rest in peace."

"Lee, Coleman is right. Boyd may be the only person who can help you."

"You can help me, Sarah Booth. You're the person I want."

"How?" I asked.

"By digging up all the dirt on Kemper you can find. I've got this all worked out. I'm going to plead not guilty, and my defense is going to be that Kemper needed killing. With your help, I can convince a jury of that. We can do it."

I saw the fire in her green eyes. She wasn't kidding. "That's not a defense," I said, holding on to the bars for support. "That's a good way to go straight down the road to Parchman prison. Maybe you could plead self-defense, get it reduced to manslaughter—Boyd might be able to get your confession suppressed."

"No! My confession stands! That bastard deserved killing, and I'll be tried on the merits of that. My only regret is that I didn't do it years ago. If I'd known how easy it was going to be I would have done it much sooner."

"Lee!" I reached through the bars and put my hand over her mouth. "Hush up! You keep talking like that and you'll die in prison."

She pulled away from my touch. "I can convince a jury that I did the right thing, but I need your help. I'm not going to be able to make bail, so I can't get out and gather evidence. You can do it, and keep an eye on Kip."

I was truly frightened for her. She had the look of Joan of Arc right before they torched the dry twigs at her feet. "This isn't about what a bastard Kemper was or wasn't. It's about killing someone. If you admit you did it because he deserved it, that could go as premeditated murder, Lee. That's murder one—that's life."

She came up to the bars and circled her hand over mine. "I didn't go into the barn planning to kill him, but I did it just the same. If I get the right jury, I can explain to them how years and years of abuse finally just piled up too high. It's been done before, and I've got the medical records to prove my case. They're filed in the barn." She walked to the back of the cell and stood under the bright glare of the fluorescent light.

I'd noticed before how thin she was. My gaze lingered on her back, the white of her thin cotton shirt, the outline of her bra, and the lack of any visible marks of a beating on her back.

Lee McBride was lying through her teeth.

The main house of Swift Level was at the hub of a circle of impressive buildings. The gracious old home had been built along the same lines as Dahlia House, and dated back before the War Between the States. Though Swift Level was older than my home, it was better maintained.

The front porch was painted and swept. Planters full of brilliant red geraniums and trailing clumps of phlox added color to the stark white of the painted brick walls.

Around the house, like the spokes of a wheel, were the stables and outbuildings. Some were new, others renovated. All were crisp white with the same green metal roof. Lush pastures spread out behind the buildings, and in the distance horses grazed. I slowed my car and simply stared at the vista. Lee had brought a dream to life. This was the exact farm blueprint that she'd drawn out in eighth-grade science class. I remembered, because while all the rest of us had sketched our "dream" homes, Lee had executed a series of architecturally accurate drawings, including all the barns, sheds, training paddocks, and living quarters for the help. She was, of course, teacher's pet for the rest of her school days.

I clearly remembered Tinkie Richmond's, nee Bellcase, comment when Eulalee unveiled her drawings. "That girl is crazy. She doesn't care about dancing or boys or anything except horses. She'll spend the rest of her life with horse manure on her shoes and trouble dogging her footsteps."

Well, Tinkie had proven almost as psychic as my other friend, Tammy Odom, better known currently as Madame Tomeka, Zinnia's answer to The Psychic Hotline. As soon as I got back to Dahlia House, I needed to give Tinkie a call. Although she was a Daddy's Girl to the max, she was also my partner in the Delaney Detective Agency. Tinkie had been my first case, and in my second run as a P.I., she'd proven to be a loyal and dependable friend. Married to Oscar Richmond, banker and deep pockets, Tinkie might be a big help in trying to convince Lee to hire a lawyer. For all of her wilting femininity, Tinkie had a good brain and amazing powers of persuasion.

I eased down the drive toward the main house with two goals in mind. Hopefully I'd find the medical records Lee had told me about, which would document the numerous beatings she'd endured. If they existed. Of more concern was my second assignment, Lee's fourteen-year-old major disciplinary problem masquerading as her daughter.

I'd *heard* enough about Kip to know difficult didn't begin to describe her. I'd *seen* enough of Kip around Zinnia to know my minimal parenting skills were going to be less than useless. In a town of fewer than two thousand it was hard not to notice a tall, slender beauty who wore a fierce look of defiance, black leather, and spiked hair dyed a burgundy red. The heavy eyeliner and shadow that she sported made her look nineteen rather than fourteen. I got the impression she was going for the look of twenty-five.

Knocking at the front door, I tried to compose a speech. I was unprepared when Kip flung the door open and glared at me.

"If she sent you, tell her to go to hell."

She tried to slam the door but I was quicker, using a body block. "Kip, I need to talk with you."

"Talk won't undo what's been done. Let 'em both rot in hell."

I had expected shock, grief, maybe even worry. The lack of all three made me testy. "Your mother's life is on the line, Kip." I pushed the door open and was surprised at her strength as she resisted. For a string bean who looked sickly pale and anorexic, she was very strong.

"She made her choices." Kip vibrated with anger. "They both did. And neither of them gave me a goddamn thought except to keep me obedient and on a horse."

"I know this has been terrible." I tried to find some way to connect with this . . . young girl. I had to keep reminding myself that she was only fourteen. "I'm so sorry about your father."

"I don't need your sympathy."

I looked at her, and she glanced back, daring me to contradict her sentiments. "I'm sorry," I said simply. "I didn't know Kemper very well, but now my concern is for Lee. We're old friends, and she's asked for my help. To do that, I'm going to need your help."

"Bite me." She turned around and started to walk away.

It took all of my restraint not to reach out and grab a fistful of that nasty spiked hair. I took a breath. "Where's the phone?"

"Find it yourself," she said, heading up the stairs.

"You might want to hear this conversation. I'm calling DHR. That's the Department of

Human Resources. As a minor, you can't be left here alone in the house. Lee asked me to take you home with me, but I have no desire to have you in Dahlia House. I guess you'll be going to juvy hall or some institution, until they can find foster placement."

She halted on the stairs but didn't turn around. She was thinking it through, wondering if I was bluffing, weighing the merits between life with me or life in an institution. It wasn't a difficult choice.

"The phone's in the library," she said, slowly turning. "But you don't need it."

"Oh, I disagree," I said softly. "I told your mother I'd look out for you as a personal favor to her. She failed to tell me that you were rude, obnoxious, and a pain in the ass. The deal is off."

I saw the fear in her eyes then, and it took all my strength not to buckle and relent. Then I remembered something my aunt LouLane had told me when she'd come into my home to finish the job of raising me after my parents had died. She said that the first encounter with child or animal sets the tone for the rest of the relationship. With Kip, I couldn't afford to lose this round.

She inhaled, thinking. "I don't want to go to DHR."

"So I have something you want—a place to stay that doesn't involve rigid rules and communal showers." I waited for her to nod. "And you have something I want—help for your mother." Again I waited for her to nod. "I think we can reach a deal, but it's going to cost you."

"How?" she asked, the defiance returning to her green eyes suddenly reminding me of Lee in her jail cell.

"You'll be courteous and polite in my home. You'll obey the ground rules I establish, and you'll work with me on saving your mother from a life sentence in prison." I held up a hand. "I don't care what your sentiments toward your mother might be. You're going to help."

"And I can have my music and a telephone." It was a statement, not a request.

"Played at a moderate level, and you can use the phone line I had installed for the computer, except when I need it for work."

She nodded. Grudgingly.

"Okay, now help me find the records for the horses," I said, not wanting to show my relief. I would never have been able to turn Kip over to DHR. Lee had already extracted my word that I would care for her.

She stalked past me, headed across the porch and down the steps. "They're in the main barn, in the office."

"How long have you been riding?" I asked, catching up with her. She was the most unlikable kid I'd met in a while, but she was Lee's daughter and her father had just been killed so I thought I'd try to engage her in some conversation.

The look she gave me was scathing. "Since before I could walk. That's my life, riding. That's who I am to Mother and what I was to my father. That's all that mattered to either one of them, those damn horses." She gave me a sideways look that was sly and cunning. "You know, sometimes at night, I entertain myself by dreaming that they all burn to death in the barns."

She was watching me, waiting for a reaction of shock and horror. It was all I could do not to oblige her. She was a cunning and manipulative young girl, and one filled with anger and hatred. Lee had not been exaggerating when she said someone needed to keep an eye on Kip. My stomach in knots, I walked past her without comment.

The barn smelled of leather and cedar, reminding me of my childhood riding lessons. I had just begun to jump when my folks were killed in an automobile accident.

Kip led me into the biggest of the barns. A central aisle split two rows of stalls. As my eyes adjusted to the dim light, we were greeted by soft nickers and neighs. Glancing at Kip, I saw that she was unmoved. She walked past the stalls without ever once looking at any of the magnificent animals.

Down the aisle a half dozen yards, an older man was mucking out an empty stall. He gave me a long, intense look.

"It's okay, Roscoe, I'm going to be staying with her for a day or two. She's a friend of Mother's. Through her efforts, Mother and all the horses will be saved." Kip didn't bother to hide her contempt for me.

"Miss Kip, don't act thataway," Roscoe said, leaning on his rake. "I know you're hurtin', but so is Miss Lee."

"At least *Father's* out of his misery." Kip stalked away, leaving me to follow or not.

"This is a sad place," Roscoe said to me. "Miss Kip's not bad, she's just messed up. Got plenty of cause to be, if you ask me."

I did want to ask him a few questions, but Kip called me down the aisle. "The records are in there," she said, pointing. "The file cabinet. Alphabetical order." She picked up a manure fork and headed toward a stall. "I have chores to do."

"Kip, I think it would be okay if you let it slide today. Maybe you should go and put some of your things together."

Her laughter was loud and brittle. "Not around here. Nothing interferes with chores and duties and responsibilities. Water, muck, turn out, ride, transport, hay, rake, bush hog, paint." She nearly spat each word, but a slant of sunlight coming through a stall window caught the glint of a tear in her eye. "My question is this. Where did Mother find the time to bash his brains out? There's always so much work to be done." She turned and walked past me.

The prospect of Kip was so daunting, I wondered if I could come up with Lee's bond myself. Maybe Tinkie would chip in some cash. I sighed and went into the office to begin my search.

Lee's medical file was two inches thick and right where she said it would be. I leafed through it. Over the last three years, there were at least fifty trips to the Sunflower County emergency room or to private physicians in the region. Flipping through the dates, I saw that Kemper's attacks against Lee had grown increasingly frequent. And vicious. I was still troubled by the lack of physical marks on Lee's back. The beating she'd described as preceding

Kemper's death would have been severe enough to leave some kind of injury, and there was solid medical evidence that he'd hurt her in the past. Why hadn't she filed charges against him long ago?

The medical records would prove Kemper's history as an abuser, but I was still troubled by the fact that Lee had lied about Kemper hitting her the night he was murdered. Why was she lying? More important, was Coleman aware of her lies?

I was so caught up in my reading that I didn't hear anyone enter the office. I sensed him before I saw him; there was that vague tingle that comes when someone is staring at you. I turned around. A man was leaning against the wall, one booted foot crossed over the other. His arms were crossed, too. It was obvious he was waiting me out.

"Who are you?" I asked.

"A good question. Why don't you answer it?" He righted himself without seeming to move a muscle. Arms still crossed, he walked up to me. He had light eyes that took me in, head to toe.

"You're not one of the ladies who come to ride. You're not a relative, and you're not media. So, who are you?"

"Sarah Booth Delaney," I said. "I'm a friend

of Lee's." I closed the file and pulled it into my lap. "So, who are you?" He wore jeans, cowboy boots, and a cotton shirt streaked with dirt. His movements blended grace and confidence, yet he wasn't what I might have expected at Swift Level.

"Bradford Lynch, but most folks call me Bud. I'm the trainer here at Swift Level."

I had never seen a man hold himself so quiet and yet so poised for action. "So you're the live-on-the-premises trainer?" I asked.

His smile was slow. "What are you, some kind of plainclothes detective?" He once again took in my jeans and camp shirt. "I remember when female cops used to look like linebackers."

"You're very good at answering a question with a question. Where's your place?"

He pointed to a staircase across the aisle. "Loft apartment."

"Were you here last night?" I asked.

"Are you viewing me as the murderer or just an accomplice? Is this the time I should confess how much I wanted him dead?"

His flip attitude was getting under my skin. "You don't have to answer my questions, but Sheriff Peters will get answers from you. It might be better if I heard them first." I looked up to see Kip standing in the doorway. The ex-

pression on her face was impossible to read.
She was staring at Bud Lynch's back.

As if he sensed her, he turned around. "Kip,
are you okay?"

She stifled a sob and turned and ran.

Bud started after her, and I was right behind
him.

Kip pounded through the barn aisle, with
Bud gaining on her. "Kip!" He called her
name. "Hold up a minute."

"Go to hell!" she shouted over her shoulder.

He was about to reach out and catch her
when I saw the wooden rake handle slide out
of a stall door. Bud's long legs tangled with the
wooden handle and he went down hard.

Rolling, he came up on his feet. For a second he stood in the barn aisle, panting, then he
turned to Roscoe. "Old man—" His voice was
filled with anger, then he glanced back at me.
Slowly he dusted off the front of his jeans.

"Leave her alone," Roscoe said. "She's been
through enough, and you and your tramp've
been little help."

Bud started to say something else, but instead he turned and walked back to me. "It's
been a pleasure, but I've got to get some horses
worked. We've got shows coming up, important shows. With Lee in jail and Kip gone, I'll
have to work all the horses."

"Where—" I started. "How did you know—"

"I overheard Kip tell Roscoe." He called back down the barn aisle to the old man. "Roscoe, the shavings are ready to be picked up. You need to go get them. Now!"

Before he could walk away, I put a hand on his forearm. "Where were you last night?" I fell into step beside him as he walked back to the office.

He faced me before answering. "I wasn't alone. All night."

"I'm sure you have witnesses to corroborate that?"

"One very satisfied witness."

"Cute," I replied, about to lose my patience with him. "I'll need that name."

He paced the room; then his gaze finally caught mine and held firm. "Are you really a friend of Lee's?"

I nodded. "I've known her since we were six."

With that answer, his entire mocking demeanor changed. "Kemper was a cruel bastard. He should have suffered a lot more. There were better ways to handle it."

I filed that away for further thought. "When did you hear of his death?"

"Lee told me this morning. She'd already

called the sheriff." He raised his eyebrows. "Messy."

His eyes were gray, with tiny flecks of golden brown around the irises. Holding my gaze wasn't a problem for him. "Can you say in court that you saw Kemper abuse Lee?" I asked.

He hesitated. "I never saw him hit her. The bastard was too smart for that. Lee would never admit that he was the cause of her injuries. At least not to me." His jaw tightened. "She knew I'd fix him."

I filed that away. "Did you see or hear anything last night that might bear on this case?" I pressed.

He shook his head.

I remembered the old man cleaning the stall. "What about Roscoe? Do you think he might have witnessed something?"

"No, I don't think so," Bud said. "Roscoe's old, and he can't half remember what he's supposed to do. You can ask him, though, when he gets back from the sawmill. Should be about an hour."

I didn't have time to wait. "I'll be in touch."

He tipped an imaginary hat in a gesture that was more Texas than Virginia. I finally placed his twang.

"How long have you been here, Bud?"

"Going on a year. Hard to imagine a cow-hand training jumpers, but I seem to have a knack for it. Truth is, horses just like to do what I ask."

Somehow I didn't think it was only horses that were eager to do his bidding.

$$\boxed{3}$$

Kip dropped her duffel bag on the floor of
the bedroom that was to be hers. She touched
the eyelet canopy that Aunt LouLane had
loved. "Sort of prissy."

"You'll learn to live with it." I wanted to
ask her about Bud Lynch, but later would be
better.

"Why don't you fix this place up more?" she
asked, going to the window and looking out.
"I'll bet it was really beautiful once."

It was the first seminice thing I'd heard pass
her lips. "It was, before my folks were killed."
She turned to see if I was trying to set her up.
"Car accident. I was just about your age." I
hadn't realized it until that moment. "Lately,
money has been kind of short."

"Money." She turned to look back out the
window. "It doesn't matter how much there is,
it's never enough, and it's the only thing in life
that matters." Turning around abruptly, she
gave me an innocent look. "Did you know you

can hire a hit man for four hundred dollars, cash?"

"Really," I said, forcing my voice to show no surprise. I was wise to her tactics, but I was also concerned. Violence was a recurring theme in everything she said. "Where?"

She waved a hand. "It isn't hard to find one, if you know where to look."

"And you would know?" I said with just a pinch of skepticism.

"I'm an excellent researcher," she said, completely unruffled. "Four hundred dollars. Of course, it's a local hit. But then, the target is just as dead, isn't he? Or she."

She refused to look at me as she talked and I wondered if she was deliberately trying to scare me. She walked around the bedroom, dragging her fingers along the eyelet bedspread. "Kids my age are killing people all the time now." She suddenly threw herself backward on the bed. "I'd like to be alone," she said. "I need to think."

I closed the door and went to my room on the other side of the house. Kip would bear watching. Careful watching. Lee had not exaggerated that need.

Kip had brought her boom box and a crate full of CDs. I wasn't familiar with a single artist or song, and I was anticipating the worst. As I closed my door, I found Jitty standing behind it like a naughty child caught eavesdropping.

"How long?" she demanded.

"Until Lee gets out of jail."

"That could be months!"

"I'm aware of that." Stepping over some clothes on the floor, I flung myself onto my bed. I heard this strange thumping and leaned down to find my red tic hound, Sweetie Pie, stuck under the bed. The only thing able to move was her tail, which was wagging furiously. She was wedged in. "How do you do that?" I leaned over further, grabbed her back legs, and pulled her out.

"What you gone do with a teenager in the house for months? You can't stand your own company for more than two hours in a row." She gave Sweetie Pie a disdainful eye. The only animal Jitty wanted in the house was a man.

"I don't know." I also didn't want to argue with her. Kip wasn't exactly my idea of fun, but she was here, and here she'd stay until Lee could get her.

"She talks dangerous," Jitty said. "Is she?"

"I don't know." Kip worried me. She didn't make threats, exactly. She'd dreamed of burning the horses and had researched finding a hit man. While not exactly what I would consider normal teen behavior, it was a far cry from actual violence. She'd also just lost her father, and her mother was in jail for murder. "I remember when my folks were killed. I was so angry. Everyone said it was an accident. They said it was a tragedy. I only knew that the two people I loved most in the world had been taken from me. Aunt LouLane . . ." I felt a rush of gratitude for my old-maid aunt. "She tried hard and she put up with a lot. I guess in some ways I was a bit like Kip."

"She walked the floor many a night worried about you," Jitty agreed.

"There's probably room for a little acting out in Kip's life right now."

"All the same, I'd keep a close eye on her," Jitty said. She pointed to the bedroom door. "Maybe you should lock it."

I shook my head. "She troubles me, but she's just a kid."

"Right," Jitty said. "Does the name Menendez mean anything to you?"

"Stop it," I whispered to her. She was spooking me.

"What about that fourteen-year-old down in Pascagoula? Killed his entire family with a bat. Or the two sisters who stabbed their mother to death. Or—"

"Jitty!" I spoke louder than I intended. I held up a hand to listen for Kip. She'd wonder who in the world I was having a conversation with. "When did you start collecting statistics on kid crimes?" I asked her.

She sniffed. "I can be useful." She pointed at the computer. "Like reminding you to check your E-mail?"

I leaned up on my elbow to give her a curious look. "I thought you hated the computer. Tool of Satan. Wasn't that what you called it?"

She shrugged. "Got to get with the times. I didn't like cars, either, but they certainly make it easier for you to get groceries to the house. Lookin' at that waistline, I don't have a doubt what a top priority food is around here."

I got up and went to the Pentium III I'd recently bought to help with my detective business. I was a long way from competent, but I'd discovered some fascinating information by surfing the Web. The little mailbox icon was blinking.

"That Tom Hanks and Meg Ryan found love by writing E-mail to each other." Jitty was hovering over my shoulder. "You've got mail!"

"I'm not Meg Ryan, and this isn't a movie."

"Obviously. When *her* hair is tousled, it looks good." Jitty sniffed. "I was hoping when you teamed up with Tinkie that she'd have some influence on your appearance."

I turned around. "Why are you wearing my clothes?"

"I thought maybe if you could see how bad you look in these things you'd go buy you a sharp-looking joggin' suit." She pointed to the screen. "Check that message."

"Jitty, think about this. If I found love on the Internet, there would be no issue. Cybersex is completely without congress." I was more than a little proud of that statement.

"Honey, normal folk use it to say howdy and then set up a time and a place to meet. Of course, *you'd* have to try to turn it into a congress." She pointed to the screen. "You've got mail."

Puzzled by her sudden interest in "demon technology," as she called it, I moved the mouse to check my E-mail. In a moment a message from Cece Dee Falcon, society editor for *The Zinnia Dispatch,* popped up on the screen. Cece had a "juicy assignment" for me. I sometimes picked up freelance work writing for Cece at the newspaper. Entrée as a reporter, I'd quickly learned, was another invaluable detecting tool. I read the message. Cece wanted me to meet her for coffee.

"Now how does this E-mail thing work?" Jitty asked.

"I don't actually know. All that matters is

that it does work." She was hovering over me. Although she looked as real as any of my other annoying friends, her touch was only a whisper, a draft passing through a room.

"There're dating clubs on computer. Big story on the news."

I turned slowly and faced her, a sudden reality dawning. "I'm not that desperate."

"Liar," she answered calmly.

"Do you know how many maniacs are out there? And what's to keep them from lying? I mean just because they say they're six four, there's no way to check it. They're all probably five two and live with their mothers."

"Who cares if they carry a step stool, as long as they're in working order," Jitty said. "This is a new millennium, Sarah Booth. This isn't about marriage or 'happy ever after.' This is about global opportunities. Show me how to work that thing."

I turned the computer off. "Never. I'm going to see what Cece wants," I said, getting up. "I'll tell Kip I'm leaving, but you keep an eye on her." That should keep Jitty too busy to meddle in my affairs.

Cece was waiting for me in Millie's Café, along with my partner, Tinkie. They were both blond, beautiful, smart, and born into old Delta families. There the similarities ended. Tinkie was everything a Daddy's Girl aspired to be, with the unfortunate—to her male family members—addition that money and security weren't enough to fill her days. Hence her association with me.

Cece, on the other hand, should have been a candidate for the Buddy Clubbers. A trip to Sweden and extensive hormone therapy had exhausted the Falcon inheritance and turned Cecil into Cece. She was one of my few wealthy friends who had actually bought a measure of happiness with her legacy. For most of them, money had become a sort of prison. One with very nicely furnished cells, I might add.

"Hello, dahling," Cece said, brushing air kisses on each of my cheeks. "You look marvelous, Sarah Booth. You've lost a pound or two, haven't you? Those love handles aren't quite so prominent."

Cece had the lean hips of a male and never failed to rub it in. "Men like something to hang on to," I said, taking a seat and signaling Millie, proprietress of the establishment and another good friend, for a cup of coffee.

Tinkie only grinned at us. "Bring some milk for the kitties," she called out to Millie. "Maybe if we feed them the fur won't fly."

Of all the folks in Zinnia, I felt closest to these three women. "What's going on?" I asked Cece. I had big news, but I wanted to get the most play out of it.

Cece scanned the room for would-be eavesdroppers. The only patrons were a few businessmen, some ladies of leisure—meaning they'd married well—and some tourists who were likely on their way to Batesville, Greenwood, or further south along the river to make the annual spring pilgrimages to old plantation homes that had become big-dollar industries.

Leaning forward, Cece finally spoke. She did know how to milk a moment. "Since you're already working for Lee McBride, I thought you might want to do some columns about what you discover?" Cece's grin was wide and wolfish.

"How did you find out I was working for Lee?" I was shocked. I'd only been hired a couple of hours ago. Looking from Tinkie to Cece, I realized they both knew.

Millie brought coffee and dishes of hot peach cobbler for four. Eyeing the café to make sure everyone had his order, she took a seat with us. "Are you going to be able to get Eulalee off?" she asked me.

"Does the entire town know?" I asked.

They nodded.

"You went out to Swift Level this morning. What did you find? Other than that little hell-cat Kip, who I understand you're baby-sitting?" Millie asked. They all leaned forward so I could lower my voice.

"Lee's medical records show extensive abuse. I can tell you that much."

"And Kip?" Cece pressed. "I've seen her around town. Trouble with a capital T."

"She's angry," I conceded. "I couldn't say no to Lee."

"And how did you find Bradford Lynch to be?" Cece said. She licked one corner of her mouth in a subconscious gesture that told me exactly how she found him.

"Evasive," I said, digging into the cobbler. "What do you know about him?" I looked from one to the other.

"He comes in on Saturdays sometimes," Millie said. She arched an eyebrow. "He has a presence. Every woman in the room stops talking and just watches him walk by. Really cute ass."

"Yes, he is one fine man," Cece agreed.

Only Tinkie looked unsure. "He's a cowboy, isn't he? I mean, I always wondered why Lee hired a cowboy to train her horses. The crowd at Swift Level doesn't chase cows, they chase foxes."

"He said something to the same effect," I said, leaning a little closer. "He also said it didn't matter. Horses do whatever he tells them."

"Honey, I'd get on my hands and knees and buck if he told me to," Cece said. When our laughter died, she looked at me. "So what about the columns? I've already heard that Lee is insisting on defending herself. She's going to try to convince a jury that Kemper deserved what he got."

Tinkie's gasp was reflected in the doubt on Millie's face. "Most of the men I know need killing," Millie said. "I don't think that qualifies as justifiable homicide."

"That's her plan," I confirmed. "She won't hire a lawyer, and she won't listen to reason, but I'm hoping Coleman can work on her." I shot a glance at Tinkie. "And you, too. She might listen to you."

Cece snorted. "If you don't remember Lee, I sure do. Once her mind is made up, she's not going to budge," she said. "Remember back in high school, when she insisted she could climb that old water tower and spray-paint her name on the side? The steps broke and she fell and fractured her arm. The day after the cast came off, she went back with ropes and some kind of harness. She was going to do it or die, and she

did. She won't change her mind about anything."

Silence settled on the table. I knew Cece
was right. We all did.

"That's why I think the columns are such a
good idea," Cece said. "Lee can present her
side of the story. By the time her case goes to
trial, we'll have everyone on her side. The jury
will acquit her in ten minutes."

"They have to select jurors who haven't
been exposed to the facts, or gossip, of the
crime," I reminded Cece.

"What planet do you live on?" she asked
archly, tapping one perfectly manicured Orange Tango nail on the table. "The more publicity Lee gets, the better her chances. As long
as it's the right kind of publicity. That's where
you come in."

I had my doubts. "I'll ask her," I agreed, because I knew that Cece was as stubborn as Lee
when it came to getting a story.

"What can I do?" Tinkie asked.

Tinkie was my wedge into society, and I had
very specific plans for her. "What do you know
about foxhunting?" My riding lessons had
been curtailed, but Tinkie, as had all the
Daddy's Girls, had ridden for years. Although
they seldom continued the sport after marriage, it was considered a social necessity to be

able to sit a blooded horse and ride to the hounds.

"I've been a few times." She shook her head. "It's a great sport, except for the fox. I don't think it can be much fun to be chased like that. Getting caught is murder."

"I need to build a list of possible suspects." All three women lifted their eyebrows. "Surely someone in that hunt crowd would want Kemper dead."

"What's that going to help?" Millie asked. "Lee's already confessed."

I nodded agreement. "I know, but I want to have a backup plan. Reasonable doubt is what I'm aiming for. If we can get Lee's confession suppressed, and if she does come to her senses, I want to be able to present at least one other person who could have killed, might have killed, or likely did kill Kemper."

"Good idea," Millie said. She sipped her coffee, but her eyes held mine over the rim of her cup. "Got anyone in mind?"

"Should I?"

"Sometimes anger can push someone right over the edge."

"Meaning?" I pressed.

She put the cup down in a saucer before she answered. "Working in a café, I hear a lot of things. Kids come in after school and talk.

Teachers get together and get a little loud." She shrugged. "About a month ago, Kip got in some trouble at the high school. Vandalism. Lee had to put her in counseling and pay the damages."

All of the women were watching me. "How much damage?"

"I heard it from the school secretary. She said Kip and another girl got into it over something. The other girl had a knife and Kip went straight at her, disarmed her, and then slapped her around some. No one was really hurt, but they took Kip down to the office along with the other girl. Kip explained that she was attacked and was protecting herself, but the principal still punished her. It was after that that Kip lost it. She waited until after school and ransacked the library. Mostly she just made a big mess, by throwing books and knocking over shelves. There wasn't a lot of monetary damage."

My gut had that knotted feeling again.

"When I see her hanging out in town," Cece said, "she reminds me of one of the lost girls. You know, an active member of the vampire cult of kids."

"She wears a lot of makeup for her age," I conceded.

"I feel sorry for her," Millie said. "She sometimes comes in here late at night. She's always by herself." She shook her head. "Teenagers don't like to be alone."

Tinkie drummed her nails on the table. "I've got an appointment with Oscar." She turned to me. "So you want me to investigate Lee's clients and associates."

"Yes. People who've been to Swift Level. Check out the hunt crowd. You can do that better than I can." I looked at Millie. "If you could keep an ear open to the conversations floating around in here, that would be a big help."

"You bet," she said. "Content and source— I'll make notes."

"I'll see what I can dig up on Kemper's past. For the obituary, you know," Cece volunteered.

For a brief moment I felt my hopes for Lee lift. She had the four ablest women in the state of Mississippi working on her behalf. And three of them were basically working for free.

4

There was one stop I had to make before I went back to Dahlia House. Zinnia National Bank was the only bank in town. I hadn't wanted to ask Tinkie to approach this matter through her father, who owned the bank, or her husband, who was director of the board of trustees. Avery and Oscar failed to take Tinkie seriously. They saw only the glitzed façade she'd been carefully trained to build—and had executed with incredible finesse. To them, Tinkie was the perfect blonde. Beautiful, animated, and pliant. Had Tinkie asked about the finances at Swift Level, they would never have told her the truth.

I had another source inside the bank: Harold Erkwell. Besides, I always enjoyed seeing Harold. Ever since my return to Zinnia from my failed career as an actress in New York, Harold and I had toyed with the idea of a relationship. Just at the point when I was ready to capitulate, fate always stepped in and threw us a curve. Still, it was nice to be desired.

His secretary, Marie, showed me immediately into his private office. Harold looked up and his crystal-blue eyes lit with pleasure. Now that was a reaction even a failed Daddy's Girl couldn't help but appreciate. The memory of his mouth on my thumb last fall gave me a delicate little thrill. I had been reduced to living on memories.

"Sarah Booth, what brings you to the bank?" A frown touched his forehead. "Everything is good with Dahlia House, isn't it?"

"For the moment." Not so long ago, Dahlia House had been hours away from the auction block. In one of his less than fine moments, Harold had offered to save my home, if he could win my hand. Had I known him better then, I might have said yes.

He rose from behind his desk and came to me. Scooping my hand up, he kissed it. "Still not claimed," he said, noting my ringless state and bringing to mind the honking big diamond he'd offered me. His lips lingered on the back of my fingers, igniting an old memory that throbbed in my thumb.

"Unclaimed and unfettered," I answered, slipping my fingers from his. Harold made the art of flirtation an Olympic-level competition. Verbal dueling was his specialty.

He waved me into a chair and called Marie to bring us coffee. Five minutes later she brought in a tray with Haviland china and silver serving pieces. A nice touch. When we both were settled with our cups, Harold nodded for me to proceed.

I'd learned that only in matters of the heart did Harold like the circuitous approach. "I need to see the financial records on Swift Level."

He was well schooled in hiding his reaction. "Impossible," he said.

"I'm working for Lee. She's hired me to help her."

Harold watched me. "She needs a good lawyer, Sarah Booth. That's not detracting from your abilities. You've done amazingly well. But her future is on the line."

"I know." I was annoyed that Harold, too, knew specific details of the case. Was someone in the sheriff's office blabbing? I intended to have a talk with Coleman as soon as I left the bank. I wasn't sure about writing columns for the newspaper, but Cece was right about one thing—the wrong kind of publicity or gossip could put the final nail in Lee's coffin.

"Lee indicated that things are tight at Swift Level. Is that true?"

Harold would dodge a question, but he wouldn't lie. "If you were asking me if you should invest in Swift Level, I would say that in the long term, it would be an extremely good move. In the short term, it could prove disastrous."

"Swift Level isn't making money?" I let it hang, watching Harold as he focused on sipping his coffee. He was deliberating on how much to tell me, scouting the boundaries of his ethics and my need to know.

"Kemper wasn't a good businessman. He was also a compulsive gambler."

The implication of this hit me like a kick to the womb—it gave Lee another motive for premeditated murder. Kemper was ruining her financially. That was a good reason to kill him, but probably not one the jury would sympathize with. "Damn," I said softly.

"Kemper spent a lot of his time down in Biloxi on those gambling boats. From what I hear, they wouldn't let him on the *Silver Slipper* in Tunica. He'd caused some problems there."

"What if Kemper owed money to someone? I hear the Dixie Mafia is all over the Gulf Coast. What if he owed them a lot of money, and they sent someone up here to collect it?"

"Very plausible story, except that Lee has

confessed," Harold pointed out. "I hear you're playing mom to Kip." His grin said it all.

"She's a thorny child." To say more would be disloyal to Lee.

Harold got up and walked to the window that overlooked Main Street. For a long moment, he stared out. Waiting is a virtue highly prized in Southern women. It is the foundation of the code of Daddy's Girls. Men act; women wait. Though I found it hard to swallow, I knew this was a moment that required all of my waiting skills. Finally he turned to face me.

"I'm talking out of school, but I think this may be important. Something wasn't right between him and Kip."

I saw Kip's fourteen-year-old face so clearly—the heavy makeup, the spiked hair. Was it rebellious youth or self-hatred? The very idea made me physically ill. I put the coffee aside.

"Are we talking physical abuse, as in beatings, or something else?"

"Something else." Harold put his hand on my shoulder, his fingers firm as they rubbed the tense muscle. "But not what you're thinking. Nothing sexual. In a way, though, it's almost as bad."

"What kind of abuse?"

"Kip played a vital role at Swift Level. As talented a rider as Lee is, Kip is better. I'm only on the fringes of the horsey set, but I've gone to some of the bigger shows. Kip is magnificent. She's been campaigning that big stallion of Lee's, Avenger, but she also had a little mare of her own, one she'd raised and trained. I think the horse was called Mrs. Peel."

I nodded that I got the reference, but I didn't want to interrupt his story.

"Last month at the Lexington show, Kemper sold that mare right out from under Kip. Kip rode the horse in a class and took second place. When she came out of the show ring, a man stepped up and took the reins, said Mrs. Peel belonged to him and his daughter now. Kemper had sold the horse while Kip was riding her in the ring." Harold frowned. "I saw Kip's face. My heart almost broke for her."

I was stunned. "Kemper was sincerely a bastard," I said. "That might explain why Kip hates both of her parents. One for hurting her, and the other for failing to protect her."

"You can check this out with Lillian Sparks. She was at the show. She overheard what Kemper said to Kip."

Lillian was the town matriarch who'd been a renowned horsewoman in her day. "Which was?"

Harold debated whether he should repeat gossip. "Ask Lillian to be sure, but I heard he told Kip that Mrs. Peel deserved a first-place rider, not a second-place."

I took a breath. "Damn it, Harold, you've just given me two more good reasons why Lee would want to kill Kemper in cold blood."

"Or Kip," Harold said as gently as he could. He sat down in the chair beside me and took my hand in his. "I know she's only a kid, Sarah Booth, but don't turn your back on her. The horse crowd is vicious and malicious. They seem to delight in character assassinations, but make no mistake about it: Kip Fuquar has a bad temper. She threw quite a tantrum."

The courthouse had suddenly become a hopping place. Parking along the entire square was full. I had to take a side street and hoof it back to Coleman's office. The morning had been made for walking. In the last days of March, it seemed that every flower in Mississippi had suddenly decided to bud. Azaleas, dogwoods, bridal wreath, the delicious magnolia frascatti, and wisteria. This was the South in her finest attire.

The fresh green of new leaves was electric, and the azaleas in purples, fuchsias, pinks, and whites were so vivid they seemed unreal. During this brief magical spell, it was easy to see where the idea of crinoline, hoopskirts, and ruffles culminated in the creation of the belle. It was simply an attempt to mimic the wonder of nature. In the South, women are still considered delicate flowers. It is a double-bladed sword.

I left the beauty of nature behind and stepped into the cool hallway of the courthouse. Television reporters were jamming the doorway of the sheriff's office. The word had spread like wildfire. I noticed a reporter from a Memphis station and another from Batesville.

Easing through the crowd, I tried to slip into Coleman's office, but I felt a hand on my shoulder and looked into the face of Deputy Gordon Walters. We respected each other, but we were not friends.

"Coleman's not seeing anyone," he said. His words were soft, but his hand was firm.

"I've got information." I wasn't sure how much I'd share with Coleman, but I'd at least tell him about the gambling. With his law enforcement connections, he could check on Biloxi gaming a lot easier than I could.

"Wait here."

I did, until the door opened and Coleman signaled me inside. He was sitting at his desk

with a stack of papers in front of him. He did
not look happy.

"Damned media," he said. "They're making
this the case of the century. Word is out that
Lee confessed."

"And how did it get out?" I asked, annoyed
and worried.

"I'll find out, and when I do, there's going to
be someone without a job."

I walked around his desk so that I was behind him. He was a tall man with broad shoulders. He'd leaned up since his high school days
on the football team. My aunt LouLane would
have said he lost his baby fat.

"Coleman, I hear Kemper owed a lot of
money down in Biloxi."

He swiveled his chair around to face me. "Is
that so?"

This was something he already knew, but he
was wondering how I found out. "That's what
I hear."

"Who's talking?"

I shook my head. "Maybe Lee didn't kill
him at all." I floated the concept. "What if one
of those Mafia types killed him?"

"Why would Lee want to protect a killer
from the gambling industry by confessing?"

It was the perfect question to lead me to

where I wanted to go. "Maybe she's trying to protect someone else."

"And who would she be protecting?" His blue eyes were alert, eager. He was waiting for me to say Kip's name. I couldn't, and I suddenly had a clearer understanding of the dangerous game Lee was playing, if indeed she was protecting her daughter.

"I don't know," I said, "but that's something I'll find out."

"When you get a line on who that might be, I'd like to hear it."

No matter his personal preferences, Coleman was saying he wouldn't cut Lee any slack. It was one of the things I admired about him. And one of the things that threatened to cost him his job, when he dared to step on the wrong toes.

"I'll let you know," I said. He bent back to his paperwork and I knew I was dismissed. I left the courthouse and headed home. I had no solid suspects, just a shadowy Dixie Mafia hit man.

And someone far more troubling: Kip.

There was also one other avenue—Bradford Lynch. He was a man with opportunity and ability. But did he have motive? That was something I had to find out. But Kip first.

Kip was on the front porch with Sweetie Pie at her feet when I pulled up to Dahlia House. Her hand was resting on the hound's head, and for a split second I could see the child Kip might have been. Then she spoke.

"There's nothing to eat here except a flat of strawberries."

"I'll make us some lunch." It was a little late, and I'd truly forgotten that Kip might want to eat. Guilt is an interesting emotion—so easy to generate and so hard to get over.

"I don't eat any of that healthy crap."

I stopped in my tracks, hand on the doorknob. "I'll make us some lunch. You can eat or not," I said as calmly as I could. "I was thinking of a grilled cheese sandwich and some tomato-basil soup." It was the only thing in the house, except strawberries. I thought of my basil plant, lying in the garden, roots exposed to the hot sun. I had murdered it even before I began. Jitty was right about me. Black-thumb Delaney. I went inside and left Kip to make up her mind. My aunt LouLane would have slapped me into next week for displaying such an attitude. Until exposure to Kip, I'd never fully appreciated the social tools she'd drilled into me.

Jitty was strangely absent. Something in the

back of my brain fluttered, but I was too intent on making lunch to pay attention. I had the soup going, two grilled cheese sandwiches in an old black skillet, and the crust for a strawberry pie in the works when Kip came in. Hunger had won out over obnoxiousness. She took her seat and I placed a sandwich in front of her. She began to eat without a word.

The phone rang and she looked up, green eyes a shade darker than her mother's. "I'll get it." She leaped to her feet, but not before I picked up the extension and said hello.

"This is Kelly Brewer with WRRK-TV in Greenwood. I'm returning your call. We've got a camera crew on the way to the courthouse."

I turned to look at Kip, who'd stuffed her sandwich into her mouth. Cheeks bulging, she stared back at me defiantly.

I hung up without a word and confronted her. "Why?" I demanded.

"Mother wants to be a celebrity. She confessed, you know."

"You're a real piece of work," I said. "I don't know if you're stupid or just plain mean."

"She confessed!" Kip was enunciating pretty well for having a mouthful of food. "She's told everyone she killed my father. She doesn't care what it does to me. She doesn't care about anything except herself and Swift Level. She wants to be some kind of righteous murderer, then let her be as famous as she wants. Maybe this confession is just a big publicity stunt to promote Swift Level. It's all over the news!"

Her face was red with fury, and though I felt a wave of pity for her, it wasn't enough to counteract my anger. "That's enough, Kip."

"No, no, it isn't enough. Mother didn't kill him. She didn't. She's taking the blame for it, though. That's what she does. She just puts herself in the line of fire. But she never thinks about me. She's my mother, and she never thinks what this is doing to me. I need her and she's in jail! Just once, just one time, I wish she could put what I need first. Just once." She threw her fork across the kitchen, missing my head by a foot or two.

"As of right this minute, you have no phone privileges."

She swallowed, and then laughed. "Right. Some big punishment. Have you noticed how many of my friends are calling to talk to me?"

She jumped up from the table, brushed past me, and ran up the stairs to her room. On the kitchen floor, Sweetie Pie moaned sadly.

5

Kip's music, a blend of Middle Eastern wails and some indistinguishable rap lyrics with a wall-vibrating beat, was still audible through my closed door. Kip was a problem, and one I had no experience in solving. I'd called Coleman and told him who the leak was. He, too, was appalled by Kip's actions. He was also relieved that none of his employees had talked to the media.

I cranked up my computer and began a search for Bradford Lynch. I couldn't exactly "hang ten" as a Web surfer, but I turned up a couple of mentions. A 1997 article in *Texas Monthly* ranked Lynch as one of the best-kept secrets of Texas. His skills in working with "problem" horses were soundly lauded. I also gathered the basics: He was born in Bandera, a small town with a population under a thousand but labeled the "cowboy capital of the world." His family had once owned the Double D Ranch, which they'd "lost." I did some quick calculations and pinned his age at thirty-nine.

Once the twenty-thousand-acre family ranch had been split and sold, Bradford had drifted around the state, training and riding horses at various ranches. End of article. There was a devastating picture of him in his faded blue chambray shirt and cowboy hat.

The other story was in the *Dallas Morning News,* a more recent account of a suspicious death. The March 1998 headline read: LAWMEN INVESTIGATE MYSTERIOUS DEATH OF LOCAL RANCHER.

Kerr County was the setting, and the dead man in question was William Talbot. He'd just filed for divorce from his wife, Tanya, whom he'd caught in the act of playing bucking bronco with a horse trainer—one Bradford Lynch.

Tiny little goose bumps began doing the boogie on my neck and arms. I read on.

Talbot, who raised cutting horses, had been found dead in a pasture, trampled in a horse stampede. Tanya had inherited everything. Though the rancher had begun divorce proceedings against her for adultery, he had not changed his will. End result, Tanya was very rich and very single.

Now that I had a source, I checked for additional articles but nothing came up. It was as if the entire matter had been dropped. Either that, or I didn't know how to work the damn computer. So I resorted to the detective's best tool, the telephone. I unplugged the computer modem and made a quick call to the daily newspaper in Kerrville. I got all the answers from a delightfully gossipy reporter named Al Redding.

Al had covered the story and was glad to gab about it. The two chief suspects with motive, opportunity, and means, Tanya Talbot, aka wealthy widow, and Bradford Lynch, had been thoroughly investigated. There was insufficient evidence to prove foul play. Tanya had inherited and sold the ranch, and Bradford Lynch had continued his drifting ways, moving out of Kerrville and into the sunset as far as anyone knew.

"They didn't go away together?" I asked.

There was a pause on the line. "It seemed that once Talbot was dead, Tanya didn't have a lot of need for Bud. It's my opinion that she dumped him and moved on to richer hunting grounds. I mean, now she had the bucks to track herself down a *very* wealthy man. Bud's a charmer, but his Dun and Bradstreet wasn't up to snuff. That was Tanya, always looking to marry up the ladder."

"So the case is over and done. Were they guilty?"

"As sin. At least Tanya was. Everyone in the county agreed she was guilty. That's why she had to sell out. The law couldn't punish her, but the community shut her out. Kerr County was once nothing but big cattle ranches. There was a code of honor, and it still exists among many of the people here."

"And the trainer, Lynch?"

"There were two schools of thought about him. Some say he planned and executed the murder for a big payoff. Others thought he was just a victim. Sure, he was bedding the boss's wife, but that's not a hanging offense this day and time. And Tanya was quite a woman. Not many men could resist her. Last I heard of him, he was down in Laredo working with some crazy stallion that had gone on a rampage and killed a half dozen of his own mares."

"The horse killed his own herd?" This did not jibe with my mental picture of the magnificent stallion protecting his herd from mountain lions, man, or other dangers.

"So I was told. He's a valuable horse, but the only cure for that kind of thing is a bullet in the brain. Once a horse kills, it's time to destroy him. Loss of marketability as a stud.

Nobody wants to breed to something crazy. That's the way it works, the unwritten horse code."

"Hey, thanks," I said.

"What's all the curiosity? Has Tanya turned up in Mississippi? I heard she had an aunt living over there."

"No, I'm writing a book," I lied. I had never conjured up a more serviceable falsehood.

"Yeah? I thought about writing about Tanya and Bud and poor ol' William. I just never got around to it. It'll make a great book, though. Good luck."

"You, too." I replaced the phone and turned to find Kip staring at me through a small opening in my door. My instant reaction was anger. She'd simply opened the door without knocking. I had no idea how long she'd been listening.

"Bud didn't do anything wrong." She wiped under her eyes where her thick black mascara was smeared. To my amazement, I saw a tear trickle down her cheek. She brushed it away with fury. "Bud can't leave the farm. There's no one else to take care of the horses."

"Kip, your mother's future is on the line. Don't you understand that? She can go to prison for life."

"She doesn't care!" Kip's voice was heated. "They were both nothing but liars. Everything was a lie. All of it. I had to listen to them fighting, to the sound of him hitting her." She put her hands over her ears. "I heard it night after night."

I gripped her shoulders lightly. "I'm trying to help Lee. It might not be the way you like it, but I'm going to pursue every avenue. You said Lee didn't kill your father. Who did?"

She took a ragged breath and stepped back from me. "I don't know, but it wasn't Bud."

"Kip, if we can point the finger of doubt at someone else, it might save your mother."

"This is what I'm supposed to want to grow up to become. Grown-ups do whatever it takes to make it work out the way they want." She shook her head, and in the blurred ruin of her face, the eyes of a terrified child looked at me. "I don't want to be part of this. I'd rather die."

She stalked out of my room, and in a moment I heard her door slam with a righteous bang.

"It's awful hard to understand how you can throw the blame on someone just to take it off another. You'd think the truth would have something to do with it." Jitty had appeared at my elbow. Her face, normally unperturbed by the trials and tribulations of mere mortals, was worried. "If you plant the seeds of lies now, there'll be a high price to pay in the future when your harvest comes in."

"I don't think Lee killed Kemper. She tells a good story, but it doesn't ring true."

"That girl is gonna suffer no matter what you do."

Jitty was correct, and I was worried. "Maybe Kip should talk to a professional. You don't think she'll harm herself, do you?" Kip's last statement seemed melodramatic and very teenlike, but she wasn't experiencing the traumas of a normal teen. She'd been hurled into adulthood.

"Doubtful," Jitty said. "If she did, though, she might want to stay here and haunt you, too. Dahlia House is big, but not big enough for two ghosts."

She was gone and I was left wondering what in the world to do. Jitty might want an heir, but Kip was enough to shrivel my Fallopian tubes. Aunt LouLane, a confirmed spinster, had been a lot smarter than I'd ever appreciated. But in the long run, what good had it done her? She'd been saddled with me.

The telephone saved me from further morbid ruminations and signaled that one of my cohorts was probably reporting in. "What have you found?" I asked, by way of hello. I was unprepared for the male voice on the other end.

"I want to see Lee," Bud Lynch said. "I've got some questions about the farm. Some serious ones."

"The sheriff won't let you talk to her?" That surprised me. Coleman wasn't exactly the type to isolate a prisoner.

"He's stalling, and right now I don't have time for it. There's someone here to pick up Avenger. She has a bill of sale signed by Kemper."

I thought for a moment. "Tell them the horse is evidence in a murder investigation."

His chuckle was rich. "I like the way you think, Ms. Delaney. The problem is, Mrs. Bishop has a bill of sale signed by Kemper, showing that she paid two hundred thousand dollars for Avenger and four of our best mares bred to Avenger. I think she's afraid the horse will be implicated in the crime. She wants him removed before that happens. Bad for the breeding business, you know, if the stud is part of a murder."

"Does Lee know about this?"

"I doubt it."

There was just enough hesitation in his voice to make me wonder—and despair.

Knowing Lee as well as I did, this was one of the best reasons yet for her to kill her husband.

"*Could* Kemper have sold the horses? I thought they were Lee's." According to Harold, Kemper had sold Mrs. Peel. I needed to know the law on this issue.

"I'm not sure of the legalities. I'm just sure that Mrs. Bishop will do everything in her power to get those horses any way she can."

"Can you stall her?" Somehow I suspected Bud would be very good at delaying a woman.

"It's March. Her mares are ready to be bred. Past ready. She's not going to tolerate much of a delay. She's on her cell phone talking to a lawyer right this minute. If this bill of sale is legal, and if Kemper had the authority to sell the horses, she's going to do her best to take them as soon as possible. That's why I need to talk to Lee."

"I'll call Coleman."

"Make it fast. She's left the motor running in her truck." He hung up.

It took a few calls to track Coleman down, but, as it happened, he was headed out to Swift Level. My call was patched through to him, and I gave him the pertinent details. He promised to check into it.

I'd just hung up when the phone jangled

beneath my fingers. "Delaney Detective Agency."

"It's me." Tinkie's voice bubbled with excitement. "What do you have to eat?"

Whereas Cece preferred cheese Danish hot from the local bakery, Tinkie liked to come to Dahlia House for empty calorie consumption. Her expensive, registered dust mop, Chablis, liked to romp on the kitchen floor with Sweetie Pie.

"As it happens, some fresh strawberry pie." It was Delaney tradition to have at least one pie with the lush, sweet berries sliced and piled high in a graham-cracker-crumb crust and covered with mountains of whipped cream. I was a slave to tradition, especially when it came to food.

"We're on our way," Tinkie said as she hung up.

I looked around for Sweetie Pie. She'd be delighted to see Chablis. They were an interesting pair—the big, gangly red tic hound and the froufrou toy Yorkie. They adored each other.

My hound was nowhere in sight. I remembered that Kip had taken a liking to her, and it was a good excuse to check on the teenager. I knocked on her door, pounding to get over the din of the music. "Kip, Sweetie Pie has a friend coming over to play. Is she with you?"

The sudden silence was startling. When the

door opened, the first thing I noticed was Kip's clean face. Without all that makeup, she looked vulnerable. Her eyes were puffy from crying. Sweetie Pie sat at her side, tail thumping the floor. In that moment she looked like only a fourteen-year-old kid who'd listened to her parents fight and had been pressured to a level of performance in the show ring that I couldn't even imagine.

"Your dog has a friend coming over?" Kip looked from me to Sweetie Pie.

"Chablis. Tinkie's dog." I hesitated, then took the plunge. "I think you'd like the little vermin. She's terminally cute, and she has a lot of heart. Why don't you come down and meet Chablis and have some strawberry pie with me and Tinkie?"

She looked as if I'd asked her to perform a ballet on a bed of nails. "I'm not hungry."

"Kip, please come down. A grilled cheese sandwich won't hold you for long. You haven't eaten enough to keep a bird alive since you got here."

"Why do you care?" Her green eyes didn't flinch, but the *please* had gotten to her.

"I won't pretend to like you, but I do care what happens to you."

"Because of my mother?"

"Partly. Also because of you. I have a feeling

that if you'd give me half a chance, we might actually like each other."

She rubbed her eyes as if suddenly aware the makeup was gone. "Why aren't you married?" she demanded.

The question took me by surprise. "I haven't found the right man." I glanced past her to see if Jitty, somehow, had invaded her room and her brain. "It hasn't been my sole mission in life."

"All the women who come to the barn talk about their husbands, or the men they're screwing. That's all they talk about." She said this with complete disgust. "What's wrong with you?"

"Now that's a question that will take at least half an hour to answer. If you come downstairs, I'm sure Tinkie will be glad to fill you in."

Her lips pressed together. "I can leave if I want?"

I nodded. "But once Tinkie starts dishing the dirt on me, you'll be too fascinated to depart."

I didn't give her a chance to refuse. I walked away. Kip was furious with everyone and everything associated with her parents. I'd found only one thing that she seemed to like—dogs. Sweetie Pie had slipped beneath her defenses. Chablis was the next tool I had to attack the wall of armor Kip had so efficiently built.

6

Tinkie's tiny fists pounded against the old oak of Dahlia House's front door. With one eye on Kip, I opened the door. As usual, Tinkie sailed past me, Chablis tucked under one arm. "I'd adore some coffee, Sarah Booth," she said. "And some pie. I'm desperate for—" The sight of Kip, standing at the bottom of the stairs, halted her.

"Is that Katrina Lee Fuquar?" Tinkie asked as she began to circle Kip as though she were some exotic animal liable to pounce at any moment.

Kip held her ground. "My name is Kip." She stared at Tinkie unflinchingly, enduring the inspection.

"As you well know, Kip is staying with me," I said, grasping Tinkie's arm and propelling her toward the kitchen. "The coffee's perking." Tinkie could almost always be distracted with food.

I looked over my shoulder and motioned

Kip to follow us. Tinkie was still craning her neck to look back at the teenager as I pushed her through the dining room and into the kitchen. Without further ado, I parked her at the table.

The afternoon sun was coming through the white lace of the eyelet curtains, which danced on a tickling spring breeze. The strawberries smelled sweet and ripe, a promise of summer. Long ago, on just such a spring morning, I'd sat at the table and watched my mother make strawberry pies. "Nothing like fresh fruit in season," she'd said, holding out a washed berry for me to eat. The white curtains had filled with her laughter, fluttering like shards of sunlight.

"Sarah Booth?" Tinkie said, her brow furrowed. "Are you okay?"

I was saved from answering by the sound of footsteps in the dining room. To my surprise, Kip pushed through the swinging door and took a seat at the table. While Tinkie stared at Kip, Kip was mesmerized by Chablis.

"She's beautiful," she said, holding out a hand for Chablis to sniff.

The miniature fluffball leaped from Tinkie's arms and skittered across the table into Kip's lap. Her overbitten little jaw worked furiously as she licked Kip's face.

Sweetie Pie butted through the swinging door, tail thumping everything in sight. She rushed to Kip, put her front paws on the chair, and joined in the frenzy. Her long tongue slurped Kip's other cheek.

"She has a way with animals," Tinkie said, fascinated. "She must get that from her mother."

"The only things I got from Mother are green eyes and the knowledge that I'll never marry." Still holding Chablis, Kip stood up. "Can I take them outside?"

"Sure," Tinkie and I said in unison.

Kip banged out the back door with Chablis in her arms and Sweetie Pie on her heels.

"That hair," Tinkie said. "I think we should shave her head. She might have lice."

"She's having a hard time," I said, putting a slice of pie and a cup of coffee in front of Tinkie.

"And what about you?" Tinkie asked. "How are you managing with her in your home? It concerns me. Have you considered another"— she knew she was treading on thin ice—"place for Kip to stay? She has a reputation for having a really bad temper."

Lee had asked for my help, and I had given my word. But Tinkie was acting only as a concerned friend. "I'm fine with Kip being here.

We set some ground rules. Kip may have a temper, but she also has a good brain. It's in her best interests to keep me satisfied with her conduct."

My reputation for stubbornness was well known. "If you say so," Tinkie said as she speared a lush strawberry and held it to her mouth. I watched in fascination as she simultaneously bit and sucked, her Tawny Port lips moving over the berry in the most extraordinary fashion. Not a hint of moisture escaped her. I was immediately thrown back into the past. Ninth grade, high school cafeteria. Tinkie eating a strawberry in exactly the same fashion. It had brought Simon Mills, the chemistry teacher, to his proverbial knees. Tinkie had a lot to teach me.

"Where did you learn to do that?" I asked her.

She looked at me, all wide-eyed innocence. "Do what?"

I shook my head. "What did you find out?"

"You're going to love this," she said, pushing the almost empty plate away and leaning forward. "The hunt season is over. There's going to be a big ball." Her eyes sparkled. "And I've gotten both of us invited!"

I was impressed. I'd never run in the hunt society, but I knew the social events were always exclusive. "This is perfect. How did you manage it?"

She shrugged one shoulder in a modest gesture that was completely sincere. "Since Lee's in jail, Virginia Cooley Davis is hosting the ball. Let's just say she owes me a favor or two." Tinkie smiled.

"Virginia?" She'd been a delicate young girl who played the piano and read novels. I couldn't imagine her riding a horse in a blood sport, and said so.

"She doesn't ride. Her husband is a whip in the hunt, and she handles the social calendar." Tinkie retrieved the pie and opened her mouth for the last strawberry. When she finished, there wasn't even a smudge of whipped cream on her perfect lipstick. A Daddy's Girl had many talents.

"This is the final ball of the season," Tinkie continued, "and Chesterfield always has a very, very elegant affair. The men will wear tails with the colors of the hunt on the collar, and the ladies"—she grinned—"we wear ball gowns fit to kill." Her expression changed to one of worry. "Can you find a date? You have to have an escort."

"Of course I can find a date," I replied, cut to the bone. "You act like no one will go out with me."

"Have you been out since Hamilton the Fifth went back to Europe?" she asked pointedly.

"I've been busy, and—" Truth was, Hamilton, the focus of my first case and the man who'd touched my heart, was often on my mind.

"So, the answer is no. It doesn't sound like your dance card has any marks on it."

I glared at her. "You know, you're beginning to remind me of Brianna Rathbone." Brianna had figured prominently in my last case—as primary suspect, primo Daddy's Girl, former schoolmate, former model, wannabe biographer, and bitch extraordinaire.

Tinkie only laughed. "Well, put your thinking cap on, because you need an escort. And don't think you can fall back on Harold. I hear he's already got a date." She tilted her head, watching for my reaction.

"Who?" My attempt to play uninterested was a failure.

"This is the other thing I found out." She slowly sat back in her chair, playing out the moment like Gloria Swanson waiting for her close-up. "Harold's taking a married woman because her husband can't attend. Carol Beth Bishop!" At my blank look, she continued with some exasperation. "She was a Farley."

I inhaled. "No!" I remembered her perfectly.

She nodded. "In fact, she's in town right this minute. Even better, she's out at Swift Level, and she's claiming that she owns Lee's prime breeding stallion and four of her best mares. She has a bill of sale from Kemper, signing the horses over as collateral for a debt."

I stood up so fast my chair spilled over backward. There was a startled yelp at the kitchen window, and I caught a glimpse of Kip stumbling away. She'd been eavesdropping.

"Carol Beth Farley! She's the person claiming Lee's horses?" Now I knew why Bud Lynch had been so desperate to talk to Lee. Carol Beth took what she wanted, when she wanted it. Anyone who got in her way was flattened.

Tinkie nodded. "She's already called the sheriff on that trainer, Lynch. He won't turn over the horses to her."

"Bravo for him." His stock rose a notch in my eyes. At least he was good for something. "Carol Beth Farley," I said, pacing the kitchen. The moment that defined her for me was a sixth-grade piano recital competition held the spring after my parents' death. She'd worn a designer gown, her mahogany brown curls piled high on her head and a glittering tiara nestled on top. She'd taken one look at the plain satin dress Aunt LouLane had made for me and twisted up one corner of her mouth. "Appearance is three quarters of the performance," she'd said, and then gone on to prove it. She'd won.

But the story was more complex than our childhood rivalry. Frankie Archey was, hands down, the best pianist in the school. Three broken fingers on his right hand had forced him to withdraw from the contest. The day before the recital, when he was practicing alone in the school auditorium, Carol Beth slammed the piano cover on his hand. She said it was an accident. Frankie said nothing at all.

"How did you find out about Carol Beth?" I asked Tinkie.

"Virginia told me. She was at Swift Level making preparations for the ball. It's still going to be held there, even with Lee in jail. Lee has insisted, though Heaven knows why. Anyway, Virginia heard the whole exchange between the trainer and Carol Beth." She bit her lower lip, then let it pop out from her teeth. I'd borrowed that little gesture to good advantage in the past.

"Good work, Tinkie."

"There's one other thing." She paused.

"What?"

"Virginia said several of our old crowd have

been taking riding lessons from that horse trainer. It seems Bud has quite a following among the ladies."

I caught a glimpse of Kip, back at the window. Judging from the expression on her face, she wasn't as indifferent to what was happening as she wanted to make out.

Once Tinkie and Chablis had gone, I went up to Kip's room. She was lying on her unmade bed, a magazine open in front of her.

"We need to talk about school," I said. I needed to keep Kip busy and out of trouble.

"I'm not going back." She didn't bother to look up from the magazine. I sat down on the edge of the bed.

"Kip, you can't drop out of school."

She closed the magazine, revealing a horse and rider clearing a big fence. "Mr. Hayden said I could do my classes on-line if I can borrow your computer. I just can't go back to school now."

"I'll talk it over with your mom," I agreed.

"Do that," she said. "She won't care. I missed school all the time to ride." She flipped the magazine open again and began to read an article. I was dismissed.

Kip was heavy on my mind as I drove to *The*

Zinnia Dispatch to see what Cece had dug up on Kemper. Because I'd already eaten peach cobbler and a modest portion of strawberry pie, I decided to forgo the cheese Danish that was my usual offering to Cece. Poor decision. Cece was always nicer when fed.

Cece's door was open, and I slowed and stopped just outside when I noticed the well-dressed man sitting in front of her desk. He was groomed to perfection, and sat with one ankle crossed over a knee, perfectly at ease.

"An industrial park isn't exactly a society page story," Cece said in a tone that showed her patience had worn thin.

"Sunflower County has *no* development," the man said patiently. "What I'm proposing will bring jobs here. And my ideas on development are far from merely industrial. I envision great things for Sunflower County. This is a land rich in history and heritage. These are all things that can be capitalized on."

"It's a news story, not society," Cece insisted.

"Mr. Erkwell, at the bank, specifically told me to talk to you," the man said.

He was not big of stature, but he had grit. Either that or he was dumb as a post. I lingered just outside the door, shamelessly eavesdropping.

"I'll have to thank Harold," Cece said. She

leaned forward on her desk. Her perfect breasts pressed against the pale yellow sweater she wore, and I saw the gentleman's gaze lock on them. "You need to talk to someone on the news side, Mr. Walz. I can't help you."

"On the contrary, Miss Falcon. One positive mention of Riverbend Development Company in your column could open a lot of doors for us. We need the support of the community." He leaned forward in his chair as he continued to talk to her breasts.

"Mr. Erkwell explained to me how so many people, especially the . . . landed gentry, shall we call them, frown on development. I concede that there have been too many unfortunate incidents in the past where historic homes and beautiful architecture have been razed to make way for progress. I want to assure the people of Sunflower County that Riverbend isn't that kind of company. You could help me get that across."

I saw a flicker of interest pass over Cece's features. "Exactly what are your plans for Sunflower County?" she asked.

"We're very ambitious. We have some major investors. We're thinking of a golf course, a PGA-level course, with a country club and a housing development. Very elite, but preserving the integrity of the original property." He had his hands on his knees and had leaned back, but the flush on his face indicated that he had not lost interest in Cece's nonjournalistic assets. "It would be the economic scoop of the year for this state. This region."

"Have you selected a location?" Cece's tone was slightly bored, but I saw the keen interest in her eyes.

"We're exploring our options, but I'd like, very much, to anchor this development in Sunflower County. I've seen several pieces of property that capture my interest," he said, rising to his feet. "Can we count on your help?"

Cece finally caught sight of me lurking outside the door. "As I said, Mr. Walz, this is a news story. Until you begin development."

He smiled at her. "I'll look forward to working with you, Miss Falcon." He came out of the office, nodding at me as he left.

"Who was that?" I asked, stepping into her office and closing the door.

"Nathaniel Walz," she said, rolling her eyes. "A short man with a persistence problem."

"Have you found out anything for me?" I asked, settling into the chair that Walz had vacated.

Cece's smile grew wide and toothsome. "You will not believe what I found." Her nails, beautifully manicured and painted a glittering shade of metallic fruit, drummed on the small space of her desk that wasn't piled with paper.

"Spill it, Cece."

"Krystal Brook, the country singer, wants to do a benefit for Lee, to raise money for her defense. Her husband, who's also her manager, stopped by to see if I would do some articles if Krystal agreed to sing."

"Terrific." Benefit was good, but I needed leads.

"You'll never guess who Krystal Brook really is." Cece was beside herself.

"Who?" I asked, not wanting to play celebrity guessing games.

"Simpson Maes Fielding!"

I was stunned. Simpson was a Daddy's Girl, not a country music diva. "Simpson?"

Cece nodded, arching one perfectly groomed brow. "Her husband, Mike Rich, is trying to launch her career big time."

"Simpson is now Krystal?" I was still in disbelief. "Krystal Brook? That's her name now?"

"She legally changed her name. It takes a lot of guts to do that—to just abandon the past and become a completely different person."

Cece would know, from firsthand experience. "It takes a little getting used to, but it sounds like a great country music name."

"This benefit could help Lee and Krystal

both. Mike said that Krystal is really talented, that she just needs a chance. She'll get total media coverage for doing this."

It was good to know that Simpson hadn't been completely transformed. She could still find the silver lining in another person's cloud. "Great. I hope it works out. But did you find out anything about Kemper that we can use?"

Not bothering to hide her miff at my lack of interest in music stars, Cece picked up a notepad and began to scan it. "I'm still digging. I haven't been able to locate his family, but I did turn up an interesting tidbit. He was expelled from Louisiana State University. Some form of misconduct. And he owned a club in New Orleans for a time." She slid her hand over the varnished surface of her desk. Her Gilded Apricot nails shimmered. "In general, a lot of false starts. Until he hooked up with Lee."

"No criminal charges?"

"None," she said, "but I'm still checking." She shuffled the papers on her desk and selected a sheet. "I have taken care of Kemper's funeral arrangements. There was no one else to do it. Thursday. Eleven o'clock. St. Lucy's Cemetery."

"Thank you, Cece." I meant it. "I know Lee will appreciate it."

"I'd have her there, Sarah Booth. For her daughter's sake and for appearances."

I nodded. "I could kiss you."

Cece held up one hand like Diana Ross stopping love. "Control yourself, Sarah Booth. We're friends, but you're not my type. Speaking of types, wherever are you going to get a date for the hunt ball? I've racked my brain, and I can't think of a single man who would take you on."

I stopped at the Pig and bought food. In concession to Kip's age, I included some chips and colas, but I also got shredded cabbage, catfish, and the makings for hush puppies and fries. I wasn't certain what type of food Kip liked, but no one in her right mind could resist fried catfish and all the trimmings. Grocery sacks in hand, I hustled in the back door. Sweetie was sound asleep on the kitchen floor, and there was no sign of Kip.

I checked in my bedroom, where the computer screen saver shifted from Mickey Spillane to Dick Tracy and a host of other cartoon renderings of detectives. Kip had been at work on the computer and failed to shut it down.

I knocked at her door. No answer. Feeling as

if I were committing a crime, I opened the door of her room. Her clothes were all over the floor, along with CDs, books, magazines, and makeup.

"She's gone."

I turned to find Jitty peering over my shoulder. "So I see."

"She's very unhappy," Jitty said.

She wasn't telling me anything I didn't know. "I'm worried about her."

"Worried that she's unhappy, or worried that she has a reason to be unhappy?"

While I couldn't confess my concerns to anyone else, I could tell them to Jitty. She couldn't repeat them, because no one else could hear her.

"What if she killed Kemper?" I asked, nudging a CD with my toe. The band on the cover looked as if they could be Satan worshipers.

"What if she did?"

It was the crux of my dilemma. Lee had not hired me to prove her innocence; she'd hired me to prove that Kemper was a bastard. The reason for this fine distinction might very well be Kip. I saw Lee's strategy very clearly now. She had confessed, which would prevent a full-scale investigation of the murder. She wanted me to provide the evidence that

Kemper was a worthless piece of work, which no one disputed. That would keep the focus of the trial on Kemper—and away from Kip. Lee had stepped onto an oily tightrope. If she could actually convince a jury of her peers of Kemper's role as abscess on the butt of the world, the right jury just might acquit her. She was correct; it had happened before. Barring that, she might get manslaughter and a sentence that amounted to county jail and probation. She could still keep Swift Level up and running and Kip safe. But it was a dangerous, dangerous game.

The thing that troubled me was Lee's first lie—that Kemper had attacked her and provoked his death. There had not been a single mark on Lee in that jail cell. A smart prosecutor, and Lincoln Bangs was not stupid, would have noticed that. That and the fact that Lee had never reported Kemper's repeated abuse of her, not one single time.

"Look at this mess." Jitty's voice pulled me back to the disarray of Kip's room. Had it not been a perfect reflection of my own room, I would have been forced to have the old "cleanliness is next to godliness" conversation with Kip. Spared by my own vices.

I turned around to leave and felt something

crack beneath my shoe. Mascara. A black makeup kit was open on the floor, the contents spilling out. A tip of blue plastic caught my eye. I looked over at Jitty.

"She's your responsibility," she said.

I knelt down. The syringe was still in the plastic case, unused. I dumped the lipstick, mascara, and eyeliner pencils onto the floor. There was nothing else. No vials of medicine, no plastic bags of white powder. Just the syringe.

The phone rang and I walked to my room to answer it.

"Sarah Booth, it's Virginia. You need to come out to Swift Level right away."

I barely knew Virginia Davis. "What's wrong?" I asked.

"It's Lee's daughter. She's out here and she's in a real state. The girl is acting crazy."

"I'm on the way."

Since Virginia had called, I went to the main house instead of the barn. There was a gold Lexus in the driveway, and a green Mercedes. The only other vehicle in sight was a big black truck with dual rear tires, parked at the barn.

I walked into a scene so thick with tension that I stopped. Kip was sitting in a chair, her

face streaked with makeup and dirt. A handsome man in casual slacks and a white shirt sat
on the sofa, chatting with Virginia.

"Sarah Booth," Virginia said, as soon as she
saw me. "Thank goodness." She gave Kip a
wary glance as she walked past her to take my
hand.

"What happened?" I addressed the question
to Virginia.

"Kip had a little tantrum," the man said. He
stood up. "Mike Rich. Pleased to meet you,
Miss Delaney. I've heard a bit about you from
my wife."

I'd heard his name, but I couldn't place it.
My focus was on Kip.

"What happened?" I asked her again.

"I was looking for something." She kept her
gaze on the floor.

"She's torn up Mr. Lynch's apartment," Virginia said with disapproval. "Her mother
would be so disappointed in the behavior."

Kip was on her feet. "Let her be disappointed! What about me? Does it matter that
I'm disappointed? She lied to me. She lied to
everyone. You can all just go to hell!" She ran
out of the room. I heard the front door bang.

"How did she get out here?" I asked.

"I brought her." Mike Rich had remained
standing. "I stopped by your home to discuss a

business matter with you. You weren't home, so I mentioned that I was coming out here to look at Swift Level for the benefit concert." He paused for a moment, his gaze on Virginia. "Kip asked for a ride out here, and I obliged."

Virginia cleared her throat. "I've already told Mr. Rich that a concert is out of the question here. We're in the midst of preparations for the Chesterfield Hunt Ball on Saturday."

That was a sticky wicket I didn't want to touch. My only concern was Kip. "Are you often in the habit of giving teenage girls a ride?" I asked. I was angry with Mike Rich. At the very least, his actions fell in the category of stupid.

"Kip isn't exactly a stranger. I knew her father," he said with one eyebrow lifted. "I'm Krystal Brook's husband."

Mike Rich, star-maker. Now I placed his name.

"What are you going to do about that child?" Virginia asked. "She's been in trouble at school. I was hoping that psychiatrist would put her on medication. There are times I worry that she's a danger to herself or some . . . one . . . else." She let her sentence stumble to a halt. "Excuse me, I need to check on the carpenters. We're installing the scaffolding for the floral arrangements."

Virginia left the room, and I found myself alone with Mike. I could feel him watching me as I walked to a beautiful old piano. I touched the ivories, drawing out a few simple chords.

"Krystal didn't tell me you were musically inclined," he said. "I thought your talent was sleuthing."

"You said you were at Dahlia House to discuss a business proposition."

"Yes, security for Krystal's benefit concert. Since you're in the private eye business, I thought you might be able to recommend some muscle. I'll need at least four trained men. One at the door, one backstage, and two in the crowd. I pay Nashville wage."

"I'm afraid I don't know any reliable 'muscle,'" I said. It was an interesting term. "Why don't you check with the sheriff?"

"He's agreed to attend the concert, of course. He's a friend of Lee's and also of my wife. But Sheriff Peters's staff is small, and he doesn't encourage moonlighting."

I closed the piano. "I'm sorry, I can't help you." I had to find Kip. I'd given her a few moments to calm down, but I was going to have to talk to her.

"I know you're not Kip's mother, but let me give you a word of advice. That girl needs to be taken in hand. She's famous for pitching fits at horse shows, refusing to ride. She's high-strung, but that's no excuse for the tantrum she threw here." He followed me to the front door. "Maybe some medication wouldn't be a bad idea. Something just to level her out for a while."

"I'll take it under advisement," I said as I walked across the porch and down the steps.

Kip was sitting on the ground, her back against the wheel of my car. She climbed into the front seat without a word. I backed up, hesitating before I put the car in gear. "Do you want to see the horses before we leave?"

She shook her head, burgundy spikes wobbling.

"Kip, what happened out here?"

She shrugged. "I lost something in Bud's apartment. I was looking for it."

"Did you ask his permission?"

"He wasn't around." She shot a glare at me. "Besides, it's my place, not his. He's just a hired hand. He doesn't own anything."

"Only a few hours ago, you were defending Bud," I reminded her.

"That was then." She turned away from me so that I could see her jawline. It reminded me of Lee's, the stubborn strength of it.

"What happened?" I asked her.

"That bitch Carol Beth Bishop was in the barn. She and Bud. Together." Her voice was swollen with hurt and anger. "He said before it was because he was trying to help Mama, but that was just another damn lie. Since Mama's in jail, I guess they can screw in the barn aisles if they want to. They all lie so they can do whatever they want to do." She reached across her seat and grabbed the seat belt. "Can we go?"

I set the car in motion, going slowly out the drive. "Was she after the horses?" I asked.

"The horses, Bud, whatever she can get. I hate her." She was staring out the windshield, and a strange blank look came over her face. "I hate her," she said slowly. "She's always here, always hanging around. I wish she'd die." The expression on her face shifted chillingly in the spring light. "Maybe she will."

My mouth went dry. "What are you saying, Kip?"

She looked at me, a long, appraising glance. "I know what it's like to hate someone, to hate them enough to do something awful."

My pulse quickened. "What kind of awful thing are you talking about?"

She lowered her chin, tucking it almost to her chest. Her glance was sidelong, considering. "You don't really want to know, Sarah Booth. Trust me, you don't. Because if I tell you, then you'll have to do something about it, and that would make Mama really upset."

7

Propped up on pillows in my bed, I tried to focus on the book I'd selected to read. It was a defense lawyer's recounting of cases, many of them involving women who'd killed their spouses. I was hoping for some help, but my mind refused to cooperate. I couldn't stop thinking about Kip.

She had hammered me with her bitter assessment of my cowardice. I'd failed to question her about the syringe in her makeup kit. She was correct—I didn't want to know the truth. Not until I had an idea of what I would do with it. What I *should* do with it. What my role as Lee's private investigator and my ethics *required* me to do with it.

I felt a chill in the room and lowered the book I wasn't reading to find Jitty standing at the foot of the bed.

"You've got yourself in a fine mess," she said softly. She sat down on the edge of the bed, her weight undetectable. "Have you figured out what you're gonna do?"

I shook my head. "I have a hypothetical question. If Lee chooses to sacrifice herself for her daughter, do I have a right to try to stop her?"

Jitty shifted, semireclining so that the moonlight falling through the bedroom window was softly gathered into the folds of her sheer nightgown. "This entire case is about the future, Sarah Booth. Lee's and Kip's. If you had a daughter, what would you do?"

Imagining the future was difficult. Imagining the future with a teenage daughter was even harder. But I knew the answer. Deep inside, there was no doubt. "The same thing Lee is doing. The same thing Mama would have done for me."

Jitty nodded. "There is no sacrifice too great for your child."

I sighed. "What about the truth?"

"Whose truth?"

There were times when Jitty's wisdom superseded her pain-in-the-ass qualities, and this was one of them. "Did you ever have children?" I asked.

She shifted off the bed in one fluid movement and went to the window. Her gown shimmered on a soft spring breeze, and I saw no trace of childbearing in her lean and supple body. But Jitty was a ghost. She was beyond the scars and failings of mere mortals.

"No children. But like you, Sarah Booth, I've had many losses. Children are the hope of the future. Kip is Lee's future. That child is what she lives for."

"What should I do?" I was firmly wedged between duty and honor.

Jitty turned to face me, and in the moonlight I saw the glint of her smile. "It seems to me your friend is hanging on to the past and trying to preserve the future. I don't think she can do it. I don't think anyone can."

She left the window and drifted to the door.

"Don't go," I said. Her words had left me with a sense of vague dread.

"I have an appointment." Jitty's moment of pensiveness was over. She did a slow turn so that the gown swirled from her hips to her ankles in one shimmering movement. "One of us has to exercise the old libido." She was gone, but her voice, faded and hardly more than a whisper, came back to me. "Be careful, Sarah Booth. Be careful."

I snapped off the light. The dark was velvety soft, the best of the Delta before the arrival of humidity and savage, biting insects. I could hear the soft throbbing of the frogs, and the chirr of the crickets, sounds I'd come to expect as part of my life, part of the first awakening of spring.

For most of my life I'd slept in this room, except for a few years of misadventuring. Jitty's comments had thrown my past and my future into sharp relief. I saw myself clearly hung on the cusp of the present. I had no past or future. One was lost in the fog of time and the other didn't exist. Would a child connect me to both, as Jitty implied? I wasn't certain.

At last I felt the pull of sleep, and I tried to shake free of the bonds of anxiety that held me in wakefulness. Eyes closed, I slipped into a dream. I was alone in the middle of a darkened room. As I glanced at a wall, a light snapped on, highlighting a black-and-white photograph. I went closer, to examine the image.

The child that looked back at me was dark-haired and smiling, a beautiful little girl holding on to a horsehair sofa for support. I knew her. She was my daughter. Her name was—

I wasn't certain what startled me out of my dream, but I was fully awake, tensed, and listening. Someone was walking by my bedroom door.

The steps were sneaky, a tiptoe on the stairs, a pause whenever a board creaked or moaned.

Easing out of bed, I cracked my bedroom door and looked out into the dark hall. A slight figure was descending the stairs. Kip.

Listening closely, I waited for her to make it to the first floor before I followed. Moving with great care, I slipped down the stairs, alert to every tiny sound. Kip had gone through the parlor and the dining room, and I heard the soft *shush-shush* of the kitchen door swinging closed. Maybe she'd gotten up for a snack. But that didn't explain her furtiveness.

I continued behind her, stopping at the swinging door. I could hear her in the kitchen, and after a few seconds I knew what she was doing. She was on the phone.

"I found out today that she has my horse," she said. There was a pause. "I'm positive. The man who bought her was put up to it by Carol Beth." Another pause. "I don't care. I don't care! I'm going to kill her."

I took a long, slow breath through my nose.

"I hate her. She's tried to take everything. She's greedy and awful, and I hate her!"

Kip's voice had begun to rise, but she got control of herself. "She's going to pay," she said in a calmer, more deadly tone. "I can't call you. My phone privileges have been revoked. She pretends not to, but she's watching me all the time."

I could hear her opening a bag of chips as she talked. "Good idea. Maybe that'll keep her off my back so I can finish what I started."

There was the click and fizz of a soda opening. "Okay, that sounds good. Whenever you can stop by. Just don't call."

The receiver was returned to the hook.

I crept back up the stairs and crawled into bed. I was not afraid of Kip, but I was afraid of what I would learn about her. Before I opened this can of worms, I needed hard facts. If Kip had committed one violent act, there was a likelihood that she might do it again.

When Kip was safely back in bed, I picked up the telephone in my room and hit star sixty-nine. I counted the seven musical beeps, a local number. The telephone rang and rang, but no one answered. Digging up the phone records to reveal Kip's partner in crime would take too long. I needed to make Lee understand that she could protect Kip from everyone but herself.

Mornings are normally my favorite time of day. There is a magic in the first moments of wakefulness, a tear in reality when anything is possible. My night had been restless, and I awoke groggy and filled with a sense of dread.

The pale yellow light of morning spilled through the window and across the foot of my bed, filling the room with a soundless presence. I realized then that Sweetie Pie wasn't beside my bed. Normally I could hear her light snoring. She was undoubtedly in Kip's room. The girl did have a way with animals.

"If you're gonna play mama, you'd best get yourself down to the kitchen and make breakfast."

Jitty was sitting in the rocker in a corner of the room. Gone without a trace was the compassion she'd shown the previous night. She'd finally changed out of my sweats and was wearing a red shorts-and-halter set. Forties? Nineties? I couldn't exactly pin down the era. Jitty had an annoying habit of traipsing through the decades in search of an identity. Whatever place in history that outfit had come from, it was definitely hot. The material was shiny and clingy. Spandex? Her white sandals were strappy, with a three-inch heel.

"You're looking anything but maternal," I said, throwing back the covers and standing up to stretch.

"Somebody around here's got to look presentable. What are you gonna do about a date for that big ball? Might be fun to conjure you up a man out of thin air. 'Course that might be the only place you'd find one willin' to be your escort."

"I have other, more important things on my mind, Jitty." I'd gone over every available man I knew and hadn't come up with a single idea for a date.

"Keep on pretendin'," she said, walking across the room with a strut that could have made a grown man cry. "You ought to get on one of those computer dating services."

I was tired of this harangue. "You do it if you're so smart."

Jitty did a three-quarter turn like a runway model. She must have practiced the move for weeks. "You know I can't type."

"Never too late to learn a useful skill." I retrieved a pair of shoes from beneath some clothes on the floor.

"It's too early for such attitude." Jitty glared at me. "It's not that I can't *type*. I *can't* type."

I had forgotten. Noncorporeal drawback. "So there is a limit to your mischief. Thank goodness for that." I went to the closet and found some jeans and a blouse.

"You gone go off and leave that young'un again today? Seems to me you might want to keep an eye on her."

"I've got to go see Doc Sawyer. I don't think she needs to hear the details of the autopsy. And I have to check on Kemper's arrangements."

Jitty nodded. "Keep it short. That's my advice. A song, a prayer, then plant him."

I gave her a dirty look. "Lee and the high-school principal agreed with me, so Kip has schoolwork to do. Don't be pestering her."

"You know I can't pester anyone but you. That's an interestin' word choice, though. Back when I was a young woman, pester was what a man did to a woman."

"I don't have time for this now."

"You're runnin' out of time, all right. That ol' biological clock is ticktocking away. Maybe you should give up on the man and just hunt you an Internet sperm bank."

"I can find a date. I can find one right here in Sunflower County. I don't have to import a man from cyberspace. Now give up on the whole Internet romance idea." I drew on my clothes. "I'll make some coffee. Kip's on her own for breakfast."

I opened the door and found Kip standing there, eyebrows drawn together in concern. "Were you talking to someone about finding a date for the ball?" she asked, looking around me at the empty room.

"Myself," I said, annoyed and embarrassed. "I

live alone. Sometimes I need stimulating conversation."

She examined the corners of the room one more time, then accepted that I was as crazy as a run-over dog. "You really have to have an escort. It's the stupidest rule. You could take a corpse, but it has to be a guy and he has to have on tails."

"I'll find someone."

"Where? All the men around here are married. Even if they don't act it."

My love life wasn't something I wanted to discuss with Kip. "I've got to get busy. Will you be okay?"

"I want to get my hair fixed. The funeral . . . Folks blame Mama because I look different," she said.

I was surprised. Kip's "look" was something she'd worked hard to achieve. "How about this afternoon? We can go to one of the salons—"

"No." Her objection was sharp. "You can do it."

"Me?" I didn't mind; it was just that she would likely turn out bald.

"I don't want to go to town. Everyone will stare."

They would, but Kip was going to have to face them sometime. She couldn't hide away at

Dahlia House or Swift Level for the rest of the year.

"Please, Sarah Booth."

Kip had taken two giant steps. She'd put her mother first and she'd used the word *please*. She was trying hard, and I had a sudden inspiration. Tinkie had aspirations of hair design. "What if Tinkie did it?"

Kip nodded. "That would be okay. I like her dog."

"Chablis is hard not to like." The dog and I had a long history. In my desperation to save Dahlia House, I'd dognapped Chablis. Tinkie had been my first client—she'd hired me to find her dog. I was still working that black mark off my karma. "I'll be back soon, and I'll have Tinkie give you a call."

Doc Sawyer's office hadn't changed an iota since the last time I was there—to get the autopsy results on Lawrence Ambrose. It appeared that even the same pot of coffee was brewing. At Doc's offer, I poured some into a Styrofoam cup. When the cup didn't dissolve, I added five spoons of whitener and enough sugar to sweeten crotchety old Mrs. Hedgepeth.

"You're here to get the results of Kemper's

autopsy," Doc said. He swung his feet down off his desk and sat forward in his chair. "Take a seat, this is going to take a bit of time. He was quite a mess."

With his magnificent nimbus of white hair, he looked like Mark Twain, and he had the wonderful mannerisms of an old Southern gentleman. A little eccentric, a lot kind. I noticed his complexion was less ruddy and his eyes were crystal clear. He'd gone on the wagon shortly after Lawrence was murdered, and judging from his appearance, he was still riding high.

I sat in the only other chair in the small, cramped space behind the Sunflower County Hospital emergency room. Doc had given up his general practice and semiretired to standby emergency work. "Doc, I need something solid. I have to talk to Lee, but I need the facts before I go there."

"You want me to tell you who killed him, right?" he said with a deep sadness.

"What I'd like to hear is that the horse killed him."

Doc picked up some papers on his desk. "I could almost say that."

I almost leaped out of my chair. "Can you? Really?"

Doc waved me back into my seat. "It's a

little more complicated than that, Sarah
Booth." His smile was tired. "But then isn't
it always. You know, I delivered Eulalee. I
watched that girl fight to carve her own identity. And then I delivered Katrina."

He looked out his window that gave a view
of the ambulance bay, which was, thankfully,
empty.

"The horse did plenty of damage to Kemper, no one can doubt that. The fatal blow was
delivered to the head by some type of metal
instrument."

"The horse was shod!"

"Avenger was wearing shoes on his front
feet. I've already checked into that."

"Then you think the horse did it?" Of all
the suspects I'd hoped to line up for Lee, I'd
never thought to pin the murder on a horse.

"He's capable of it. He attacked Kemper in
November. Bit him seriously. I know because I
treated the wound. Lee said Kemper brought
the injury on himself, and I don't doubt it.
Kemper reaped what he sowed."

"I haven't met a single person who doesn't
agree that Kemper needed to die. Unfortunately, that isn't a very good defense for Lee. If
we could prove that it was accidental, that Lee
and Kemper fought, maybe even that she
struck him, but that the actual deathblow was

delivered by the horse . . ." My mind was churning with possibilities. "Avenger has a reputation as a dangerous animal, doesn't he?"

Doc shrugged. "Lillian Sparks would be the woman to ask about that." He said this with some reservation.

"You recommend Lillian, not Lee. Why?"

"She's not personally invested in the horse. Lee is. Avenger is the horse Lee's been looking for all of her life. She can't see how dangerous he is. Every time there's an injury, she blames everyone but the horse."

Doc stood up. "I'll have more forensic answers when my tests come back from the state lab. I have to determine what type of metal instrument struck Kemper in the head."

"But you're positive that blow to the head was the cause of death."

He nodded.

"Do you know the time of death?"

"I'll know more when the tests come back."

"When might that be?"

"This afternoon. Tomorrow." His head gave a quick tilt to the right, a gesture of impatience or evasiveness.

"Doc, you treated Kemper for the horse bite. What about Lee? Did you ever treat her for injuries?" He knew where I was headed.

"Yes."

"For accidents?"

"Yes. And I can't say more than that. Doctor-patient privileges." His tone was terse.

He'd delivered Lee. She was one of his. I took a gamble. "What about Kip? Did you treat her?"

"No. Not for physical injuries." He stood up and walked to the door. "I heard Kip was staying with you. That's good for her. She needs someone now. Someone who can hold the line." He stood in the open doorway, looking beyond me. "Be careful, Sarah Booth. Kindness can be both generous and foolhardy." There was more to this than he was going to say. "Lee has better answers for you than I have."

"I'll check back with you," I said.

Doc's smile was tired and sad. "I'm sure you will, Sarah Booth."

A confrontation with Lee was inevitable, but I managed to delay it a bit by stopping at Lillian Sparks's home. I'd been there during the last holiday season to deliver one of Lawrence Ambrose's orphaned cats. I was delighted to see Apollo perched in the front window when I pulled up.

Lillian answered the door and ushered me back into the kitchen, where she was making tomato aspic for a dinner party. I settled at her kitchen table while she made tea for both of us.

"Tell me about the horses at Swift Level," I said.

Using exact movements, Lillian put the tea leaves in a cerulean ceramic teapot. "Avenger is one of the most magnificent performance horses of the century," she said. "Lee really has something with him."

"Doc says he may have killed Kemper."

Lillian snorted. "No wonder Lee confessed. She'd sell her soul to save that stallion. Without him, there is no Swift Level." She poured the boiling water over the leaves. "But Lee's story doesn't make sense. Kemper was an idiot, but he'd never have gone into that horse's stall, not even in a fit of rage to hurt Lee. Avenger hated him. People think of horses as big, dumb animals. They aren't stupid. They're fully capable of recognizing someone who hurts them. Avenger was gentle as a kitten, unless Kemper was around. Avenger saw into Kemper's soul. He saw the blackness, and he hated him."

"Tell me about Kip," I asked.

Lillian was settling the teapot lid. The lid flipped from the pot, landing with a clatter on the stovetop. Her hand shaking, she ignored the implication of my question. "Kip's the most accomplished rider I've ever seen."

"I need to know the truth, Lillian." She knew far more than she was saying.

"Whose truth?" she asked, and I felt the vague uneasiness of the night before.

"The plain truth."

Lillian poured the tea into thick mugs painted with horses that looked like cave drawings. "Ask yourself why Lee *confessed*," she said. "What would make her risk her future and her dream? When you know that, you'll know the truth."

Kip was in my bedroom on the computer when I got home. I'd bought groceries and I made dinner and waited, setting the table in the kitchen. She came down the stairs at a gallop with Sweetie Pie right behind her.

She asked no questions of my day or about her mother, and I let the silence fall over the meal, until she looked up at me.

"Kip, where were you the night your father died?"

She was putting the last bite of her sloppy joe into her mouth. She chewed and swallowed. "What did Mother say?"

"It doesn't matter. I need the truth."

"I was in my room," she answered, getting up and putting her plate in the sink. "May I be excused?"

"No, you may not. What were you doing in your room that night?"

Kip stared at her fork. "I was doing my homework. Biology."

"Alone?"

She finally looked up. "Yes. Alone. Now may I be excused?"

I had to press harder. "This afternoon, I went in your room looking for you. I saw a syringe in your makeup bag. Why do you have it?"

Anger touched her eyes and the corners of her mouth. One hand slipped to the back of her chair for support. "I *thought* you were snooping around."

"I wasn't snooping." My own anger rose. "Why do you have a syringe?"

"For the horses," she said with a look that held pity and contempt. "If you knew anything about a horse farm you'd know that syringes are all over the house, in the barn, in the horse trailers, all the vehicles. We all have them, because in an emergency you don't have time to go out and find a drugstore that's open."

One side of her mouth lifted. "You think I'm doing drugs?" She laughed. "They drug test the horses, but not the riders."

"Kip, are you taking anything?"

She was openly amused at me, and terribly angry. "Other than the prescribed drugs, you mean?"

"Prescribed?"

"The Prozac and the Paxil. The stuff Dr. Vance gave me. To keep me calm. To keep me in school and on the circuit. To keep the pressure from getting to be too much when my parents screamed and fought."

I knew Dr. Vance. He was a child psychiatrist in Memphis, the preferred magician for the youth of the Sunflower County wealthy.

"You're seeing Dr. Vance?" Lee hadn't mentioned this minor detail.

"Since the school incident. I had to agree to counseling before they'd let me back in school."

"And Dr. Vance prescribed those drugs?"

"You didn't know? Mother didn't tell you? She didn't warn you that I was highly unstable? The diagnosis was severe depression and extreme anxiety." Her smile was bitter. "I'm crazy, Sarah Booth, but not too crazy to ride in the show ring for Swift Level. Now may I be excused?"

I nodded. Kip was no longer the focus of my thoughts. They had shifted to Lee, and the many things she'd failed to tell me.

By the time the dishes were put away, I was exhausted. I wanted nothing more than quiet and the luxury of a good book. The technicalities and hairpin curves of murder trial tactics were too much for me. I picked up my new copy of Kinky Friedman's latest mystery and climbed the stairs like a woman twice my age. Emotion is frequently worse than aerobics as far as wear and tear goes.

Settling beneath the comforter, I opened the book and allowed myself to be a silent participant in the New York City loft where Kinky cogitated and, above us, the lesbian dance class tapped their way to bliss. I read Kinky for fun, but there was also the hope that I might learn a few tricks of the P.I. trade from the eccentric sleuth.

My last thought was that Kinky would have a lot more success with women if he got rid of his cigars. Or maybe I would have more success with men if I smoked a good Cuban stogy.

8

It was still early on Wednesday morning when the ringing telephone pulled me out of a foggy dream about a golden-eyed cat batting a puppet head around the floor of a New York apartment. Both red telephones on the desk of Private Investigator Kinky Friedman were ringing.

And so was mine. It was a long flight home from Kinky-land to my bedroom.

I fumbled the phone to my ear and heard Cece talking a mile a minute. "—and bring Danish. Hurry!" Click. She'd hung up.

It was time to get up, so I dressed. On my way out, I tapped lightly at Kip's door. There was no answer, so I cracked it open. She was flung across the bed, one hand dangling on the floor, her back lifting softly and rhythmically with her breathing.

Who and what was this child? Lee owed me some answers.

I hurried out of the house and to the

bakery, per Cece's specific order. With a white bag of cheese Danish in hand, I entered the newspaper office.

"Bribing Cece again?" Garvel LaMott asked with a sneer.

Garvel had been the high-school tattletale. He was the police beat reporter for the paper, and he had shoes that ate his white socks, exposing pasty ankles with scattered black hairs.

I ignored him and entered Cece's private office without knocking. Only when I closed the door did she look up to see who'd arrived. She was so eager to tell her news she ignored the bag of Danish. "I tracked down an old girlfriend of Kemper's, circa 1970's, over in Louisiana."

"And?" I put the bag on top of a pile of papers on her desk.

"She wasn't surprised to discover someone had killed him. She said the reason Kemper made such stupid decisions was because he thought with his penis and there wasn't a lot there to work with."

"*Aye-yi-yi-yi,*" I said, laughing. "I hope you print that. Remember, you can't slander the dead."

"Don't tempt me." Cece's teeth were large, even, and dazzlingly white. She was showing a lot of them.

"Anything else from the Bayou State?" No one had ever met Kemper's family. Lee had brought him home from Lafayette, Louisiana, an unknown entity.

Cece snagged a Danish, took a large bite, and then daintily wiped the corners of her mouth with one elegant finger. "Odd that you should ask. Leshia and Henri Fuquar live in St. Martinsville, about thirty minutes from Lafayette. According to his ex-girlfriend, they disowned Kemper when he was sixteen. They had him emancipated and cut him loose. Prior to that, they'd petitioned the Church for an exorcism."

"You've got to be kidding." She was, but not completely.

"The exorcism was my personal touch, but Kemper made quite an impression on his hometown. His ex-girlfriend said he set a teacher's car on fire at the high school. He ran with a tough crowd, displaying all the traits of a true sociopath. She said he showed no remorse for any of his acts. The phrase she used was 'bad seed.'"

The term "bad seed" was like a tumbler of ice water down my spine. I knew from my studies that some mental disorders were genetically transmitted. Or at least the tendencies for them. "Did you speak with his parents?"

"I called twice. They won't talk to me." She pushed a sheet of paper across her desk to me. "They said their son died years ago, and the man using his name has no relationship to them. You might have better luck."

I went around the desk and gave Cece a big hug. "You go, girl," I said. "This is the kind of stuff that may actually help Lee if she insists on the defense that Kemper just needed to be killed."

"There is one other small thing." Cece extricated herself from my hug, licked some white icing off her fingertip, then looked me dead in the eye. "Your date for the ball. Tinkie went to a lot of trouble to get you invited. The Chesterfield Hunt Ball is very formal. It would be better if it were someone who could ride, but that's asking the impossible."

"Cece!" I was shocked at her lack of faith in me.

"Oh, I didn't mean it that way. It's just that there aren't any suitable men around. Except Harold, and he's going with that witch Carol Beth." She leaned forward, perfect eyebrows arched in animation. "Can you believe her, showing up to take Lee's horses before Kemper is cold in the ground? She should be at the top of your list of suspects."

"If Kemper got in her way, she'd hammer him," I agreed. "She always believed that whatever she wanted was there to be plucked." I didn't have a single good memory of Carol Beth. "Men, money, jobs, cars, whatever. She pointed and her daddy had it delivered to her door."

This was not an exaggeration. Our senior year, Mr. Farley had a hunter-green Jaguar XKE driven through the marble hallway of their home, Magnolia Lane, and parked in front of Carol Beth's bedroom door.

"She's got enough money to buy any horse she wants. Why is she determined to take Lee's horses?" Cece asked.

It was a brilliant question. Even if what Lillian and everyone else said about Avenger was one-hundred-percent true, there were still other fine horses. Some of which were for sale.

"If I find out anything new, you'll be the first to know," I promised Cece.

"Where are you headed today?" she asked.

"To see Lee." I studied the slip of paper Cece had given me. It was just a phone number.

"Better wait until after lunch. Coleman or

someone has arranged for her to speak with a psychiatrist."

My gaze snapped up to hers. "Lee?"

She nodded. "Insanity, of the temporary sort, might not be a bad plea for her."

"Lee's not crazy. She's just stubborn."

"Sometimes, Sarah Booth, stubborn just slides right into crazy. You should know."

On my last drive out to Swift Level, I'd failed to notice the beauty of the land. The cotton fields were freshly planted, the brown earth furrowed in long rows that merged in the distance. The smell of the newly turned soil was distinctive. Fertile. The men who farmed it said it smelled like money.

I drove the fifteen miles without passing another car. County Road 11 was narrow and straight, like so many of the Delta roads. Swift Level came up on the horizon like a diorama.

As I turned down the lane, a herd of magnificent horses came running toward the fence. There were at least a dozen of them, and they ran with the grace and spirit of young athletes. As they neared the fence they turned, a choreographed movement of such startling beauty that I stopped the car and watched them continue in the other direction, weaving a pattern that looked deliberately designed, yet was a perfect expression of freedom. Horse dancing. Whatever else Lee had done, she had bred something of beauty.

I parked in front of the house. The plants on the front porch still bloomed perkily, but they hadn't been headed or watered. I made a mental note to do that before I left. There was no one in the house, so I went down to the barn, alert for Bud Lynch. The man could move like a shadow, and I didn't want him sneaking up on me again.

The black truck with four rear tires was still parked at the barn. As soon as I entered the main barn where the office was located, I recognized Carol Beth's demanding tones. She was back at Swift Level and engaged in a shouting match with the trainer.

"You're hired help," Carol Beth fumed.

"That's right. You hired me, and I delivered. At the time, you weren't complaining about my services. In fact, you were mighty complimentary." That little statement was followed by a purely male chuckle, smug and amused.

"You goddamn son of a bitch."

"That's not what you were calling me—"

"You are a dead man. Do you hear me? I'll see to it that you never work again. You won't be able to get a job riding ponies at a fair by the time I finish with you. My husband—"

"Now, *Mrs.* Bishop, I wouldn't do anything rash. There're a lot of angles to consider here. I can give as good as I get, as you well know. I don't think your husband would enjoy the details of our . . . partnership."

I walked into the office doorway and saw them faced off at each other. Carol Beth had aged well, which meant she hadn't really aged at all. With her hair pulled back in a ponytail and her body encased in skintight riding breeches, a sleeveless white shirt and the de rigueur black boots, she looked as if she might still be the haughty seventeen-year-old who'd refused to date a single Zinnia High School boy. Not only did she refuse to date them, she told them why. She had her sights set higher than Sunflower County. She wanted out of Mississippi, and she managed it, too. She graduated with honors from Ole Miss, and two days later married a Virginia lawyer. From all tales, she was the crème de la crème of Richmond society and the darling of the Bridgeport Hunt there.

Neither of them saw me, so I had a chance to examine the tableau that presented itself. Lynch lounged in the office chair at the desk, and Carol Beth stood two feet away from him, her chest moving rapidly with anger. Her mahogany hair caught window light, and it seemed to glow like the finest old furniture. Her dark gaze was focused on Lynch, and I expected his bones to melt at any moment.

"You bastard. You can't threaten me."

"Oh, I can."

She took a step forward. She was close enough to kiss him. "I will ruin you."

"You can try," he said with a slow drawl and an easy smile.

"You are insufferable."

"You're a greedy bitch. Greedy and completely unprincipled. Don't push me too hard."

"You'll pay for this." She heaved a deep breath.

"Don't think you can play with me." Lynch's smile was gone, and his face lifted closer to hers. "We were together when Kemper was killed. Remember that. You can phrase it any way you'd like, but just don't try to change that fact."

"My memory isn't all that good, Bud." Carol Beth smiled.

"Try some ginkgo biloba. I've heard it stimulates the brain. Just do it fast. Remember, Carol Beth, if I don't have an alibi, neither do you."

"And who would a jury in Sunflower

County believe—a horse trainer implicated in a Texas murder, or the daughter of Littleton Farley?" Her laughter was cold.

"I've tied up with people a lot smarter, richer, and tougher than you. And I always come out on top." Bud appeared unperturbed.

"We'll see about that." Carol Beth whirled, and then halted dead in her tracks when she saw me.

"What are you doing here?" The question was a spear hurled across the room. "I wasn't aware that Dahlia House was in such dire straits that you'd been reduced to mucking stalls to make ends meet."

Her attack was surprising, but not necessarily unexpected. Carol Beth hadn't changed a bit. "Lynch said he had a way with horses. I guess he doesn't have the touch with a jackass." What the hell, there was no reason for me to hold back. I was rewarded with a crooked grin from Lynch that sizzled with charm. Part of his appeal was the ease with which he established a connection. I felt a desire to move physically closer to him.

"Get out of my way." Carol Beth stormed toward me.

"Wasn't that what Sherman said on his way to Atlanta?" I stepped aside and turned to watch her stalk down the barn aisle. In a moment, there was the sound of a big diesel engine starting, and her rig pulled away. The old man, Roscoe, peeped out of a stall and grinned at me.

"I gather you know Mrs. Bishop," Lynch said in that slow Texas twang.

"Since first grade."

"I'm sorry," he said.

He had a quick wit and a bit of malice. "What was that all about?" I asked as casually as I could manage. The conversation I'd overheard involved more than equines. Bud Lynch and Carol Beth Bishop had only each other for an alibi the night Kemper was killed. Although Kip was my primary suspect, Bud was close behind her.

He shrugged a shoulder. "A woman with regrets is never a pretty sight." Although his attitude was cavalier, his tone belied his worry. "How's Kip?" he asked.

"She's managing." Although his concern seemed genuine, I had my own questions. "What was Carol Beth doing here? Why does she want Avenger and the mares? She has enough money to buy any horse she wants. Why Avenger?"

"That horse is worth a lot more than the bill of sale Kemper signed for him and the mares. After this show season, when his first crop of babies demonstrate their stuff, Avenger will be getting ten thousand a pop for a stud fee, and that's just starters." He shifted one lean hip. "Of course, that's if everything goes as planned. In the horse business, risk is the only certainty."

He motioned me over to a chart on the wall that listed names of horses, breeding dates, foaling dates, sales.

"Avenger's potential is unlimited. The mares who are bred to him carry foals that will bring millions. Four of his babies are on the Olympic team, eight on the Grand Prix circuit. If any were available on the market, they'd command prices up to half a million dollars each. Carol Beth recognizes the possibilities and she has the three hundred grand to seize the opportunity. That's the answer to your first question. In simple terms, she wants what Lee has. Carol Beth's eaten up with jealousy of Lee. Everything Carol Beth has, someone else actually owns. She went from her father's largesse to her husband's. Lee's made her own way."

"You make Carol Beth sound just a little psychotic," I said.

"Not psychotic, but certainly obsessed. Ever since she first showed up out here under the guise of taking riding lessons, she's been planning on how to get Avenger. That fool Kemper played right into her hands."

I could buy that explanation. Now for the more unpleasant chore. "I want to see where Kemper was killed."

He motioned me to follow him. As he went through the door, it was impossible not to let my eyes wander down his body. He had a fine butt. Was it riding that made it look that good? I forced my eyes up to his shoulders and saw the good posture, the strength. He was a total package. Remembering the facts I'd dug up on him—not least of all his possible implication in the murder of a Texas rancher—I wondered if all that charm and masculinity were what might be considered a lethal package. It occurred to me that I was alone in a barn with a potential killer, but what was worse was that another suspect was living under my roof. It wasn't exactly what the private eye handbook cited as an example of wise investigating techniques.

We left the main barn and walked down a path of raked gravel to a smaller barn with only a few stalls—all empty—but a lot of sunlight and fresh air. He led me directly to a huge box stall cordoned off with the remains of yellow crime-scene tape. "Help yourself," he said. "The sheriff's come and gone."

I slowly opened the door and found only what I had anticipated. Blood had been spattered everywhere. The shavings were soaked in it. It looked as if a terrible battle had been waged within the confines of the whitewashed boards.

There was nothing for me to learn in the stall except that Kemper had been brutally murdered, but I had other questions. "Are you involved with Lee?"

Instead of answering, he walked into the sunshine. Leaning against the barn, he turned his face to the sun. I caught up with him, growing more annoyed. "I need an answer. After all, this wouldn't be the first time a woman you were involved with ended up with a dead husband."

He ignored the gibe. "Involved can cover a lot of ground. I'm the hired help. Of course I'm involved in part of her life."

Hedging was his specialty. I could be more direct. "Are you in love with Lee?"

"Why do you want to know?"

"It speaks to motive. I won't be the only one asking."

"Kemper was a cruel, sadistic bastard." He looked beyond me, down the aisle to where a horse called a soft greeting to him. "A long time ago, if things had gone differently, she might have fallen in love with me. If Lee had given me a single sign that there was a chance . . ." He turned slightly away. "Things would be a lot different now."

He forestalled my next question by pointing down the lane where old Roscoe was leading a huge gray horse. The animal shook his head and called a soft greeting.

"That's Avenger." He straightened up and waved at Roscoe. "Put him back in the stallion barn. Use the spare stall. We'll get his cleaned up tomorrow."

As the horse was led away, I couldn't help but notice how every muscle seemed defined. He was breathtaking. His sculpted head nodded up and down on an arched neck. A forelock of black hair tossed against his gray hide as his hooves beat a tattoo on the gravel. My eyes lingered on him, captured by his magnificence.

"Do you remember Spartacus, Lee's big gray stallion from her teen years?" Bud asked.

"Yes." I had a vivid memory of her riding down my drive on a cold Christmas morning.

"Avenger is his son. Kemper wanted to sell all the horses, take the money, and start some new business. What that actually meant was that he would gamble it away. Lee, of course, refused. It would have killed Kip."

That was a sentiment I questioned. "Kip doesn't seem all that fond of her life at Swift Level."

"That's where you're wrong. Kip loves these horses as much as, or more than, Lee. Her love was always the weapon used against her. Is there anything else you need to know?" he asked, obviously ready to conclude my visit.

"Where were you the night Kemper was killed?"

"I told you, I was with someone."

I merely looked at him. "I heard. Carol Beth. But there seems to be some disagreement there."

He shrugged one shoulder. "Carol Beth is trying to play the odds. If she can implicate me, she'll try it. With Lee in prison and me out of the way, she'd be up here with an eighteen-wheeler and load up everything with four legs."

"Who killed Kemper?"

"Lee didn't."

"Is this a theory or a fact?" My heart was beating fast. Was Lynch going to confess to murder? "It's not so different from Texas."

His chuckle was slow and easy. "Yes, a setup similar enough that it would be very convenient to pin this on me. You're hoping I'll say I did it." His eyes caught the light, a pure, clear blue. "Or maybe you're afraid I'll say I did it."

He let that hang between us, the possibility that he was a killer. Smiling, he shook his head.

"I didn't. Like I told you, I was with Carol Beth. Believe it or not, I'd do anything I could to help Lee." He paused for effect. "Anything."

I arched my eyebrows, waiting.

"I can't confess," he said slowly.

"There's bound to be a good reason here."

"The night Kemper was killed, Carol Beth showed up intending to claim the horses. She showed me the bill of sale. She put it in the glove box of her truck. It was the only evidence she had that Kemper had sold her Avenger."

There was a long pause as he let me work it out for myself. "Once she was asleep, sated with pleasure, you were going to steal the bill of sale."

"Not my most noble act, but yes. That was my plan. Unfortunately, it seems a succubus doesn't need sleep. I must have dozed off. When I woke up, Carol Beth and her rig were gone, along with the bill of sale."

9

The sycamore trees along the drive were budding out with tight, green leaves. Against the pale blue sky they were almost chartreuse. Sycamores are messy trees, but they're also graceful. I love them at all seasons, even in the winter when their pale trunks rise like ghostly bones into the sky.

My mind was still back at Swift Level. Two things intrigued me. Number one was that Carol Beth had lowered her standards enough to sleep with someone who wasn't landed gentry. Second—that Lynch had survived the experience. "Succubus" was a perfect word to describe Carol Beth.

A little added jolt was Lynch's vocabulary. He was a lot better read than I'd ever thought.

I was halfway down my drive when I saw a man sitting on the front porch of Dahlia House. He held a glass of something, and he was reading a magazine. He looked up as I parked the car. My first thought was that a

Flannery O'Connor character had jumped out of the pages of her stories and come to sell me a Bible. His suit was shiny and black, and the thin tie reflected his own physique. There was even a briefcase at his feet. Glass eyes? Wooden legs? What was he after? His slick smile did not bode well.

"You must be Sarah Booth," he said. "I got here as quickly as I could. Your niece was kind enough to give me some sweet tea." He took a sip and smacked his lips. "Perfect."

"I don't have a niece." Very slowly I walked up the steps, taking him in full measure. He was tall, oiled, and impeccably ironed. I was sure his underwear had a crease. His hair, probably a sandy blond, was slicked back in an eighties style, and a pair of aviator sunglasses was folded into his shirt pocket.

"You said to bring a set of tails." He pointed to a suitcase leaning beside the door.

"Who are you?"

He looked puzzled. "Malone."

"Malone?"

"Malone Beasley." He grinned. "You said you were in dire need of a man, so here I am, tails in hand and ready to dance."

"Where did you come from?" I felt as if I'd gotten trapped in a nightmare. Had I conjured him up from the hell pit of my subconscious?

"Wetumpka, Alabama." He was looking at me as if he were suddenly concerned.

"Wetumpka," I repeated. It was a hole-in-the-road town within driving distance. I looked around and noticed that he didn't have a car.

"I took the bus," he said. "Leave the drivin' to them!" He laughed. "You have a Mercedes." He rolled the word as if it had tremendous flavor. "That's car enough for the both of us." He walked past me down the steps to the car in question. "She's a real beaut." His lips thinned as he said very slowly, "Cher-ry." His fingers trailed over the Chinese red paint in a way that was purely sensual. He was in love with my car.

"Beasley," I snapped.

Hand still proprietarily on my car, he grinned. "You don't have to be formal. You can call me Malone."

Just my luck, a weasel with two last names and suffering from autoerotica. "Why are you here?"

His brows drew closer together, almost meeting in a worried point. "For the ball. You know, I'm your date."

Immediately I detected the fine hand of Cece Dee Falcon. She'd dredged this creature up from the mud of the Mississippi River and expected me to take him to the Chesterfield Hunt Ball.

"I've already got a date," I told him.

Disappointment registered all over his face. "You do? Then why—"

"I don't know," I said. "I have no idea why. But when I find out, I'll send you a postcard. I think you should take the bus back to We-tumpka. Send a travel voucher to *The Zinnia Dispatch* for reimbursement."

Anger crossed his features like a storm. "You can't do this. There's some kind of law. It's . . . false advertising."

His voice was growing louder, and I saw a curtain move in the parlor. Kip, Jitty, or the spring breeze, I couldn't be certain. Two of them would be enjoying this little scene far too much.

"Leave or I'll call the sheriff. He's a close personal friend."

He walked stiffly back up the steps and picked up his suitcase and the briefcase, heft-ing them with a huff. "And I brought you a present," he said. "Dang chocolate's probably melted all over my clean underwear."

I felt a momentary pang of guilty horror. It wasn't his fault that Cece had invited him here with the promise of a ball and a date. None of this could be laid at his door. But I knew where the big bad wolf of guilt was going stalking for dinner tonight.

Malone cast a covetous glance at my car. "How about a ride to the bus station? You can't expect me to walk back to town."

I hesitated. Common decency dictated that I give him a ride. Then again, he might salivate in the front seat of my car.

"I'll call a cab." That was the best I could offer. And I acted on that, going inside and calling Burtis Wade, the only cabby in Zinnia. He wasn't actually a cabby, but he had a 1963 Ford Fairlane that he used on prom night to drive the seniors around so they could drink. He was groggy from a nap and reluctant to work, but I told him it was an important story for Cece, whom he should bill for the fare. He said he was on the way.

I wanted a hot bath and a locked door. When I went into my room, Kip was sitting at the computer. She clicked off the screen she'd been looking at. "Where's Mr. Beasley?" she asked.

"He's gone." I examined her fourteen-year-old face. She was growing more innocent by the second. "Did you tell him you were my niece?"

"No. I told him I wasn't your daughter, that you'd never been married. He just assumed I was your niece." She was finding it hard to hide her amusement. "He had a box of cherry cordials for you. He showed me. I thought it was kind of sweet."

I wanted to murder Cece. I was prevented from rash action by the sound of high heels tapping through the parlor and toward the kitchen.

"Sarah Booth! Kip! I'm here!" Tinkie called out.

I'd forgotten all about the hair appointment. I went down to the kitchen to find her pulling boxes and bottles out of a pink plastic bag. She already wore a pink plastic apron. Kip had followed me, and Tinkie signaled her over to the table. "I think something with auburn highlights, but very subtle." She was already touching Kip's hair. To my surprise, the thorny teenager sat in a chair and let Tinkie have her way with her burgundy head.

Afternoon light slanted through the kitchen window illuminating them, and for a moment I saw clearly how Kip craved the attention of a woman, the feminine skills that Lee had put at the bottom of her list of priorities. Kip needed a mother.

I walked to the window and looked out at the family cemetery plot some fifty yards away. The Delaneys, including my parents and Aunt LouLane, were all buried there. Five generations. Around LouLane's grave a star-burst of daffodils was blooming. They'd always been a favorite of hers.

"Sarah Booth, what do you think of this style?" Tinkie pointed to a magazine on the table.

I walked over and looked at the crisp, clean cut. "I like it."

"Just make me look completely different," Kip said.

"Okay, then we'll do that cut, and this color." Tinkie held up a box.

"Great," Kip said. "No one will recognize me."

I gave her a close look, but she was staring at the hair-color box.

"By the way, Sarah Booth, Margene, my cook, is bringing over a roast for dinner. I hope you don't mind." Tinkie was whipping strands of hair into the air.

"Thanks," I said, meaning it. Without the duties of chef, I could take care of pressing business. "I need to run an errand or two." I hesitated. Was I leaving Tinkie in danger?

"That roast will be here in half an hour," Tinkie said. "We'll just have time to put the color on." She rolled up the sleeves of her Chanel suit. "You go on, Sarah Booth. We'll have a surprise for you when you get back."

All of the courthouse offices were winding down for the close of day, but Coleman was still at the sheriff's office, and I noted that it seemed he seldom went home anymore. I walked in to an unexpectedly big grin.

"Well, Sarah Booth," he said. "You've been on my mind." He could barely contain his amusement. "There was a man here about half an hour ago. One Malone Beasley. He says you lied to him. That you deceived him in a deliberate effort to make a jackass out of him. He wanted to press charges against you. Date fraud."

My ears flamed with humiliation. "Maybe you should talk to Cece. This is her idea of a joke." I would never, never live this down.

"Now I've heard of date rape, but date fraud is a new one on me. What, exactly, does that entail?"

"I just said no," I answered glumly.

Coleman's chuckle was soft and easy. "I needed a laugh," he said. "Mr. Beasley didn't have bus fare, so I loaned him some cash and sent him on his way."

"Thanks." I felt my body shrinking.

"You didn't ask him to Dahlia House?"

"Coleman, I'm not an idiot. Absolutely not."

"How did he know about the ball and you?"

It was a logical question, but logic is never a girl's best friend in moments of burning shame. "Cece told him."

Coleman laughed again. "I'd kill her, Sarah Booth. But take a word of advice, don't confess if you do."

"May I borrow your phone?" I asked. Alternately steaming and burning, I dialed the newspaper. Cece was out, and no one knew where. I suspected she was hiding in her office, but I didn't have time to drive there and hunt her down. It would have to wait until tomorrow, when I was fresh and ready for mayhem.

"Can't find her?" Coleman asked.

I shook my head. He signaled me into his private office and closed the door. When he sat at his desk, all traces of his earlier humor were gone.

"Have you found anything?" he asked.

It was a strange question coming from the sheriff. Coleman was good at his job. He didn't need my help, and more often thought of me as an interference.

"Nothing concrete," I said. More than anything, I wanted to talk to Coleman about Kip. He was rational, logical, a man who'd learned to look at evidence and not emotion.

But I couldn't. Coleman was sworn to uphold the law. If Kip had broken it, he would arrest her.

Fel Harper knocked at the door, his face deliberately expressionless as Coleman motioned him into the room. He extended an envelope, turned abruptly, and left.

Fel was still sore at me about my first case, when he used to be county coroner before he was recalled from office for misidentifying bodies and other small infractions of the law. Now he worked as a gofer for the Sunflower County Funeral Home. I'd already made it very clear to Tinkie and Cece that should anything happen to me, my body was not to be left alone with Fel.

The envelope was heavy, and Coleman opened it and dumped the photographs onto his desk. At first I didn't recognize what they were pictures of. Then I realized it was Kemper Fuquar—or what was left of him. My first reaction was to acknowledge that Doc Sawyer had not been exaggerating. Avenger's hooves had done tremendous damage. I looked through the stack, willing my stomach to stay calm and my emotions to remain cool. I knew one thing, though: If those photographs were allowed into the courtroom, Lee would lose a lot of sympathy. It wouldn't matter that Kemper was dead when the horse stomped him. The prosecution would put those images to good use.

Coleman gathered up the photographs without a word and slid them back into the envelope.

"I need to see Lee," I said.

"Talk some sense into her if you can," Coleman said softly. "The prosecutor had her evaluated by a psychiatrist this morning. She was found competent to stand trial. She won't tell me a damn thing except she killed him, and that she's prepared to stand up in court and say he got what he had coming to him." Coleman held out the pictures. "These don't prove anything, but they're emotionally damning."

Coleman didn't have to tell me that Lee's situation had just gone from bad to worse.

He led me to the door of the jail, opened it, and then closed it behind me. I walked toward Lee's cell with a heavy heart. The vacancy rate in the Sunflower County jail was high. At times, Coleman was jammed to overflowing with state prisoners who were "boarded out" in county jails—by court order. And there were the drunks, parties to domestic violence, burglars, and such. Since Lee's arrival in the jail, though, Coleman had done his best to give her as much privacy as possible. I wondered if she even realized it.

She was sitting on her cot, her elbows on her knees and her chin in her hands. She didn't hear me as I approached.

"Lee?"

She straightened her back and rose to her feet. "Sarah Booth," she said. "How's Kip?"

"Tinkie's giving her a makeover."

Relief showed in every line in her face. "She hasn't been to see me. She's okay?"

"She's fine. She hasn't asked to visit," I said. "She's angry. With you and everyone else."

Lee nodded. "I can imagine." Something dark passed over her features. "She's only a child," she said with such urgency that I wondered what she was really saying.

"She wants to do her schoolwork via computer. She doesn't want to go back."

Lee nodded. "Thank you, Sarah Booth. Kip's a whiz on the computer. That's how she kept up with her classes when she was on the show circuit. It's been hard on her. A lot harder than it had to be." A note of iron crept into her voice. "But she's an all-A student. She'll have the scholarships I never had a chance at. You know, scouts from the Olympic team are looking at her this year. She's only fourteen!"

I watched Lee closely. Except that she was framed through the bars of a jail cell, she could have been any proud mother listing her daughter's accomplishments. That and the fact that she was crushing her right hand with her left as she talked.

"Lee, what happened at school?"

She swung on me. "How did you find out about that?" She got a grip on herself and consciously grew calmer. "It was nothing. Kip got in an argument with another student. It got out of hand. She knocked some books over in the library and tore up a locker." She shrugged. "It's over."

"Kip said Dr. Vance prescribed some medication for her?"

Lee blanched. She was already pale, but what little color there was in her face completely drained. "She told you that?"

"She did. She said she was taking Prozac and Paxil. Those are both pretty strong."

"It's also a crock of shit. Kip doesn't take those drugs. That moron Vance prescribed them. That's what he does—cure all the problems of kids with a few prescriptions. Kip went to him; she had to, or they were going to expel her from school. He gave her the prescriptions, and we get them filled every month. The school can check to make sure she's following his medical advice. But she doesn't take the pills. She flushes them down the toilet."

I wondered if she was just naïve or if she was deliberately lying to me. "I found a syringe in Kip's makeup."

Lee hesitated. "It wouldn't be uncommon for her to have something for the horses."

"That's what she said."

She paced the cell. "That's what it is. It has to be for the horses if she said so."

"Lee, did Kip kill Kemper?"

She was at the bars so fast that I actually stepped back.

"Don't say that, Sarah Booth. Don't even think that again. Kip didn't do anything. I told you, I killed him. I did it and no one else."

I knew she was lying, just as Coleman did. Just as a jury would, but they would still convict her if she insisted she was guilty.

"Then I have some questions for you. Why didn't you report the past beatings to the sheriff? Why not plead self-defense? Why didn't you divorce Kemper before it came to this?" I peppered her with the questions. "Who are you protecting?" I asked softly. "If it's Kip, there may be a better way."

Lee's fingers tightened on the bars. "Leave Kip out of this. I mean it, Sarah Booth. Leave my daughter out of this. She's suffered enough.

Now don't ever mention this to me again, or to anyone else."

"If it were only me, it wouldn't matter. I'm on your side, Lee, but I'm going to point one thing out to you. The night Kemper was killed, he never struck you. There wasn't a mark on you, and I'm not the only one who noticed. That's why you aren't pleading self-defense. You didn't kill Kemper. You're covering for—"

"I don't have to answer your questions. You need to know one thing and that is Kemper died by my hand. By all that you hold dear, if you try to sacrifice my daughter, you will re-gret it until the day you die."

Although Lee hadn't killed her husband, I had no doubt that she would do serious dam-age to me or anyone else who tried to harm her child.

10

Tinkie was in the kitchen, washing the last of the supper dishes, when I got home. A heaping plate of roast, new potatoes, carrots, onions, and fresh shelled English peas waited on the counter for me under a stainless steel cover.

"Kip's upstairs setting her hair. I showed her how." Tinkie took a dishcloth and wiped the counter. "Under all of that bad hair and makeup, there's a lovely young girl."

I sat down at the table and began to eat. "Thanks, Tinkie. This is wonderful."

"Margene's been cooking for me since she was eleven. Her mama, Mazy, cooked for Oscar's mama. I stole Margene right out from under Mother Bellcase. Lord, she threw a famous hissy fit at The Club and almost got us all thrown out, but that's water under the bridge now. She's glad enough that Margene is cooking for Oscar now."

The roast was so tender it almost melted in

my mouth. I was so busy eating I could only nod and chew.

Tinkie sat down at the table, reached into the pocket of her fitted jacket, and brought out a sheet of paper. "I had lunch today at The Club with Carol Beth. I picked up some interesting gossip." She held the page out to me.

"Carol Beth?"

She nodded. "She is such a bitch, isn't she? She said you were at Swift Level. To check out Bud Lynch's services." Tinkie giggled. "I couldn't help myself. I told her that you were engaged to Hamilton Garrett the Fifth, and that he was so smitten by you that he was thinking of moving back to Mississippi since you wouldn't leave your home."

"Tinkie! You are the best girlfriend! That was brilliant."

"She was so aggravated about the romantic trip to Paris you're taking in April that she said a few things she might regret." She nodded at the page I held.

I looked at the list of names scribbled in Tinkie's hand. At the top was Bud Lynch, followed by a series of names—all female, I noted—that included some of the shining lights of Delta society, all former schoolmates of mine.

"Mary Louise Bellington, Elizabeth Cooper, Susannah Adair Fitzgerald, and Krystal Brook?" I finished the list on a big question mark. "Simpson—that Krystal?"

Tinkie nodded slowly. "She's been taking riding lessons from Bud. Her husband doesn't seem like the type to tolerate those kinds of antics."

"I've met him," I said. "He definitely likes to manage." I studied the list. "Are you're telling me that Carol Beth fingered these women as possible murderers?" I knew all of them—all former Daddy's Girls who'd married well, lived well, and had the finer things in life handed to them on silver platters. "Why would they kill Kemper?"

"They were all taking *riding* lessons from Bradford Lynch."

My eyes opened. "*All* of them?"

"Every single one of them. Sometimes five times a week." Tinkie's Sun-Kissed-Peach lips slowly curled into a wicked smile. "Rumor has it that the horses at Swift Level never broke a sweat, but the trainer was another matter."

"Lynch! He was—"

"Riding them hard. And with incredible skill."

"That would be twenty times a week." Math wasn't my strong suit, but in this case I could multiply.

"His stamina is legendary."

I took my dishes to the sink. "So Carol Beth thinks one of these women killed Kemper because they were being serviced by Lynch?" I still didn't get it. "She was taking lessons, too."

Tinkie refilled our coffee cups as she talked. "Carol Beth believes that Kemper was trying to blackmail these women, and one of them decided to do something about it. They're all married. They all have a lot to lose if it becomes public knowledge that they're sharing the services of a philandering horse trainer. I mean it would be different if he were just seeing one of them. But all of them! It looks so . . . desperate. I mean, at thirty-three, we're all past our prime. But to have to pay for riding lessons just to get . . . some attention."

Desperation was never a good look on a Daddy's Girl. I was finally getting the picture Tinkie's list painted. In all of the DG training, the most unacceptable thing was to appear desperate. Cute, temperamental, manipulative, helpless, brainless, malleable, flighty, and just plain blond—all were high art forms in the hands of a DG. Desperation was for lesser mortals. When a DG looked desperate, it was the end. She'd blown all the work of building her lifelong façade. Ask Blanche DuBois. "You might be on to something," I agreed. It didn't explain Lee's confession, but it did give us more suspects and motives to muddy the water.

"Besides, Kemper was a total piece of shit." Tinkie got up and walked to the window. I knew she was looking out over the darkened vista of the cotton fields, which had been recently tilled and planted. I'd leased the land to Willie Campbell, a local farmer who'd been a few years ahead of me in high school. Tinkie could see none of my land. It was an internal landscape she viewed.

"Anyway, you have the list," she said. "Every single one of those women will be at the hunt ball. We can tackle them there." She bit her bottom lip in her signature gesture. "I have to get home. Oscar had a late meeting, but he'll expect his cocktail to be waiting for him."

"Thanks, Tinkie. You did great."

Her smile was a million watts. "We'll figure out a way to keep Lee out of prison, won't we?"

"We don't have a choice," I said, putting my arm around her shoulders and leaning down to whisper. "If we don't, Kip will have to go and live with you."

Tinkie's remark, harmless enough at the time, that at thirty-three we were all over the hill, began to work on me at about midnight. I sat straight up in bed from a sound sleep, slightly disoriented by the bass thud of Kip's music. I wondered if she'd fallen asleep with her boom box on, or if she was still up.

"What are you muttering about 'over the hill'?" Jitty's voice drifted to me from the old rosewood rocker that my mother had used to soothe me when I was a babe in arms. Generations of Delaneys had been lulled into sleep by the rhythm of that old chair, and as annoying as I found Jitty, I was comforted by the gentle creaking.

"I'm not even close to being over the hill," I said. "If you'll remember back to the research done in the 1970's, women don't reach their sexual peak until their late thirties. Or even the late forties."

"Dream on." In the darkness Jitty sounded bored.

I snapped on the bedside light. "You read enough of those old *Cosmo* magazines in the attic to drive me crazy. There were dozens of articles in them about how women sexually peak out so much more slowly than men."

"Poppycock."

She was in a difficult mood and dressed to show it. She had on a slinky jumpsuit of what could only be tomato-red spandex. It was sleeveless, with capri-length legs that emphasized her trim ankles and killer-spike sandals. Her hair was straight, à la Vanessa Williams, and she looked like she might be twenty-two. I hated her.

"Get out of my bedroom."

"We need to talk."

"Go away." I pulled the covers over my head, but I knew it wouldn't do any good. I couldn't sleep, because I was worried. Forcing Jitty out of my room wouldn't quell my bout of anxiety. I threw back the covers and went into my bathroom. Beneath the bright lights of the mirror, I examined my face. Yes, there were the first signs of wrinkles. My left side, creased by a fold in the sheet, was worse. Crow's-feet. Laugh lines. Squint marks. I had them all. I turned profile to see if a wattle was developing.

"Better find you a man before you have to use spackle."

"Shut up." Jitty was enough to send me to look for the razor blades.

"Sarah Booth, why do you think you're still single? I mean, just as a point of curiosity. Why aren't you married?"

This was more soul-searching than I could stand. "Because Prince Charming has ridden all around Mississippi and somehow managed to avoid Zinnia?"

Jitty snorted. "You didn't give Malone Beasley a chance. You didn't even offer him a cup of coffee."

I turned to her. "Why should I entertain some reject Cece dredged up?"

"Maybe he was a nice man."

"He wanted my car, not me."

"What? You think he should have walked up to you and rubbed your bumper?"

She had a point, which only made me more adamant. "Cher-ry," I mimicked.

"You seriously need to get you a life." She frowned her disapproval.

"I may need a life, but he needs a car. He rode the bus from Wetumpka."

She sighed.

"He didn't have money to get home. That's exactly what I need. Another mouth to feed around here."

She sighed more deeply.

"He was—" I didn't get to finish. There was the sound of a guitar outside my bedroom window. It was a good riff that ran full ahead, broke, flowed, and continued into low-down and dirty blues.

A very low and sexy voice blended in with the guitar. "I sent for my woman, da-da-dum; she came to my side. Da-da-dum. She whis-

pered so sexy, da–da–dum; you been drinkin'
and you lied! Yeah, my baby's gone, and she
took all her lovin' when she went!"

"I think you got company," Jitty said, stepping back against the wall. "He might not
have a car, but he's got one helluva way with a
guitar."

She was gone, and I was left with the trou-
badour beneath my window. I could only pray
that Kip was asleep. What would she think?
Malone Beasley and now this.

I hurried to the window and leaned out. In
the darkness I couldn't see him, but he saw me.

"Sarah Booth, I've come to crown you as
the queen of the blues."

"Who are you?" I whispered as harshly as I
could.

"John Bell Washington, or the ladies call me
J.B., the original blues man from Greenwood.
At your service, ma'am."

I gritted my teeth. "Come around to the
front door," I said sweetly.

"Whatever you say."

I grabbed some jeans and a shirt and hurried
barefoot down the stairs. He was waiting there,
guitar in hand, when I opened the door. He
was better than six feet tall and had a grin that
would charm Medusa. Long, dark hair was
neatly queued.

"I apologize for arriving so late," he said as he stepped past me and into the house. "I had a gig at the Delta Blues Bar in Greenwood. It would have been a breach of contract if I didn't show. But here I am, and I'm ready to sing, dance, and generally make your life a pleasure. You look like you could use a massage."

"Who are you?"

A look of consternation passed over his face. "I told you. John Bell Washington. You know, JBBLUES, all caps."

I didn't have a clue what he meant, but I was going to absolutely kill Cece. Malone Beasley wasn't bad enough. Now I had a musician standing in my foyer. No, headed into my kitchen. And who should greet him with a wagging tail but Sweetie Pie.

"What a great dog," he said, bending to pat the stomach she offered for his touch. "I'm about famished. You said you'd have something good to eat when I got here, and I think I smell roast."

He pushed straight into the kitchen and unerringly opened cabinets, drawers, and the refrigerator until he had a plate, flatware, and food. He served himself and sat down at the kitchen table. "Mmmmm, this is good," he said, spearing a half potato. "You are some kind of cook, no doubt about that. I'd say you were running neck and neck with Mother in the category of kitchen expertise."

"I didn't actually—"

"Lots of women lie about that kind of thing, but a lie always catches you in the end. That's what Mother says, and that's why I never lie. Now tell me about this ball we're attending."

In the light of the kitchen, I could see he cultivated a rugged look—he'd deliberately not shaved. His dark eyes watched me with mild curiosity. If I were forced to tell the truth, I'd have to say he was quite attractive.

"The Chesterfield Hunt Ball?" I knew without a doubt that Cece had been at work again.

"Yeah, all those ritzy ladies and gents. Lots of money and no fun. That's what you said, and I agree. Well, we're going to show them what it means to have a good time at a ball."

He polished off his plate of food with such blinding speed that I served him another without thinking. I cut a hunk of roast and offered it to Sweetie Pie, who broke off her adulation of John Bell Washington long enough to swallow it whole.

"So, are there any good blues clubs in Sunflower County? I haven't spent much time over here."

"One or two," I said.

"Well, I'll find something to keep me busy until Saturday. Don't you worry about it at all. I'm good at entertaining myself. You know, I've never met an actual, honest-to-God private investigator."

Whether it was charm or calculation, I felt myself smiling. John Bell Washington, for all the fact that he was probably a manic-depressive on the upswing, was irresistible.

He laid his knife and fork properly across the plate. "I know this is kind of strange, so I'll mosey on down to the local hotel and park it until tomorrow. I'll rent some tails in town, and we'll make us some plans for that big ball."

He pushed back from the table and stood up. "Good night, Sarah Booth." He squeezed my fingers gently.

There was not the thumb throb of Harold, but there was a warm tingle. "I do love the blues," I said, unwilling to commit to anything more.

"I'm your man, then," he said with a lop-sided grin. "Call me John or call me J.B., just be sure and call me tomorrow."

He left by the back door, whistling a down-and-dirty tune, and I was left alone in the kitchen with Sweetie Pie and the empty platter where once a roast had lain.

Trudging back up to my room, I stopped by Kip's door. I almost tapped on it with a reminder that it was long past her bedtime. Instead, I went to my room. Kemper's funeral was set for tomorrow morning, Thursday, at eleven. No matter how it played out, it was going to be an ordeal for all of us.

Lying in bed with Kinky for company, I paused in my reading to listen to the wails and throbs of Kip's music. Perhaps her desire for a new hairdo was a sign she was coming around. I was certain of nothing. I only knew that I was deeply troubled and that my bedroom door, for the first time in my life, was locked.

Sleep settled over me, a thin blanket of forgetfulness troubled by strange images and a suffocating sense of urgency with an undertone of blues guitar.

I'd been asleep for what felt like a few minutes when I heard Sweetie Pie's soft whines. She was outside my door in the hallway. She'd taken to splitting her time between me and Kip. Apparently she was now ready for the midnight shift change and annoyed that my door was closed. I got up and opened it.

Instead of coming into my room, Sweetie barked and headed downstairs. At the landing, she waited for me. Curious, I followed. The tile of the foyer was cold beneath my bare feet as Sweetie led me to the front door. Looking at me, she began to bark.

I saw the headlights then. They were halfway down the drive, yellow beams in the dark night, too far away for me to distinguish the make of the vehicle. A slender figure passed in front of the headlights and got into the passenger side. Backing among the sycamores, the car turned around and left.

I didn't need to check Kip's room to know she was gone, but I did. Her bed was empty. With her things scattered all over the floor, there was no way to tell what, if anything, she'd taken with her.

I walked out onto the landing and sat down on the stairs. Kip was fourteen, a troubled girl with a history of instability, and possible violence. Her mother was in jail. I didn't know what I should do. Coleman was the logical answer, but I resisted. I had not yet resolved my role.

Jitty slipped beside me and sat. "You were fifteen when you ran away," she said.

"Fifteen and four months," I responded with a wry smile. I'd forgotten the incident. Aunt LouLane had forbidden me to attend a dance with a high school senior. Angry with her, and embarrassed that I was being treated like a baby, I'd run away. "I only went over to Annabelle's house."

"Yeah, only to Annabelle's. You had it all planned, didn't you? Your girlfriend loaned you a dress, and you had that boy pick you up there, and you went to the dance."

"I remember," I said. The dress had been a deep, rich russet, a beautiful silky dress with a matching shawl. It had been late September, when the weather was still warm. "Taylor Williams. That was his name." I smiled at the memory. He'd gone on to college the next year, disappearing into one of the law firms of the Northeast. "He married a Yankee. I think Aunt LouLane's fit scarred him for life."

Jitty was not amused. "Your aunt about stroked out. She was drinkin' bakin' soda fizzes, 'cause she thought she was havin' a heart attack. She had the sheriff, the highway patrol, and all five constables lookin' for you. Ever' time the phone rang, she thought it was the kidnappers callin' with a ransom request."

I couldn't help but smile, though the memory still caused me deep guilt. "I danced all night. The last disco party."

"And then you didn't sit down for several days."

"That was the only time Aunt LouLane ever spanked me. She used a hairbrush, as I recall."

"Lucky for you she didn't use a baseball bat."

"True." I sighed. "So what are you trying to tell me?"

"Somebody had to know when and where to pick Kip up." Jitty leaned back on her elbows. "This ain't no rash runnin' away from home. It was planned, just like yours."

"Maybe Tinkie overheard her on the phone." I had a lead.

"That would be my first suggestion. Then I'd check that computer. There's a whole world out there that she's conversin' with, and some of those folks may not be safe."

If Jitty intended to frighten me, she was successful. I jumped to my feet. "Internet predators! Do you think she's talking to some killer?"

Jitty rolled her eyes. "More likely she's talkin' to some hired hit man, but I'd use what few skills you got to find out. And first thing tomorrow, I'd sign up for some computer classes."

"Like I have time to learn anything new," I retorted.

"You gone be old, wrinkled, with shriveled ovaries and no technology skills. In other words, you're racin' toward extinction with the lumberin' speed of a dinosaur!"

I finally turned to look at her. She looked dressed for speed. "You learn it," I said. "I have to call Tinkie."

The clock in the kitchen, where I put on a pot of coffee, showed two in the morning. Oscar was not going to be happy with me. Not at all. Oscar had been amazingly pleasant about Tinkie's involvement with the detective agency, but I suspected a dead-of-night call might be the straw that would break the camel's back. Still, there was no help for it.

Tinkie answered on the second ring, her voice sleepy.

"Kip just ran away," I said.

"Where? How? With whom?" She was wide awake and asking all the right questions.

Unfortunately, I had no answers. "I just saw her get in a car. The driver was smart enough not to come all the way down the drive."

There was a long, low rumble of complaint and I knew Oscar had awakened, and not in the role of Prince Charming.

"Honey, Lee's girl has run away. I've got to help find her."

There was a garbled, mumbled discussion that I wasn't intended to hear. At last, though, loud and clear, came Oscar's voice, surprisingly pleasant. "You promise?" he asked.

"Baby, I'm going to rock your world when I get back," Tinkie said. She spoke into the phone. "I'm closer to Swift Level than you. I'll stop by and check there on my way."

"Thanks." I hung up, pondering Tinkie's many skills. She'd taken the lesson plan of a Daddy's Girl to new and dizzying heights. In fact, as I pondered it, I came to the conclusion that she was breaking the major rules and bending all the others. In her own way, she had become a rebel.

I was on the front porch with coffee when she pulled up. She got out of the car and I almost choked. She was wearing a flowing tiger-print silk robe over a matching teddy. On her tiny feet were five-inch spike heels with a little ruffle of fuzzy tiger fur.

"You actually wear that to bed?" I asked. My own sleep-shirt was faded and sagged in all the wrong places.

Her answer was a critical eye that lingered on each sag. "You need help," she said. She reached into the backseat and brought out a black leather bag. "There was no sign of Kip at Swift Level. Pour me some coffee while I change. I was afraid if Oscar really woke up, he'd say I couldn't come, so I just grabbed some things and ran." She was walking toward a downstairs bathroom as she talked.

By the time I had her coffee, she was back on the porch in jeans and a sweater, waiting for me. I filled her in, telling her everything, from the syringe to the phone call I'd overheard to the psychiatric diagnosis. Confession didn't bring the release I sought. Tinkie's face was as worried as mine.

"Kip was on phone restriction except for schoolwork. Did she talk to anyone last evening?" I asked.

Tinkie nodded. "She went upstairs to her bathroom. I was cleaning up the mess and setting the table, and I started upstairs to check on her. I overheard her whispering."

"Do you remember what she said?"

"She said, 'Can you find her? I'll do whatever I have to.' Then there was a long pause, and she said, 'Whatever you say.' And she hung up."

"Did she see you?"

"No, but I asked her what was wrong." Tinkie sipped her coffee. "She said it was a school friend who lost her dog. I should have told you

SPLINTERED BONES 167

this, Sarah Booth, but teenagers always have so many secrets. I didn't give it a thought."

I put a hand on her shoulder. "I should have gone to Coleman long ago, when I first suspected."

"Suspected what?" Tinkie asked. Her blue eyes were large with concern.

"That Lee is protecting Kip."

Tinkie looked down at her feet, now encased in sensible Italian walking shoes. She fiddled with the shoelace. "He already knows," she said. "I was worried about you, Sarah Booth, alone here with Kip. I'd heard a few things. I talked to Coleman." She looked up with tears in her eyes. "I had to."

"What did he say?" Instead of being angry, I was relieved.

"He already knew all of it. He's been keeping an eye on you and just waiting and watching, hoping that Lee will recognize the futility of what she's doing. I think we should call him now."

"Let's give it until morning," I said. It was only another few hours. "If she's not back by six, we'll call him."

Tinkie stood up. "I hope you made a big pot of coffee."

We were sitting on the porch when Kip came walking down the driveway. A low fog had covered the ground in dense patches, and Kip walked out of one, materializing like a specter.

"Kip!" Tinkie stood and called her name.

Kip froze, then started walking again. She came straight on, stopping at the steps.

"Where have you been?" I asked.

"There was something I had to take care of," she said, green eyes holding mine with sheer will.

"We've been worried sick," I said, slowly rising.

"I'm sorry. I knew you wouldn't let me go. I had to do it."

"Do what?"

She swallowed, glancing at Tinkie and then back at me. "I can't tell you."

"Who picked you up?" I asked.

"A friend."

"I want a name."

She shook her head. "I won't tell you. Send me to DHR or wherever you have to. I won't tell."

"Go inside and clean up," I said with as much control as I could muster. The new hairdo that Tinkie had created had done a lot to improve Kip's look, but she was still the same rebellious kid.

"I'll be ready for the funeral," she answered, walking past me and into the house.

"What are you going to do?" Tinkie asked.

"I don't know," I answered.

The casket, covered with a blanket of white roses, was on a stand beside the open grave. Father McGuire stood at the head of the silver coffin, his black robes fluttering in the March breeze that carried the dizzying fragrance of wisteria.

Lee stood beside Coleman. I almost didn't recognize her in a black dress, hose, and heels. Her long Viking hair had been piled into a very sophisticated chignon. Tinkie, with her yen for hair sculpting, had been by the jail. For all of her Daddy's Girl upbringing, Tinkie had a way with hair. Had she been born into different social circumstances, she could have been the Sassoon of the Delta.

Though I scanned the tiny group twice, Cece was not to be found. Garvel LaMott, camera dangling from his neck and grubby notepad in his hand, was representing the *Dispatch*. Cece was not only a meddling hussy, she was also a craven coward. She was afraid to show up and fess up to sending those two men over to Dahlia House.

Tinkie had agreed to bring Kip. As they approached the green tent, I took note of Kip's miraculous makeover. The short haircut was perfect, and the color was dazzling. She had the strength of Lee's features but a darker skin tone. In her black dress, she looked older and more sophisticated than her fourteen years. The traces of a long night without sleep could be seen in the circles beneath her eyes, and I caught the look of pain on Lee's face as she devoured her daughter with her gaze.

As soon as Kip spotted Lee, she abandoned all pretense of aloofness. She ran across the tiny cemetery and flung herself into Lee's open arms.

"Mama," she said, crying.

"Oh, baby." Lee kissed her head repeatedly as her hands moved over Kip as if to make sure none of her parts had been stolen.

"I miss you," Kip cried.

"I miss you, too. But it won't be for much longer."

Kip pulled back from Lee. She was a tall teenager, but she still had to look up at her mother. "Tell them the truth! You didn't kill him. Just tell them," she begged.

Lee's features froze as she looked over at Coleman. I turned to look at him, too. I couldn't be certain if he'd heard what Kip said or not.

"Kip!" Lee's voice was sharp.

"Tell them!" Kip's voice grew louder. "I don't care. Tell them, or I will!" The new haircut and makeup were superficial changes. The rebellious teenager was back in the set pattern of her face.

"Kip." Lee had lowered her voice. Now it was soft and deadly. "Stop this." She looked around. "Stop it now."

"You're always the big martyr. The only problem is that it's always me who suffers. I'm going to tell—"

Lee's hand was so fast I never saw the slap coming. I heard it and saw Kip's head rock back. She gave her mother one long stare, and then turned and walked back to Tinkie's side, the imprint of her mother's hand clearly discernible in her flesh.

"I want Kip in my office. Tomorrow," Coleman said, leaning over to me. "No excuses, Sarah Booth, or I'll have you in the cell right beside Lee."

My first impulse was to strangle Lee. It would save the taxpayers a lot of money if she didn't have to be tried. To control my emotions, I had to turn away. As I did, I saw a big black dually diesel turn off the road and aim toward the church parking lot. I walked out of the cemetery with the direct intention of heading Carol Beth off at the pass. Whether her motivation in coming was greed or curiosity, she wasn't welcome.

I was almost to the church when I got a good look at the truck. The front windshield was broken out, and someone had spray-painted the word "Bitch" in white paint on both sides of the truck.

Bud Lynch stepped out of the shadows of a big cedar tree and made a beeline for Carol Beth. I stopped. Bud could do a much better job of ass-kicking than I could, and it would be fun to watch.

Carol Beth was in her riding togs and came out of the truck like she had ants in her skintight pants. "If you call my husband one more time, I swear I'll . . ."

She didn't conclude the threat, and I wasn't sure if it was due to lack of imagination or the sudden realization that Bud Lynch wasn't a man to threaten.

"What will you do, baby doll?" Bud asked. "Let's see. Slander is out of the question, since what I intend to tell your beloved husband is the truth. He'll be able to recognize that little mole shaped like Italy on the left side of your . . . coccyx."

Ah, Bud did have a vocabulary.

"Leave Benny out of this." Carol Beth advanced toward Bud.

"I think a man should know what his wife's about. I mean, Benny provides you with a terrific lifestyle and a lot of cash. Maybe if he knew how you spent your evenings away from home, he wouldn't be so generous. And I believe if Benny weren't so generous, you wouldn't have so much free time and money to make mischief in Lee's life."

"I'm going to get Avenger and those mares. Legally, they're mine. No matter what you do, you can't stop me."

Bud pointed to the truck. "Haven't you caused enough trouble around here? I see Kip found out you have Mrs. Peel. I wondered how long it would take her to figure out who bought her mare."

"Kemper sold her for top dollar."

"That was Kip's horse. She'd raised her from a foal." Bud's voice was ugly. "Everything can't be valued in money, Carol Beth. One day you'll learn that. It broke Kip's heart."

"She has a dozen other horses to ride. Mrs. Peel is mine now."

Bud shoved his hands into his pockets. "You obviously haven't thought this through very well, so I'll help you. Even if you get all the horses, you won't keep them. Legally they'll be *your husband's* horses." He laughed at her shocked expression. "Consider the fact that if Benny Bishop divorces you, you'll have to get a job. How binding is that prenup you signed? When you signed it, you never imagined that your daddy would have such awful luck in the stock market, did you? Sounds to me like you'll be headed straight to the secretarial pool."

"I'll have my own money, and you can bet I'll never put myself in a position of relying on a man again."

"You can have all the money in the world, Carol Beth, and it won't be enough to fill that black hole in your heart."

"You'll pay for your part in this," Carol Beth vowed as she hopped back in the big truck and started the engine. The window rolled down smoothly. "I don't know why you want to protect Lee. She hasn't paid you in months, and probably won't ever be able to. She's going to prison for the rest of her life, and then we'll see who ends up with Avenger."

The window rolled up and the black truck wheeled in the parking lot and lurched through the ditch onto the blacktop. Bud was left standing in the parking lot alone, chuckling.

I thought I was hidden by the shadow cast by the church, but Lynch spotted me when he turned to go.

"Are you detecting or spying?" he asked as he walked over to where I hid.

"Was that blackmail or simple conversation?" I countered.

"Blackmail, I hope. I think the only thing that will stop her for good is a silver bullet."

"Kip vandalized Carol Beth's truck?" I asked.

"With good reason." He took my elbow and led me back toward the cemetery, where Father McGuire was getting ready to start the service. "Carol Beth won't press charges."

"She knows it was Kip?"

"She caught her and brought her out to Swift Level. I drove Kip back to your place and let her out at the drive."

"Did you pick her up last night?"

He slowed his pace so we could finish our conversation before we entered the cemetery. "No, and she wouldn't tell me who did, or who told her about Mrs. Peel."

"Any guesses?"

"Kemper knew, of course. I found out.

Neither of us told her." He touched my elbow, moving us forward.

I scanned the small gathering. About twenty yards past the graveside, three men in dark suits stood watching. "Recognize those men?" I asked Bud.

He steered me away from them. "They've been out to the farm. I would call two of them collection agents. The third one is Tony La-Coco, the gamblers' bank. Kemper owed him a lot of money. I suppose they're wondering how to collect."

The men simply stood and watched, and I thought of the big blackbirds that once sat on the telephone lines up and down the county roads. I was still looking at them when the gold Lexus pulled up. A beautiful redhead and Mike Rich got out of the car.

The redhead, who had to be Simpson/Krystal, stopped by the three men long enough to sign autographs. It was both crass and fascinating to see the brief exchange, and at least Mike Rich had the manners to be annoyed. Even from a distance of a hundred yards, I could tell that he wasn't exactly cordial to them. Then he grasped his wife's arm and ushered her away.

"So, the celebrity has arrived," Bud said.

"Yes, you know Krystal well, I hear." I

watched him closely, but he ignored the implication in my tone.

"I was referring to her husband," Bud said. "Krystal's a piece of cake compared to her spouse. He thinks he's the talent and she's just an accoutrement."

Bud and I took a place in the back of the small gathering, behind Coleman and Deputy Gordon Walters.

"We've come to say good-bye to Kemper Fuquar," Father McGuire intoned. "He has left us here to begin his immortal journey."

One of the men in a dark suit stepped to the head of the casket. In the startled breach, he said very calmly, "And he left owing Mr. LaCoco a lot of money." He looked around at everyone, his gaze lingering on Lee. "Mr. LaCoco has asked me to deliver his condolences, and to tell you that he hasn't been able to convince the sheriff to let him talk to you in jail. The sooner he talks to you, the sooner Mr. LaCoco can leave town." The last was spoken to Coleman.

He gave Kip an appraising glance before he looked at Lee. "Mr. LaCoco will be in touch." Nodding once, he rejoined his friends, who remained standing beside a big Town Car. They got in and drove away.

"Father," Lee said softly.

The priest concluded the brief service, and we all turned to leave.

"Sarah Booth," Coleman said, putting a hand on my shoulder. "Wait up. Gordon can take Lee back to the jail."

The sheriff and I waited at the cemetery until everyone was gone. Mose, Rake, and Elijah, the three old grave diggers, leaned on their shovels and stared at me. Coleman, too, was staring at me. He took my arm and we walked slowly away from the grave and toward a small pecan orchard that was just budding out.

The sunlight was warm, and the day promised to be truly beautiful.

"How stable is Kip?" Coleman asked.

This was a question I dreaded. It seemed that he and I were running down the same tracks. "I don't know." I turned to face him. "I don't know anything about kids. What about those men at the funeral? That guy all but came out and threatened Lee and Kip. Who is this LaCoco?"

"They're exactly what they look like. They're from Biloxi. Kemper owed them money. I'm checking them out." He put a warm hand on my shoulder. "I still want to see Kip tomorrow."

"Coleman, I don't—"

"Billy Appleton, the Security Life agent, was in my office this morning. Kip is the beneficiary of the primary insurance policy on Kemper." His blue eyes held trouble. "Kemper changed the policy just two weeks before he was killed. He upped it considerably. Prior to that, Lee had dropped a lot of the policies. She was having financial difficulties."

In the silence I could hear the unsettling call of a whippoorwill, normally a nighttime bird. We turned back the way we'd come, and we walked in silence.

"Don't forget about tomorrow," Coleman said as we parted.

The three grave diggers were still waiting. "Bury him deep," I told Mose. "We don't want him crawling out of the grave."

The body was lowered into the ground, and the men threw in the first shovelfuls of dirt. I suddenly thought of stopping the entire process to open the casket and apply the required wooden stake. Even though I'd seen the gruesome photographs, I just didn't trust Kemper to stay dead.

12

I stopped by Dahlia House to check on Kip, only to discover a note from Tinkie. She and Kip had driven over to a small restaurant on the Tallahatchie River for lunch. They would be gone for an hour or two.

"Bless you, Tinkie," I murmured as I kicked off one high heel and then another. At the sound of the shoes falling, Sweetie Pie bolted out from under the dining room table and snagged a shoe. She had the fastest jaws in the South, and I lunged across the floor to grab it before she could begin the process of digestion.

"Sweetie!"

At the reproach, Sweetie dropped the shoe, lowered her head, tucked her tail, and slunk away. I heard the kitchen door swing open and shut. She'd gone to console herself with a bowl of food.

Just as I reached up to unzip my dress, I felt a

chill. I didn't have to turn around to know that
Jitty was in the room.

"Maybe you could just leave that dress on
for a little while. Legs are good. Men like 'em.
Folks around Zinnia think you got gorilla hair
or somethin'."

Jitty was wearing a gold body-stocking with
a sheer black overdress threaded in gold. It was
a stunning outfit that did justice to her beautiful skin tones and made me think of *Star Wars*.
Gold streaks had been glitzed through her dark
hair. I decided to trade insult with compliment. "You look great." It was hard not to be a
little jealous.

"Your partner is good at playin' mama. You
should take notes."

"Tinkie does seem to have a way with that
girl." I stepped out of my dress and walked upstairs, shedding hose, slip, and bra. What was
called for was a completely different outfit—
something denim and down-home. Jitty could
be fashionable and Tinkie maternal; I was
happy playing Elly May Clampett.

"That blues man's not so bad." There was a
hint of mischief in Jitty's voice. "You like the
blues. The man was outside your window *sere-
nadin'* you! What more could you want?"

I rummaged through my closet and found

some clean jeans and a red cotton top. It was spring outside, and I suddenly wanted to put the top down on the Mercedes and take a spin in the sun.

"He seems nice," I said, because it was true. Against all good judgment, the blues-singing John Bell had piqued my interest. Once the case with Lee was concluded and things had settled down, I was going to make it a point to go and listen to him play. As Jitty pointed out, I did love the blues.

"Sarah Booth, you gone give that man a chance?"

A touch of wistfulness in her voice made me turn around and look at her. I caught the hint of sadness in her eyes. "What's wrong?"

"It's a long road between thirty-three and eighty-three. You keep on like you are and it's gonna be a long, *lonely* road. You ever wonder why you're so afraid of a relationship?"

I had wondered what era Jitty would assume, once she was done with the fifties. Now I knew—after a bit of hopping around she'd settled on the future. She was Princess Leia, spouting the latest pop psychology on why love hurts.

"I'm not afraid," I said, perhaps without total conviction.

"Delaney women have always been headstrong, opinionated, full of the devil, ornery, and driven by the needs of their wombs. But they ain't never been afraid to take a chance." She gave me one of those long appraising looks that put me in mind of Aunt LouLane when she was disappointed in something I'd done. In this case, it was what I hadn't done.

"You want me to seriously consider taking John Bell Washington to the Chesterfield Hunt Ball?"

"I haven't seen any other prospects beatin' down the door." Sensing victory, she arched an eyebrow. "He's a fine-lookin' man."

She was right, on both counts. "I'll think about it."

"So you don't know a thing about him. The future is a risk, Sarah Booth. Walkin' down the street, goin' out to work on a case, anything you do is takin' a risk. Look at that Bud Lynch. Could be he's a killer, but you talked to him."

"That's a case, Jitty." The difference was clear to me, if not to her.

She snorted. " 'Cause it gives you a *reason* to do something. Like that would make a bit of difference if he cut off your head. We could put it on the tombstone. She was workin', not so-cializin', when he killed her. But you'd still be just as dead."

"What, exactly, is it that you want me to do?" I asked.

"Open yourself to the possibilities of the future. Times are changin', and if you don't adapt . . ." She arched one eyebrow in a gesture I envied. "Dinosaur bones," she whispered, leaning closer. "Take a chance. Live a little. What could it hurt?"

"It could hurt a lot. Loss hurts. You never got over the loss of your husband. You never remarried." She'd once told me the story of how her husband had gone to war with my great-great-grandfather. Neither had returned alive.

"You great-great-grandma and me, we never had time to worry about findin' a man. We were worried about survivin'. Gettin' through each day didn't leave room for no other worries."

"Okay," I agreed. I was dressed and ready to go. "You've guilted me into it. I'll talk to him."

"You better think about payin' him a *visit*. He's at that motel, waitin' for you. Maybe you two could 'do' lunch."

I was spared answering her by the ringing of the telephone. The caller ID showed it was, at long last, Cece Dee Falcon, the woman I deemed responsible for my current predicament.

"I'm going to break your neck," I said sweetly as my form of hello.

"How nice, dahling." Cece didn't even take a breath. "I've found out the most interesting thing. Guess!"

"Could it be about one of the men you've drug out of the cotton fields and brakes and sent over to Dahlia House to devil me?" My sarcasm was thick.

"All you ever think about is men, Sarah Booth," she said, with some ill humor. "I don't know why I bother, but I've been working on your case."

"Right."

"I called to tell you something important." Cece was annoyed. "I thought it might be of interest to you that Tony LaCoco is in town. He's a gangster, Sarah Booth. He owns The Golden Corral, biggest gambling house and den of pleasure on the Louisiana-Mississippi line. He's been in town the last *four* nights."

That tidbit of news did stop me in my tracks. "The last four nights? *Before* Kemper was murdered?"

"That's what I've been trying to tell you."

I could imagine Cece moving her shoulders back and forth in that little maneuver that showed off her exquisite collarbones, and her impatience. "That makes him an excellent—"

"Suspect," Cece supplied. "Those Mafia types take it seriously when a debt isn't paid. For a little debt, they just break kneecaps. For a big debt, like what Kemper owed, it's death. They have to make an example of people who don't pay, so all the others are afraid and do pay."

"LaCoco was at the funeral. His man made a veiled threat to Lee." As mad as I was at Cece for playing Chuck Woolery in my life, I couldn't help but be delighted with her information. "Good work, Cece. Why weren't you at the funeral?"

"I had a little run-in with Mr. LaCoco at Millie's about half an hour before the funeral. I went in and started to ask a few simple questions about his business in Zinnia. It isn't every day that a gangster of Mr. LaCoco's repute visits a small town for a collection."

"What happened in Millie's?" Cece had a way of making a person beg for the punch line.

"Mr. LaCoco doesn't care for journalists," she said dryly. "One of the bodyguards, the least cute one, threw a plateful of biscuits and redeye gravy at me. I'm afraid that wonderful Dior suit is ruined."

"And I thought you were hiding from me."

"*Moi?* Hiding? Whatever for?"

So she was going to play innocent. I could crack her, but it would take more time than I had. Besides, I was more interested in LaCoco. "Where's LaCoco staying?"

"There's only one place to stay. The Holiday Breeze."

"Excellent work, Cece."

"Thank you, dahling. One does the best one can. Now I have to dash. Kisses."

The line went dead and I replaced the receiver.

Although in at least a tiny corner of my heart I wanted to be a victim of love, slain by the power of romance, and addicted to passion, I also had an ulterior motive for speeding over to the Holiday Breeze. I hoped to get an up-close look at Tony LaCoco. John Bell Washington, blues man, was a good secondary reason.

Just now, the Breeze had more patrons than I could remember ever seeing there, with the exception of 1999 when the monster truck competition was held in Clarkesdale and Zinnia ended up with the overflow of fans.

I heard the slide guitar as soon as I parked the Mercedes near the motel office. I didn't have to ask the desk clerk what room John Bell

Washington was occupying. My destination, and according to Jitty my destiny, was room 8.

Zinnia had once boasted one of the grand hotels of the South, the elegant old Sunflower Hotel. But it was long gone, and with it had faded the tradition of afternoon tea and the evening story hour. The Breeze was more a place of mid-morning Millers.

Built in the 1950's along the distinctive architectural lines of a prison, the motel was flat, low, and painted a monotone shade of gray-yellow.

The small, empty pool nestled between the V-shaped wings was depressing. Eighteen-wheelers roared by on 61 Highway—the route many blues musicians and blacks had taken north—blasting grit against my legs.

A red Chevy van was parked in front of room 8, and there were three other cars in the parking lot, one of them Tony LaCoco's Town Car. There was also a red Mustang convertible and, to my surprise, the gold Lexus I'd seen Mike Rich driving.

Just as I was pulling in, a silver Taurus pulled out. The strange, dapper little man I'd met in Cece's office, Nathaniel Walz, developer, was leaving the parking lot.

I tapped on John's open door and peeped inside. He was in a chair, guitar in his lap, singing the blues. He nodded and put aside the guitar. "Come on in, Sarah Booth."

There were twin beds in the room, both of them rumpled. He was rumpled, too, his dark hair unbrushed. He wore baggy shorts and no shirt, though his chest was not a bad view.

"How's the case?" he asked. "I'm fascinated by this private eye business."

"My friend's in a lot of trouble," I conceded. It was something of a relief to talk to someone who didn't know Lee, someone who might just respond to the case as a set of variables.

"So your friend owes Tony LaCoco a lot of money," he said, frowning. "Maybe LaCoco had her husband killed."

I liked the way this man thought. I also wanted to know where he'd gotten those details, so I asked him.

He pointed at the headboard of the bed. "Yesterday, Mr. LaCoco had his goon practicing the speech he was to give at the graveside. I hope after all that work that the delivery was good."

"Convincing."

John glanced at the bathroom door for a split second. "What are you goin' to do? The kid's stayin' with you, right?"

His drawl was soft and easy, a voice that could be a comfort. "Yes, Kip is with me. The sheriff is aware of the threats, and he's watching out for her."

"And what about yourself? Who's watchin' out for you?"

I couldn't help but smile back at him. "If you've read any mystery books, you'll know that the private investigator always looks out for herself. It's one of the rules."

John laughed. "I want to know more about the rules and regs of being a private dick. I don't normally like rules, but it seems you're workin' with some interestin' by-laws. When I was a kid, I wanted to be one of the Hardy boys. I didn't care which one, just so long as I got to get in on all the adventures."

John's voice was like a down comforter on a cold winter night. I felt myself relaxing, loosening up. "I read Nancy Drew *and* the Hardy boys," I told John. Although few would consider it a mutual literary heritage, John and I had more in common than most of my married friends.

"Have a seat," he said, nodding at one of the beds.

My gaze fell on the suitcase, a sort of floral-patterned bag with what looked like a bit of pink quilted robe poking out. "Why don't we go to Millie's and grab something to eat?" I was only slightly uncomfortable. Jitty had

urged me to take a risk, but loitering in a motel room with a man I didn't know the first
thing about went up hard against Aunt
LouLane's oft-repeated code of conduct for a
Delta girl.

"Sure," he said, putting his guitar in a case.
"Food sounds good. We had a big breakfast,
but that wore off a while ago. Mother loves
to eat."

It was no Daddy's Girl ploy when I repeated
the word. "Mother?"

He nodded. "Mother always travels with me.
Of course, she knows she can't go to the ball,
but we can fill her in on the details when we
get home. Since Dad died, she isn't interested
in dating, but she enjoys meeting my friends."

Looking at John, I had no sense of danger,
but my gaze slid to the bathroom, to the place
where the shower waited so innocently. I
couldn't help but wonder if the shower curtain
was opaque or clear. I could feel my muscles
tensing for action.

He gave me a puzzled look. "What's wrong?
Mother will be out in a minute."

"John, where was your mother last night?" I
asked as calmly as I could.

"Oh, she was asleep in the car. I wanted to
meet you and see what you looked like. I
mean, people do lie about themselves on the

Internet. Some women I've met claimed to have an athletic build." He winked. "Yeah, right, sumo wrestling would be the sport. Now me, I never lie. What you see is what you get."

"What are you talking about?" I was torn between trying to figure out what he was saying and worrying that when I stepped outside the door, Norman Bates would probably be standing there.

"The Internet. Your profile. You know, where you tell what you look like, what you do, what movies you like. Yours was *V.I. Warshawski*. Not a terrific flick, but appropriate."

I suddenly *knew* what he was talking about. "What else did my profile say?" I asked.

His grin was charming. "Is this a test? You're thirty-three and hangin' by a thread, never been married, a blues lover, mystery reader, especially books by Kinky Friedman, and you're an equestrian."

And I knew where the profile had come from. Kip was in big, big trouble. All along I'd blamed this on Cece, but not even Cece would think of listing me as "an equestrian." "I'm sorry, Mr. Washington, but I didn't fill out an Internet profile. Someone else did this. You've been duped, and so have I."

He picked up his guitar and played a few riffs. "Sounds like we're talkin' the blues. Might be a song in this somewhere." He began to sing. "I profiled my baby, da-dah-dum. I found her on-line, da-dah-dum. But when I got to Zinnia, for a date she was dis-inclined!"

He was laughing as he put the guitar down. "So I guess the Chesterfield Hunt Ball is out of the question."

"I'm afraid so." I stepped through the door. "I can only promise you that there's going to be one very sorry teenager." I was eager to find Kip.

"At least meet Mother." He called out to her. "Hey, Mom, Sarah Booth's agenda has changed. Come out and say hello."

Good manners rooted me to the spot, though I only wanted to flee. When the bathroom door opened, a short, white-headed woman in a lavender plaid dress stepped into the room. She looked at John Bell and then at me.

"You must be the woman Johnny came to date," she said in a pleasant voice. "I'm his mother, Lydia Washington."

Having been haunted by a ghost, I knew the difference between a figment and a real, live human. Lydia was real enough, and a relief. But a line had been crossed in my mind that I could not step back over. "It really is a pleasure to meet you," I said. "Something has come up in the case I'm working on, and my plans have changed." He might be the most normal, kind-hearted son in the universe, but I couldn't help it. I stepped further into the sunshine.

"Oh, dear," Mrs. Washington said. "I'm glad we didn't rent tails in Greenwood."

"I have to be going." There really wasn't anything else I could say.

The minute I walked out of the room and toward my car, the middle of my back began to tingle. Very slowly I turned around. One of the dark-suited men stood in the open door of room 10, next door to J.B.'s room. Tall and lean, the man watching me had worked on his physique, and not necessarily for aesthetic reasons. His gaze was hard and direct. He started walking toward me with intent.

"You're the one keeping the kid, aren't you?" he asked. He didn't give me time to answer. "I hear she inherits. You might want to remind her that Mr. LaCoco expects his debts to be paid. In a timely fashion. In this case, since the payments are so far behind, that means Mr. LaCoco would like his money yesterday." He grinned before he walked back in the room and closed the door.

I saw the motel curtain drop back into place. Someone inside the room had also been watching.

When I got back to Dahlia House, Kip was in the kitchen. Pasta was boiling in a big pot, and she was stirring some delicious-smelling sauce on the stove.

"Do the names Malone Beasley and John Bell Washington mean anything to you?" I asked, standing behind a chair, my hands gripped on the back of it. I was angry and trying not to show it.

"Mr. Beasley was a mistake. He lied on his profile." The tiniest hint of remorse faded completely as she kept talking. "But John Bell Washington is cool, Sarah Booth. He'd be a great date. He had some of his music on his profile, and he's really good. He wants to help you with your cases. What could be better, a blues-singing private eye?"

"Kip, you got those men to come here under false pretenses. You tricked them, and you used me to do it. It's humiliating for them and me, and it was wrong."

She put the wooden spoon down. "I tore up Carol Beth's truck. That was bad, and I meant it to be. Going on the Internet for you wasn't bad. I heard everyone giving you a hard time. I know what it's like when everyone expects things and you can't make it happen like they want. I thought it would be great if you showed up with a handsome guy who was fun and cool. It would show them."

Maybe she was a great actress and maybe I was a fool, but my anger was leaking out. "You can't do things like that, Kip."

"I heard you talking to yourself the first night I was here. You were debating about going on-line to find a date. That's where I got the idea. It worked for Meg Ryan; why not for you?"

In her own way, Kip was paying me a compliment. "This is life, Kip, not a movie."

"What did it hurt? Beasley was a loser, but Mr. Washington would be fun. Why not take him to the ball?"

"In his profile, did he mention that he travels with his guitar—and his mother?"

Kip's eyes widened. "No!"

I couldn't help but grin. "Yes, he does. She's charming, and so is he, but just a little too strange."

She picked up the spoon and stirred the sauce some more, her total concentration on the bubbling pot. "I'm sorry, Sarah Booth. I really was trying to get your friends off your back."

"Kip, there are a lot of things we need to talk about, but this can wait until Lee is out of jail. Just don't do it anymore, okay?"

She nodded. "I'll delete your profile."

"Thanks," I said. "And that's it for the computer. Use it only for schoolwork and nothing else. And no phone. And no music. That's punishment for leaving the house last night and worrying me to death."

She looked up, surprised. "That's it? That's the punishment? What about Carol Beth's truck?"

"I know why you vandalized the truck. What you did was wrong, but I'm not willing to punish you for it. When your mother gets out of jail, the two of you can sort it out. I'm not your warden, Kip. But there is something I want you to do for me."

"What?"

"Who told you that Carol Beth had bought your horse?"

Her gaze slid back to the pot of sauce, which she began to stir with a vengeance. "I can't say."

"I certainly can't torture the name out of you, but I will tell you that whoever did it was either very irresponsible or very cruel. Does knowing where Mrs. Peel is make you feel better?" She didn't say anything, but I knew she was getting my point. "Has it helped your feelings in any way? Or has it just made it worse?"

"Worse," she whispered. "Before I found out

Carol Beth had her, I could pretend that the young girl was riding her, and loving her the way I do."

"Who told you where the horse was?"

"Mr. Rich." She spoke the name so softly I wasn't sure what she said.

"Mike Rich?"

"Yeah." She picked up a pasta spoon and pulled up several spaghetti strands to test them. "He didn't know it was a secret."

"And did he pick you up last night?"

The look she gave me was desperate. "Don't get him in trouble. I lied to him. I said I had to talk to Carol Beth about something else. Mike was the only one of the men who came to the house who was ever nice to me. He came to the shows, too, and sometimes he'd sit at the trailer and talk to me. He knew I loved Mrs. Peel. He thought I'd want to know she had a good home."

She was holding back the tears by sheer will. "Okay, Kip," I said. "It's okay."

"Carol Beth is a bitch. She wants everything. She hung out at the barn, chasing Bud and wanting all of the horses. She took Mrs. Peel because I loved her, and Mrs. Peel loved me!" Red splotches bloomed on Kip's cheeks, and her throat was an angry red. Her eyes glittered, but not from unshed tears. She was furious. "I hate that bitch. I hate her! I hate the two of them, Carol Beth *and my father.*"

She dropped the spoon she held and ran out of the kitchen and up the stairs. I heard her door slam.

When dinner was ready, neither Kip nor I had much of an appetite. We toyed with the pasta and salad before we decided to call it a night. Before I saw Coleman in the morning, I had to decide what I was going to tell him about Kip.

I crawled into bed, book in hand. Instead of ideas for my case, I had only worries. LaCoco's man at the Holiday Breeze Motel had ignited my anxiety fuse. Kip was more than I could manage, and another day had passed with Lee still in jail.

Since there was nothing I could do until morning, I opened my book. Kinky was in rare form, as author and as character. I slipped into the story, hoping that somehow, somewhere, I'd find a bit of detecting that might help me with my own case.

I was too tired to even turn off the light when I felt the book slipping from my fingers. I simply let loose of consciousness and fell into a deep sleep.

The smell of baking muffins teased me

awake, and I discovered that I was fully dressed and already pushing through the swinging door into the kitchen.

Coffee perked on the counter, a sound and smell that offered good possibilities. What I didn't expect was the black-hatted stranger sitting at my kitchen table, twirling a cigar.

"Jitty said you'd be down soon," Kinky Friedman said, and I knew that I was dreaming. "And by the way, some women find cigars sexy."

"How'd you get in?" I asked.

"You should get a puppet head to hide your key," he recommended. "Of course, that won't do much good if you don't lock your doors."

"What are you doing in Mississippi?"

"I heard you were having trouble with your case. I thought I'd drop by. Mind if I smoke?" He didn't wait for a reply. He fired up the cigar and puffed to the ceiling. "From what I gather, you have a friend who's confessed to the murder of her worse half."

"She's innocent," I said.

"All the best ones are."

He wasn't as sympathetic in a dream as he'd appeared in a book. "I need to *prove* she's innocent," I told him.

"She's bound to be guilty of something. All the best ones are."

I poured us both a cup of coffee and sat down at the table. "If you aren't going to help, then let me sleep in peace."

"What's she guilty of?" he asked.

"What kind of question is that?" I demanded.

"The right kind. What's she hiding? Why's she lying? The question I'd get an answer to first is why she stayed with her louse for all this time. Once you know that, maybe you can pick up the scent of other interesting things. And remember, if at first you don't succeed, ask and ask again."

He was gone, leaving only a curl of cigar smoke wafting in the early morning light.

I woke to the sound of Sweetie scratching on my bedroom door, and in my brain the humming of a question that demanded an answer.

13

On Friday, Kip had her own date with destiny in the form of Coleman Peters. Although she had a new do and better makeup, the sullen demeanor on her face was old and familiar.

Kinky's nocturnal visit had reignited my faith in myself, and I tried hard to be firm yet comforting with Kip. "Just tell Coleman the truth," I reminded her as we turned toward the courthouse square.

"Why do I have to talk to the sheriff?" she asked for the fifth time, as we pulled into a parking space at the courthouse.

"Because he wants to talk to you." I was losing patience, though I was trying hard not to.

"I don't know anything."

"It sure sounded like you did at the funeral. You accused your mother of lying. 'Tell them the truth.' I think that's a direct quote. It made your mother look very, very bad."

She fell silent, staring down at her hands in her lap. We were parked beneath oak trees, and the young leaves were apple green. Even the shade cast by the trees seemed dusted by green.

"Kip, if you know something, please tell me now, before you tell Coleman."

"He won't do anything anyway."

"I wouldn't be so sure about that."

"He used to come out and see Mama. Last year." Her face was lowered and she cut her eyes over at me with a slanting, knowing look. "They were very good friends."

She knew exactly what she was implying. "Coleman? Are you sure?" Call me naïve, but I was dumbfounded.

"Sheriff Peters," Kip said. "He would come when Daddy was gone. They'd build a fire in the ladies' parlor and drink brandy or something. Sometimes Mama would play the piano."

This was too much. I'd never taken Coleman for the type who'd play country gentleman in a parlor with a piano, especially not to another man's wife. I knew that he and his wife, Connie, were having a rough time. They'd been near divorcing for the past five years, but Coleman wasn't an adulterer. He just wasn't. This went further than a gut instinct—it went all the way to the womb.

When we arrived in the sheriff's office, Coleman was at his desk on the phone, but his gaze studied Kip. I searched his features for guilt, but saw none. Men were somewhat immune to the feelings of guilt, remorse, and regret. That was the holy trinity of the female.

Coleman put the phone down and motioned for Kip to enter his private office. I got up to follow.

"I'd like to speak to Kip alone," he said pointedly.

"Lee has made me Kip's unofficial guardian. I think it would be better if I stayed with her." I looked to Kip for confirmation, but she was sunk beneath her own thoughts. She sat slumped in a chair, refusing to acknowledge either me or Coleman.

"It's within my right to question Kip," Coleman said.

"Yes, it is." I hated to play hardball with Coleman. He could squash me like a gnat. "But it may be in your best interest to have a witness."

He caught my drift, and I saw a splotch of red touch his cheeks. Guilty! He motioned us both into his office and closed the door.

"Kip, you said at the funeral that you wanted your mother to tell the truth. What truth is that?" Coleman sat down behind his desk as Kip and I took the two remaining chairs.

"I just wanted her to say she didn't kill

Daddy." Kip spoke in a monotone. "She didn't."

"Who do you think killed your daddy?" Coleman's tone was far gentler than I expected. I glanced surreptitiously at him. He was leaning forward, elbows on his desk, face earnest. "I'd like nothing more than to let your mama go home. She and I have been good friends for a long, long time. You know that."

"Yeah, good *friends*." Kip didn't bother to hide her sarcasm.

Coleman ignored her. "I don't think your mother killed your father. I don't think she's capable of it. So who would want to see your father dead?"

Kip snorted and finally looked up, her green eyes blazing with fury. "He owed money all over the place. You saw those men at the cemetery. What do you think they wanted? Daddy lied to everyone. He treated everyone like shit. He hit Mama, and he hit the horses. He only pretended to care about people when he needed them for something." Her eyes filled with tears. "He was going to hit me, once, at a show. But Bud told him he'd kill him if he laid a hand on me."

Coleman kept his face very composed. "Did you ever see any of those men from the funeral at Swift Level?" he probed.

"No. Daddy's *friends* came late at night and they went to the barn." Her voice was barely audible and her gaze was once again on the floor. "I don't know anything except that Mama didn't kill him. She should have, but she didn't."

Coleman changed directions. "What do you know about insurance policies?"

I sat up and began to pay attention. LaCoco and his men were still very much on my mind.

"I don't know. Nothing. Daddy's office was in the barn. All the important papers were kept in a safe there." Kip shrugged. "Ask Bud."

"Did your father ever talk to you about insurance?"

"Like he talked to me about anything but winning. Riding and winning, that was what we discussed. Or that's what he talked about. I never got a chance to say much."

"He changed his policy two weeks ago, and made you beneficiary. Did you know that?"

Kip looked puzzled. "He did?"

Coleman nodded. "Okay. I only have one more question. Why did your mother stay with your father if he abused her all the time?"

It was almost as if Kinky had also visited Coleman. He was asking my question.

"Ask Mother." Her voice was a monotone.

"I have. She doesn't have an answer. I thought maybe you would."

Kip picked at the seam in her blue jeans.

"Kip?" Coleman pressed.

She looked up at me. "I don't know."

Coleman wasn't going to back off. "That's a lie, Kip. You won't help your mama by lying, and you might get yourself in trouble."

"Coleman . . ." I didn't intend to let him frighten her or use guilt to pry answers from her.

"Stay out of this, Sarah Booth. Lee could have divorced Kemper. This is a question the prosecution is going to ask, and Kip had better be prepared to answer it."

Kip's confusion was evident as she looked up at Coleman. "You said you were Mama's friend. If you think she's innocent, why do you keep her in jail?"

That cut Coleman to the bone. He sat back in his chair. "I have to uphold the law."

"Even when it's wrong?"

He picked up a pencil and twisted it. "Lee confessed to murder. I didn't go out and arrest her, you know."

Kip stared at him, and the teenager disappeared before my eyes, replaced by a cold, angry young woman. "You were part of the reason she didn't divorce him. Whenever she threatened to, he'd say how he would counter-sue and blame you. He said he'd ruin you politically and also ruin your marriage. He told her the damage he would do could never be repaired." Her nostrils widened slightly as she leaned toward his desk. "That isn't the answer you wanted, is it?" She stood. "Am I done?"

The door of Coleman's office slammed shut behind Kip. I was left sitting in my chair and staring at the floor. When I finally looked up, Coleman was watching me. His voice was low when he finally spoke.

"Lee and I were always good friends in high school. About three years ago, we both found ourselves in a bad place. I started going out to Swift Level when I knew Kemper was gone. He spent a lot of time down on the Gulf Coast." He held my gaze, though I wanted to look away. I didn't want to hear this. I didn't want to be Coleman's priest.

"We'd have a drink and sit around the fire and talk. It was good for both of us. Connie and I couldn't—can't—pass a civil word. It was worse with Lee and Kemper, though I didn't know he was hitting her."

"Please stop," I said abruptly. "This isn't my business."

"Yes, it is, Sarah Booth, because I care what

you think about me. I care a lot. I didn't want to question Kip, but it had to be done."

"Why? You didn't learn a damn thing worth knowing." I was suddenly angry, and I stood and began to pace. "You've hurt her and Lee and yourself. For what? Just so you could say you did your job? That's a crock, and you know it." He had also hurt me. I believed in Coleman. I believed he was a man who knew the difference between right and wrong, and stayed on the side of the angels.

"My job is the only thing I have right now," Coleman said so quietly that it made me halt. "Connie's seeing a lawyer. She's filing for divorce. We're legally separated. It's just a formality now."

"Is Connie naming Lee?" That would be too much.

He shook his head. "The grounds are incompatibility. Connie wants kids and I don't. I work all the time. I neglect her. Connie's list of complaints is longer than my arm."

"I'm sorry, Coleman."

He shrugged. "My marriage was dead a long time ago. We should have ended it then."

It was ironic that now Lee's marriage was dead, too. Dead because someone had killed her husband. "You make a pretty good suspect in Kemper's death," I said. I meant it as a joke, but I also recognized the truth of it. So did Coleman. He dropped the pencil and stared at me in silence.

"If I were Jack Webb, I'd have to ask you where you were on the night that Kemper was murdered." I tried to make it sound like a joke.

"I don't have an alibi," he said, and he was not joking. "I was riding around out by Opal Lake. Connie and I had another fight and I just got in my truck and started driving. I didn't go home until nearly dawn."

A strange lump had worked its way into my throat. Coleman was throwing himself in front of the train. He was willing to become a suspect to take the heat off Lee. "If you want to help Lee, it would be a lot more beneficial if you said you had her in the truck with you. Even better, you could really give her an alibi by relating gritty details of making love on the seat like some teenager." I didn't understand why I was so mad at him.

He stood up. "I wasn't with Lee. There was a time, back in high school, when I thought we were suited to each other. Both of our lives would have been very different." He opened the door to his office. "But that's not what happened." His mouth set in a firm line, closing that avenue of conversation. "Boyd Harkey stopped by to see Lee this morning. She was crying when he left."

"What about those men at the funeral? Did you find anything?"

"Tony LaCoco has gambling interests in Mississippi and Louisiana, most of them illegal. Kemper owed money, a lot of money. LaCoco has stated a claim to funds, once the will is probated, but I don't think he'll give Kip any trouble."

"I wouldn't be so sure." I told him about the brief encounter at the Holiday Breeze. I could tell that he didn't like anyone threatening Kip.

"I'll have a talk with Mr. LaCoco," he said. "What were you doing at the Holiday Breeze?"

That was a question *I* didn't want to answer. I ignored it. "How much did Kemper owe those men?"

Coleman sighed. "About four hundred thousand."

"How much is the insurance policy?"

Coleman got up and walked to the window so that his back was to me. "A million dollars. But there's some question as to whether the policy will pay off if Lee's convicted of the murder."

"But Kip is the beneficiary?"

"Yes," Coleman said. "There's another thing you need to know. Swift Level belonged to Kemper. From the very first. Lee's name was never on the deed."

14

My intense desire was to get in my classic convertible and drive through the open fields of Sunflower County until I came to terms with at least some of the issues that were troubling me. My brief stint in the study of psychology at Ole Miss had given me an understanding of the complexity of emotions—and the ensuing damage that came from *not* sorting through them.

Unfortunately, I was missing one emotionally volatile and very angry teenager. There was an old bench in the shade of an oak on the courthouse lawn. I sat down, knowing that it was useless for me to hunt Kip and that when she was ready, she would find me. The cement bench was cool, and I enjoyed the contrast between my cool seat and the warm sun on my shoulders as I watched the cars circle the courthouse square. Some were looking for parking while others were merely exercising the American right of curiosity. The courthouse was still the hub of Sunflower County. It was where the action was.

When I was a kid, I loved to ride my bicycle around the courthouse square and the town, flying along the sidewalks and less busy streets. My father had hauled the old Schwinn from Dahlia House in the trunk of the car. Daddy was a circuit court judge, a man of influence. My mother was a character, a woman ahead of her time.

"Lovely day, isn't it, Sarah Booth?"

The sonorous tones of Boyd Harkey made me sit up straight on the bench. I felt as if I'd been caught naked. I didn't like Boyd, and he didn't like me. He was a shark, and he only came around when he smelled blood. The fact that he was being pleasant to me made the hair on the nape of my neck stand.

"It is a nice day, Boyd." My early training as a Daddy's Girl dictated that I maintain the veneer of pleasantness.

"Since you're on Lee's payroll, that means you're working for me now. I'm her lawyer, in case you haven't heard."

I tried to hide my surprise. Lee had emphatically stated she would handle her own defense. She also held Boyd in the same contempt I did. "When did she hire you?"

"Today. I'm in charge of her case, and that means you work for me."

I looked up to see if he was kidding. He was staring at the courthouse, his leonine head lifted, chin forward. He was a big star in the local theater, and he was adept at striking poses. This was one of his better ones.

"Mrs. McBride is not as clever as she thinks," he said.

No surprise there. Only Boyd was as clever as he thought. Still, the fact that Lee had gotten professional help was a relief. "Can you prove she's innocent?"

He stared at me, his eyes too wide apart in his large head, his flowing gray hair groomed to a sweeping perfection. "I don't even think about it. I'm not paid to think about guilt or innocence; I'm paid to get my client off. That's why I'm talking to you. If you want to help Lee, find me a scapegoat, someone I can point the finger of blame at. I need a Plan B for this case, Sarah Booth, and I've decided that you're the person to give it to me."

"Has Lee agreed to this?" I had my doubts. "She hired me to gather evidence showing that she had justifiable reasons to kill Kemper. I tried to convince her to help me find other potential murder suspects, but she was adamantly *against* that kind of defense tactic."

Boyd's smile was more of a sneer. "Lee is a fool. She's perfectly suited to breed horses and

216   *Carolyn Haines*

cowboys. Anything else is out of her league. I'm in charge of this case. She's already stupidly allowed herself to be evaluated by a psychiatrist. Now temporary insanity is out of the question. I have to have something else by next Friday, when we go before the grand jury. Reasonable doubt is the next best thing."

"Lee's not going to accept the idea of fingering someone else as a possible killer," I pointed out. When the finger of blame moved away from Lee, it would point directly at Kip, and Lee would not tolerate that.

"You can take your marching orders from me, or you can clear out of the way. I won't have you screwing things up." He put his hand on my shoulder and then let it slide down my bare arm. "Find me a scapegoat and be quick about it. Her current defense is ridiculous. Everyone in town is relating it to that song. A Dixie Chick defense," he added in disgust.

I knew the song about Earl and why he had to die. The lyrics had struck a chord with women across America—and ignited the ire of a certain kind of man.

"Instead of strategizing, why don't you—"

"Find me suspects. Check out that group of horsewomen. They're a talented lot. They've figured out how to screw their husbands in all the classic ways. Surely you can find me a motive for murdering Kemper in that group. Reasonable doubt is all I need." He squeezed my hand so tight that it took all my restraint not to pull away from him.

There was a soft, feminine laugh from behind us. "Boyd, I see you're still ordering women around. And using physical force, when necessary. I suppose that's why you always married children. A mature woman wouldn't put up with you for thirty seconds."

I turned to find Lillian Sparks leaning against the huge oak tree that shaded us. I had no idea how long she'd been listening, but her presence made Boyd drop my hand as if my skin had suddenly become too hot. Instead of hot, though, I felt cold. Boyd's touch was not sexual; it was even more intimate, more obscene—the witch feeling Hansel's finger to see if he was fat enough to eat.

"Lillian," Boyd said with fake joviality, "I was going to call on you later today. We may need an expert on horse behavior. Would you consider it?"

Lillian came toward us. I often forgot she was in her seventies until she moved. Her ankles were so badly swollen she could hardly walk, and I wondered how she'd sneaked up. "I'll be glad to testify in Lee's behalf. But about what?"

Boyd's smile was superior. "Perhaps we'll throw suspicion on that horse. Paint a scenario where Kemper was alive in that stall."

"The forensic evidence—" I tried to say.

"Juries don't want forensics. They want a good, dramatic story."

Lillian exchanged a look with me. "I'd like to believe the average citizen is more intelligent than you obviously think, Boyd."

He laughed out loud. "They're morons. Fools to be led to whatever conclusion the best lawyer conjures for them. The jury is the ignorant masses, and the lawyer the magician that makes them believe in illusion. You know it in your heart, Lillian." He laughed again. "All of you dreamers, wanting things to be different. Well, they aren't, and they won't ever be. You just have to figure out how to make the best of the situation and turn it to your advantage."

"Thanks for the lesson in life," I said. I had things to do. Nothing Boyd had told me was news, except for the date of the grand jury. Next Friday. A week from today. What he had accomplished was to sharpen my focus. Lee did need a Plan B, and I was going to have one ready for her. One that wouldn't risk her daughter or Avenger.

Boyd walked away, striding across the greening lawn. Lillian, sighing, took a seat on the bench.

"I saw Kip. She looked upset," she said.

"She is." It occurred to me that Lillian would probably know the details on Swift Level. Her father had been one of the premier horse breeders in the Southeast at one time.

"Do you have a financial line on Swift Level?" I asked.

"Historical or current?"

I considered. "Both. It's for the case."

"Kemper bought the Parker estate, and it was a good thing, too. He had money, but he was gambling like mad. Lee insisted that he buy the property. She was about to have Kip, and it looked like her parents were actually going to finally accept Lee for who and what she was. Then something happened. I'm not sure what, but the rift between Lee and her folks was permanent. She'd obtained some of her inheritance, enough to get Swift Level remodeled and the pastures and barns up and running. The rest of it, Lee earned on her own, by the sweat of her brow and by sheer, damned determination."

"So Kemper owned the physical property—"

"Which Lee has vastly improved."

"And she owned the horses and everything of value."

Lillian nodded. "It was a stalemate. She couldn't really divorce him, and he didn't want to divorce her. She was his constant source of income, and Swift Level was the showplace that Lee had created out of a dream. They were twined together in a terrible partnership."

As Lillian got up to go, I couldn't help but wonder if there wasn't something else there, something more than money.

I was still sitting on the bench when Kip found me. She was sullen and uncommunicative, but she followed behind me when I stood and walked to the car. We drove slowly back to Dahlia House, each of us staring at the passing scenery and trapped in our own thoughts.

There was a call on my answering machine from Millie. She was brief and to the point—the gossip about Bud Lynch and his riding students was all over town. Carol Beth had set up camp in a back booth of the restaurant and spent the morning slandering Bud. It crossed my mind that Carol Beth was laying the defense she planned to use to her husband. I wondered how smart Benny Bishop could be.

I made a quick call to Tinkie. I didn't have

time to wait for the Chesterfield Hunt Ball to talk to the four Daddy's Girls who comprised Bud Lynch's personal stable.

Tinkie picked up on the first ring, a little breathless. "Sarah Booth, I've been driving all over town looking for you."

I was curious to know why, but I shifted back to first priority. "I need phone numbers on Elizabeth, Mary Louise, Susannah, and—"

"Krystal's fund-raiser for Lee is tonight. At the Crystal Pistol."

"How appropriate. Krystal plays the Crystal."

"Don't be tacky," Tinkie said. "I've already talked Oscar into going."

"Not Oscar the banker." I couldn't help but tease her. "Oscar must hold the mortgage on the bar."

"Sarah Booth, that's too mean. What's wrong with you?"

I'd actually hurt her feelings. Normally Tinkie didn't mind a few jokes at Oscar's expense. "Sorry, I thought for a minute I was a comedienne."

"It's okay."

Tinkie got over a huff faster than anyone I knew. Rapid forgiveness was a Daddy's Girl ploy, but in Tinkie's case it was for real.

"Is Simp . . . Krystal really trying to help Lee?" I asked.

"Help her or gain attention, I can't say for sure."

"Tell me what you know." Every passing day proved to me that my decision to take Tinkie in as a partner had been the right one.

"Her husband has rented the Pistol for the whole night. There's going to be a hundred-dollar charge at the door per couple, and Krystal's going to actually record the whole session for a possible album called *Jail Bail*. She's going to allow local talent to play and sing with her, and the proceeds from tonight and the album will go to Lee's defense fund."

"Brilliant." It was. Whoever did PR for Krystal deserved a big salary increase. I could almost guarantee that media from Nashville to New Orleans would be on hand for this event. I could see the headline: SINGER RAISES MONEY TO HELP JAILED FRIEND. Krystal would become a saint. "The only thing better would be if she could get the Dixie Chicks as backup."

"She tried. They're on tour in Biloxi. Conflicting schedules."

"No kidding." I was impressed. "I need to talk to Krystal."

There was a pleased giggle. "No problem, Sarah Booth. You've got a backstage pass and thirty minutes to talk privately."

"How did you arrange that?"

"Oh, I just used that lie you made up about the book. I told her husband you wanted to put her in your book. He was a little confused because he thought you were *only* a private investigator. I straightened it all out."

"Tinkie, you are terrific!"

"Well, it was your original lie. I just borrowed it."

"When we make some money, remind me that you need a raise."

Her laugh was musical, an attribute many Daddy's Girls aspired to but few achieved. "Sarah Booth?"

"Yes." I didn't like the new tone in her voice.

"The Chesterfield Hunt Ball is tomorrow night."

"I can't conjure a man out of thin air." I sounded defensive, but I couldn't help it.

"Let me handle this. Now, I left a catalogue in the kitchen when I brought Kip home yesterday. Pick out a dress and order it. My credit card number is written on the front."

"I can't—" I was still redeeming my credit rating after a rough couple of years, but Tinkie wasn't my fairy godmother.

"Don't argue. I know your credit rating got a little confused before you became a detective. You can pay me later. Right now we need fast action, and the store will express deliver if they can charge an account. Just pray you don't need alterations. With that in mind, the less material the better, if you get my drift. Don't procrastinate, Sarah Booth. Just do it."

15

The Neiman Marcus catalogue was on the kitchen table, along with the digits of Tinkie's platinum charge account. I put on a pot of coffee and managed to avoid picking up the catalogue for all of ninety-seven seconds.

While the coffee brewed, I slipped into a chair, grabbed the wish book, and opened it to the gowns. Jitty took a seat beside me, silent while I flipped the pages.

At last she spoke. "Go back a page. That red number has your name all over it."

It was exactly the dress I wanted. As if it had been created by Tinkie's prediction, there wasn't a lot of material involved. The front was a low V and the back was scandalous. "I don't know . . ."

"Fine time for you to decide to act like a lady." Jitty pointed at the dress. "Order it. Just remember, this is one ball where you need to take your own prince, Cinderella."

She was right; the dress was the least of my

problems. The ball required a date, and one in tails, no less. I had about twenty-four hours to conjure up such a masculine masterpiece.

"You could ask one of the Buddy Clubbers. They're old enough to be your father, but they all have full dress suits in their closets."

Instead of getting my ire up, Jitty's comment deeply depressed me. "This is what I've come to, finding a man as potential date material because he has the proper wardrobe." I closed the catalogue. Tinkie would have to manage the ball without me. Even if I ordered the dress, I couldn't just order up a man.

"That blues singer isn't so bad. So he has a mama. Ever'body knows a man treats his wife the same way he treats his mama, and looks to me like John Bell Washington sure treats his mama good." Jitty studied her fingernails as she talked. They were a strange metallic color. Her outfit was rather futuristic, too—a form-fitting tunic with a flared skirt. Very short! And leggings. Jitty had definitely left the June Cleaver image behind. Her hair was a smooth upsweep that made her look like . . . Lieutenant Uhura. I gave her ears close scrutiny. No points—yet.

"Earth to Sarah Booth. Earth to Sarah Booth. I said that blues singer, John Bell whatever, was kind of good-lookin'. I think Kip did a pretty good job findin' you a date."

"I have to face facts. I don't have a date to-day, and I won't have one by tomorrow night."

Jitty walked around me, her Star Trek outfit looking like a second skin. She stopped in front of me and narrowed her eyes. "You go any deeper down in the ditch of de-spair, you gone need to call nine-one-one to get a ladder long enough to get you out." Jitty studied me. "What's wrong?"

"It's the case. I can't seem to do anything to help Lee. The more I dig, the worse it looks. Kemper was ruining her financially, and he actually owned Swift Level. It won't be hard for the prosecution to make a case that she certainly stood to benefit financially from his death. There's not a jury in the world that would feel compassion for a premeditated murder. The thing is, I think she's protecting Kip."

"Let me tell you somethin', Sarah Booth. Somethin' I don't want you to ever forget. Your mama would have gutted anybody who ever tried to hurt you. She would have cut out his gizzard with a bread knife. I'd be a lot more worried about Lee if she *wasn't* protectin' Kip. Now quit mopin' around and order that dress," Jitty instructed. "It can be here tomorrow. If you don't wear it, you can send it back."

"I don't have a date." Back to square one.

"I guess I better go up in the attic and look for my fairy godmother wand." Jitty grinned. "Now, I forget. What else do I need? A pumpkin, six mice? Wasn't there a lizard or two in there?"

"I have a perfectly fine carriage. What I need is a prince."

"Order the dress. Miracles do happen, Sarah Booth."

The Crystal Pistol was off Wade Hampton Road, a strip of narrow asphalt that connected Zinnia to the greater community of Blue Eve. The locale was somewhat appropriate, seeing as how the community was named after a woman who caught her man cheating and then knifed him to death. Her guilt was never proven in a court of law, so she remained a free woman. But it was said she wandered the flat Delta back roads for the next thirty years, looking for him in all the joints and shanty shacks where he'd drunk and gambled. He was dead, but she was a long way from over him.

Of course, her name was Eve.

Blue Eve was a hub of the cattle-and-hay industry in the Delta. These were the hardscrabble farmers who'd pieced together four hundred, six hundred, or a thousand acres, in contrast to the cotton plantations, which often stretched for miles. While the Delta aristocrats rode their thoroughbreds to the hounds, the men of Blue Eve rode their tractors into the sunset.

I'd passed the Crystal Pistol a thousand times, but had never stopped in. Tonight, the pickup trucks were liberally laced with Mercedeses, Lexuses, a scattering of Volvos, and six television trucks. One reporter was doing a live stand-up in the parking lot, while a crowd of beer drinkers yelled and yee-hawed in the background. The band was muffled but not smothered by the windowless cement-block building. A big, hairy man was sitting on a stool with a cash drawer on his lap.

"That'll be fifty dollars, little lady."

He had white teeth and brown eyes. Everything else was covered by hair. But they were perfect teeth, and they showed even more when I held up the backstage pass Tinkie had finagled for me.

"So you're the book writer. Mike said to be on the lookout for you." He pulled open the heavy door, and a blast of music and cigarette smoke nearly knocked me back into the parking lot. "Miss Krystal won't go on for nearly an hour, so you might get to talk to her a bit. Just take it easy. She gets a little tense before she performs. It makes her . . . snappy." He grinned even bigger.

"Bitchy" was the word he wanted, but he valued his job. I waded into the music and felt as if a physical presence were resisting me. The lights were dim and it took a moment for my eyes to adjust. Gradually, I began to make out a few people I knew. Lillian Sparks was at a table with Boyd Harkey and Lincoln Bangs, the man who would prosecute Lee. I wondered at Linc's presence at a fund-raiser for Lee's defense. The Delta is indeed incestuous.

The house band was playing a fair rendition of a country song I'd heard on the radio but didn't know. On the dance floor, a thin blond woman was dancing alone, her body moving in a way suggestive of the horizontal salsa, eyes closed and hips thrusting. She was holding on to a support beam covered in red indoor/outdoor carpeting. Three men at the bar were staring at her with their mouths hanging open and their thoughts clear for all to read.

I felt a hand on my shoulder and turned to face Bud Lynch. Murder suspect he might be, but he was a charming one.

"Want to dance?"

"Now?" I didn't want to match moves with the blonde.

His answer was a laugh as he took my hand

and led me to the floor. With one hand on my hip and the other firmly holding my hand, he swept me into the beat of the music.

"Just relax," he said. "I'll make you look good."

And he did.

"Will you bring Kip out to ride?" he asked.

"Sure, if she wants to go. She hasn't mentioned it, but seeing the horses might be good for her." We twirled until I was breathless.

"Avenger needs her. She's the only one who rides him. He hasn't been ridden in a week, and he's about to tear his stall down."

"I'll bring her if she wants to go. I have to say, she didn't seem overly fond of the horses in her conversation."

Bud shook his head. "She loves them, just like her mother. Kemper was always putting heat on her to ride, but Kip would have done better if he'd left her alone. She's a natural, a real, honest-to-God talent. You should see her on Avenger."

We finished with a twirl and a dip, and I found myself in Bud's arms and staring over his shoulder into Harold's silvery eyes.

"Why, Sarah Booth, you look terrific." Harold held out a hand. "Care to dance?"

"I'll catch up with you later," Bud said, turning me over to Harold.

We stepped onto the dance floor and into a two-step. Harold moved with grace and a firm lead that showed me to advantage. "I'm taking Carol Beth to the ball, but I wish it were you," he said.

I felt a rush of blood to my thumb. Harold had the power to move me, at times. "Why are you taking Carol Beth?" I asked. "She has a husband."

"Benny can't make it. I was asked to be her escort." He spun me, caught me tight, and whispered in my ear. "I'm doing a little investigating of my own."

"Harold?" I said, spinning and ending by his side for a few quick steps before he twirled me again.

"I need you to do something for me," he said.

"What?"

"You've met Nathaniel Walz, haven't you?"

"In Cece's office." I was talking in short sentences. Harold was giving me a workout on the dance floor.

"Make it a point to talk to him. He has some interesting ideas, and he thinks you're pretty."

I frowned at Harold. "Date bait?"

Harold shrugged, but his crystal eyes were alight with amusement. "A good P.I. uses all of her tools," he said, his hand sliding up my ribs and sending a chill down my spine.

Carol Beth stepped out onto the dance floor, blocking us. "And Madame said you'd never be able to dance. It just goes to show you *can* make a silk purse out of a sow's ear. *With enough effort.*" Bud had walked up holding two beers. She looked at him. "Sarah Booth can't afford you, honey."

"Neither can you," Bud said easily. "Though you tried your damnedest."

"What are you doing here, Carol Beth?" I asked. "I thought for sure you'd be signing checks for the prosecution, in the hopes you might be able to play carpetbagger and just step in and steal Lee's entire farm."

Harold captured Carol Beth's hands. "They're playing a waltz," he said, steering her onto the dance floor. Over his shoulder, he gave me a long look that I couldn't decipher in the dim light.

I took the beer Bud offered. "I can see why Kip hates Carol Beth. What I don't understand is why you were spending time with her."

"Would you believe me if I said it was a long story?" His grin was wry.

"Where did you and Carol Beth hold your little rendezvous the night Kemper was killed?" It was too loud in the bar for subtlety.

"You're back to checking my alibi."

"Maybe. Or maybe I'm checking Carol Beth's." I held his gaze. "Who else has been hanging out at Swift Level?"

"Kemper did a lot of business in the barn. He owed money, and that's where he met his creditors. I never hung around to hear the conversations, but I got the idea that some of them were men who wanted money and were determined to get it."

"Could you identify any of them, in a lineup?" It was stretching, but Boyd Harkey had said his plan was to inundate the jury with potential suspects.

He nodded. "One or two of them." He hesitated. "I got a call out at the farm this morning. It isn't good news."

"What?"

"Coleman's been turning the office inside out looking for something. I finally figured out what—insurance policies. I had a little visit from the insurance agent yesterday. What a strange man he is. Kemper took out additional life insurance about two weeks before he died. Seems like he thought an awful lot of himself."

"I know," I said. "Why would he take out a policy on himself? It would seem more likely he'd take one out on Lee and try to kill her." I was thinking aloud.

"That would be more in character," Bud said.

"Were there any other changes in policies?" I asked.

"He wouldn't say, but someone else has been looking for something. Things have been moved, little things. I haven't been able to catch them at it. Yet."

Bud Lynch was a capable man. It would take some fox to sneak into his henhouse and get out alive. "Any clues?"

"Papers in the office have been moved around. Someone had a key to get in the office, and the combination to the safe. No way for me to tell who's doing it."

"Was anything missing?"

"Lee would know better than me. It appears all of the important papers are still there." He shrugged. "Lee's the business manager. I'm just the trainer."

"What about Lee? Does she have any idea?"

Bud frowned. "I had a talk with her this morning and she says no, and I believe her. She said she and Kemper had the only keys, other than mine. All three of those keys are accounted for."

A woman who'd been eyeing Bud from the bar sauntered over to us and planted a kiss on Bud's cheek.

"It's been too long, honey. Where you been keepin' yourself?" she purred. She attached herself to his side and gave me a purely feline glare.

"I'll see what I can find out," I said, slipping away for my meeting with Krystal. It had been more than ten years since I'd talked with her.

The backstage area was tiny, but she had her own private space. There was even a vinyl star with her name plastered on the door. I tapped and waited.

"It had better be important."

The voice still held traces of a Delta Daddy's Girl, but it was overlaid with Nashville twang and a polyurethane coating of hardness. As I recalled, Simpson, as I had known her, had been good at French and Spanish, too.

"It's Sarah Booth."

"Oh, Sarah Booth, come in." The door opened and a smiling Krystal Brook greeted me.

Red hair flamed out from beneath a white Stetson hat, and her makeup was flawlessly, though heavily, applied. She was wearing a hot pink silk blouse with white fringe that outlined her enhanced bosom. A white-and-silver belt with a big buckle circled her tiny waist, and tight pink pants swelled over her hips and down her long legs. She even made the white cowgirl boots look good.

"Simpson! You look . . . terrific." And she did. She just didn't look like Simpson. She was, indeed, Krystal Brook.

"I know. Sometimes I look in the mirror and I think, who is that woman looking back at me?"

Her voice was musical, filled with implied heartbreak and treacherous secrets. She'd always been a very private girl. Of all the Daddy's Girls, I knew least about her. I couldn't remember even once being invited to her home.

"Krystal, baby." I turned to the door as her husband strode in.

"Sarah Booth, this is my husband, Mike Rich." Krystal's introduction was flawless, but something changed the moment her husband got near. I realized it was her eyes. They were suddenly Barbie's—beautiful but without life.

"Yes, we've met."

"Sarah Booth, I hear you're going to put my wife in your book." Mike shook my hand in a pump that was guaranteed to bring water in less than thirty seconds. I would have gushed if I could have.

This was going to be tricky. The old line "Never con a con" came to mind. "That's my goal. Sometimes I wonder if I'll ever finish this darn book." Artful Dodging, lesson number thirty-two in the DG training manual, was coming in handy.

"You should try singing," he said. He perched on the edge of Krystal's vanity table. "My wife goes out there every night and takes the temperature of the mob. She can sing her heart out and get nothing. She can put every inch of her soul out there for them to stomp on. A writer has it easy, compared to that. And you can't imagine the money that's tied up in launching a singing career. Krystal better pay off soon, or I'll have to get a new model."

Gritting my teeth, I smiled. "You seem to know everything about everything."

Krystal went to her husband and put her arm around him, giving a big squeeze. "Sarah Booth wants to ask me some questions."

Actually, I wanted to ask him what he was doing picking up a teenager from my home in the wee hours of the morning, but now wasn't the time.

"Sure, go ahead." He inched his butt further up on the vanity, knocking over a bottle of perfume. He ignored it.

"I'd like to talk to her alone," I said sweetly.

"Sorry. As her manager, I don't think that's a wise idea."

I nodded. "I see your point, and I certainly

understand. Thanks." I started toward the open door.

"Mike, baby, Sarah Booth and I are old friends." Krystal tilted her head up at him. "We've got some old gossip to dig up, and we don't want you hearin' it."

"I think we need to control the things that are printed about you," Mike said as he watched my reaction. "The wrong kind of publicity can do tremendous damage."

"Sarah Booth wouldn't write a harmful word about me," Krystal said, putting her hands on her hips. "Now go on and let us talk for a few minutes."

"I don't understand why I shouldn't listen to the interview," he said, standing up.

"I'm afraid my interviews are conducted one on one. That's the premise of my book," I ad-libbed. "I appreciate your viewpoint, though. A star has to protect her privacy. No hard feelings; I'll just find another singer to interview."

"You won't put her in the book if you don't talk to her alone?" He was incredulous.

"Structure, you know. It's everything in a book. I'm sorry, but I have to follow the structure I've established."

His eyes narrowed, and he looked at Krystal. She shrugged and made her expression helpless.

"What kind of questions?"

"Oh, just about her recording career, where she started, that kind of thing. Fans want to know the basic details of a celebrity's life. It makes the star more real, more human."

Mike studied me. "Nothing personal. You're not going to ask why she doesn't have kids or that kind of thing that's nobody's business but mine?"

I shook my head. I didn't have to ask that question. He'd just given me the answer. "Strictly professional questions."

He pursed his lips. "Okay. But I'll be outside the door. Krystal, you know the rules."

"Yes, Mike." She gave him a smile that should have set his clothes on fire. Krystal had added a full measure of sexual heat to the talents of a Daddy's Girl.

He stepped out of the room, and I walked over and closed the door. When I looked at Krystal she was about to laugh out loud. "Mike's got his good points, but Lord, he can be a trial. He thinks if he doesn't have his finger in every pie, none of them will bake."

"Thanks for doing this for Lee," I said. "She's in a real mess."

"What is it you want to ask me?" She sat down at the vanity and began to check her makeup.

"What can you tell me about Bud Lynch?"

She darkened an eyebrow, her hand never faltering. "We can't talk about that here."

"Then where?"

There was a knock on the door. "Five minutes, Miss Brook. Mike wants you to do a sound check on all the equipment."

Mike had left the room, but he'd made sure there was no time for real questions. I watched Krystal closely. Her back straightened, her shoulders drew back, and she tipped the cowboy hat on her head.

"Honey, this will have to wait. We'll talk later. Right now, though, it's show time." She grasped my shoulders and leaned over to kiss my cheek. "Sarah Booth, it was sure good seeing you."

16

Mike was standing outside the dressing room, hands in pockets and silk tie loosened. His compulsion had not allowed him to go further than the closed door. "How'd it go?" he asked.

"Fine. I can't wait to see Krystal's performance." I thought of the star/manager marriages I'd read about in magazines. Mike fit the stereotype to a T. His claim to fame was controlling the talent. Living as the-man-behind-the-woman had to be tough on his fragile ego.

"Got all your questions answered?" he pressed. Sweat glistened on his forehead.

"All except one." I shifted so that I could look him directly in the eye. "What were you doing, picking Kip up at two in the morning?"

He was startled, but only for a second. "The kid called me and asked me some questions. I knew she was having a hard time, so I talked to her a little and one thing led to another." He shrugged.

"She just called you up, out of the blue?" It wasn't hard to generate disbelief in my voice.

Mike's face darkened. "I was suffering from a guilty conscience. Krystal's just getting into the horse thing, but we're figuring it won't do her career any harm if she learns some rodeo stuff. That Lynch is teaching her. Sometimes I go watch her take lessons, and I overheard some things I shouldn't have repeated."

I raised my eyebrows. I wondered if he knew exactly what Bud was teaching his wife.

"I let it slip that Carol Beth had bought that mare of hers. Kemper never should have done that to the kid."

"Kemper was a total bastard," I agreed. "But Kip is in my care. Didn't it occur to you that I would be upset if she left in the middle of the night?"

"Hell, she said she told you that she was going out with a friend." He frowned. "I guess it's different with boys. We used to take off at all hours."

"And you didn't have a clue she was going to vandalize Carol Beth's truck?"

He was surprised. "I didn't know. She just said she wanted to talk to Carol Beth about the horse. Make sure it was doing okay. She said Carol Beth was expecting her, so I let her out at the motel and left. That's all I had to do with it. Honest." His grin was all charm. "Sorry if it worried you. I won't do it again. This time I promise."

The girls I'd grown up with had made interesting choices in spouses. By comparison, I didn't mind being single.

"How'd you get into the music business?" I asked, pulling out a notepad that I'd brought as a cover. There was something in Krystal and Mike's relationship that niggled at me. He didn't have the finesse required for the truly big league, and I was vaguely curious as to why Krystal kept him around. Maybe he had her tied up in a contract.

"I started out in real estate, some car dealerships, insurance, HMO groups, services for the homebound, those kinds of things. I still dabble a little, but now I'm a record producer and manager of Krystal's career. She's going to be the toast of Nashville by this time next year. She has the talent, and I have the money to make it happen."

So, he was the capital investor. "She's certainly reinvented herself," I agreed.

"Do you think there's something wrong with that?" he asked with more than a hint of aggression.

I almost stepped back. "Certainly not. I

think the ability to go after what you want without being hampered by the past is a sign of real strength. I admire Simpson."

He laughed without humor. "My God, she hated that name. She hated everything about her childhood. Her mother was the ice queen, and her father was a lush. She was lucky she found me. We're the best thing that ever happened to each other."

"I'll be sure to note that in my book," I said as I made my escape.

When I went back out front, the joint was so jammed I had to push for fifteen minutes to get close enough to the bar to order a drink. With a bourbon-and-water in hand, I perched at the edge of the bar and watched the stage.

Krystal came out on a roll of drums and blew two kisses into the audience. She didn't waste any time. Long strides carried her across the small stage as she belted out an old Janice Joplin song, redone in country style. She was damn good.

The more I watched her, the more I liked her act. She'd blended the look of the Grand-Ole-Opry-cowboy-glitz with the heart of traditional rock'n'roll, and in the process had harnessed something hot. She also looked and moved like a star. She possessed that legendary "it" quality.

Everyone who had known Simpson would be stunned at the transformation. The only thing that could begin to compare was Cece's sex change. Even then, everyone had always sort of thought of Cecil as feminine.

No one could ever have imagined Simpson as Krystal.

The song ended to wild applause before Krystal calmed the crowd. "If y'all will listen for just a minute." She held the microphone and waited. Gradually the audience quieted. "As you know, my good friend Lee McBride is in a little trouble. I want to thank you all for comin' out tonight and puttin' some money in her legal kitty. Lee's a good woman." She said it again with emphasis. "A . . . good . . . woman."

She paused dramatically. Her eyes searched the crowd but didn't linger on anyone. She began talking again and I was amazed at the down-home syntax.

"Life takes some strange twists and turns. I know that for a personal fact. Sometimes we find ourselves in places that, a year before, we would never have dreamed we could stumble into, much less stay in. I know I sure have."

That private revelation sent a wave of applause through the crowd. Obviously, everyone in the bar had been someplace that wasn't a comfortable fit. It also gave me some insight into exactly how good Krystal was at working the crowd. She'd connected with everyone in the room on a personal basis.

"Lee and I go back a long way. All the way to high school. *Where we were good friends!* I only wish she'd called me sooner. I know The Beatles aren't country, but they still had a lot of good things to say, and one of the truest was that you can get by with a little help from your friends." She nodded and her red hair shimmied around her shoulders, catching the lights. "With all of that said, there's only one other thing to say. . . ."

The lead guitar did an introduction that was picked up by the rest of the band. Then Krystal began to sing. "Maryanne and Wanda were the best of friends, all through their high school days."

The audience picked up the words to the Dixie Chicks' song that had touched a national nerve. When they got to the part where "Earl had to die," the entire place was shouting out loud.

The only two not singing along were me and the prosecuting attorney.

For the entire hour that Krystal performed, she never let the audience settle down. She gave a show that was one of the best live performances I'd ever seen. It gave me plenty of opportunity to seek out the other DGs.

I wasn't too surprised to find that Mary Louise was the only one in attendance. She looked more than a little out of place in her spit-polished paddock boots, jeans with a crease, and diamond Rolex, but she was trying. In fact, she was on the dance floor in the tight embrace of a local when I found her. When the song was over, I made my move.

"Mary Louise," I said sweetly as I went up to her. "It's been years."

"Sarah Booth." She smiled, but it didn't hide the worry in her eyes. "You haven't changed a bit."

It was a lie, but a nice one. "Can we talk outside for a moment?"

"Sure." She led the way into the relative quiet of the parking lot. My ears were still ringing, and I could feel the bass throbbing in my bones.

"What's going on?" she asked.

"Bud Lynch." I had decided on a frontal assault. It was the one method of attack a Daddy's Girl would never use.

"Oh." She didn't look away. "Bud Lynch." She gave a half laugh. "How'd you hear about that?"

"Carol Beth has been very, very busy," I said.

Mary Louise shrugged a shoulder. "Hell, she wants everything at Swift Level, including Bud. Susannah and Elizabeth and I were mostly having fun, driving Carol Beth crazy. We'd just sit around and talk about Bud so she could overhear." She shrugged again. "In case you haven't kept up, my track record with men hasn't been so great. Why are you so interested in Bud?"

"Because of Kemper's murder."

She looked at me hard. "You think Bud murdered Kemper?"

By her tone I could tell *she* didn't believe it. "Maybe. That's what I'm trying to find out."

"Lee confessed," she pointed out. If she wasn't truly puzzled, she was a damn good actress.

"She's lying," I countered.

Her eyebrows rose in sudden understanding. "To protect someone. Lee would do something like that." She thought a moment. "But I don't think it's Bud. She knew him for what he was, a terrific trainer and good in the sack. But he's what my therapist would term emotionally unavailable. Lee always wanted more than that. She wanted a partner. What a crock of happy horseshit."

Mary Louise had developed a salty tongue

and a pragmatic attitude about life. She also had some insight into Lee that I didn't. "If Bud is emotionally unavailable, what would your therapist term Kemper?"

"Earl." She smiled, but it was sad. "See, we all knew Kemper was knocking her around, but Lee wouldn't let anyone help her. She wouldn't talk. She'd just show up in the barn with another black eye, another cast. Hell, if I said anything she got all pissy. Even Bud gave up trying to talk to her."

"It's hard for me to picture Lee taking that kind of abuse."

Mary Louise rolled her eyes. "The worst was that poor kid. She was caught between it. If she didn't win a class, Kemper took it out on Lee or one of the horses. I'll tell you, that bastard Kemper should have been strung up. Getting stomped to a pulp was too easy for him. And the fact that it was Avenger sure is sweet revenge. He hated that horse. Kemper knew Avenger's value, so he couldn't really hurt him, but he didn't spare the riding crop. Not on the horse or on Lee."

"A jury is going to want to know why she didn't simply divorce him."

Mary Louise belted back her drink. "You've never been married, Sarah Booth. Once you say those magic words of bondage, you open the door to suffering. If it's not physical abuse, it's emotional. Derk never hit me. That would have been too clean and simple. No, he liked to tell me how inept I was . . . in bed, in the kitchen, at parties, in business, in providing for his many needs. Lucky for me he found an eighteen-year-old who could take the pressure off me."

That was a whole minefield of emotion I knew I couldn't step into without setting off a dozen bombs. "Would you testify in Lee's behalf? About the beatings."

"Sure."

I had to make certain of one other thing. "What if your relationship with Bud comes up in court?" I kept going. "It occurred to me that perhaps Kemper was blackmailing you and the other women because of Bud. Was he?"

"Blackmailing *me*? No. Like I said, Bud is one in a long line. It won't hurt my feelings to have it pointed out in a court of law that I'm an idiot with piss-poor taste in men. As for Susannah and Lizzie, I don't think they'll testify. They're still pretending that they have a marriage." The ice tinkled in her empty glass.

"Is it possible Kemper was blackmailing them?"

She shook her head. "They would have told me if he tried."

"What about Carol Beth?"

She laughed out loud, and this time with a bit of humor. "Now, I'd pay a lot of money to hear what Carol Beth would have to say about her relationship with Bud. I hear she signed a prenup with Benny. Adultery is grounds for walking off without a dime." She mimed concern. "Carol Beth can't afford to admit to bedding down with Bud. She'd quicker own up to murder."

"Thanks, Mary Louise. I'll be in touch."

I mentally scratched Mary Louise off my list of suspects. She was many things, but she wasn't a candidate for blackmail, so she no longer had a motive to kill Kemper. More shocking was the fact that she'd voluntarily left the tribe of Daddy's Girls. Somewhere along the road of life, she'd grown up and turned into a woman I would probably like to know a lot better.

She went back inside the bar, and I stood outside in the parking lot, glad to have some fresh air and reassured that my ears might eventually readjust to normal.

I was almost ready to go back in when the door opened and a tall man whose walk I recognized came out into the starry night. He came straight toward me.

"Good evening, Coleman," I said, glad to

see him. Leavening the gladness was an image of him sitting on the floor in front of a fire with Lee.

"Sarah Booth, it's a relief to be out here."

"Have you found anything new about Kemper's murder?"

"I've been meaning to talk to you," he said, leaning against the side of a car. "I talked with the prosecutor. *I* know Lee's protecting someone, and *you* know she's protecting someone. Lincoln Bangs thinks she's protecting her accomplice."

"What?"

Coleman shrugged. "She's been in jail for nearly a week, Sarah Booth. She's sticking by that damn confession, even when she knows I know she's lying."

I stood up straight. "Does Linc know who she's protecting?"

"He thinks it's Bud Lynch."

I tried not to show my relief. "Does Bud know he's the latest suspect? He seemed pretty carefree all evening."

"Not yet, and don't tell him. Lee has raw emotion behind her. You saw the crowd tonight, all of that 'Earl had to die' stuff. Linc's decided to go for the other end of that emotion—greed. If he can portray Lee as a greedy woman, then he can counteract the victim emotion."

Coleman had it figured out pretty well.

"What can I do?"

He sighed. "Keep working for her. Keep talking to her. She's afraid, and too proud to show it." He swallowed. "She won't even talk to me now."

I wanted to point out to him that it wasn't so surprising that she wasn't in a humor to confide in him; he'd locked her up for murder. I kept my mouth shut. There was no point rubbing salt in a wound.

"How are you, Coleman?"

"Me?" He sounded surprised. "Tired of all of it." He put a warm hand on my shoulder and gave it a squeeze. "I know Lee is innocent, and I may end up being a big liability to her."

He was referring to his relationship with Lee. He was right; it could be trouble for both of them.

"I'll keep an ear to the ground," I told him.

His hand moved around my shoulders and pulled me to him for a gentle hug. I smelled whiskey on his breath as he leaned down and whispered, "Thanks, Sarah Booth." He straightened up. "Let's go back inside and dance. I have a proposal for you."

A dance and a proposal. Coleman was definitely up to something. He spoke to the bouncer at the door as he pulled it open for me. Once inside, a path parted for us to enter the dance floor.

"I haven't danced with anyone but Connie for ten years," he said as he tentatively put a hand on my back. "Hang on."

And I did, surprised to discover that Coleman was better than fair on the dance floor. The fact that we'd both been drinking helped ease us past the initial awkwardness of body touching body. In a few steps we were moving easily together. I closed my eyes and let Coleman waltz me around to the old Hank Williams number the house band was playing.

"Sarah Booth, will you be my date to the Chesterfield Hunt Ball?"

The question came out of left field. "What about Connie?" The question was out of my mouth before I could stop myself.

"She's not in the mood for a date. She's filing for divorce. Besides, this is work-related. For both of us."

Strange how flat that made me feel. "Sounds like a plan," I said breezily, though my blood pressure had skyrocketed. "I accept."

His hand tightened on the small of my back, bringing me into slightly closer contact. "I like your style," he said, and to my surprise he kissed my temple, a soft, gentle kiss.

After Coleman's strange behavior, the rest of the night was anticlimactic. I made it home by three, danced out and fueled up by the attention of my close personal friend, Jack Daniel's. Krystal had done another set, equally as good as the first. She was a bona fide Nashville singer and had all the makings of a star. I had no doubt she'd one day be at the Grammys with a trophy in each hand. My advice would be for her to dump her husband first. He was nothing but deadweight.

I checked on Kip, took a shower, swallowed three aspirin and two glasses of water, and slipped beneath the cool cotton sheets. Although my body demanded sleep, my mind was whirling. I'd pretty much written both Krystal and Mary Louise off my list of possible Kemper-killers. They both might have wanted him dead on general principle, but I couldn't see them doing the job.

Bud was still a strong suspect, for me as well as others. Linc was contemplating the horse trainer's involvement as part of a capital murder charge. Bud did have a past history of being at the bloody scene at the wrong time, but it was possible that Linc had dug up something more. I hoped to find out the details from Coleman at the ball.

That left Susannah, Elizabeth, and Carol Beth from the horsey set. The gamblers. And Kip.

My stomach growled, and I realized I was hungry. In a few short hours it would be morning. Maybe I would bake muffins. Then I'd eat two, swimming in butter.

Sleep was playing hard to get, so I picked up my Kinky book. I snuggled deeper into the bed. At last my eyelids grew heavy, and I put down the book and snapped off the light. I had my own case to solve, and I knew I needed all the rest I could get.

The smell of muffins teased me awake, and even as I felt myself get out of the bed, I knew I was dreaming. In that strange mode of dream travel, I was suddenly in my kitchen. The muffins were on the counter, already buttered, waiting for me with my favorite white coffee cup beside them. Steam rose from the coffee.

Sunlight filtered through the kitchen curtains and struck the table in a hazy yellow shaft. I had started toward the muffins when I realized someone was sitting at the table.

Two someones.

"It's 'bout time you got down here to see to your company," Jitty said. She nodded at the black-hatted cowboy. Kinky Friedman was once again in residence at my kitchen table.

"I was about to find my guitar and play you a song," Kinky said. "Jitty tells me you're partial to a good serenade." He and Jitty exchanged a good laugh.

Jitty had obviously felt compelled to share all of my latest traumas with him. I did not like this new coalition. My head was throbbing, an excess of Jitty, Jack, and Kinky. "Why are you here?" I asked him.

"Checking on your case. Any new developments?"

I flopped into a chair. "None that are good."

Two cups of coffee steamed on the table in front of us. Jitty didn't ever lift a hand, so I knew it was dream coffee. I took a sip anyway.

Kinky sampled his and made a face. "Where's the real coffee? This is flavored water."

"I don't have an espresso machine." His predilections were clearly listed in all of his books. As a big fan, I knew them by heart.

"She don't have nothin' that chugs, bubbles, or foams," Jitty threw in.

I glared at her, noticing that while I was in

my rumpled nightgown, she was dressed in a snappy little capri outfit. Damn her.

"I'm going back to bed," I said. "I've suffered enough abuse for one dream."

"Hold your horses," Kinky said. "In fact, why not pin it on the horse? Last I heard, they couldn't strap Trigger in the electric chair. The straps aren't big enough. Pin the murder on the horse and get your friend out of the hoosegow."

"I've already thought of that," I said irritably. If Kinky was going to disturb my sleep, at least he could arrive with fresh bad ideas. "Lee won't go for it. If she says the horse killed him, then it ruins Avenger as a stallion. Not to mention it contradicts her confession."

Out of the corner of my eye, I saw Jitty glare at me. She wasn't fond of surliness, except when she was the one who surled.

"What if it was an accident?" Kinky pressed. "It's a simple thing for her to change her story. People do it all the time. It's pretty much a job requirement for politicians."

His idea was growing on me. So was he. I found it comforting to have someone to discuss my case with.

"She could just say she was protecting the horse, but wants to tell the truth now. Kemper attacked her, she hit him in the head, he fell in the stall, she tried to drag him out but he was too heavy, she went to get help, when she got back he was dead, the victim of a tap-dancing horse."

"Doc Sawyer only says it was a blow to the head that killed Kemper, not necessarily a hoof to the head," I reminded him.

Kinky waved a hand as he flipped open the front flap of the hunting vest he wore. Instead of bullets inside, it was loaded with cigars. He selected a stubby one. "Details. Simple details. Forensic evidence is always fascinating, but there is always room for a good lawyer to introduce reasonable doubt. Think about it, Sarah Booth. You saw the photos of Kemper. Can even a man of science really deter-mine that *one* specific blow killed Kemper Fuquar?" His grin was wide as he leaned for-ward and motioned me closer. "Would that same man of science, Doc Sawyer, *want* to prove that?"

He let me digest it all.

"Everyone agrees Kemper needed to die. No one really wants Lee to go to jail. Reason-able doubt. That's all you have to have."

"Thanks, Kinky." His idea had merit.

"Professional courtesy," he said, flicking his Bic and lighting the stogy. "Call on me any-time."

He was gone in a puff of cigar smoke.

I found myself sitting straight up in bed. Sunlight streamed into the room, and Sweetie Pie, snoring loudly by the side of my bed, rolled over and began to wag her tail. The bedside clock said nine. I inhaled deeply and caught the scent of blueberry muffins.

Not bothering with a robe or slippers, I ran down the stairs with Sweetie Pie hot on my heels. The dream had been so intensely real that I felt compelled to make sure the Kinkster was not actually in my kitchen.

Pushing through the swinging door, I stopped in my tracks. It was almost as if I'd walked into the dream again. Hazy sunlight struck the kitchen table. On the counter across the room, two muffins on a saucer swam in butter, and beside them a white cup of coffee steamed.

"Boll weevil!" The phrase slipped out.

"What's wrong?" Kip stood up. She'd been wiping something off the floor. "The muffins aren't poisoned. I thought I'd make you some breakfast."

I picked up a muffin. Blueberry, my favorite. I eyed it suspiciously.

"Are you okay?" Kip asked.

"Just a dream," I said, sighing. "I thought Kinky Friedman had paid me a visit."

"Kinky Friedman?" Her expression said it all.

"He's a mystery author."

She backed up a step and looked harder at me. "Maybe you shouldn't party so hearty, Sarah Booth."

17

Although quelled, my appetite wasn't completely killed by the dream of a nocturnal liaison between Jitty and Kinky. I ate the muffins while my bathwater ran, then washed up, jumped into a pair of jeans, and got ready to go.

Kinky's suggestion—to blame Avenger for Kemper's *accidental* death—was roiling around in my mind. If Lee recanted her confession, saying she'd offered it to protect Avenger and save Swift Level, then there was a possibility a jury could be convinced that Kemper's death had been an accident, of a sort. Doc Sawyer wouldn't lie, but he wouldn't split hairs, either.

I tapped on Kip's door. "I'm going to Swift Level. Want to come?"

Her feet hit the floor with a loud thud and in two strides she had the door open. "I'm ready!" Her boots were in her hand and her face was flushed with happiness.

"Why didn't you ask to go home before now?" I asked. "I would have taken you at any time. You said you wanted the horses to burn—"

She shook her head. "It was never the horses. It was . . . everything else." For the first time since she'd moved into my house she voluntarily touched my arm. "Will we have to sell Swift Level?" There was worry in her voice. "There are so many debts. That man, Mr. La-Coco, says we owe him a lot of money. I don't think he's going to wait much longer. There were men in the barn a lot just before . . . Kemper was killed." She spoke so softly I had to lean toward her to hear. "There were phone calls, and I could hear him talking. He was angry and scared. I think they were threatening him."

I noticed her use of Kemper's name. She was distancing herself from him, and it was a sad thing to witness. "Did you hear any of those conversations?" I wasn't certain Lee would go along with Avenger accidentally killing Kemper, so a Mafia hit was also still an option. It wasn't lost on me that I had completely shifted from finding the truth to finding the best story that would free Lee.

Kip shook her head. "I could have. I could have walked right up to the door and listened, but I didn't. I ran away instead. I'd go ride Mrs. Peel or Avenger so I didn't have to hear." She caught her top lip with her teeth and pressed until I could see the skin turn white.

"No one can blame you for not eavesdropping on your father's conversations, Kip." I was careful not to show my disappointment. It was clear to me that Kip had often been made to feel that she'd disappointed a lot of people. "If you'd known what was going to happen, you might have tape-recorded the calls," I said, trying to inject a light note.

Her green gaze was so sad and so filled with hurt. "But I did know. I knew exactly what would happen. He would hang up the phone and go up to the house. Then he'd start yelling at Mother. Then he'd start saying which horses would be sold to pay his debts, or else he'd sell the property. Then he'd start hitting Mother. That's what always happened when he got angry and scared. He hurt Mother or one of the horses." She swallowed. "I didn't listen because when I heard it start, I knew what would happen and I wanted to kill him."

Kip was on the edge. She had crept as close to a confession as she could get. She only needed a little nudge. I thought suddenly of Coleman, and wondered how he could stand this part of his job. The truth would only bring more pain and hurt to people who had suffered far too much, yet I had to ask.

"Kip, what really happened the night Kemper was killed?"

"Can you save Mother and Swift Level?"

"I won't promise you anything, except that I'll try."

Kip assessed me with eyes far older than her fourteen years. "Mother has some good friends. You and Mrs. Richmond. And that newspaperwoman. Miss Millie at the café. You've all tried to help Mom."

"I don't believe Lee killed Kemper. But even if I did, I'd still try to help her. Lee's idea of a defense, that she's just going to prove Kemper deserved killing, makes a great song, but I'm scared for her."

"She didn't kill him," Kip said without dropping her gaze.

"Who did?" The question was effortless, without planning. Kip and I had finally reached a level of honesty that I trusted implicitly.

"You know he sold Mrs. Peel to Carol Beth?" she asked.

I nodded.

"I was sick. I was so angry that I thought my head would explode. But there was nothing I could do. Nothing. Except not give him what he wanted. I refused to ride in a big show. Avenger has to be shown and campaigned right now. It's vital to keep him out there as a performance horse, if we're going to be able to ask the high stud fees."

I nodded again that I understood all of this. "Lillian and Bud have explained a lot of this to me."

"I refused to ride. I told him I would never ride any of the horses again because of what he'd done with Mrs. Peel." She blinked back tears. "She was my horse. Mine. Mother gave her to me when she was born, and I trained her all by myself. Every day. She wasn't as strong as Avenger, but she was as good." She wiped a single tear from her cheek. "She loved me. She would do anything I asked of her, and no one else had ever been on her back."

Kemper Fuquar did deserve to die. By any measure of fairness or justice, his death would not be another reason for this child to suffer. There were no adequate words, so I said nothing, waiting for her to take a deep breath and regain control.

"He came up to my bedroom, angrier than I'd ever seen him." At last she dropped her gaze, staring at the toe of her sock. "He said he'd beat me if I didn't ride. He said he'd make me regret the day I was born, because he regretted it." She wiped at her cheeks. "He hated me."

"Kip, I'm—"

She shook her head and when she looked up at me, the old tough exterior was back in place. "I always knew it. This didn't come as any big shock. He said a lot of other hateful things. Mean things that he thought would upset me. Then he said if beating *me* didn't work, he'd beat Mother. He said I was going to ride and I was going to win, or he would make me sorrier than I'd ever been. That's when Mother came home. She ran into the room and told him that if he ever threatened me again, she'd kill him. She had a knife from the kitchen, and he knew she'd do it. He stormed out of the house and went down to the office in the barn."

"Where had Lee been?" I'd heard none of this. Lee had fabricated a story, and told only what she wanted us to hear.

"She'd been out in the pasture with one of the mares. There was difficulty with a foal, and she and Dr. Matthews had delivered the filly."

"Did she hear Kemper threaten you?" I asked. I made a mental note to talk to the vet. He might have written down the time he left.

"I don't know. She only came home at the last. She heard some of the mean things he said to me. She was more upset than I was."

"After Kemper went to the barn, what happened?"

Kip clamped down on her top lip again until I thought she was going to bite through the skin. "Mother told me not to tell this part."

"Your mother could go to prison for life, Kip."

"She knows that. If I tell the truth, can we save Swift Level?"

"If Lee is found innocent, the insurance company will have to pay off. There'll be money to pay Kemper's debts. Lee inherits Swift Level, from what I understand." I turned up both palms. "I can't make any promises. I won't lie to you."

She tucked her chin once, then stared me in the eye. "I went down to the barn. I'm not really certain what I intended to do. I wanted to talk to Bud, and I wanted to kill Kemper . . . my *father*. I heard him talking on the phone. I peeped in the office door and saw him, his legs up on the desk, leaning back in the chair, and talking. He had some papers in his lap, and he was talking about the payoff. He said he knew what he was doing and he'd have money in two weeks at the latest. He was drinking and laughing loud. He did that all the time, showing off. I just stood there and thought how much better everything would be if he were dead. I could get one of the sur-gical knives that we kept for emergencies and just slip up behind him and—" She made a slashing motion across her throat.

"But you didn't do that?"

"No, I heard something behind me." Her mouth hardened. "It was that bitch Carol Beth. Her and Bud."

Bud, at last, had a witness to corroborate his alibi. "What were Bud and Carol Beth doing?" I prompted.

"She was all over him, just crawling on him. She'd been after him for weeks. She was telling him how she had the signed bill of sale for Avenger, and how she was going to have the best breeding program of performance horses in the nation, and that it would be all hers, and how she needed him to help her. They would be partners, she said. He wouldn't be just a hired hand." She spoke the words as if they were dusted in bitterness.

"What did Bud say?"

Kip's hands clenched around the tops of her boots so tight her knuckles burned white. "He was telling her she was smart, that she'd finally gotten what she wanted. He said that she'd outsmarted everyone else and that he wanted to see the bill of sale."

"Did she show him?"

"Oh, yes. They went back to the truck and she opened the door and showed him. She'd finally gotten everything she wanted. Bud, the horses. All of it." She fell silent. "Then they went up to Bud's apartment."

"And Kemper?"

"He was still on the phone."

"And what did you do, Kip?"

"I decided to kill him." The words were spoken without emotion. "I decided it would be better to sneak up behind him and stab him with a shot of Rompum. I knew if I could push the whole syringe of Rompum into him, it would kill him. So I got the syringe, and I got the medicine out of the cabinet, and I went in Mrs. Peel's stall and waited for everyone else to go to sleep."

"Rompum?"

"It's a sedative. Enough of it would stop his heart."

Surely Doc would have found a huge dose of sedative in the autopsy. I wasn't any kind of forensic expert, but something like that would have been obvious. "Did you inject Kemper?"

"I don't know what I did," she said. "I fell asleep. When I woke up, the medicine was gone. I still had the syringe in my hand, but the bottle of medicine was completely gone." She looked up at me with bleak eyes. "I don't know what happened."

"What do you remember next?" I was as

gentle as I knew how to be. Kip was scared. I believed she had no recollection of events. Her eyes were haunted by the possibility of what she might have done.

"The next thing I remembered was Mother calling for me. It was just dawn, and I was asleep in the stall. Mother was frantic. I didn't know where I was, and I didn't know what had happened. When Mother found me, she told me that he was dead and that she'd taken care of everything."

"What had she taken care of?" I asked.

"I don't know," Kip repeated. "When I have one of the blackouts, I don't remember anything."

"You've had these blackouts before?" I remembered the medicine Dr. Vance had prescribed. Prozac and Paxil. Heavy-duty stuff.

"Only a few times. Only lately. It's from the stress and anxiety, the doctor said. When I can't handle it anymore, it's like my brain just takes a vacation."

That was as simple an explanation as I'd ever heard for a psychotic break. But what had Kip done while she'd blacked out? "What's the next thing you remember?"

Kip smiled. "My blue robe. It's falling apart, and Mother bought me a new one, but I like the blue one. Mother took me up to my room

and ran a hot bath. She put the blue robe on
me and put me in bed and told me to stay in
my room and not to talk to anyone. She said
that everything would be fine now. That he
was dead and everything would be just fine."
Kip stared at me. "She lied, didn't she? It isn't
going to be fine."

Kip was silent on the ride out. When we
turned on County Road 11 and approached,
she pressed closer to the window.

Sunlight stretched golden across the mead-
ows of Swift Level. The green grass rippled as if
gilded by the hand of Midas. In a far pasture, a
herd of fifteen horses raced and cavorted.

When she smiled, she was a normal-looking
child of fourteen, not a potential murderer suffering from blackouts and dark desires. She
pointed at the horses, and I stopped the car for
a moment so we could both watch the herd.

"That's Grange and his herd of mares," Kip
said. "He's a Connemara. Many of the mares
we're breeding to Avenger have his blood in
them. A Thoroughbred/Connemara cross."

"They're beautiful," I said. "You know, I always wanted a horse."

"You did?" Kip studied me. "You're pretty
weird, Sarah Booth. You talk to yourself and

dream about fictional characters who come to visit you."

I put the car in motion. As the beautiful old antebellum home came into view, I saw the cars in the drive. So did Kip.

"You'd think that with Mother in jail, they'd cancel this stupid ball. I hate those people. They all pretend to be so refined. They're just trash."

It was a pretty accurate summation of some of the folks who belonged to the Chesterfield Hunt, but not all of them.

"Your mother gave permission for the ball to be held here."

"I know. I don't want to go to the house. Please take me to the barn."

I was relieved at her choice. I wasn't in the mood for Martha Stewart chitchat from the women preparing for the ball. I got enough decorating grief from Jitty.

We pulled in beside the smaller white barn where Avenger resided, and beside Coleman's brown patrol car. I hadn't expected to see him here. I glanced at Kip to see how she would react. Their last meeting had been rather emotional.

"I want to ride Avenger," she said, opening the car door. She dashed into the small barn.

Coleman walked out of the shadows of the show barn and came up to me as I got out. "Morning, Sarah Booth."

"Hi, Coleman. What's going on?"

He leaned back against the car, turning his face up to the warming sun. "I'm looking forward to tonight. I'll pick you up at eight."

His statement caught me enough by surprise that I answered before I had censored my own feelings of excitement. "Me, too." My personal anticipation cooled, though, as I remembered why Coleman was probably at Swift Level. "Are you here to see Bud?"

"To question him." He looked past me, toward the barn. "Let's go for a walk."

I fell into step beside him as we walked along one of the gravel paths. We passed the barn where the office was, moved on past the stud barn where Kip was saddling Avenger, and continued toward a white fence where we could watch a dozen young foals playing in the sunshine while the mares grazed. We stood for a while without talking.

"Bud has an alibi," I reminded Coleman.

"Sarah Booth, you're too old to be so naïve."

My retort was diverted by the sound of a shrill scream. I wasn't certain where the sound came from, but Coleman started toward the show barn, which contained an indoor riding arena.

"Avenger!" Kip's voice held authority. "Stop it!"

The horse's scream of rage came again. Every story I'd heard about Avenger came back to me. He was a dangerous animal, and Kip was in trouble. Coleman and I ran toward the indoor arena at a dead run.

Coleman got there first. He ducked under the white rail and rushed into the center of the ring. I stopped at the rail in horror. Bud was standing by a red-and-white jump, and not ten feet away, Avenger danced on his hind legs. Kip clung to his back, her face grim and determined as she leaned forward on his neck, arms extended, putting all of her weight on the reins in an effort to push the horse back down to the ground.

"Avenger!" she cried. The horse dropped to the ground and shook his head, almost flinging Kip off. Then he reared again, and this time I saw what he was after.

Roscoe lay on the ground in front of the jump. He was on one elbow, while he held up his other arm in an effort to ward off Avenger's front hooves as the stallion pawed the air and struck at him.

"Right rein, Kip. Pull the right rein." Bud was tensed for action, but there was nothing he could do.

Kip twisted one hand in the horse's mane and grabbed the right rein with the other. Avenger's hooves windmilled.

"Avenger!" Kip's face showed nothing but determination. She gave the rein a mighty tug. It was enough to unbalance Avenger, and he dropped his front feet to the ground not ten inches from Roscoe's prone body.

"Push him forward!" Bud's voice carried, strong and assured. "Push, Kip. Push!"

The big gray horse danced dangerously as an enraged scream tore from his throat.

"Avenger!" She pulled hard on the right rein, physically turning the horse's head and neck. With great skill, she clapped her heels into the horse's sides and sent him forward, away from Roscoe's prone body. The old man fell back on the ground, and I couldn't tell if he'd been struck or not.

Coleman rushed to Roscoe as Bud caught up with Kip and Avenger. The trainer caught the stallion's reins and put a soothing hand on his neck, but his attention was on Kip.

"Are you okay?"

She nodded. "Is Roscoe hurt?" She was fighting back tears. "I don't know what happened. He was working fine. I didn't know Roscoe was in here painting the jumps, and when he stood up, Avenger went up to him for just a moment, like he wanted to be petted, and then he went nuts."

"It's okay," Bud said, patting her leg. "It wasn't your fault, Kip. You rode him like the champion you are. You saved Roscoe's life. If he'd come down on top of him . . ." He didn't finish. He didn't have to.

Coleman was helping Roscoe to his feet. The old man was shaky, but seemed uninjured.

Roscoe ducked under the rail and then stopped to catch his breath. He was panting as he pulled a bandana from his pocket and wiped his glistening forehead. "Thanks, Sheriff." He turned to look at Kip in the arena. She had Avenger back on the rail, and under Bud's guidance was circling to put him at a jump. I watched in awe and some trepidation as the big gray seemed to fly over the jump, which was at least five feet high. He made it look effortless, and Kip looked like she'd been born to do nothing but sit on his back. They were truly a magnificent team.

With Kip easily taking the series of jumps, Bud came over to the rail where Coleman, Roscoe, and I stood.

"I'm sorry, Roscoe," Bud said. "I didn't know you were in here or I wouldn't have brought Kip in."

"I was painting the jumps, like Miss Lee told me."

I saw the paint can, then. The bloodred paint had been kicked over and was soaking into the dirt.

"Nobody was hurt, and that's the important part," Roscoe said. He started to brush off his jacket, pausing a moment as he examined the worn fabric. It had once been a very expensive coat. His gaze traveled back to the horse, but he didn't say anything.

"Is Kip safe?" I asked Bud; I could see that Coleman was wondering the same thing.

"Avenger would never hurt Kip," Bud said. He went to the center of the ring and motioned for Kip to bring the horse to him. She rode up, executed a perfect halt, tossed the reins to Bud, and then vaulted to the ground. Avenger lowered his head and nuzzled Bud's chest.

"No wonder Carol Beth's determined to have that horse," I said to Coleman.

"He is something." Coleman turned his attention back to the ring, but I could see he wasn't watching Avenger. He was watching the interaction between Kip and Bud. "Maybe you could take Kip for a walk," Coleman suggested as he slipped under the rail.

"Kip," I called. "I need to talk to you."

She saw the sheriff and must have known what was coming. She looked at Bud, turned, and ran off in the opposite direction.

"Damn," I said under my breath. "Damn it all to hell."

Doc Sawyer was in his office, and he gave me a tired smile when I tapped on his door and entered. I'd dropped Kip off at home. I didn't want her with me to hear this conversation.

"I've been trying to call you," Doc said.

"What's going on?" The same pot of coffee seemed to be sitting in the stained coffeemaker. I eyed it carefully to see if it had come to life yet.

He came around the desk and put his arm around my shoulders. "I got Kemper's blood work back. There's something strange there."

"What?" My heartbeat surged, but I forced my body to remain relaxed.

"There was insulin in Kemper's body."

"Insulin? Was he diabetic?"

Doc slowly shook his head. "No, he wasn't.

Sarah Booth, I haven't told Coleman yet, but I'm going to have to."

"So there was insulin. What exactly does that mean?"

He gave my shoulders a squeeze before he walked back behind his desk and picked up some papers. He was looking down when he spoke again. "I'm not a detective, I'm just an old country doctor, but I'd say someone injected Kemper with the intent to kill him."

"What about the blow to the head?"

"That's what killed him," he said slowly. "I'm still not certain what kind of instrument. Nippers, a hammer. Coleman never found the weapon."

"Was insulin the only thing you found in his blood?"

He paused. "Should I have found something else?"

My gaze fell to my lap. "How should I know?"

He cleared his throat. "I would have to say that Kemper was unconscious from the insulin when he was struck a fatal blow in the head. That's what I'll have to testify to."

The scenario Doc described was one of premeditated murder—and one that couldn't be blamed on a horse.

18

Thunderclouds were massing outside the driver's window as I drove home. On either side of the car, cotton fields, sprouting with the tender new growth of spring, stretched to the horizon. Only to the west, where the clouds marshaled, did there seem a finite end to the fields. Slowing the car, I watched the clouds. They took on the shape of a cavalry charge, and in the distant rumble of thunder I could hear the horses' hooves racing toward me. It was a fantasy of childhood, and one I always associated with Lee.

The storm perfectly matched my mood. I'd thought carefully about my role in this case. I was going to have to go to Coleman with what I knew. Counting the seconds between the thunder and the forks of lightning that followed, I calculated the distance of the approaching storm. It would be nice to be at Dahlia House for a turbulent spring storm. I'd never felt less than safe within the walls of my home, and I loved to watch the wind twist the sycamore trees into a dance of strength and beauty. I notched the speed up to eighty-five, relishing the handling of the car, and raced the storm home.

The first strong winds were whipping the tender leaves of the sycamores when I turned down the drive. Dahlia House, in need of paint and other cosmetics, stood like a grand lady at the end of an aisle. The sense of coming home was one of the best emotions I'd ever felt. I could only pity those people who'd never loved a place, had never felt the satisfaction of roots holding firm in land that nurtures both the past and the future. I was home.

I made sure the convertible top was latched down and the windows rolled up before running up the steps just as the first big drops of rain began to fall. I almost tripped over the large package that was tilted against the doorway, the overnight delivery box a bright orange and purple.

My dress! In the emotional turmoil of the day, I'd forgotten that Neiman Marcus was going to FedEx my Cinderella outfit for the ball. I snatched it up, ran inside, and headed straight for the kitchen and some coffee. I forced myself to wait until the coffee was brewing before I opened the package.

The red dress, featherlight and so delicate that the tiniest movement sent the material rippling, was beautiful.

"Good thing you're goin' to this ball with the law, otherwise the vice squad would be on your ass like a duck on a June bug."

Jitty was leaning against the wall, a smile of satisfaction on her face.

"Isn't it beautiful?" Looking at the dress, I could even forgive her for ganging up against me with Kinky in my dreams.

"Put it on," she suggested.

I didn't need a second invitation. I stripped out of my clothes and let the dress whisper down my body. The sheer sensuality of the material sliding over my skin made me shiver. It was one helluva dress. Jitty confirmed it with a whistle.

"You 'bout over the hill, Sarah Booth, but that dress makes you look like you got a few good years left."

"Thanks," I said, unable to feel anything except delight, even if Jitty was being a troll. "I'm going to have to rush out and get some new underwear," I said. Any excuse for new underwear was a good one, but this dress was the best.

"Yes, ma'am, panty lines would sure ruin the

effect." Jitty sniffed. "Maybe you could just go without."

There was a hint of devilment in her eyes. "Maybe," I agreed, my own imp of mischief ready to play. I stepped out of the panties I was wearing and felt the delicious slide of the dress against my body. "I need my red high heels." They'd been an extravagance when I bought them in New York, but now they were going to pay dividends.

"Yes, indeed. Better find your red garter belt and some of those shimmery stockings." Jitty sighed. "Harold is going to regret asking Carol Beth instead of you."

"I certainly hope so." I huffed. "You'd think after Brianna he'd have learned his lesson about cavorting with man-eaters."

Jitty's chuckle was warm. "You sound a little jealous."

"I just hate to see Harold roasted on a spit." If Jitty were still in her fifties mode, she'd be harping on family values and the immorality of married folks going out with single folks. Unfortunately, it wasn't a road I could travel for long, seeing as how Coleman was also married. Of course, going to this ball was just part of the job. For both of us, I reminded myself.

"I'll expect a full report." Jitty began to fade.

"Hey, don't go." I needed some guidance, and Jitty had been around for a hundred and fifty years. She'd worked elbow to elbow with my great-great-grandma Alice and a host of other Delaney women, surviving war, famine, and Reconstruction. Surely she could come up with some ideas for this case. But it was too late; Jitty had vanished.

The knock on the back door almost made me jump out of the dress. I glanced out the window and met Harold's silvery gaze beneath the rim of an umbrella. Rain spattered and jumped off the stretched cloth.

"Let me in," he said. "Do you have company?"

It was almost as if I'd conjured him up with my conversation. There was nothing to do but kick my discarded clothes into a pile beneath the kitchen table and open the back door.

He walked in and scanned the room, stopping dead center on me. "Sarah Booth." His breath came out in a rush. "You look ravishing!"

Ah, Harold had a way of expressing himself. "Do you like it?" I did a spin that set the dress in motion.

"I think that dress could be classified as a lethal weapon."

I laughed with pleasure. There was nothing

like a well-paid compliment to make a woman happy. Money isn't even good coin in comparison. I could almost forgive him for asking Carol Beth to be his date. Almost.

"What brings you to Dahlia House?" I asked. I got two coffee cups and put them on the table.

"Kip. Where is she? I'd like to have a word with her." Harold's visit was serious, not social.

"I'll get her." I went upstairs, only to find her room empty. I checked around, stopping in my room. My computer was still on, and several of Kip's notebooks were beside it. A page was taped to the computer screen.

"Amy Winslow invited Sweetie and me to spend the night. I knew you were going to the ball, and I didn't want to be alone. Kip."

I took the note back downstairs and gave it to Harold. While he read, I watched his face. He was truly disturbed about something.

"What is it?" My initial pleasure at the thought that Kip had been considerate of my feelings in leaving the note began to fade.

"A check came through Lee's account. It had been forged with Lee's signature. I'm fairly certain Kip wrote it."

"What are you going to do?" I asked, suddenly weary.

"I took care of it, for now."

"Thank you, Harold. I think."

"It's not that simple." He looked up, and his silvery gaze was worried.

"Who was the check made out to?"

He walked to the kitchen window and looked out at the rain. "I *should* go to Coleman with this."

Who in the hell was Kip writing checks to? Harold wouldn't tell me. He had a rigid sense of ethics when it came to banking business, but he was doing his best to give me fair warning that Kip was in big trouble.

"I'll talk to Lee. And I'll talk to Kip. In fact, I'll go bring her home right this minute."

Harold shook his head. "Leave her at the Winslows'. She's better off there than alone here."

"I suppose." He had a point.

He stood up. "Talk to her in the morning, Sarah Booth. There wasn't money in the bank to cover the check she wrote. She has to understand the gravity of her actions."

"I'll take care of it. It would help if I knew—"

He leaned forward and brushed his lips

across my cheek. "I can't tell you. Save me a dance tonight."

With each passing hour, my anticipation for the ball increased. By seven-thirty, I was a red, shimmery frenzy of nerves. But I was ready. Jitty had given her seal of approval, and I decided to spin some discs in the parlor while sipping a little bourbon to calm my nerves.

Jack Daniel's and my mother's old Percy Sledge album were a fine combo. I'd mellowed enough to answer the door with a smile when Coleman knocked. My smile froze as I took in the figure he cut, his body taller and leaner in his tails. I stepped back and allowed myself a head-to-toe exam while he did the same.

"My, oh, my," I said.

"Sarah Booth, you look terrific."

We spoke simultaneously and ended up laughing. "I think we both need some dating practice," I said, ushering him inside. I poured him a drink and refreshed my own. I could tell by his demeanor that Doc Sawyer hadn't spoken to him about the insulin. I considered my options, and decided that tomorrow was soon enough to tell him what I'd learned.

Coleman finished his drink in three swallows.

He paced the parlor, nervous as a cat. "Are you ready?"

The minute I reached for my handbag-cum-briefcase, I knew I was destroying my dress.

"Make another drink. I'll just be a minute," I said, rushing up the stairs to find my sequined evening bag. I dumped the contents of my purse on the bed and was busy picking out lipstick, blusher, compact, brush, and—I froze. Half hidden beneath my wallet was a syringe. Very carefully, I examined the syringe and needle—identical to the one I'd seen in Kip's makeup bag, except this one contained nearly eight cc's of clear liquid.

"Sarah Booth?" Coleman called. "Is something wrong?"

"I'm coming." I looked at the syringe. I didn't have to wonder where it had come from. I knew. Swift Level. Someone had slipped into my car and put the syringe into my purse.

"Do you need some help?" Coleman called.

I heard his tread on the stairs and I pushed the syringe and contents of my purse under the pillow on the bed. Snatching up the sequined bag, I hurried across the room to meet him at the door.

"I had some trouble finding my purse," I said, holding it out as evidence.

He smiled. "Women. Even the smartest ones can act a fool over a handbag."

I was so upset I didn't even try to defend my gender. "I'm ready," I said, slipping past Coleman.

Who had put the syringe in my purse? Bud? Kip? Anyone on the property could have done it. Bud had said earlier that someone was snooping around.

The questions whirled in my brain until I felt dizzy. Coleman's hand at my elbow stead-ied me at the bottom of the stairs.

"Are you okay? You're acting strange," he said.

"Party nerves," I answered, trying hard to be calm.

He turned me to face him. "What's wrong?"

It was the moment of truth. By all rights, I should turn the syringe over to him. "I'm not certain what to do," I said in all honesty.

His hands slid down my arms to capture my hands. He held them lightly. "I only know that I've never been out with a lovelier woman."

I found a smile. "Thank you."

"Don't look so sad, Sarah Booth. We have time to finish our drinks before we go. I'll freshen yours up."

He went to the bar and poured a little bourbon over the ice. "Remember, we're working,"
he said as he handed me the glass.

"Are you ever off work?" If he would ever
go off duty, maybe I could confide in him. I
wanted to—needed to. But I couldn't risk the
outcome.

"You sound like Connie. It's hard to turn it
on and off, you know." He sipped the drink
and regained a friendlier tone. "Do you find it
that way?"

My cases had come back-to-back, with
hardly a moment for thinking in between, but
I could see where detecting could become a
lifelong habit—or vice, as the case may be. "So
far, yes."

"Once your trust in human nature is gone,
it's hard to find it again."

I spun the ice in my glass. "Is it the trust of
others or of ourselves that we lose?"

"That water's a little too deep for preparty
chitchat." Coleman put down his glass and offered his arm. "Are you ready? If you ask really
nice, I'll let you turn on the siren."

The night was magnificent. The rain had
cleared the atmosphere of everything except
the magic of the stars. A billion of them
winked anticipation as we drove the narrow
county road.

"I want you to keep an eye on Bud tonight," Coleman said.

"Bud? Why?" I asked.

Coleman pulled up in the circular driveway of Swift Level, restraining me with a gentle touch on my arm. "There's more to Bud than Lee lets on. You've got a good eye. See who he talks to, what he does."

The valet opened my door and helped me out. Coleman walked around the car and handed over the keys, with instructions to keep it close. With my hand on his arm, we walked into the ball.

Swift Level was elegant and gorgeous unadorned, but with the huge arrangements of lemony-smelling magnolia blossoms hanging from the ceilings and along the crown molding, and the blooming rose vines that climbed the walls, it took on the appearance of an enchanted garden.

An orchestra, hidden behind a screen of potted, blooming azaleas, played a seductive melody. The floor was crowded. Coleman was not as flashy as Bud in the dance category, but he was sure and steady and smooth. As we swirled around the floor, it took only a few seconds for me to realize he was scoping out the room. Coleman could dance and detect—a multitasking fool.

Amidst a gentle scattering of applause when the song ended, Coleman whispered that he was getting to work. He gave my hand a squeeze as he left me to my own detecting.

I felt daggers in my spine and turned to find Carol Beth glaring at me. I gave her the royal wave, a cool turn of the hand that we'd all practiced in seventh grade.

"Want me to kick her ass?" Bud asked, slipping up behind me.

"Really hard. In public." I turned to face him, and smiled at his concession to hunt club dress: black jeans with a razor-sharp crease and western tails, string tie, and black hat. He had managed both handsome and eccentric with great finesse.

He laughed, and I felt the tug of his charm. Unfortunately, charm had no place in the evening. "I need to talk to you," I said, steering him out to the patio where the light was still good but we had a bit of privacy. "Did you put something in my purse today?"

He lifted his eyebrows in surprise. "Like what? You already know my phone number."

"Don't play with me, Bud. This is serious."

"The answer is no."

I believed him.

He grinned. "I didn't leave you a present, but you're going to get one tonight. I called

Benny today. I invited him to the ball. He should be here by . . ." He checked his watch. "Ten. And he didn't sound like he was in a good humor."

"You didn't!" My gut reaction was glee. "I'd better warn Harold." I didn't want to see him caught in the cross fire.

Bud shook his head. "Don't bother. Your banker friend's no fool. He knows the score."

"What is that supposed to mean?"

"He isn't with Carol Beth for the pleasure of it. Watch him. He's taking care of business."

"I'll check it out," I promised, curious as to what Harold was actually up to.

The patio door opened, and Krystal Brook stepped out in a dark green sheath that hugged every inch. "I was wondering where you got off to, Bud." She came toward us. "Sarah Booth, have you seen Mike? He went to get me a drink an hour ago." She rolled her eyes. "I'm going to have to put a training collar on him."

She laughed and Bud smiled, but I could manage only a weak smile. Lillian Sparks stepped out on the patio, easing the silence that had suddenly developed. Lillian carried three drinks; she handed one to me and one to Bud.

"Krystal, I didn't know you were out here," Lillian said.

"No problem. I'm headed to the bar. My husband is probably behind it," Krystal said. "You owe me a dance, Bud. Just wait until we're sure Mike is too crocked to care."

"Lillian's my date," Bud said, putting his arm around the older woman. "Most sensible woman I've ever met."

Lillian was still laughing when Krystal left the patio, her hips undulating to the music as she wove through the dancers on her mission to the bar. Krystal still owed me a conversation, but now wasn't the time or place.

Lillian leaned against the patio wall beside me. "Bud asked me to tell you why Avenger can't be involved in a crime. In performance horses, temperament is half of everything. If Avenger were to be labeled a dangerous horse, a horse that injured humans, his value would drop radically. A horse that's dangerous, a rogue, is often destroyed."

"It doesn't matter, anyway," I said, thinking of the insulin.

Lillian turned to Bud. "Harold is signaling me for a dance. I doubt my ankles can take more than four or five measures. Do you mind?"

Bud kissed her cheek. "Show 'em what you've got, Lillian."

When she was gone, I picked up my conversation with Bud. "If you were a betting man, where would you lay your odds on who killed Kemper?"

He took my arm and led me to the stone wall, where Bud brushed off a place and we perched. "Eliminating me and Lee, I'd say that puts Carol Beth up to bat. To be honest, though, she doesn't really have a motive. She has a bill of sale. She didn't need to kill Kemper."

"And Kip? What about her?" I'd finally gotten to the real question. Kip had admitted that she was in the barn with intent.

Bud sipped his champagne. "If anyone had a *right* to kill Kemper, it was Kip. But she couldn't do it. She can't kill a roach."

I didn't believe it. "Does Lee keep a lot of drugs in the barn?"

He gave me a questioning look. "Just the typical drugs for emergencies. Rompum and Ace for tranquilizers. Banamine for colic. Why?"

"Is Carol Beth familiar enough with the barn to find the drugs?"

He frowned. "Anyone could. They aren't under lock and key. Most of them are in the little refrigerator in the office."

"Are any of the horses diabetic?"

"What are you getting at?" he asked.

I shook my head. "Better you don't know. Just answer the question."

"None of the horses are diabetic."

"Would it be possible to confuse Ace or Rompum with insulin?"

Bud stared at me, drawing his own conclusions. "I'm not that familiar with insulin. I'd assume they're all clear, injectable liquids. But we don't keep insulin around, so I couldn't say for certain."

"What did Carol Beth tell Coleman about your past?"

"Plenty. He had a lot of probing questions about Texas."

"And?"

"And I'm not worried. I was with Carol Beth, no matter what she says. She'll eventually tell the truth." He grinned. "Some mares take a little longer than others to bring under saddle."

I couldn't help but smile at his confidence. A confident man is truly irresistible.

"Now I've been on the hot seat long enough. No more questions unless you're going to explain the big interest in insulin," he said.

"I can't," I answered.

"Okay, then, a toast." He tipped his glass against mine. "To finding the truth, which shall set Lee free."

"One more question? This one is strictly personal." As Cece had pointed out, there wasn't a woman still breathing who wouldn't be attracted to Bud, but my question was more than nosiness.

"One more. That's the limit." He sipped his champagne.

"Have you ever been serious about a woman?"

"Once."

He answered without hesitation, and there seemed to be a hint of remorse in his tone. Bud Lynch had loved and lost. "What happened?"

"Hell, we were both too young. She said I wasn't capable of love. The ugly truth is that I got scared and ran."

I wondered if Bud was being honest or shooting me a line of bull that worked on all of his conquests.

"Was she right?"

He looked through the open doors of the patio into the ballroom, as if the answer might be found in the dancing couples or the floral arrangements. "That's the third question, but I'll answer it anyway. Yes. She was. And the real tragedy is that she won't believe I've changed."

There were a lot of things I started to ask, but something caught his eye. He abruptly stood up. "Excuse me, I need to have a word with someone."

I followed the direction of his gaze and saw Carol Beth with the other two women I sought—Susannah Adair and Elizabeth Cooper, the Daddy's Girls who were now members of Bud's mounted posse. Bud walked right past the women and disappeared among the throng of people. Tinkie, who looked ravishing in a coral Versace dress with three straps across the back, had Krystal in a corner. I'd catch up with Tinkie before the ball was over.

I needed to talk with Susannah and Elizabeth, though. "Hi," I said, rushing up with air kisses for them. I ignored Carol Beth, who was glaring at me.

"Sarah Booth." They both angled a skeptical look at me. "When did you take up hunting?"

"I'm a guest," I said. Age had used a tender hand to touch them. There were fine lines and a few sags, but all in all they hadn't changed since high school. Both had married Delta boys, though not from Sunflower County.

"This ball isn't the same without Lee," Susannah complained. "If she was going to croak Kemper, she should have done it with poison. Kemper loved that andouille sausage. Hell, you could add just about anything to that and no one would ever be able to tell."

"I think a good old-fashioned medical emergency would have been the way to go," Elizabeth countered. "What I don't understand is why Lee wasn't smarter. She knew how to kill him and get away with it. There's enough medicine in her barn to kill a small village. She could have made it look like a heart attack." She rolled her eyes. "It was just plain stupid to hit him in the head."

"Lee was never known for her brains." Carol Beth finally broke her silence.

"You're just jealous of her," Elizabeth said. "You always have been. She has everything you ever wanted."

"But not for long," Carol Beth said with a cold smile. "Not for long." She walked away and reattached herself to Harold.

I seized my opportunity. "Ladies, I need an answer. Was Kemper attempting to blackmail either of you about your relationship with Bud?" My question was direct and to the point. I watched them closely. Elizabeth cut her gaze at Susannah and a silent message was exchanged.

"No," they said in unison.

Elizabeth rolled her eyes. "You know, he would have if he'd thought about it. He just wasn't that smart."

"We can say he was, if it will help Lee," Susannah offered.

"Thanks," I said. "I'll get back with you on that."

Funny, everyone who knew Kemper was willing to lie to save Lee. I headed back into the thick of the party. My teeth gritted as I watched Carol Beth hang on Harold's arm. She was so busy flirting that she didn't see a short, plump man with a big scowl stalk up behind her. His balding head was red and his face a dark thundercloud. He grasped Carol Beth's arm, and when she turned, the look on her face was priceless.

"Benny, darling," she said. "I thought you were in Berlin."

"I gave you everything a woman could want," Benny said calmly, coldly. "You had credit cards, checking accounts, horses, lessons, barns, grooms, the finest farm in Virginia." He slipped a finger under the strap of her gown. "You have excellent taste, Carol Beth, and I indulged it. And what is my repayment?" He looked around the room, noting that everyone was staring at him. "You've made me a fool, a cuckold." He reached into his coat pocket and pulled out some papers. "My lawyer will be in touch."

Carol Beth grabbed at his coat. "Benny, give me a chance. Let me at least explain."

Benny turned away from her, then slowly turned back. "The worst part is that I truly care for you. Even knowing how greedy and manipulative you are, I still care."

"Benny, we can work this out," Carol Beth said. She glanced around her. The party had come to a halt, and everyone was staring. Even the band had quit playing. Blood rushed up Carol Beth's neck and into her cheeks. "I'm begging you, Benny. Just talk to me."

Benny turned away from her. For a short man, he was walking tall. He went straight out the front door.

"Benny," she called after him. She started to go, but Harold grasped her wrist. Putting an arm around her, he led her out onto the patio.

A soft murmur rippled through the guests, and I looked toward the door. Cece Dee Falcon was standing in the doorway in a black evening gown that was absolutely fabulous. Her escort was the short and dapper Nathaniel Walz.

"Hello, dahlings," Cece said in her low, throaty voice. "After all this work to make a grand entrance, Carol Beth has stolen my thunder with a bit of tacky adultery. Somebody hand me a drink."

Several waiters rushed to place a champagne

flute in Cece's waiting hand, but my attention was diverted back to Carol Beth. She had extricated herself from Harold, and she was moving across the room like a jungle cat. She went straight at Bud. Never saying a word, she slapped him as hard as she could, a crack that echoed in the big room.

"You low-down son of a bitch." She slapped him again on the other side of his face. "You bastard. I'll make you pay."

Bud stepped closer to her. "I told you not to screw with me, Carol Beth. You should have stuck with the truth."

"You want the truth!" She looked around the room at the faces all turned to her. "He loves Lee. He has forever. He came here because he loved her, and he killed Kemper because he was in the way."

"You're pathetic," Bud said, walking away.

Carol Beth grabbed a champagne flute from a passing waiter and threw it at Bud's back. The glass struck him between the shoulders, splashing champagne on several bystanders. Striking the floor, the glass shattered. Bud never turned around. He walked out the patio door and into the darkness.

Coleman's hand captured my shoulder. "We have to go," he said.

I looked around. The party was in full swing. "Why?"

He took my arm, a steady hand that I didn't fully appreciate until he spoke. "Mrs. Winslow called. Kip is missing. She took their car and disappeared."

19

The moon had risen, full and pale in the eastern sky. We drove toward it in silence. Coleman turned south toward Zinnia.

"Did Mrs. Winslow say anything else?" I asked Coleman, hoping for some word that would stop the painful thudding of my heart. Kip had more on her than any kid should face.

"Nothing useful. Kip talked with someone on the phone. Amy didn't know who it was. A little later, Kip said she was going to take Sweetie Pie for a walk. No one thought anything for at least an hour. Then when they started looking for her, she was gone, along with the car. Why would she run?" Coleman countered, and I was reminded that I hadn't been truthful with him.

I knew full well why she might run—bad checks and a blackout, just for starters. I was terrified for her. For what she might do and what she might have done. My decision not to be honest with Coleman was haunting me far worse than Jitty ever had.

Coleman reached across the bench seat of the patrol car and put a hand on my thigh. Through the thin material of my dress, I could feel the calluses at the base of each finger. "Maybe she's just out for a lark. You know how teenagers can be."

"Kip isn't a normal teenager. Her mother's charged with killing her father."

"Point taken," he said. Instead of driving to the courthouse, he headed out toward Dahlia House. "Maybe she left you a note or something," he said by way of explanation.

"Or maybe you think you're going to leave me behind," I said.

He took a long breath. "That might be for the best, Sarah Booth. Consider that."

"We'll check Dahlia House and then I'll decide."

We pulled to the front of my home and both rushed up the steps and inside. The foyer was empty of clues, and I asked Coleman to search Kip's room while I went to the kitchen. The thump, thump, thump of Sweetie's tail against the floor told me Kip had been there. She'd brought the dog home from the Winslows', which probably meant she wasn't planning on returning anytime soon.

"Sweetie," I said. Bending down to pet the hound, I saw the pale paper attached to the dog's collar. Snatching it off, I tore it open and unfolded the single sheet of lavender-scented stationery that so bespoke youth and innocence. I began to read with great trepidation.

"Sarah Booth, Mother didn't kill Kemper. I did it. She's been trying to take the blame for me, but she can't protect me any longer. I did what I had to do, and now I'm going to finish it. Kip."

The note fluttered out of my numb fingers and landed on the floor. Sweetie Pie nailed it with one paw, her tail working overtime. I picked it up and read it again.

Kip had confessed. There it was in black and lavender. No explanations, no reasons. No room for doubt. A confession as brutal as her mother's, but with less detail.

"No sign of her upstairs." Coleman stopped just inside the kitchen. His gaze took in the note in my hand. "Where is she?"

"She confessed to killing Kemper." I handed him the note, surprised that my hand wasn't shaking.

"Damn it all to hell," he said softly as he read. "Where would she go?"

I shook my head. "Lee might know."

There wasn't time for a change of clothes—or even to grab something. Coleman and I, with Sweetie hot on our heels, dashed back down the steps and into the patrol car. Coleman didn't object when I opened the back door for Sweetie to ride with us. If it came to it, Sweetie might be helpful in tracking Kip.

Coleman picked up the radio. Deputy Walters's voice crackled in answer from the courthouse.

"Kip Fuquar has run away," Coleman said. "She's in a 1998 Volvo sedan, blue, belonging to Mark Winslow. You've got the tag number. Put out an APB and alert the authorities in the surrounding counties."

Siren wailing, we flew across the black Delta night.

"Do you have any idea where she might have gone?" he asked.

Like it or not, I did. "The Holiday Breeze," I said. His reaction was exactly what I expected.

"Why would she go there?"

"Harold stopped by this afternoon to tell me that Kip had written a check on Lee's account. She forged her mother's signature, but the bank caught it. I suspect Kip may have been trying to pay Tony LaCoco the debt Kemper owed him. She was trying to save Swift Level."

Coleman didn't say a word or utter an accusation. His silence was worse than anything he might have said.

That compelled me to keep talking. "Harold wouldn't tell me who the check was written to. I'm just guessing about this. And don't blame Harold. He was going to talk to you about it."

"It might have been helpful if he'd told me sooner."

Coleman was angry, and I didn't blame him. There were other things I needed to tell him, too. "Coleman, I—"

"If she *is* with LaCoco, she could be in real danger," Coleman interrupted. "He's been hanging around town, waiting to see how Kemper's will would fall. The best thing about Lee remaining in jail is that there's been no pressure for disposition of Kemper's will. Now Kip may have walked into real trouble."

My chest ached with worry and dread. I'd lost all sense of time and place, and looked out at the vista of field and darkness. The road seemed to have stretched into an endless journey. "How much further?" I asked. Sweetie harmonized a low whine in the backseat.

"Not far. Hang on and keep your fingers crossed."

True to his word, Coleman pulled into the

Holiday Breeze in less than five minutes. The big black Town Car was still parked in front of room 10, but all the other vehicles were gone. There was no sign of a blue Volvo.

We got out of the car, and I let Sweetie out of the back. She rushed past us and went straight to the door of room 10. Barking twice, she hurled herself at the cheap wood.

One of the bodyguards opened it up. His hand was inside his coat, obviously on a gun. When he saw Coleman he didn't move. He remained blocking the doorway while he called back inside the room. "Mr. LaCoco, the sheriff and his date are here to see you."

"Let 'em in."

As soon as the bodyguard stepped aside, Sweetie rushed in. Coleman was right behind her, and I was on his heels.

Fully dressed in a dark suit, Tony LaCoco reclined on the bed. Glancing around the room, I noted the absence of the second bodyguard.

"What brings you to the Holiday Breeze?" LaCoco asked Coleman. His gaze swept over Coleman and then me. "You're a little overdressed, I'd say."

"Where's Kip?" Coleman asked.

"Interesting kid. She has a lot of . . . heart." The pause was deliberate, a cat tormenting its prey.

"Where is she?" Coleman asked. He was very, very calm. That made me very, very nervous. Coleman was extremely controlled, but the antithesis of such control is lack of it. I had no doubt that if he ever let his temper go, Coleman could make Tony LaCoco regret the day he was born.

"She was here. She made me an offer I *could* refuse." LaCoco laughed, and his bodyguard laughed with him. "Very cute kid."

"Where did she go?" Coleman asked.

LaCoco shrugged. "She was upset when she left. I had to explain to her that debts have to be paid. Since there's some question whether Kemper's insurance policy will be paid off because of the circumstances of his death, there will have to be another means of payment. And not another check that bounces. I had to explain that my clients who try stunts like that end up shopping for prosthetics."

"She's a kid," Coleman reminded him.

"A kid who inherits, from what I can find out." LaCoco made a face. "I tried to help her. I suggested that perhaps she should consider finding a way to come up with some cash before something happens to that horse she's so fond of." He grinned. "Blame it on the movies. That's where guys like me get all of our best ideas."

Coleman's fists were clenched, and I put a tentative hand on his arm. The muscle beneath my fingers was rigid.

"You're a real tough guy, LaCoco. Frightening teenage girls, threatening children. You'd better hope that Kip is okay. If something happens to her, it's going to be a very personal issue."

The bodyguard took a step closer to Coleman. LaCoco shook his head. "The girl came here of her own choice. As you can plainly see, she isn't here now. She left. What she does next is no concern of mine. Now take that ugly dog and get out of here."

Sweetie Pie had come to stand by my leg; I laced my fingers through her collar.

"LaCoco, if Kip is harmed in any way, I'll spend the rest of my career finding the dirt that puts you away." Coleman took my elbow and walked me out into the night. As soon as we were out of the room, Sweetie tugged away from me. Nose to the ground, she began sniffing the parking lot.

I was trembling when we stopped beside the car. Beneath the starry sky, Sweetie circled the lot, returning repeatedly to one spot where Kip must have parked the stolen Volvo.

"Was he actually threatening to kill Avenger

if Kip didn't come up with the money?" I asked.

"That's exactly what he was doing."

"Kip must be terrified." Her note kept running through my mind like a ticker tape. *I'm going to finish it.* "I'm afraid she's going to do something foolish," I said. "She hates Carol Beth."

"Get the dog and let's go," Coleman said brusquely.

Another time, under different circumstances, I would have flatly refused such a high-handed request. This was not another time. I fell into step beside Coleman like a well-trained DG. "Where are we going?"

"Back to Swift Level. My gut tells me that's where Kip would head. She'll go to protect that horse. If I can find her, get her to talk to me, maybe we can resolve this case once and for all." He seated me and got behind the wheel.

Slinging gravel, we went roaring off. No subject seemed adequate, so the silence between us grew as the miles rolled under the wheels. I kept glancing at Coleman, but his focus was on the road and his thoughts somewhere far away. We were only a couple of miles from Swift Level when the radio squawked again. Far, far away came the sound of a siren. I gritted my teeth. Perhaps Kip had already been run to ground.

"Coleman, here." The radio was swallowed by Coleman's hand.

"Better head on over to Swift Level," Gordon said.

"I'm on the way. They found her?"

"Nope. There's a fire. From what I can tell, the stud barn is burning."

Coleman swerved abruptly, dodging an armadillo. With practiced skill he corrected the car. "Is the fire department on the way?"

"Both of the city trucks." Gordon's voice seemed to come from a long way away.

"What about Mount Tildon and Blue Eve? Did they send a truck?"

"Both volunteer units are en route," Gordon said. "Full teams responding. I hear it's a disaster out there. Lots of confusion. Bud Lynch has disappeared and there's a chance he might be trapped in the barn."

"I'm on the way." Coleman replaced the radio and stepped hard on the gas. The big V-8 in the patrol car responded with a forward surge. I'd only thought we were going fast before.

"LaCoco's other bodyguard was missing." I didn't have to spell it out for Coleman.

"I noticed," he said, intent on the road.

"What about the horses?" I asked. Movie images of flames and screaming animals tore through my head. "Avenger." I whispered his name.

The sound of the sirens grew louder, and in the distance I could see the orange glow of the fire. It was the stallion barn, the place where Avenger lived and where Kemper died. Set against the starry night, the fire gave me the sensation that hell was waging direct war with heaven. The faster Coleman drove, the more I wanted him to slow down. I didn't want to confront this tragedy. In the back of my head, a mantra was spinning—the horses are safe; Bud is alive. I repeated it over and over.

We turned down the drive in front of one of the fire trucks, but we didn't slow at all. Coleman drove like a demon. In the headlights of the car we saw elegantly clad women and men, shoulder to shoulder, working a bucket brigade. The arrival of the fire truck was greeted with a hail of cheers, but even I could see that the stallion barn was a total loss. The roof was collapsing, falling away from the main timbers in huge sheets that burned hotly in the black night.

So far, the fire had not spread to the other buildings, but men and women were evacuating horses from the other barns, moving them to pastures where they bolted and ran to safety.

I got out of the car and ran toward the front of the line. To my surprise Carol Beth was closest to the fire, her beautiful gown ripped and torn. She stumbled toward the blaze with a bucket of water, flinging it, then turned back for another.

I felt something brush my leg and watched in horror as Sweetie Pie made a dash for the blazing barn. I started after her, knowing I would be too late. Harold rushed out of the shadows and grabbed her by the collar.

She tried to break free of him, and when she realized he was not going to let her go, she lifted her head and howled. It was a sound unlike any she'd ever made. It echoed over the night.

"I'll put her back in the patrol car," Harold said, dragging Sweetie past me and Carol Beth.

"Did they get Avenger out?" I asked her.

"I don't know." She rubbed her eyes on her forearm, smearing soot and makeup. "Bud went in to get him, but he hasn't come out." She spoke the words as if the events had happened a hundred years before. "That kid, too. She was standing in the doorway."

Dread is the most peculiar of sensations. It

moved from my ankles up my legs with icy fingers, freezing me even as I stood in the intense heat of the burning barn. "The kid?"

"Yeah. Lee's kid."

"Kip?"

Carol Beth nodded. "She just stood in the doorway with the flames behind her. We were all running down here, but we were too far away to do anything. I called out to her. She turned and walked into the fire, like she didn't feel any of it. Like she was already dead. That's when Bud ran into the barn."

Another section of barn roof collapsed, sending a shower of sparks in a spiral that was as deadly as it was beautiful.

I grabbed Carol Beth's shoulders and shook her, forcing her to look at me. "Are you sure it was Kip?" Maybe there was a mistake.

"It was her." Carol Beth twisted free of me. "It was her, all right."

"How did the fire start?" I asked.

"The sprinkler system was turned off. Some bastard did this deliberately," she said. "May his soul burn in hell for all eternity." A broken sob escaped her.

I felt a hand on my arm, and Lillian pulled me out of the way as another fire truck arrived.

"What happened?" I asked her.

"I was outside on the patio. I saw the fire." She turned to look at the flames. "I told Bud, and he ran down here while I called the fire department. Everyone came down to help, but it was too late. The whole barn was engulfed. I'm afraid they're dead."

20

Lillian was still standing beside me when Krystal walked up. Her dress and makeup remained perfect, but her eyes were glazed from what could have been alcohol or shock.

"I can't find Mike," she said in a flat tone. "I've hunted and hunted." She looked beyond me at the barn. "Where in the hell is he?"

"I haven't seen him all evening," Lillian said. "I'm sure he's around somewhere, though."

The fire trucks were bringing the flames under control, but there wasn't going to be much of anything left standing, except the huge support beams.

"Krystal!" Mike came out of the darkness, his white shirt stained with black soot and his eyes and hair wild. He put his arm around his wife. "I was worried sick. I looked for you everywhere."

"Where've you been?" she asked him in a sharp, accusing tone.

Mike's arm tightened around his wife. "Hey,

it's okay. I'm fine." He kissed her cheek and whispered something in her ear as his arm tightened around her.

"Bud Lynch is in that barn," Krystal said, shrugging away from him.

Mike made a sound of disbelief. "I heard. Can you imagine that stupid bastard running into a burning barn to save a horse? To save a horse! The damn thing was insured."

Krystal stepped away from him. "You can be such an ass," she said, stalking away.

Mike looked at us and shrugged. "Temperamental artist." He went after her.

I felt as if I were swimming deep beneath the ocean. The fire was a roar in my head, a primal sound like surf. The people around me moved in slow motion. I heard and saw everything, but it was as if some layer of clear, pure water surrounded me, protecting me from the nightmare of the burning barn.

I listened for the sounds of dying horses and heard nothing, thank God. I also listened for the cries of a teenager and the shouts of a grown man. Nothing. The fire had worked its destruction, and all that remained was the charring of the bones.

Another volunteer fire truck arrived. The worst was over. The worst of the flames, that is.

It would be many hours before investigators

could begin to sort through the ashes to recover those who'd perished. My God, who was
going to tell Lee? She'd lost everything of any
value to her.

I walked over to an old oak shrouded in
darkness so thick that the flames didn't pene-
trate it. I needed something to lean against,
something solid and permanent to shelter under. The party-goers slowly began to leave.
With the flames dying, there was nothing else
for them to do.

Carol Beth lingered, her stance somehow de-
fiant and defeated as she stared at the smoldering
timbers. At last, Harold appeared at her side and
led her away. He was disheveled and filthy, too.

Only the firemen and Coleman remained.
He was walking the perimeter, talking with
Ory Jones, the Zinnia fire chief.

"Miss Sarah Booth?"

The voice that called me was soft, worn by
time. I turned to find old Roscoe standing behind the tree. "Are you okay?" I asked. I hadn't
even thought to wonder if he was safe.

He nodded. "I was asleep in one of the other
barns. I got the foals out just in case. They got
it under control now."

"And Avenger?" When the old man didn't
respond, I had my answer.

"I saw Kip. In the barn," he whispered.

How could a name so perky belong to a dead girl?

"She was with Avenger," he added. "She was saddling him up to take him for a ride."

"How did the fire start?" I asked.

He looked around, as if he expected someone to be listening. "In the hayloft. I smelled it first. Then I went to check and saw the flames. It was in the hay. Someone lit it."

"You're positive the fire was deliberate?"

He looked around again. "I smelled gasoline."

"Who started it? Did you see?"

He shook his head. "No, I didn't see anyone. But I have something for Miss Lee. Will you give it to her?"

"Sure."

He held out his hand in a fist. I held mine out, palm open. The thing he dropped into my hand was light, and he closed my fingers around it. When he turned my hand loose, I opened it. Examining the thing by feel, I recognized it instantly. It was a butterfly hair clip that Kip had worn a lot.

"Give it to Miss Lee. It'll mean a lot to her."

"I will," I said.

He backed away. "Come see me tomorrow. Come by yourself."

He disappeared into the night.

I found Tinkie sitting on the front steps of the house. She held a damp washcloth that someone had given her clenched in her hand as the tears slipped down her face.

"Oh, Sarah Booth," she said. "What are we going to do?"

"I don't know." I sat down beside her. I heard footsteps behind us and looked back to see Oscar, her husband. He was as disheveled as everyone else. Concern for Tinkie was evident in his eyes, but he nodded to me and went back inside the house. Like I could offer comfort to anyone.

"How did Kip get here?" Tinkie asked.

"She stole a car from the Winslows. She went over there to spend the night with Amy." I was miserable. "That's it, down by the show barn." It was easy to see since all the other vehicles were gone.

"They said she walked right back into that burning barn." Tinkie was in shock.

"I'm sure she was trying to save Avenger." I thought of Tony LaCoco and his cruel threat to Kip. I wanted my shot at him before Coleman got there.

"Who would burn a barn?" Tinkie asked. "Especially a barn with a horse in it. As awful as it is, it's lucky only Avenger was stabled there."

Tinkie daubed at her eyes and held the cloth out for me. I wiped my face and gave it back to her. "Did you see anyone here who might be capable of doing this?"

Tinkie drew in a deep, ragged breath. "No. I was keeping an eye on Carol Beth. I thought she might try to kill Bud." Tinkie sighed. "It's like we were all playing some kind of stupid parlor game while real danger was waiting just outside the door."

"I know." I still held Kip's hair clip in my hand, and I pressed it deep into my flesh, imprinting it in my palm. The job of telling Lee was one I couldn't begin to imagine.

"Are they sure the fire was deliberately started?" Tinkie asked.

"I believe someone did it deliberately. Carol Beth said the sprinkler system was turned off. Someone meant to kill Avenger. Bud and Kip just got caught up in it. They were at the wrong place at the wrong time."

"Why kill a horse? Who could hate Lee that much?"

I knew the answer to that, and I suddenly knew where to start looking for the culprit. "Because Avenger was insured," I said, slowly rising to my feet. "That horse was insured, and I'll bet it was for a considerable sum of money. That's what that creep Tony LaCoco was saying. If the horse died, there would be money to pay Kemper's debts."

"What are you going to do?" Tinkie asked, rising also.

"Tell Coleman. Tell him some things I should have told him long before now."

When I got back to the place where Coleman had parked the patrol car, I found that he had left me and Sweetie Pie in Harold's care. Coleman was gone, headed into the night to do God knew what.

Harold had found a piece of rope and was using it as a leash to keep Sweetie Pie from trying to hurl herself into the still-burning remains of the barn. He pushed my hair back from my face and leaned over to kiss my cheek. "I'd offer you a drink, but I think a hot bath would be more helpful."

"Harold, how much money would it take to pull Swift Level out of the red?" I asked.

Even in the unreliable light from the fire I could see that my question had startled him.

"I don't think Lee can make it without Avenger. I don't think she'll want to try without Kip. My God, this is awful, Sarah Booth. It's going to kill Lee."

I simply could not allow myself to think about Kip or Bud or I would start to cry. I was afraid I wouldn't be able to stop. "What about another one of the horses? One of Avenger's sons?" I asked.

Harold seemed to understand my need to veer away from the horror of the deaths. "I'm not sure. Lillian's right over there. Ask her."

Lillian was sitting in the open door of Cece's car, her feet still on the ground and her head bowed. It seemed only her indomitable will kept her from falling over.

"Lillian." I spoke softly so as not to startle her.

She slowly looked up. "I thought when Father had to sell our farm that that was the worst thing I'd ever face. Maybe time has dulled the horror of it, because this is surely more awful." She brushed a tear away. "Kip and Bud. Avenger. It's just too hard."

My own eyes were filling with tears, and I struggled to maintain control.

Harold put a hand on Lillian's shoulder, giving her a sympathetic rub. "With Avenger gone, can Lee reorganize and build on one of Avenger's sons? I'm sure she must have some colts by him."

Lillian looked out toward the dark pastures. "It all depends on the horse," she said. "The problem is the time. She's spent nine years promoting Avenger's reputation in the ring, buying the right mares, breeding them, raising those foals, getting them in the right position to show that his traits have been passed on. It would be like starting over, almost. It would take years, and hundreds of thousands of dollars." She made a derisive noise. "It wouldn't matter if she had Trigger, Silver, and Black Beauty. Without Kip, Lee won't last a week out here. This is the end of Swift Level."

"Would you like me to take you home?" Harold asked her.

"No," Lillian said. "I'm waiting on Cece. She's got that awful man, Nathaniel Walz, with her. I wonder if it's too late to throw him into the fire."

"Lillian!" Harold said with feigned shock. "What has poor Nathaniel done to earn your ire?"

"He breathes," Lillian said, pushing herself up onto her swollen feet. "He breathes, and there's a horrible chance he might reproduce. At least that won't happen with Cece."

"Cece is smitten with him?" I asked, remembering the day he'd come into her office looking for publicity. He'd certainly played to her sense of power.

"They're thick as thieves," Lillian said, visibly making an effort to pull herself together. Though her voice was still shaking, she continued. "Cece's been busy driving him around the area, introducing him to people who might want to invest in one of his developments."

I knew Lillian's attitude toward developments. It ran a close parallel to mine. We were antiprogressives, lovers of the soil instead of asphalt. We were troglodytes.

"What exactly does he want to develop?" I asked.

"Quaint inns, bed-and-breakfasts, culturally stimulating things such as a working plantation, maybe a racetrack. To hear Cece talk, Nathaniel is popping with ideas. Like a big fat bloodsucking tick."

Harold kissed Lillian's cheek. "It does me good to hear you so riled up. Otherwise, I'd be worried about you. I'm going to take Sarah Booth home. Last chance to ride with us."

"I'm staying," Lillian said. "I'd better go look for them. Nathaniel's probably staking out the burning barn as a great locale for an ice-skating rink surrounded by discount shopping stores."

Harold stood beside me as we watched her move slowly into the night.

"Come on, I'll give you ladies a ride home." Harold still had Sweetie on the rope. He grasped my elbow with his free hand and led me toward his car. He put Sweetie in the back and me in the front, and he walked around and got behind the wheel. He drove very carefully away from Swift Level.

"Coleman went to tell Lee, didn't he?" I asked.

Harold hesitated. "Yes. He thought it would be best if he could tell her alone." He drove for a few moments before he spoke again. "Listening to Lillian was very interesting. I should tell you that Nathaniel Walz came by the bank a couple of days ago. He was asking about Dahlia House."

I had thought I was numb, incapable of feeling any emotion. I was wrong. A bolus of fear and anger zoomed through me. "Asking what about Dahlia House?" I'd come so close to losing my family home only the year before. At that time, a developer had been interested in the land for a strip mall. The idea of seeing Dahlia House razed and leveled, the rich soil entombed beneath asphalt, still haunted me. Harold had tapped into the main line of my fears.

"Asking if you might sell it."

"I'm not behind in any of my notes. How dare—"

"I told him that Dahlia House was not, under any circumstances, up for sale."

The pressure inside my skull eased, allowing for some brain function. I'd been about to jump down Harold's throat, and he was protecting me.

"Sorry. Hot button."

His chuckle was amused. "Sarah Booth, I always thought it was your thumb that was your hot button."

If I had ever doubted that he knew what effect he'd had on me the night he'd seduced my thumb, I now knew the truth. I was struck simultaneously by a weak throb in my thumb and a hot flush in my face.

I decided that I would fall back on some Daddy's Girl training and ignore the gauntlet that Harold had thrown down. "I wonder how Nathaniel knew to ask about Dahlia House." Cece would never, never divulge my financial difficulties, not even if Nathaniel Walz were the last man alive.

"He knew a great deal about a lot of property in this area. Inside information. I asked him where he got it, and he only laughed. He said it was his business to know these things."

"But you let him know Dahlia House

wasn't in any danger?" I needed the reassurance of repetition.

"I did." Harold reached over and brushed my hair from my face. "Sarah Booth, as hard as you've worked to save your home, I couldn't let you lose it."

Once again, tears threatened. My emotions were raw, my thoughts jumbled. Out of the clear blue, Harold had made an offer so generous that I couldn't begin to thank him. But I had to try.

"I can't tell you what it means for you to say that."

He picked up my hand and brought it slowly to his lips. "Sarah Booth, you've won my admiration and respect. Be careful, or you're going to have to decline another marriage proposal from me."

"I'll think about being careful," I answered.

We were almost to Dahlia House when I spoke again. "Why did you invite Carol Beth to the dance?"

Harold thought for a moment. "The finances at Swift Level are of interest to Coleman. He has never believed Lee's confession, and he believes that Kemper's death was because of financial difficulties. He asked me to keep an eye on Carol Beth, to see what her interests were at Swift Level. She isn't a client of mine, so whatever she told me in social conversation could be passed on. Taking her to the dance gave me a reason to call on her. For all the good it did."

"Did you learn anything?"

"She was determined to have that horse. 'Obsessed' may be a better word. I won't say she set Kemper up to lose money gambling, but I know she encouraged it. She loaned him money, which only put him deeper in the hole. When he was in over his head, she cut off his funds and demanded Avenger. Kemper's ace up his sleeve was Tony LaCoco, or so Kemper thought. LaCoco is a businessman with only one business: high-interest loans. Carol Beth wasn't above dealing with LaCoco if she thought it would help her get Avenger." He seemed to be searching for the right words. "Carol Beth can't seem to see the difference between taking something from someone else and building something of her own."

"She lost a lot tonight. At least financially. It looks like her husband is going to divorce her."

"She put Bud Lynch in a corner, and he jammed her back. I have to say Bud gave her fair warning, repeatedly."

"I told Coleman about the check Kip wrote."

He patted my hand. "I know. He was upset with me, but in time he'll get over it."

"In time, will I?"

Harold pulled up in front of the house. Reaching back, he opened the door and let Sweetie Pie out. "You have no choice, Sarah Booth. You'll either recover or die. And dying isn't as easy as you might believe."

He leaned over and kissed my cheek. "Good night, Sarah Booth. Drink some whiskey and try to sleep."

Instead of going inside, I sat on the front steps and watched Harold's red taillights disappear. I didn't have the heart or the energy to go inside. Sweetie had undoubtedly gone to the back and gained entrance through her own personal doggy door.

I heard the sound of footsteps coming across the wooden boards, and I was glad Jitty had decided to stay home and wait for me.

"Sarah Booth, are you okay?"

The voice was unexpected—masculine, yet full of warm Mississippi nights. In the darkness, I couldn't see the man's features.

"Who are you?" I demanded.

"Chill, it's me, J.B."

"J.B.?" I was on guard. The night had left my nerves a ragged jangle, and this man had nearly scared my dress right off my back. "What are you doing here?"

"I saw you at the motel earlier tonight. I saw you go into that gangster's room with the sheriff."

"What are you still doing in town?"

"I got a gig over at Smokin' Blues, out on the highway. I played there Friday night, and I'm doin' a brunch this mornin' at Playin' the Bones."

The porch light wasn't on, and I still couldn't see him. "Where's your mother?"

"She went on back to Greenwood. She doesn't care for the nightclub scene. I guess she freaked you out a little, huh?"

"Maybe just a little." I was too tired to lie. "She was lovely, though."

He came forward and took a seat on the steps. For some reason that made me feel better, and I relaxed beside him, arms folded on my knees.

"You look like you lost your best friend, ran over your own dog, and got gut-shot by the revenuers."

"Thanks, you have a way with compliments."

He chuckled. "I couldn't help but overhear some of what was goin' on tonight. You ever find the kid?"

Tears burned in the back of my throat, but I

managed not to cry. "There was a fire. One of the barns burned. Kip went in to save a horse. No one saw her come out."

J.B. put a hand on my shoulder and began a slow, easy massage. "I heard all the sirens and wondered what was going on. That's sort of why I'm here. I talked to her a few minutes at the motel. She was hangin' out at the Coke machine by the office, tryin' to get up her nerve to see that gangster. I tried to talk her out of it, but she was determined. She was a gritty little thing."

" 'Gritty' is a good word for her. Did she say what she was doing with LaCoco?"

"Not in any detail. She said she was stayin' with you, and that she was the one who'd put your profile on the Internet. She was tryin' to help, you know."

I nodded, fighting a lump in my throat. "I know. What else did she say about LaCoco?"

"She had the idea that he was going to try and hurt her horse. She said she'd tried to pay him so he'd leave town, but that something had gone wrong. Then she said she'd fixed everything so her mother would be set free." He sighed. "I guess it didn't work out the way she planned."

"She didn't say what she'd fixed?"

"No. But when I came up on her, she and

that little guy were talkin'. He'd really pissed her off."

J.B. kept working the knots in my shoulders. "What little guy?"

"The one in the neat suits. Some kind of deal-maker. He's staying at the motel. Likes to talk loud on the telephone."

"Nathaniel Walz?"

"I'm not sure of his name." John chuckled. "He's so lazy he won't walk over to talk to anyone else in the motel. He calls them on the phone. Can you believe that?"

Knowing that Walz was the kind of man who looked to destroy the past to profit from the future, I wasn't surprised at any aberrant behavior. "Did you hear what they were saying?"

"The kid just told him to go to hell. That's all I heard from her, but I've heard other things. Those walls are thin."

"Like what?"

"He found a place for that singer to move to. She wants to put in a sound studio and things like that. He found an old house that's cheap, something that has the space for everything she wants. I'm a blues man, but she's got the look of a country star. I wouldn't mind playin' some backup for her."

"You're talking about Krystal Brook?"

"Yeah, Krystal. She's pretty nice, too. Anyway, that Nat guy talked to her and her husband. I'll bet he's turnin' a pretty penny on that deal. He was talkin' to that gangster, too, and some other folks. I couldn't always hear too good. Somethin' about a piece of property that would come on the market soon at a really cheap price, due to some kind of economic screwup."

John was a wealth of interesting information. "You came here to tell me all of this? Why?"

"I saw you and the sheriff go in LaCoco's room tonight. I figured it was about the girl. I don't really know much, but I thought I'd come tell you what I know. I thought it might bear on your case. Like I told you, being a detective was always a fantasy of mine."

I had not treated this man with any measure of fairness, and yet he'd come to my home to tell me something he thought might be useful.

"Thank you, J.B."

"No thanks necessary. I hate it about the kid. If you need some cheerin' up, come by Playin' the Bones about eleven. I'll play a song just for you."

He walked down the steps and disappeared into the night. In a moment I heard the sound of his car, and then his headlights cut the darkness as they sped down the long drive toward the road.

I forced myself to get up and go inside. No matter how weary, how defeated, I was going to make someone pay for what had happened to Kip.

Jitty was sitting at the top of the staircase. She wasn't her vibrant self. Her skin tone was a little on the ashy side.

"Girl, you've talked your way through most of this night, but what are you gonna do now?"

"I don't know," I said, stepping past her.

She followed me into my bedroom. "Will Coleman let Lee go free, since Kip confessed?"

"I don't know." I let my red dress fall to the floor and stepped out of it. Jitty didn't even raise an objection when I left it where it fell. "It's odd. Now that Kip's confessed, I'm not so certain she killed her father." There were a lot of things niggling at me.

Jitty sank down in the old rocker that my mother had used when I was an infant, and generations of Delaneys before that. She rocked slowly. "Any other detective would be glad to have things neatly wrapped up."

"If this case were neatly wrapped up, I'd be happy, too."

"Kip confessed to the murder. What could be neater?" Jitty persisted.

I went to my purse and got out the hair clip. Roscoe had never said how he came by it. "Kip, Bud, *and* the horse are gone," I reminded Jitty. "Lee will collect the insurance on Kemper and on the horse."

"Are you saying that Lee benefits from all of this tragedy?"

I slowly paced my bedroom. "I don't know what I'm saying. I'm too tired to think right now."

"I know," she answered softly. "Crawl up in that bed and go to sleep. I'll just sit here and watch over you."

I sank into the bed, aware that Jitty was seldom so nice. It was something that, like Scarlett, I would have to worry about tomorrow.

21

I awoke to the sound of fists on the door. Not Tinkie's normal little knock, but more of a "rise and shine" pounding. I pulled the pillow over my head and ignored it. There was no one I wanted to see. No one I cared to talk to.

The pounding didn't stop, so I got out of bed and stormed downstairs, Sweetie Pie at my heels.

I opened the door with a glare that turned into amazement. The King stood before me, in tight black jeans and a sky-blue silk shirt, open just enough to reveal a tantalizing bit of chest.

"Howdy, ma'am," he said. "I hear you're havin' a rough time. I'm here to help."

Elvis died in 1977. He could not possibly be standing on my front porch. I peered around him and saw a magnificent pink 1957 Cadillac in my drive. I had a weakness for classic cars. "Jitty!" I yelled. "Jitty!" My resident haint had to be behind this visitation.

"Easy, ma'am," Elvis said. "You're 'bout to

have a conniption." He put a hand on my
shoulder. A real, warm, human hand.

"Who the hell are you?" I asked.

"I'm Tom Smith. You know, Tomcat Tupelo.
As soon as I got your E-mail, I rushed right
over here."

I looked down at my ratty sleep-shirt.
Maybe a timber had fallen on my head. Maybe
I was dreaming, but for the past week my midnight hours had been claimed by visits from
the Kinkster, not Elvis. For the life of me, I
couldn't figure out what this man was doing
on my porch.

"What E-mail?" I asked.

"The one that told me to get right on over
A-S-A-P. And I thought, W-W-E-D. That's
short for 'What would Elvis do?' He would
have rushed right out to help a lady in distress,
so here I am. Oh, yeah, Kip said to tell you not
to worry."

"Kip?" The name slipped from my lips.

"Your secretary." His handsome face was
creased with worry. "She sent the E-mail. She
said there'd been a fire, and that you were very
upset. I can see she didn't lie."

I backed into the foyer, motioning him to
follow. "Coffee," I said, leading the way to the
kitchen. "Coffee," I mumbled. I had gone from
dreaming to hallucinating, but I had the

strangest sensation that Tom Smith was real. If *that* was true, then Kip was alive. It was more than I could absorb.

"Coffee," I repeated for the third time.

"Sounds like you *need* a cup of java." He fell in behind me.

I needed something stronger than coffee. Kip had sent this man an E-mail mentioning the fire, and he had come to help me. It was her way of letting me know that she hadn't burned to death.

I turned so suddenly that he stepped back. "What time did you get that E-mail?" I demanded.

"I got in from a show and it was there. Musta been about three this morning. I went right home and put all my gear in the car. I haven't had a wink of sleep, but Elvis had a lot of stamina."

"What time was it sent?"

He frowned. "I can't rightly say. I didn't look. But it had to come in during the wee hours. I checked my mail about midnight and cleared out my mailbox. Ask your secretary when she sent it."

A brilliant suggestion, except "my secretary" was supposed to have died in a fire. I pointed to a chair at the kitchen table and put on a pot of coffee. While it perked, I held on to the kitchen sink and stared out the window at the family cemetery.

"I brought all of my things for the audition."

"What audition?" At least that was a question that might have a sane answer.

"At noon. At *The Club*." Tom's voice rose with excitement, which only made his drawl extend. "I can't wait. Everyone in Tupelo has heard about The Club. I never thought I'd be goin' there. I've been rehearsin' and rehearsin'. My act is down pat. I don't think there's an Elvis who can possibly beat me out this time."

A dim bell began to jangle in my memory. The Club, exclusive hangout of Daddy's Girls and their older male counterparts, the Buddy Clubbers, was hosting some kind of fund-raiser for charity. An Elvis impersonator contest.

I chanced a look at him out of the corner of my eye. He was the spitting image of Elvis Aaron Presley in his lean and mean days. He caught my glance and smiled, and I knew why millions of girls had fallen in love with him.

"I know you're on a case. You're tryin' to save your childhood friend, and I want you to know how much I admire that. Elvis stood behind his friends. It was loyalty to the death."

He was talking as if he sat in my kitchen every morning of his life.

"That was one of the things that intrigued

me about you. I guess because of my vocation, I meet a lot of women who sort of wait for life to happen to them. You're not like that. You go out there and make it happen."

The coffee was only half perked, but I poured two cups and put one in front of him. He lifted the mug in a toast.

"Might as well tank up," he said agreeably. "Coffee doesn't make me nervous. You know, before Elvis got all strung out he took every appearance seriously. He studied for each show, and rested, and made sure that he could give it his all. That's how I do it. Just like he did."

"Is there any way you can check when you received that E-mail?" I asked him.

"Sure. I got a laptop out in the car. Once you get the hang of those things, they're terrific. Keeps my bookin's straight and all my taxes. Or I can use your computer. Six of one, half a dozen of the other."

"How did you know I had a computer?" I asked.

He laughed. "You've been sendin' me E-mail for a week now. If it hadn't of been for you, I never would have known about the competition at The Club."

"Let's check my computer," I suggested. "It's right upstairs."

With Elvis at my side, I went to my bedroom. Kip had left the modem plugged in, saving me from having to crawl under the desk.
He sat down in front of the computer and
within seconds had accessed his E-mail. "Let's
see here." He made a few more clicks. "I received that E-mail at two-ten in the A.M."

I walked over to the bed and sat down. Kip
was alive. There was no doubt about it.

"Are you okay?" he asked me.

"I'm better than okay." A strange joy had
taken hold of me. Kip was alive! If I got my
hands on her, she might not be for long, but
she had not burned to death.

"You look plumb delighted," he said. "I
sometimes have that effect. Folks often ask me
how I got into this business. My mama used to
dress me like Elvis when I was a little baby boy.
I could always sing, and they got me a little
guitar and she made me some clothes with a
bit of flash and dazzle, and they'd take me
around to the state fairs and things and I'd perform." He stood up. "And that's what I've got
to do right now. Perform. I've got to get on
over to the competition. The original plan was
for me to come by here *after* I won the competition. Is that still a go?"

He smoothed back his hair on one side,

careful not to disturb the single strand that hung in his eye.

"Mr. Smith, my secretary is missing, and my friend is in jail charged with murder. I think it would be best if we postponed our . . . meeting. At least for a while."

"I can see you've got your hands full. I know what it's like to be caught up in your work." He smiled, and he'd never looked more like The King. "If I make it big as Elvis, I'd like to come back here and court you."

"You call me. On the telephone," I added hastily, pulling out an official Delaney Detective Agency business card from the pile of papers on my computer and handing it to him.

"Good day, Sarah Booth. Now you call me if you need me for anything," he said, doing a courtly little head nod before he walked out of my bedroom. I heard the front door close behind him. Elvis had left the building.

It had been days since I'd been on the computer. I went to my E-mail and took a shaky breath. There were 173 unopened messages. I began to scroll through them, noting the names. TopDog, SweetHome, Chester, Dancinfool. Kip had been very, very busy in my behalf, but there was no message from her.

I opened the file that contained sent messages.

There were three to Malone Beasley, two to JBBLUES, and three to TomcatTupelo, among a half dozen others to such interesting cyber addresses as Utopia and UncleHenry.

"I tol' you that you had mail!" Jitty said at my shoulder. "If you weren't stubborn as a mule, you'da been prepared for some of your gentleman callers." Jitty perched on the edge of my desk. "This is the future, Sarah Booth. There are more men out there than you can shake a stick at. You just got to find one that can shake a stick back!"

She slapped her thigh, laughing at her own joke. Kip's resurrection had lifted the pall. Jitty was out of black and wearing a lime-green mini.

"You put Kip up to using the computer, didn't you?"

Jitty made a face of surprise. "*Moi*?"

"*Moi* my ass," I said. "How'd you do it? You can't talk to anyone but me."

"You did it yourself," she said, standing and walking toward my bedroom window. She did a half-turn and looked over her shoulder. "You're always fussin' at me, and Kip just overheard you. She's a smart girl. She put two and two together and decided on her own that you needed a date for that ball. She didn't do too bad, either. Two outta three."

I couldn't argue the statistics, but I wasn't going to concede the battle. Especially not to Jitty. "Your fingerprints are all over this."

She smirked and strutted, hips swaying like a gentle tide. "Teenagers are very open to suggestions from . . . beyond. Poltergeists and demons love 'em." She arched one eyebrow in a gesture that I coveted.

"You are a demon," I pointed out.

"Honey, that's not always a bad thing." She winked. "A man likes a woman with a little bit of devilment. If you got Harold smokin' in the right places, he'd find that big honkin' ring he offered you and you stupidly gave back."

Harold was one place I didn't want to go, but I had a point to make. "If Harold decided to ask me out again, I wouldn't be averse to that. Unlike gentleman callers from cyberspace, Harold is a known quantity," I said carefully. "I'm comfortable with that. I know who he is."

"Because he lives here in Zinnia?" Jitty asked.

"Because I know how he treats people, how he thinks. I know his values."

Her eyebrows were almost in her hairline. "Sarah Booth, maybe you should invest in a tape recorder and use it on yourself. You're talkin' like a traditionalist. You only want to risk a man that you can pin like a bug and

examine. You *think* you know Harold because
he's familiar. Because he's *geographically known.*
You think 'cause he's from right around here
that you share values with him." She paused for
effect. "That's a mighty big assumption, young
lady."

"I have a history with Harold, and I'm not
talking about that thumb-sucking incident."

"Too bad your aunt LouLane isn't around to
hear this." Jitty rolled her eyes. "I remember
many a night she worried herself silly that
you'd hurt yourself takin' a foolish risk. While
you were out cuttin' a rug, she'd be pacin' the
floor in her room, worried that some boy
would break your heart."

"I was only having fun," I said, remembering
the days when I had Aunt LouLane to come
home to. I'd been free then just to enjoy the
boys and young men who waltzed through my
life. "I wish Aunt LouLane was here now. Used
to be a girl could count on her family to introduce her to nice men."

"Oh, I remember that!" Jitty said, not bothering to hide her sarcasm. "Yeah, those were the
days, when a nineteen-year-old spinster was
packed into a wagon and sent from relative to
relative in the hopes that someone could find a
man to take her off their hands. Oh, I know exactly what you're talkin' about. If Cousin Ida

can't find a man for the poor thing, send her on to Illinois and Cousin Belle. Surely she can find some desperate corn farmer to take a wife."

"That's not what I mean." Jitty was wearing me down. "There used to be a time when a man's reputation meant something. Family members took the time and trouble to check those things out."

"Are you hearin' yourself?" Jitty asked. "You want a consensus on the man you have feelin's for? Girl, you better get one thing straight right now. The only person who can judge the right man for you is you. No one, livin' or dead, can approve your feelin's and make them right or wrong."

"Not approval, Jitty." She was missing the point.

"You're just afraid to risk. Does the word 'dowry' mean anything to you? Too bad your daddy didn't arrange a marriage for you when you were born. That would certainly make it easier now, wouldn't it?"

"You've stepped over the line," I said with as much huff as I could muster. "I don't have time to argue this right now. Since Kip is alive, I've got to find her." I shut down the computer and stood up.

"You can change the subject, but this conversation ain't over until the fat ghost sings."

"Finding Kip is more important than a discussion of my nonexistent love life." I pulled some clothes from the closet, determined to get out the door before Jitty could start a new harangue.

"Who was the last person to see Kip alive?" Jitty asked.

"Bingo!"

I bathed, dressed, and hurried out to the car. I put Kip's hair clip on the passenger seat, and beside that, the syringe in a plastic Baggie.

As I drove up to Swift Level, the site of the barn was a charred and blackened skeleton. Except for the deputy Coleman had left at the scene, the farm appeared deserted. The yellow crime-scene tape fluttered in the quickening breeze. No one was there searching for bodies, which told me a lot.

I parked in the shade of an oak and made my way over to the deputy, a new recruit I didn't know.

"Where's Coleman?" I asked. I had a lot of things to tell him.

"Gone." He gave me a long look. "You're the detective, aren't you?"

"Sarah Booth Delaney." I held out a hand for him to shake.

"You can call me Dewayne. Deputy De-wayne Dattilo," he said. "Sheriff Peters went back to town."

"Did they find anything?" I was really asking how much Coleman knew.

"Best to talk to the sheriff," Dewayne said. "He told me if I said a word to anyone, he'd skin me alive."

No amount of badgering was going to pry a single tidbit from Deputy Dewayne Dattilo. The fact that Coleman was gone already, though, pretty much confirmed my suspicions. Neither Kip, nor Bud, nor the horse had been in the barn when it burned, and Coleman knew it.

I went down to the main barn where the of-fice was. The white paint on the outside wall had blistered and begun to peel from the heat of the fire. I brushed a few flakes off as I walked past.

The office door was unlocked, and I found the medicine cabinet with ease. All of the vials and bottles were clearly labeled. There was no insulin, though there were a number of unused syringes the size of the one I possessed.

Bud had lived in an apartment above the of-fice, but I wasn't certain where Roscoe lived, or if he even resided on the grounds.

"Miss Delaney?"

Roscoe's soft voice called to me from a stall,

and as I drew closer, he stepped into the hall-way, manure rake in hand. "I didn't know if you'd come."

"Where's Kip?" I had no intention of beat-ing around the bush. "What about Bud and Avenger? Are they alive, too?"

Roscoe leaned the rake against the wall with great deliberateness before he spoke. "Kemper was gonna kill that horse."

"What are you talking about? Kemper's dead."

"Avenger. Kemper had been plannin' on killin' him. That Kemper Fuquar was a mean bastard. He owed those men money, and they weren't gonna wait no longer. They come up here one night, three of them. They showed him a little bit of what it felt like to be knocked around. The next day, I heard him on the phone, gettin' insurance on Avenger. But he had to kill the horse in a way that no one could tell, or the insurance company wouldn't pay up."

I'd heard of people who killed racehorses for insurance money. It was a highly profitable scam. Horses were shot in pastures and labeled "hunting accidents," or beaten to death with metal pipes and reported as "accidents in the starting gate." It was a dirty, ugly business, and one I'd always associated with the lowest class of scum. The problem in my thinking was that just because Kemper lived at Swift Level, I hadn't actually seen him for what he was.

"Did Lee know about this?" Unfortunately, here was another motive for her to want him dead.

He shook his head. "He worked on it while she was gone to shows. He planned it all out, but I was watchin' him. And Bud was watchin', too. Bud shoulda killed him."

I didn't disagree.

"Even the horse knew. Avenger hated Kemper. Hated him. He could smell him a mile away. That's when he'd get crazy." Roscoe shifted his weight. "I was wearin' Kemper's old jacket yesterday when Avenger took out after me in the arena. I shoulda known better, but I wasn't thinkin'."

"Do you know how Kemper was going to kill the horse?" Maybe the horse could take the rap and plead self-defense.

His gaze was intent when he looked up at me. "Insulin injection. I knew how he was gonna do it, I just didn't know when. He had to wait until Miss Lee was out of the way. I guess when Dara had trouble foalin', he saw his chance. I found the insulin in the syringe in the stall, before the sheriff got here. I know I shoulda told the sheriff, but things looked so black for Miss Lee, I thought that would look like another good reason she wanted to kill Kemper. I didn't know what to do for a while. I was afraid whatever I did would only make it worse. Then I thought, you were Miss Lee's friend and you'd know best what to do."

"You've given me too much credit, there. I'm not certain what to do either," I admitted. "Please continue."

He took a long breath. "I figured it out, you know. I found the twitch he was using. Kemper thought he could put the chain on Avenger's lip and hold him while he gave the shot, but he didn't know Avenger. He's a smart horse. He knew to act like he was caught. When Kemper went to pop him with the needle, Avenger knocked him down. Kemper never stood a chance. Avenger got him." He lifted one hand, clenched in a fist. "The horse got him first. He stomped him to death, and Miss Lee is takin' the blame."

I heard Roscoe's ragged breathing and knew it was caused by the fury and frustration he felt. If only the scenario he had presented were true. But it wasn't. I watched dust motes dancing on the weak sunlight that filtered through the stall windows, and a part of my brain registered that the thunderstorm was holding off.

"Kemper had insulin in his body," I finally

told him. "The horse couldn't have given him an injection. Someone else killed Kemper."

Roscoe shrugged. "Maybe he fell on the needle. It's happened more than once around a strugglin' horse."

"Can we find evidence of that?" I asked him.

"Even if we can, Miss Lee won't allow it. She won't let Avenger take the blame." Roscoe picked up the manure rake.

"Then Avenger *is* alive?" I'd finally circled back to the question I'd come to ask.

He stopped, his back still to me. "I didn't see nothin'."

Roscoe pulled a wheelbarrow out of the stall and pushed it down the aisle to the next stall. "All I'm gonna say is that I believe that little girl, her daddy, and her horse have all gone to a better place. I wouldn't worry about those three."

"Her daddy? You think Kemper went to a better place?" I was just a little startled by that sentiment. Most folks were soothed by the idea that Kemper was likely toasting at the feet of Satan.

Slowly he turned around. His wrinkled face held many secrets, but this was one he was going to share. "Kemper's not her daddy. Bud Lynch is."

22

My first impulse was to rush back to town. Coleman had figured out that Bud, Kip, and the horse were alive. He was probably tracking them down right this second. While I was at Swift Level, though, I wanted to look for a little more evidence. Coleman had searched the premises looking for evidence of Kemper's murderer. He hadn't been looking for the leavings of Cupid.

Bud's apartment was sparsely furnished, reflecting what little I knew of his nature. There were over a hundred books neatly stacked on shelves, many of them showing the signs of having been read more than once. I glanced through the titles, surprised at the names T. R. Pearson and Pete Dexter, and a host of Mississippi classics from Welty to Faulkner. Based on Bud's vocabulary, I'd known he was well read, and yet I was still surprised at the scope of his literary taste. Horse magazines were piled beside a chair and lamp.

There were no photographs on the shelves, no mementos of past good times. Several pairs of cowboy boots were neatly lined up in the closet, and his clothes hung above them, cleaned and ironed. Even the bathroom was ordered. Shaving gear, toiletries, all pushed to the back of the counter.

The queen-size bed was covered with a patchwork quilt. I recognized the Rose of Sharon pattern, and wondered if it was his or Lee's. The bed was an old iron frame, painted white and butted against an exterior wall. Beside the bed, curtains with a bronco motif fluttered in the light breeze.

The drawers were my next line of attack. I shuffled through his personal items and found an old wallet, empty of everything. I couldn't help but contrast his living quarters to my own. In Dahlia House each piece of furniture had a family history. Photographs and letters had been passed from generation to generation. The details of my character could be found scattered along library shelves or hanging on walls. Every item in the house was hooked to someone or something of importance to me. Even the pots in the kitchen could be linked to Aunt LouLane's cheese grits or my mother's cornbread. Bud had deliberately eradicated any trace of his past. No photos of favorite horses, no old postcards or movie ticket stubs. Nothing.

I decided to check between the mattress and the box springs, so I pulled the quilt off the bed. Military corners on the sheets. It was the most revealing thing I'd found so far. As I lifted the mattress, I heard the tinkle of something hit the floor. There was nothing under the mattress, so I let it drop and searched for the item I'd heard fall. I saw it sparkling against the polished wood floor. A gold pendant.

It was beautifully crafted, an elegant horse's head, wild mane flying over a magnificent emerald eye. Certainly not Bud's, but one of his conquests'. It could easily belong to any of the women who took riding instruction from Bud. Any of them. But the unique design of it told me otherwise.

I tucked the pendant in my pocket and took one last look around. I had not found what I was looking for, but I'd found something else.

The need to talk to Lee pressed hard on me, but I went back to the barn office and went through every file again in a search for the insurance papers on Avenger that Roscoe and Mike had mentioned. Those papers could prove crucial to Lee. After an intense search, I had to admit defeat.

Coleman was not in the sheriff's office, and I didn't bother asking Deputy Walters for permission to visit Lee. I opened the door to the jail and shut it behind me. I had to see Lee, and I had to see her alone.

"Sarah Booth," she said, rising from her cot. She was so pale she was almost ethereal.

I held out the hair clip, my hand stuck through the bars at her. She took it very carefully. "You know they're alive, don't you?" I asked.

"I had hoped," she said. Her fist curled around the hair clip, holding it tightly. "Thank God."

"Where are they?"

Her green eyes slowly lifted until our gazes met and held. "I don't know."

"Don't know or won't tell?"

"I don't know, and I wouldn't tell if I did. It doesn't matter where they are, Sarah Booth. They're safe. That's all that matters."

"So many secrets, Lee. So many unnecessary secrets." I reached into my purse and brought out the insulin syringe.

"What's that?" she asked, a pulse jumping in her throat.

"You tell me." I waited. Lee was an accomplished liar, but she wasn't as good at hiding her fear.

"I don't know," she said.

"One more time. I need the truth. What is this?"

She reached for it, but I withdrew it. "An injection of some type." She made a gesture to show it was of little importance to her.

"My best guess would be insulin. Now tell me one more time how you killed Kemper. This time don't forget the part where you injected him with insulin."

Lee didn't move. She was frozen in place. Her gaze clung to mine, searching for some sign that what I was saying wasn't true.

"You weren't even in the barn when Kemper was killed, Lee. You've been lying all along. It's time for you to tell Coleman the truth."

"No."

"We need to find Kip and bring her home. We can get help for her."

"No." She slowly shook her head. "No. She's safe now. She's with Bud. He'll look out for her, make sure she doesn't . . ." She stopped.

"She doesn't hurt someone else?"

"She's not like that. You know she isn't."

"Coleman knows they're alive. I'm sure of it. He's hunting them now, and he'll find them.

Lee, help Kip. Tell the truth, get out of here, and help us find her."

The movement of her head was minute, but it was still a no. "She's only fourteen."

"And she needs her mother."

"Bud will take care of her."

"Because he's her father." I knew all of her secrets now, and I was using them to tear her down, to bring her to her knees so that she would have to accept the truth of what had happened—what was going to happen.

Her gaze was fixated on the syringe in my hand. "I should have killed him long ago, before he sank us in gambling debts. He wouldn't stop. Nothing could stop him. He was going to tell Kip he wasn't her father. He was going to hurt her because she'd disappointed him."

So Roscoe was right. Bud was Kip's father.

Lee's chest moved in and out, but she didn't look away. "I got pregnant, and Bud didn't want to marry. We were young and wild. He wanted to live the cowboy life, which isn't conducive to a wife and home. I was trapped, and I was prideful. When Kemper came along, he was so greedy for what he thought I would inherit. I thought I could make it work." Her hands clenched in her lap. "It's a mistake I've paid for every day of my life since."

"Would it have been such a terrible thing for Kip to know Bud was her father?"

"Yes. Yes, it would have. Things were bad enough for Kip, but that would have been worse."

"I don't see how," I said. "Kemper was such an S.O.B. At least Bud didn't beat you."

She turned on me. "You don't know anything about not belonging, Sarah Booth. Don't lecture me on what it's like to discover that you're a bastard child. Don't ever try to tell me how it feels when you have your nose rubbed in the fact that the man you called Daddy has nothing for you but contempt. Every beating I took was for Kip. Every time Kemper struck me, it was only the thought of Kip's face that kept me from killing him on the spot. Weston McBride isn't my father. I don't know who my real father is, but when I came home pregnant and told my mother the truth, that was the end of me.

" 'Like mother, like daughter,' *my father* said. Those were the last words he ever spoke to me."

23

A large crack of thunder greeted me at Dahlia House. The old porch seemed to vibrate as I walked to the front door.

"Keep that storm outside—the rain *and* that thundercloud on your forehead," Jitty said before I could clear the threshold.

"I'm not in the mood for a sassy ghost who"—I checked out her black jumpsuit with the red racing stripes—"looks like an escapee from some sci-fi movie."

She put her hands on her slender hips, accentuating the spandex that clung in all the right places. "You've got mail, and somethin' tells me you'd better read it," she said defiantly.

"Not another word," I warned her. I went to the kitchen and began to rummage through the refrigerator for something to eat. I was angry, and any strong emotion required calories. I found a platter of leftover fried catfish and put it on the table. Catfish po'boys were an option.

I turned back to rummage for other possibilities.

Faster than a speeding bullet, Sweetie Pie made a lunge for the fish. Her houndish jaws snapped shut on all four pieces as she passed by, and before I could blink, there was nothing left on the platter but a couple of cold fries, some stray pieces of onion, and a puddle of grease.

"Sweetie!" I started after her, but she was out the doggy door and free.

"I told you that hound was gonna be nothin' but trouble." Jitty had come through the wall and was standing by the refrigerator.

"Jitty, I don't want to be chastised or lectured. Save it for a rainy day."

Prophetically, another deep echo of thunder rattled the windows, and raindrops the size of marbles began pelting down. Jitty walked past me, just a cool whisper blowing by. She went to the window and looked out at the Delaney family cemetery in the distance. I didn't have to look; I knew by heart the outline of the old tombstones, and the newer ones that marked my immediate family. I suddenly wondered where Jitty's bones had been buried. I was about to ask when the telephone rang.

I answered it, fully expecting Coleman. Cece's voice was low, as if she were whispering.

"I've just heard that Kip is alive."

"Your sources are accurate," I said. I wondered who was tickling Cece's ear with whispers.

"I think we should keep this quiet," she continued.

My agreement was total, but my curiosity was piqued. "Why?" I asked innocently. "So many people were traumatized by the fire, I would have thought you'd be rushing to press with a banner headline."

"Sarah Booth, dahling," Cece said with some contempt, "a true journalist knows the difference between a good story and the *seed* of a good story. This is just a tiny little sprout."

"And what do you see growing from this sprout?" I asked.

"A girl can't give away all of her secrets. Just tell Coleman to keep this hush-hush. I'm positive he'll agree with my assessment of the situation. I presume Lee is still in jail?"

"Yes."

"Good. She should stay there." Before I could respond to that, she continued. "She's protecting Kip, isn't she?"

I couldn't answer that question. As frustrated as I was with Lee, I couldn't violate her trust.

"Never mind answering, I don't need confirmation. What are you going to do?"

"Try to find Kip and the horse."

"And that delicious trainer," Cece said. She smacked her lips. "When you find him, tell him if he needs a place to stay, I have plenty of room."

"You're getting greedy, Cece. Can you handle Nathaniel Walz *and* Bud Lynch?" I couldn't help teasing her just a little. The developer was so definitely not her type, and yet she'd taken him to the ball as her date.

"Talent comes in surprising packages," Cece said somewhat coolly. "By the way, your entry in the Elvis contest was quite impressive. What was his name, Tom Smith? I hope you have a percentage in him. That man is going places." She cleared her throat, and her voice dropped to low and sizzling. "How far did he make it with you, dahling?"

The wickedness in her voice was the only thing that saved her. It was impossible to get angry with her when she was being so bad. "I don't kiss and tell." I'd actually forgotten about Tom. "Did he do well?"

"First place. By a large margin. Congratulations. He said to tell you he'd be in touch." I could imagine her smiling. "So what gives with you and the man with a badge?"

"Business," I said too quickly.

"I'm sure."

"Coleman's married." Even to me I sounded defensive.

"Not for long, from what I hear."

"So tell me, Cece, what is it about Nathaniel Walz that holds your interest?" I had to refocus the conversation, or Cece would soon ascertain that my feelings for Coleman, though confused, weren't all professional.

"He's a man with ideas," she said. "I like the way he can see into the future. That's a talent, Sarah Booth, as real as writing or painting or singing."

"What does he see?" I had to be careful. Cece sounded as if she really liked this man.

"Beautiful buildings, places that bring back the elegance of the old South."

"Does he have any locations in mind?" My heart rate increased, even though Harold had assured me that Dahlia House was safe.

"He's very secretive. That's one of the things I find so interesting about him. He knows a lot about this area, and he reveals only what he must."

"Does he have backing, or is he . . ." I almost said "a lot of talk." I had to remember that Cece had feelings for this man. While I'd barely spoken to him and didn't like what gossip I'd heard, Cece might have invested emotionally in him.

"He has yet to fully confide in me, but when he does, if there's a good opportunity, I'll let you know. Ta-ta, dahling, one of my best sources is on the other line."

She hung up, and I replaced the phone. Cece was not behaving normally. I couldn't help but wonder if her talk of secrets and withheld revelations had more to do with what she'd failed to tell Nathaniel Walz about herself than vice versa. I'd never known Cece to have an emotional attachment, and I'd never considered how hard it was going to be for her to reveal her past.

I looked around for Jitty. She'd taken herself off on some ghostly business, and I was spared having to confess that she was right about one thing—while I found safety in the past, Cece had hurled herself into a new future. Neither one of us was doing great in the romance department, though.

I was hungry, but had neither the energy nor the inclination to do anything about it. It took the very last of my strength to drag myself up the stairs and run some bathwater. When all else fails, a soak in a tub is the only alternative.

I used a liberal amount of some delicious foaming vanilla bubble bath that a friend in New York had sent me, lit candles, and got myself a hefty measure of Jack Daniel's on the rocks. I had a gut feeling that Jack and I were going to become good friends before the evening was over. If I'd belonged to the elite society of Daddy's Girls, I would have drunk white wine. Lucky me, as an outcast I could keep company with the rowdy boys.

I sank beneath the bubbles, forcing my body to relax one part at a time. Underwater, sound is completely distorted, but I thought I heard someone at the front door. I rose up out of the water and listened. The only thing I heard was the water dripping from my head and pattering into the tub. Sweetie Pie, though a food thief and shoe-chewer, was a pretty good watchdog. If someone had been around the house, she would have barked.

Tinkie had given me an inflatable bath pillow, and I made good use of it, reclining back. The Jack Daniel's had a bite, and I felt it burn all the way down. It was Sunday, and I'd been through an emotional wringer with the thought of Kip burning to death, and now her resurrection. Lee was lying through her teeth, but I didn't know how to save her without sacrificing the thing she loved most. I wanted to get very, very drunk, and I intended to do exactly that. I took another long swallow, rattling the ice cubes.

Not even whiskey could rout Kip from my

thoughts. I hadn't realized how disturbed she truly was. Was she mentally unbalanced enough to risk burning down Swift Level? Had she actually turned off the sprinklers? The fire had been contained to the stud barn, but one gust of wind and the flames could have been spread to the mare and foal barn, then on to the main barn or the covered show ring. Kip was fourteen, a child. But she was intelligent and surely capable of understanding the danger of starting a fire, and the consequences of murder, even for a man who so soundly deserved to die.

She was terribly disturbed, and I had to accept it. Lee, too, would have to come to terms with the truth. And soon.

I sponged water down my back and sank against my pillow. I polished off one drink and poured another from the crystal decanter of amber liquid. The storm had passed, and weak sunlight came through the window by the bathtub. I held the decanter aloft, enjoying the play of light on the glass and whiskey. I knew I had to call Dr. Vance in Memphis. I wondered if I could find him on a Sunday.

Sweetie Pie's toenails scrabbled on the oak floor in the foyer, and I listened for her to head up the steps. She was mostly a meat-and-potatoes kind of dog, but she also had a fondness for bathwater. I suspected she, too, was missing Kip. We could have a little drink together and commiserate.

Suddenly, there was a low growl that ended in a snarl. I had the sensation of an icicle dragged slowly up my spine. I eased out of the water, grabbed a towel, and slipped to my bedroom door. The extended growl came again from the landing of the stairs.

Someone was in the house.

Leaving sodden footprints behind me, I tiptoed over to the computer and picked up the telephone on my desk. The phone was dead. The damn computer modem was plugged in. Dahlia House needed an entire wiring facelift.

There was no time to scrabble around tracing a snarl of wires. My clothes were scattered over the floor, and for once it was a good thing. I found jeans and a blouse and slipped into them, stepping into some sneakers as I zipped my pants.

Outside, the day was ending on a note of fresh-washed glory. The storm had passed, and pink clouds burned to the west. The intense light gave the room a glow that made everything seem more vivid, as if the volume of color had increased, saturating everything. My blood was pumping hard as I looked around my bedroom for a weapon. I picked up a heavy candlestick and inched back to the door.

Sweetie's growl was even lower, more deadly, finally ending on a snarl and a snap. I heard her moving slowly up the stairs until she took her stand outside the open bedroom door. Crouching low, she readied herself for the attack.

She was not a hound who would back down in a shoot-out. She'd already rescued me twice, and in the process had taken a stab in the gut and a grazing wound from a bullet, not to mention having her sutures ripped open.

I pressed myself against the wall by the door, ready to rush out as soon as Sweetie made her move. If she could knock the intruder down, I would deliver the coup de grâce. I gripped the candlestick tighter, listening to the very soft tread on the stairs.

"You are one ugly-looking dog."

The voice was casual and feminine, not at all what I expected. I leaned against the wall and exhaled. Not that Krystal Brook wasn't a dangerous woman, but I didn't think she'd come to kill me while talking a blue streak to advertise her presence.

"Sarah Booth Delaney, call off this dog!" Krystal yelled.

"Have you ever heard of knocking?" I

asked, stepping into the doorway. "I was ready to bash your brains in."

"Seems to be a bad habit in this part of the country." She stayed on the top step, her gaze shifting from Sweetie to me. "I did knock. Repeatedly. The serving staff seems to be in a coma. No one came to the door. What kind of dog is that, anyway? I've never seen anything that ugly."

"Watch it," I warned her. "Sweetie Pie is a red tic, and she's mine. I happen to find her quite lovely."

She rolled her eyes. "There's no accounting for taste."

"How true. I never in a million years thought I'd see you prancing on a stage in white boots."

"Honey, my wardrobe is the least of my problems. You should try being married to your manager." She made a rueful face. "I stopped by because I wanted to check on you, and we never got a chance to talk. I suppose Bud's a moot issue, now." She shrugged, but it didn't hide the slight tremble in her voice.

The ice was melting in my drink, and a good hostess always offers her guest refreshments. "Let's go to the parlor and fix a drink," I suggested, pointing her back down the stairs.

"Bourbon on the rocks. It's five o'clock

somewhere in the world, as the old saying goes."

Following her down the stairs, I couldn't help but notice that a lot more had changed about Simpson than just her name. She'd developed a real fondness for whiskey.

She took a seat on the horsehair sofa in the parlor, and I poured the drinks. "What's going to happen to Lee?" she asked.

"I'm not sure," I said, taking an old wing chair. "No one really believes she killed Kemper, but she won't retract her confession."

"It's hard to believe that someone should be punished for killing Kemper Fuquar. If anyone ever deserved killing, it was him."

Her statement sadly echoed the defense Lee clung to so hardheadedly. "The law says that someone has to pay. Lee volunteered." I watched for any reaction.

Krystal held out her glass for a refill. I did the honors and resumed my seat.

"Kemper was a piece of shit from the first time I met him, and that was twenty years ago." She sighed. "I couldn't believe it when I found out Lee had married him."

"You knew him *before* they married?"

"Actually, Mike knew him. They went to school together. I only met him once. But from what Mike said, Kemper could be quite charming with the ladies. He would draw them over, and Mike would benefit from the varied selection. Mike said he was very surprised when Kemper married. I suppose someone should have warned Kemper that Lee had a real talent for pissing her daddy off."

Krystal had confirmed my darkest suspicions of Kemper's motives. He'd married for Lee's money, and then when it didn't come through, he'd set out to punish her every day for the rest of her life.

Krystal reclined on the sofa, putting one leg over the back in a pose that was both girlish and provocative. "Mike can be a bastard, too, but he knows how to make money." She finished off her drink. "That's his only talent, and the only reason I keep him around. Once my career is launched, he's history." She looked into the empty glass for a moment. "I'll have one more before I go, if you don't mind."

I didn't, and I got up and made her drink. I held up my own glass. "To Bud. I didn't know him well. Tell me about him." I was hoping she might know something that would lead me to where Bud had taken Kip and the horse.

Krystal's face softened. "Bud was all right. I took some riding lessons, hoping that there might be something there." She shook her head. "He liked to flirt, but I think he did it to aggravate the rest of his harem. If you want to know the truth, I think Carol Beth hit the nail on the head. He was in love with Lee. And that ate at Carol Beth."

"Any clue as to why Carol Beth was so jealous of Lee?"

Krystal tinkled the ice in her drink. "Lee asserted her independence. She just told her parents to kiss off, and she set about making her own life. They disinherited her and moved to Italy, and she never let it slow her down. Carol Beth has always made it off someone else. Her parents, her husband. She never stepped up to the plate and proved her own worth. I think that made her just a little bit crazy."

Krystal wasn't a psychologist, but she was smarter than the average bear, and her opinion confirmed what Harold had said.

"So what about Carol Beth and Bud?" I asked.

"Honey, she would have given up her wealth, her security, everything she had, just for a shot at Bud. I think he gave her just enough to make her crazy for him." She put her empty glass on a coaster and stood up. "Now, that's a talent more men should develop—giving a woman just enough. Sounds like the perfect title for a new country song. I think I feel a visit by the muse coming on. I guess I'd better go back to the stimulating creative atmosphere of the Holiday Breeze. Thank God, Mike used some of his real estate connections and found me a place. I'm moving to a house this afternoon. You know, I never expected to feel like coming home, but I think I'm going to enjoy living back here in Zinnia."

"It'll be good to have you home," I said, meaning it.

She stood up. "Let's plan on spending some time together. Right now, though, I've got songs to write."

I walked her to the door and watched her drive away. I took my half-filled glass and her empty one to the kitchen sink. Watching the whiskey slip down the drain, I wondered how it would feel to have just enough of anything. It was, indeed, a great song title.

24

Dusk had fallen, and I had miles to go before I slept. Krystal's visit had made me realize one thing: like my literary hero, Kinky Friedman, I couldn't abandon a friend in need. The Kinkster would never leave Ratso or Rambam or McGovern or any of his buddies in jail. Lee was innocent, and I was going to prove it.

My investigation had focused on everything but the victim, if Kemper could be described by such a term. Cece had made a few initial phone calls and determined that Kemper was something of a bad seed growing up. I hadn't pursued that avenue, and I didn't think Coleman had, either. Kemper had lived in Sunflower County for fifteen years. It was hard to believe anything in his past could be relevant, but maybe there was something.

I found the piece of paper Cece had given me with the telephone number for Kemper's parents on it. I dialed and listened to the ringing of the phone.

A woman answered in a voice both refined and tired.

I introduced myself and waded right in. "I'm working for Lee McBride."

"The woman who killed Kemper." The statement was made without emotion.

"Yes, ma'am. Lee's an old friend of mine."

"There's nothing we can tell you," the woman said. "Don't call again, or we'll be forced to pursue legal recourse for harassment."

"Mrs. Fuquar, my friend may spend the rest of her life in prison—"

"She shouldn't be punished. Kemper set out on this path long, long ago. I'm sorry for your friend, but there's nothing we can do to help. Our son has been dead to us for many years. We know nothing about him, except that he was a bad person."

"Please think about it," I said. "Lee has a daughter, a fourteen-year-old. She needs her mother."

There was a long silence. "We haven't spoken Kemper's name in this house for nearly twenty years. We can't help you, but there is someone who may be able to. Her name is Veronica Patriquin. She's a newspaper reporter." She gave me a telephone number. "She knows things about Kemper."

The line went dead.

Veronica Patriquin turned out to be a whiskey-voiced chain-smoker who knew her territory like a shark knows a coral reef.

"Kemper Fuquar, yeah, the name rings more than a bell," she said into the phone. "I heard a rumor that he was killed."

"He's dead," I confirmed.

"Let me think." She exhaled, and I wanted a cigarette with an intense craving. "I'll have to go back to some of my files. Can you hang on? None of that stuff is on computer now."

"Sure." I settled at the kitchen table to wait.

She was back in a few minutes, and I heard her turning pages as she talked. "I remember now. He and some partners bought an old estate. They were going to renovate it, make a resort. They sunk a lot of money in it, and then the place burned."

No big alarms were going off in my head, but a few bells were tinkling. Big estate. Fire. "And there was a huge insurance policy on the place, correct?"

"That about sums it up. As I recall, there was some speculation that the fire was arson, but no charges were filed. Shortly after that, Kemper disappeared. I guess that would be about the time he moved over your way."

"I think so."

"Why are you curious about Kemper's past?" she asked.

"His wife is a friend of mine, and she's charged with his murder."

"And you're hoping to dig up enough dirt from the past to develop reasonable doubt."

"Something like that," I said.

There was a long pause. "You want a list of the other investors in the resort?"

"Sure." I got a pencil and pad from a drawer. "Shoot."

"There were three of them. Kemper, a small-time gangster named Tony LaCoco, and somebody named Mitchell Raybon. LaCoco has gone on to local fame and fortune as what passes for a true mob figure around Louisiana."

LaCoco's name stopped me dead. "Thanks, Ms. Patriquin," I said. "You've been more help than you'll ever know. By the way, how much was the insurance settlement?"

"Three million. It was a nice, tidy little scam."

"And the insurance company?"

"It's right here in the story. Let me see . . . Liberty Associates. I think they're out of business now."

"Thanks again." I hung up the phone.

I placed a call to Billy Appleton at home. Billy didn't have to talk to me, but he didn't know that. I pressed my advantage. "Coleman asked me to check and see what you'd found on the Fuquar insurance papers," I told him.

"I was about to give him a call," Billy said. "I've searched high and low. As I told him earlier, I have the original policies, which were taken out in June of 1986. I remember Lee wanted policies that would provide re-placement values, but . . . Anyway, the policy will pay something toward the barn that burned. . . ." His voice faded away.

"And the horse?"

"Ah, no. There was nothing on the horse." He cleared his throat. "I wish I could say dif-ferently, Sarah Booth. I know how much that animal meant to Lee and her financial future. I called the home office just to see if maybe a policy had been filed through another agent. Nothing."

"You're sure?"

"Positive. We don't normally insure horses. If there was a policy, the home office would have known."

"And Kemper? What about his revised life insurance policy?"

"Ah," he cleared his throat. "Ah, there's a snag there. Ah, murder is sort of a different matter."

"As in?" I wanted to stick him with a cattle prod.

"There's a reluctance to pay off a claim when there's a charge of murder. See, the policy is designed to provide financial compensation in cases of natural death, acts of God . . . See, murder is very different. Especially murder to obtain the insurance."

"Kip was the beneficiary, not Lee."

"Very true," he said softly. "Ah, but Kip is dead. Lee now benefits."

I'd known Billy since he was six years old. In the first grade he'd gone through the desks in the entire classroom and stolen the red crayon from everyone's pack. He'd hoarded them in a cigar box, taking them out one at a time and sharpening them until there was only a box full of crayon curls.

"Are you saying the policies are invalid?"

"The home office makes those decisions, Sarah Booth." His words were rushed. "I'm only an agent. I'm not a policy maker."

"What's the good of insurance if it doesn't pay off?" I asked him pointedly.

"It's not supposed to be an inducement to murder."

"Lee didn't kill Kemper."

"No matter what you *think,* Sarah Booth, Lee has confessed."

"And if I prove someone else, or something else, killed Kemper?"

"That's another story."

"You'll be hearing from me."

"You'd better stop threatening me. I sell insurance policies, that's what I do. I don't make up the rules and I don't enforce them." He slammed the phone down.

Puzzled by Billy's panicked behavior, I dialed Tinkie. I didn't recognize her voice when she answered the phone.

"Oh, Sarah Booth," she said through a stuffy nose. "I was trying to get up the nerve to call you. I don't think I'm cut out for this private eye business after all. I'd better resign."

"Tinkie?" In the last few months, I'd grown to admire Tinkie in a number of ways, and a big one was her commitment to seeing something through. She wasn't a quitter. "Is Oscar giving you grief?" Her husband had a very narrow view of the Richmond family role in Delta society. I'd been blown away when he'd allowed her to become my partner in the first place.

"Oh, no, Oscar says I shouldn't quit." She sniffled. "It's just . . . Kip." She choked back a sob.

"Don't quit on me, Tinkie. I need you." I needed to tell her Kip was alive, but I had wanted to do it in person so I could impress on her that she had to keep it top secret. Tinkie had many valuable assets as a partner, but keeping a secret was not one of her strengths.

There was a long sigh. "Really?"

"Now more than ever. Lee needs us both, even if she won't admit it. I need you to do something." This was one she'd like. "Find out exactly what Mary Louise, Elizabeth, and Susannah did with Bud Lynch."

"Did?" Tinkie paused. "You mean *did*?"

"That's exactly what I mean."

"Why?"

"I have a theory, but I don't want to prejudice your investigation by saying it. Just find out."

"Okay," Tinkie said slowly. "I can do this."

"I'm certain you can. The only person who ever doubts your ability is you, Tinkie. You're the best partner a P.I. could ask for."

"Thanks, Sarah Booth." Tinkie lowered her voice. "What about Carol Beth and Bud?"

"Leave Carol Beth to me," I said with some malice.

"Oscar heard up at the bank that Benny is filing for divorce. And there is an ironclad prenup. If Benny can prove infidelity, Carol Beth won't get a penny from him."

"Oscar told you that?" Ever since Tinkie had begun to pump Oscar during nooners, he had become a gushing fount of informative tidbits.

388 *Carolyn Haines*

"Oscar said Benny may be mild-mannered on the surface, but he's a barracuda when he's protecting his assets."

"You do good work, Tinkie."

"I seem to have a little talent, don't I?"

"Absolutely. Call me as soon as you have anything," I said.

The ruins of the stud barn were visible from the county road. Carol Beth's big dually was parked at the main house, but I knew she'd be in one of the barns. I parked at the house, and took great care in walking quietly down to the main facility. Whatever Carol Beth was up to, I wanted to find out as much as possible before she saw me.

Hay was scattered down the central barn aisle, and as I entered, several horses lifted their heads, hay sticking from their mouths. They continued chewing, a comforting sound.

The office was empty, and there was no sign of Carol Beth in the feed room. I slipped up the stairs to Bud's loft apartment. The door was open, and I could hear someone inside. Using all the stealth I possessed, I slipped through the stark den to stand in the bedroom doorway. Carol Beth was straining to heave the big mattress up and over.

"Need some help?" I asked.

She screamed, dropping the mattress and whirling on me as if she would attack.

I slipped my hand into the pocket of my jeans and pulled out the gold pendant. Dangling it from thumb and forefinger, I held it aloft. "Looking for this?"

"Give it to me." She made a lunge at me, but I was quicker. The pendant slid back into my pocket.

"Not until you answer some questions."

"Look, Benny is going to divorce me and leave me without a penny. I need that pendant. Where did you find it, anyway?" She pushed a strand of hair out of her face, and I realized that she was in a state of complete disarray. Her shirttail was pulled from her breeches, and dirt smudged the fawn color of her pants and white shirt.

"You know where I found it." I looked at the bed pointedly. "I want some answers, Carol Beth. Now."

"People in hell want ice water. Give me that jewelry. It's mine."

I stepped back. "Okay, if that's the way you want to play it." I turned and walked out of the apartment and down the stairs. After only a few seconds I heard her clattering behind me.

"What do you want?" she demanded.

"Where are the insurance papers on Avenger?

Kemper took out a policy on that horse, and now it's conveniently disappeared." I never turned around, just kept walking down the barn aisle. "I was thinking maybe you didn't want Lee to collect."

She grabbed the back of my shirt. "I don't know. I never saw a policy. Why do people keep asking me that question?"

"Could it be because you're perceived as a chronic liar?"

"If I knew where the papers were, I'd tell you. They don't mean anything to me. I wanted the horse, not the money."

I doubted that, but there was a hint of desperation in her voice. "Why didn't you say that you and Bud were here, in the barn, the night Kemper was killed? Why did you lie?"

She paced down the aisle and back. Her face was composed when she finally looked at me. "The only thing I wanted was the horses. Benny will never believe that, though. I did what I thought I had to do." She tapped her fingers on the top of a stall. "None of that matters now. Bud is dead. My husband can never prove that I slept with him."

She was indeed cold-blooded, but she had a point. Now that she believed Bud and Avenger were dead, she'd be heading back to Virginia to mend fences with the man who paid her bills. I

had a few more questions. "What's your relationship with Tony LaCoco?"

Her fingers stilled, and her dark eyes focused
on me with the intensity of a laser. "I already
had a bill of sale on the horses. They were mine.
Legally. But Kemper was going to try and cheat
me out of them. The double-crossing bastard
took my money and apparently was going to
try to collect on an insurance policy. Kemper
owed LaCoco a whole lot of money. I thought
I could work out a deal with LaCoco."

"What really happened that night?"

She turned so that she was in profile to me.
"Bud wouldn't help me. I had to get him out
of the way, so I went to bed with him and put
something in his drink. Once he was unconscious, my intention was to load up Avenger
and the mares and take them. I could have
done it, too, but that moron Kemper was in the
barn office, and he wouldn't leave." Her tone
was laced with bitterness.

"You had the bill of sale. Would Kemper
have tried to stop you?"

"He had no intention of honoring the debt.
I couldn't risk it. He would have called Lee
down to the barn. She would have taken steps
to have my case disputed. There was a legal
point. The horses technically weren't Kemper's
to sell. I knew if the horses were in my posses-

sion, I'd stand a better chance in court." She turned to me. "Legally, they were mine—payment of a just debt."

"And the pendant?"

Her mouth twisted up at one corner. "Bud must have pulled it from my neck." She reached up to her throat. "I didn't realize it was gone until the next day."

"What else did you see that night?" It was out of character for me to believe anything Carol Beth said, but this story had the ring of truth to it.

"Kemper was in the office, from about eight o'clock until I left at one. I waited and waited for him to leave. He was on the phone, talking to someone he owed money to. They were threatening him."

"How could you tell?"

"He was lying, saying that he would have the money in a few days. He said he had a plan. A guaranteed plan. Then he laughed. He said he'd get the money and show his bitch of a wife who was boss. He said he'd kill two birds with one stone."

"Did you see him try to kill Avenger?"

She shook her head. "Bud started to come around. I knew I had to leave then."

"And you never saw anyone else in the barn?"

"You mean Lee?" She pushed a strand of mahogany hair behind her ear. "I wish I could say I saw her bash his brains out, but I didn't see anything."

"Lee confessed that she and Kemper were fighting, that she went to the barn and he followed her."

Carol Beth walked slowly toward the office door. She pointed inside. "He was there, at the desk, alone. That's what I saw." Anger crept into her voice. "If I'd taken Avenger, he would be alive now. Think about that. Kip would be alive. Lee would have her daughter. It's all such a stupid waste."

Pulling the gold pendant from my jeans, I tossed it over to her. She caught it and clutched it in her fist.

"This is the only bit of evidence that could possibly prove I had anything to do with Bud Lynch," she said. "I'm home free with Benny."

It was almost more than I could stand not to tell her that Bud was alive and still very capable of giving Benny the fine details of her sexual misconduct. Instead, I said nothing.

"I'm going back to Virginia," Carol Beth said. "Give Lee a message for me. Tell her she's a fool. Everyone in town is gossiping about her kid and what a psycho she was. Tell her that if she'd listened to that Memphis psychiatrist and put Kip in an institution, Avenger, Kip, and Bud would still be alive today."

She spun around and walked down the barn aisle, a long, lean silhouette who'd turned her back on what she'd once hoped was her future.

25

Driving through the darkness, I pondered
Carol Beth's cruel words. As Cece often
pointed out, it was impossible to keep secrets
in a small town. If it was true that Dr. Vance
had recommended institutionalization for Kip,
then it was time for Lee to face the truth. Sacrificing herself would not save her daughter.

The parameters of my case had changed
drastically. My original assignment had been to
dig up the details of Kemper's life that would
prove he deserved killing. I'd accomplished
that, and more. No one could dispute that
Kemper needed to die.

Now I had to convince Lee that she should
let Kip stand trial for the act she'd committed.
Temporary insanity was still a viable defense
for Kip, and a legitimate one, from what I'd
been able to discover. With some professional
help, Kip might stand a chance of holding on
to a portion of her future.

I doubted that Dr. Lazarus Vance would talk

to me at all, especially not late on a Sunday evening, but I was determined to give it a try. This was a call I dreaded making. I'd grown fond of Kip, and I didn't want to confront the possibility that she was mentally damaged.

I got Dr. Vance's home phone number from Information and placed the call. I was surprised when he answered the phone, identifying himself immediately.

I explained who I was and why I was calling, expecting the standard line about doctor–patient privilege. Instead, the psychiatrist cleared his throat.

"I've been very worried about Kip," he said. "I was so sorry to hear of her death."

"She isn't—" I stopped myself. He'd never talk to me if he thought she was alive. "How did you find out about the fire?" A barn fire in Zinnia hardly seemed the kind of story the Memphis newspaper would cover.

"Another of my clients told me. I've tried to contact Mrs. McBride, but she isn't taking my calls."

"As you can imagine, Lee's horribly upset. I'm trying to help her," I said. "What can you tell me about Kip?"

"I'm afraid I can tell you nothing."

"Dr. Vance, Kip is gone. I need information if I'm going to help her mother. I'm sure this isn't a violation of any doctor–patient privilege. Kip would want you to talk to me. She left a note clearing her mother of the murder."

"Since she's dead, I suppose there's no harm in talking," he answered, and I imagined that he was settling back into a comfortable leather chair, a pipe close at hand.

"Kip was a brilliant child. Too smart for her own good. And too conscientious. She carried the weight of that farm on her shoulders. The turmoil of her circumstances affected her more severely than it might another teenager, because of her need to protect her mother and the farm."

I didn't doubt any of this. "Kip said she was having blackouts."

"Yes, a minor break with reality when she couldn't bear any more. She'd just slip away, deep into a safe place in her own mind. It isn't that uncommon, really. Many of us do a similar thing in the form of daydreams. We're bored or uncomfortable, so we slide just beneath the surface of the mind. The danger is when such incidents become a frequent pattern, and when the break from reality is so deep that reconnection is difficult or time is lost."

"Could a person commit an act he or she didn't remember in such a state?"

He chuckled. "You're building a case, aren't you, Ms. Delaney?"

"I'm exploring a possibility."

"The answer is yes. In extreme cases."

"And was Kip an extreme case?"

"The answer is . . . yes. Kip was extreme, in more ways than one."

I didn't like the undertone of what he was saying. "What does that mean?"

"I got the feeling that Kip was frequently playing with me. She was a very clever girl. Of course, our relationship had not fully developed. She was my patient for only a few months."

My stomach knotted. "Playing with you how?"

"*Pretending* to be emotional, volatile. It did occur to me that Kip didn't actually suffer from blackout periods, that, perhaps, she was establishing an alibi for something. As I said, she was very clever. Quite a challenge."

"You prescribed several drugs for her." I kept my tone neutral.

"Standard practice. Kip had acted aggressively and violently toward another pupil. She was in danger of expulsion. Our public schools have become a battleground for many things, Ms. Delaney, among them the rights of certain students to disrupt the rights of others to learn.

It isn't an easy choice, for a parent or a doctor. Kip needed to stay in school, and the school needed some assurance that she would not attack another student."

"Attack? Is that an accurate description of what happened?"

"The classmate was taken to a doctor's clinic for eighteen stitches and a broken wrist."

"What?"

"Suffice it to say that Kip believed it was an accident. In her mind it was a shoving match, and the other young lady fell into an open locker. I have no way of knowing what actually occurred, but as you can clearly see, Kip was in serious trouble at school."

"Was Lee aware of the seriousness of Kip's condition?" Even if I didn't ask it, someone else would.

"We had several conversations about Kip. Mrs. McBride resented the fact that Kip was required to see me. She felt that Kip's anger and frustration were justified."

"Thank you for your time, Dr. Vance." I hung up the phone consumed with a gnawing dread, and a slow burning anger at Lee. Her attempts to protect Kip from the truth had only made things much, much worse.

Dr. Vance had spooked me. Badly. The one thing I knew for certain was that if Kip was

brought to trial for Kemper's murder, somehow Lee was going to have to prevent Dr.
Vance from testifying.

I got up and replaced the phone. The blinking red light on the answering machine indicated that I had missed calls. On the off chance
that someone had something good to report, I
punched the play button.

"Sarah Booth, it's J.B. here. Sorry you didn't
make it to Playin' the Bones this mornin'. I
was lookin' forward to seein' you. But I do
have something to tell you. Somethin' important. The rats are really runnin' around here,
and you'd be surprised who's head of the pack.
Why don't you give me a call, or even better,
drop on around by the Breeze to talk with me.
Maybe we can have a drink afterward. I'll keep
my ear to the wall until I hear from you."

A drink with J.B. sounded like the best offer
I'd had in a while. He'd also proven to be an
accomplished eavesdropper in the past. It
sounded like he'd overheard something big.

The clerk at the Holiday Breeze connected
me with J.B.'s room, and I let the phone ring
ten times before I gave it up and decided to
drive over.

The motel vacancy sign buzzed neon orange
as I turned off the highway just before an
eighteen-wheeler rolled over me. The suction

from the truck made me wonder how anyone slept in the motel. There were about five cars pulled up to the front of the rooms, including the black Town Car. I drove past the manager's office, where I could see a slender man leaning forward intently into a television.

J.B.'s room was dark, and I knocked loudly. Zinnia wasn't exactly a hotbed of late-night activities, so when there was no answer, I knocked again. Another truck roared down on me in the night, and I tried the doorknob. To my surprise, it turned easily.

The room was dark, but the truck lights briefly illuminated the double beds, the disarray of clothes, the television on the floor, and beside it a pair of legs that disappeared behind one of the beds. The black-and-white images were seared into my brain.

The passing truck suctioned the air out of my lungs as the lights faded and the room was returned to blackness. My hand was frozen on the doorknob. I stood there, breathing, unable to move. At last I reached inside and flipped on the light. This time the images were full color—a vivid bloodred.

Blood had soaked into the carpet beside J.B.'s outstretched right arm. I forced myself to move forward, to look at him. The blood seemed to come from a wound on the back of his head. His eyes were closed and his face was very, very pale.

"J.B." I whispered his name as if I didn't want to disturb him from a light sleep.

In my entire life, I'd seen only a handful of bodies. Finding Lawrence Ambrose dead last Christmas had been a trauma, my first view of fatal violence. Before that, my experience with death had been relegated to the paneled, carpeted chapels of the local funeral homes where the dead reposed with painted faces and crimped hair.

My impulse was to run, but I knelt beside him. Hand shaking, I touched fingertips to J.B.'s neck, surprised that he was warm. Beneath my fingers a thready pulse flickered.

"Nine-one-one!" I grabbed the phone by the bed and got the clerk on the line. "Nine-one-one," I repeated. "Call them now. Send an ambulance and call the sheriff."

"We don't have no trouble in the Breeze," the clerk said gruffly.

"There's a man injured. Call an ambulance now!" I hung up and went back to kneel beside J.B. "Hang on, J.B. Help is on the way."

I forced myself to look around the room. I tried to think of the things I should do—the actions a private investigator would take in such circumstances. My job was to observe, to note details, to register the small things that might be useful in determining who had attempted murder. I touched nothing, but I did note the suitcase thrown against the wall, clothes spilling out everywhere. J.B.'s possessions had been searched. The bathroom door was off the hinges.

The weapon was easy enough to identify: the base of the bedside lamp. It was a heavy, ugly piece that now lay beside J.B.'s cracked skull.

He moaned softly, and I pressed lightly on his chest to keep him from moving. I didn't know the extent of his injuries, but I was afraid that if he began to struggle, he would only do more damage to himself.

"Find her," J.B. said. His hand clamped suddenly over my wrist in a painful grip. "Find her!"

"I will, J.B. I will." I looked again at the bathroom. Had his mother returned? Was she injured, or dead, in the bathroom? "Everything's fine," I said, attempting to soothe him.

In the distance, I could hear the sound of sirens approaching. It seemed to take forever before the flashing blue lights stuttered through the window blinds of the room.

Coleman came in first, his hand on the butt of his gun. As soon as he saw me, kneeling

beside J.B. in all that blood, he called the paramedics into the room.

J.B. stirred again, his brow furrowing as he
tried to open his eyes. "Find her," he said again.
"They're goin' to kill her."

"It's okay," I said, "we'll find her." I nodded
at the bathroom, and Coleman instantly moved
toward it. This time he drew his gun. It took
only a few seconds to determine that the room
was empty. By then, the paramedics had arrived with a stretcher and were busy stabilizing
J.B. so they could transport him to the hospital.

"I'll follow the ambulance," I told Coleman.

"Then I want to talk to you," Coleman said.
"I'll be waiting at the courthouse."

It was long past midnight when I left the
hospital. J.B. had not regained consciousness,
and there was talk of transferring him to
Memphis. I had not wanted to leave him,
but there was nothing else for me to do, and
Coleman was waiting. I had no doubt of that.

Rumpled and tired, Coleman poured fresh
coffee and pushed a cup across to me. We were
standing in the main office, the counter between us. I was on the side of freedom, he on
the side of the law.

"This is just one big tragedy," I said, wondering what, exactly, Coleman wanted to talk about. He was a perceptive man, and the telephone interview with Dr. Vance weighed heavily on my mind. While Coleman was sworn to discover the truth, I was hired to protect Lee, which meant protecting Kip.

Coleman said nothing. His blue gaze merely held mine. His scrutiny made me even more uncomfortable. Putting down his coffee cup, he leaned across the counter and took my hand. He held it, palm open to the light. He studied it for a long time, then drew a finger lightly from my wrist to the tips of my fingers. The power of his touch caught me by surprise.

He looked back into my eyes. "I get the sense that no one has told the complete truth in this case. If you know something you haven't told me, now would be the time."

He still held my hand, the lightest of touches, and I had to admire his tactics of interrogation. They were incredibly effective. "Kemper was involved with Tony LaCoco in an insurance scam in Louisiana before he married Lee. It was the two of them and a third man named Mitchell Raybon."

"Mitchell Raybon," he said. "Should I know the name?"

"I don't. I got it from a newspaper reporter in Lafayette."

Coleman nodded. He smoothed his thumb across my palm. "Good work. Now tell me where Kip is, and the horse."

"I don't know."

He gently bent my fingers back as if he might find the answer to his question in my palm. "I have to find her, Sarah Booth. For her sake. Was J.B. Washington talking about Kip when he told you to find her?"

I sighed. "I really don't know what he meant. He left a message at Dahlia House. He's been snooping around a little, eavesdropping, that kind of thing."

"And reporting to you," Coleman finished, making it sound as if I were responsible for J.B.'s condition.

"He liked doing it."

"It had nothing to do with him liking you?"

Putting it that way made me sound even more responsible. "He didn't really know me."

"But he wanted to, didn't he?"

I could only stare at our hands on the countertop. "The message J.B. left said something about how the rats were really running now. He said he'd overheard something important. I went to the motel as soon as I got his message."

Coleman eased my hand to the counter.

"Whoever struck him meant to kill him. That's an extreme measure to take if he was merely hanging around the motel, picking up gossip."

"I guess it depends on who the gossip involves."

Coleman leaned forward on his elbows. "That's true. Be careful, Sarah Booth. Somehow the stakes in this case have changed."

"Coleman, did you run across anything that might indicate Kemper had insured Avenger?"

He picked up his coffee cup. "Billy Appleton said he spoke with you, so you know his story. The horse wasn't insured."

"Not by Billy."

"There are companies that specialize in insuring horses. I checked all of them. There's no record of a policy taken out by Kemper Fuquar on a stallion."

"Could it be in Kip's name? Or someone else's?"

He shook his head. His hand on the counter moved toward mine, but stopped less than halfway. "This case doesn't add up. We're missing something, Sarah Booth. Something very important. You need to know that Lee talked to Boyd earlier this evening. They're trying to come up with some kind of involuntary manslaughter plea bargain. She's decided to plead guilty and avoid a trial altogether."

My frown must have tipped him off as to my thoughts.

"It isn't what I want, but Lee refuses to help herself. This would be better than risking a trial for murder. She can do a little time, get paroled out, and pick up what's left of her life without losing anything more."

There was an element of sadness in his voice that chilled me. "I don't know," I said. I wasn't willing to give up.

He gave me that lopsided grin that made him look about fourteen. "You can be a bulldog, Sarah Booth."

I took it as a compliment, which showed how far I'd fallen from my Daddy's Girl ways. In my former incarnation as a DG, the only reference to a dog that would have been a compliment was being called a real bitch—in the sense that my high standards for a man were hard to meet.

"Connie called earlier. I've got to run home for a while. She's been doing some thinking, and she wants to talk. Try not to stumble on any more wounded bodies tonight."

"You got it," I said as I walked out of the office and into the empty halls of the courthouse. My footsteps echoed hollowly off the vaulted ceiling, and I looked up the double set of staircases that led to the courtroom. This was the place where my father had told me that justice balanced the scales. He'd never told me how hard it was to find the evidence.

Jitty was sitting on the front porch steps, and I was relieved to see her. Sweetie Pie, too. The hound was stretched out, sleeping off the adventures of her day. Since Dr. Matthews had removed her regenerated ovaries, she was a more relaxed—and better-smelling—pet. Not too far in the distant past, when a man had a "disobedient" wife, he'd take her in for a bit of surgery. Once her ovaries were snatched out, she might get a little weird, but she lost all of those unfortunate impulses toward sexual identity.

Of course, a Delaney, like Sweetie Pie, would just have grown a new set of ovaries. I, personally, had regrown my tonsils after they were surgically removed. Regenerating body parts. It was a fine genetic tradition to uphold.

I sat down beside Jitty.

"Pretty bad day, huh?" she asked.

It didn't take me long to fill her in on the graphic details of the assault on J.B.

"If I could hold a glass, I'd make you a drink," she said.

"Grand idea!" I went inside and made a

double, because it was only polite to drink for her, too. I rejoined her on the steps and stroked Sweetie's silky hound ears. I'd neglected the water in my "Jack and water," and the bite was harsh and welcome.

"You've done everything you could do," Jitty said in the gentlest tone I'd heard her use in a while.

"I suppose." I didn't have it in me for an argument. J.B. Washington's battered body was wedged on the edge of my subconscious, and I intended to drink that image away. Arguing would only hamper the process.

"Sarah Booth, I've been giving this some thought. What do you see in your future?"

Jitty had been on this kick about the future all month. Even tonight, she was tricked out in some glistening fabric that caught the moonlight and spangled it in the amber weave. Still, the future was better than her prior obsession—the fifties, where she'd taken the wholesome image of June Cleaver to the point of making me want to hurt her. The problem with her question was that I had no clear view of the future. "I see Dahlia House painted and looking like she used to look. I see me sitting at the kitchen table paying my bills, writing out checks without having to wonder if I might be arrested when they bounced."

"And who do you see with you?"

That question opened a black hole in my heart. "Jitty, I don't have that kind of imagination."

"Harold would look nice standing there beside you."

My smile was fleeting. "He's a good man. You were right about him."

"And?"

"And nothing."

"If you had Harold sitting here beside you, there wouldn't be a need for discussion. A man has a way of takin' a woman's mind off her troubles."

"And, if everything is working properly, producing an heir to Dahlia House at the same time, right?" Jitty was as single-minded and pigheaded as all of my other acquaintances.

"That sheriff is a good-lookin' man. Why don't you find a reason for him to apprehend you? A thorough search might be fun."

"Jitty!" I gave her a hard look, and realized that in the outfit she was wearing, a man wouldn't have to touch her at all to get a list of her assets. "Where'd you get that dress? It barely covers possible, as Aunt LouLane so delicately referred to the female anatomy."

"I love these modern fabrics. All suction and no ironing." Jitty smoothed her hands over her torso. "But I'm not the focus of this conversation. You are. You and the future, which is pretty bleak if it only includes paint for Dahlia House and money in the bank. I want to hear the pitter-patter of little feet, and no matter how independent you are, Sarah Booth, you can't get pregnant alone. That Coleman, now, he'd make a good daddy."

I gave Jitty a sideways glance. "Perhaps you've missed the fact that he's married."

"Yeah, I guess one of us missed that fact." She stood. "Maybe you should go to Paris and visit Hamilton. If you time it right, you could come back with the goods."

"I can't afford to give birth to 'the goods,' as you so charmingly call it. I can't private detect *and* raise a baby. Besides, I wouldn't use Hamilton that way."

She rolled her eyes. "Please don't throw Mr. Hamilton into that mean ol' briar patch!"

She'd used her height as an advantage, so I stood and moved up two steps. "Jitty, I've had a really bad day. Can we talk about men tomorrow?"

"Fine, put it off 'til your innards are as black and shriveled as your heart. The future is just one second from now, you know."

"Jitty, why don't you focus on the present?" I thought it was a brilliant retort.

"Huh! You're a fine one to talk. You cling to the past like it's your favorite pair of sweat-pants."

The arrow of truth struck with a sting of pain. I did have a habit of living in the past. How could I help it, with a ghost from the 1850's lurking in my home and the curse of tradition in every corner of the house? But there was more to Jitty's accusation. I knew what she meant, and the truth of it was fright-ening.

"I don't want to get hurt again. Loss is something I have no desire to experience again."

"I know that, Sarah Booth. I know it well. I lost people I love, too. But the only thing that makes all the sufferin' worthwhile is bein' able to love again."

Jitty's words held wisdom. I turned to thank her, but I was alone on the porch with a gently snoring Sweetie Pie and the darkest hours of the morning ahead of me.

I got up and went inside. I couldn't remem-ber the last time I'd had a meal, so I went to the kitchen and made two peanut-butter-and-jelly sandwiches. Dr. Matthews had fussed at me about Sweetie Pie's rapid weight gain, but then the good doctor was thin as a rail and didn't have to suffer the emotional flux of the

Delaney womb. Chocolate would have been best, but peanut butter was a good second choice.

Sweetie and I smacked our way through the sandwiches, and I took myself off to bed and the Kinky Friedman novel that had seen me through the last long night. Like Kinky, I was blessed with good friends. Tinkie was the perfect partner. Her only drawback was that she was married and didn't frequent bars.

I took my book and settled beneath the covers. The night was still chill enough to make the comforter a real comfort, and I immersed myself into the cigar-smoking, espresso-making world of the Kinkster.

26

When I woke on Monday, I was surprised to see the sun streaming in the bedroom window. Only seconds before, I'd been in a dark New York City bar sharing a bottle of Jameson with Kinky.

He'd had on his black cowboy hat, black shirt, black vest, and a purple boa that hailed from his days as opening act for Bob Dylan. The dream had been brief, but pointed. He'd used his first and second fingers to do a little Broadway dance number along the bar while he sang, "Let your fingers do the walking."

I groped for the phone book even before I headed downstairs to make coffee. It was just after eight, and I called Dr. Matthews, Zinnia's top veterinarian and the man who'd saved Sweetie Pie's life.

"Where would a person get enough insulin to kill a horse?" I asked him without preamble.

"Funny you should ask," he said. "I'm missing some drugs."

I was suddenly wide awake. "What kind of drugs?"

"A bottle of Banamine and the insulin. I try to keep some on hand. I didn't notice it gone until yesterday."

"When was the last time you saw it?"

"Last Sunday, I was out at Swift Level on an emergency call. Lee was having trouble with a foaling mare. The drugs were in the truck. I remember because I had to rummage around to get the things I needed to help deliver the foal."

There was no delicate way to proceed. "Who could have taken them?"

"Anyone there, except Lee. She was with me the entire time." His voice was firm, and I was reminded that his friendship with Lee spanned two decades. He was playing it as she had asked him to.

Still, I had to try. "Speaking of time, when did you leave Swift Level?"

There was a long pause. "I'm sorry, but I'm a little confused on that point. It was a long and difficult birth, and I was very tired. I wasn't paying attention to the time."

"Thanks, Dr. Matthews." Caught between loyalty and the law, he wasn't going to contradict Lee's story—at least until he was under oath and forced to do so.

I placed a second call to the hospital to check on J.B. His condition was stable and the doctors had decided not to transfer him. He was still unconscious, but I would be allowed to visit.

I was dressed and walking out the front door when Tinkie pulled up. She'd changed cars, upping her trademark Caddy to the latest model in a handsome hunter green.

"I heard about that musician. My goodness, Sarah Booth. Are you okay?" she asked as she came up the front steps. She made the art of high-heel walking look easy.

"I'm fine. I think J.B.'s going to be fine, too." That was more wish than fact, but I was clinging to it.

"I have some news for you," Tinkie said.

"I have some for you, too." I took a breath. "Kip and Bud are alive. So is Avenger."

Tinkie moved gracefully to one of the rocking chairs on the porch and sat. "They're alive?" Her blue eyes were wide.

"Tinkie, you can't tell a soul. Not even Oscar. Everyone has to believe they're dead. Kip may be in real danger." I told her what J.B. Washington had said as he gripped my arm. "I think he overheard some plan to hurt Kip. I think that's why he was attacked."

"Where is Kip?"

"That's the million-dollar question. Coleman's searching for her. Lee says she doesn't know."

I gave Tinkie a few moments to digest the news. In the fields on either side of the veranda, flocks of crows settled onto the newly plowed earth. Willie Campbell was getting ready to plant. Would it be cotton or soybeans? I hadn't asked him.

"Coffee!" Tinkie demanded. "Make it strong."

"I'll get us a cup," I said. I knew just how she felt.

When I returned with the coffee, Tinkie was staring out into space. "Are you okay?" She was still too quiet and too wide-eyed.

"Who burned the barn?"

"I'm not certain," I said. It was a damn good question.

"Did Kip set that fire?"

"Maybe," I admitted. "I'm just not sure."

She rocked for a moment longer. "My news is a bit anticlimactic. Bud never slept with Mary Louise or Elizabeth or Susannah."

My discoveries into Bud's relationship with Lee and Kip had somewhat prepared me for the truth. This was the theory that I'd hoped Tinkie could prove for me. Bud was a man women wanted, and when they didn't get him, they simply lied. It was an interesting bit of psychology to chew on at a later date. Right now, it confirmed my belief that Bud, though he had slept with Carol Beth in an attempt to save Avenger, was deeply in love with Lee. "Did the girls actually admit they hadn't slept with him?"

"With much chagrin and a lot of begging that I keep this to myself," Tinkie said. She narrowed her eyes as she stared at me. "You aren't surprised? Everyone in town had the idea that he had a revolving door into his bedroom."

"Bud is Kip's father."

Tinkie sat back in her rocker so hard she hit the wall. "Holy shit." She threw a hand up over her mouth. "Excuse me, that just slipped right out. Bud is Kip's *daddy*?"

Repeating a fact is also a DG method of emphasis and backhanded flattery, showing that a real juicy and unexpected tidbit has been revealed. The original spokesperson can then repeat the fact for additional effect. I was glad to oblige.

"Lee admitted it."

"Why in the world didn't she dump that loser Kemper and marry Bud?"

"It's a long story," I said. "A long, sad story that has a lot to do with living up to others' expectations. That and the fact that Kemper owned Swift Level and Lee's secrets. He was a master at emotional blackmail."

Tinkie had grown pensive, her lively face settling into an expression of sadness. "What a terrible waste. Bud and Lee are a lot better suited for one another. And Kip adores Bud." Tinkie used her tiny little feet in their child-size, lime-green high heels to push her rocker gently back and forth. "What a hell it must have been for Lee. Kemper was ruining her financially. Kip was being forced to watch her parents eviscerate each other on a regular basis, including physical abuse, and, down in the barn, Bud was doing his best to make everyone believe he was screwing everything that walked."

"To keep Kemper from realizing Bud's true motivation for being at Swift Level, I can only presume," I said. "And to save Avenger, where Carol Beth is concerned."

Tinkie shook her head in bemusement. "All of those women thought the others were screwing Bud, so they said they were doing it, too. No one wanted to be the one left out, so they all just started lying, and with each lie they upped the ante."

I felt the beginning of a laugh build. "It's almost too good," I said. One-upmanship was the basis for most conversations among DGs, but this was the extreme. Normally, competitions had to do with the most expensive gift, most boring husband, most doctor's appointments in a week's time, and most disciplinary actions taken against their children at school that required parental intervention and unconditional defense.

Now, headed toward their mid-thirties, the DGs were feeling the pinch of time and had added sexual notches to the competition list. At least Bud was a trophy worth bragging about.

Tinkie was getting angrier with the women as I grew more amused. "That Susannah! We had a couple of drinks at The Club, and she told me how good Bud was in bed. She gave me details that actually made me blush. And she'd made every bit of it up." Tinkie rocked faster. "Those girls!"

"You did an excellent job, Tinkie."

"They tricked me."

I leaned forward in my rocker so she had to look me eye to eye. "Only because they so effectively tricked themselves. And me, and Coleman, and half the town. I thought they were sleeping with Bud, too. He was as guilty in that little charade as the women were."

Tinkie sipped her coffee. "I guess. The bottom line is that none of that really matters. We've just been chasing our tails."

Tinkie had a way of cutting to the heart of the matter. "I have another assignment for you." I told her my theory that Kemper had tried to kill Avenger for insurance money. "Both Mike Rich and Roscoe, the stable hand, mentioned an insurance policy on the horse. There has to be one. The person named as beneficiary will have a lot of explaining to do, assuming it isn't Kemper, and I'm pretty positive the policy is in someone else's name. Do you think you could make any headway with Billy Appleton? We need to find that policy."

"Billy's kind of weird, but he isn't a liar. If he says there isn't one, I think we have to accept it as fact."

I nodded agreement. "I don't think he's lying, but maybe you could convince him to look a little harder. I know there's a policy. We just haven't been able to figure out how to find it."

"I can do that. Oscar went out on a limb and helped Billy secure a loan for his new insurance office. You know, the interior is entirely red. Remember when he stole all the red crayons in first grade? It's like he wants all the red in the world."

I did remember. "Talk to him, Tinkie. Getting men to do your bidding is your forte."

She smiled. "That's not a talent, that's a knack."

"Where's Chablis?" I asked. Tinkie hardly went anywhere without the dust mop.

"At Canine Curls. She just had to have a lift to her color. It was getting plumb mousy." Her gaze slipped past me and toward the door of the house. "Don't take this the wrong way, Sarah Booth, but I made an appointment for Sweetie Pie. They have this wonderful new cosmetic veterinarian from France! I've booked a consultation for Sweetie Pie for a breast reduction." She held up a hand at my protest. "I know she's had puppies and that just naturally makes the breasts sag, but she's still a young dog. And I'm paying for everything. I'll even pick her up and take her myself."

When I turned around, Sweetie was standing in the open doorway of Dahlia House. She'd slept in, and her ears were a mess. My gaze shifted down her body to the rounded belly and the telltale shadow of dangling nipples. "Don't worry, Sweetie, no surgery. I promise."

The hound stepped into the sunlight, blinked, then began to bark as a silver Taurus pulled up behind Tinkie's new Caddy. Nathaniel Walz got out of his car and began to walk toward us.

"Tinkie, don't leave," I whispered. "I'm afraid if I don't have a witness, I may kill him."

"What does he want?" she whispered back as we both watched him approach.

"He was asking Harold about the possibility of buying Dahlia House for one of his development projects."

"Get the garlic," Tinkie said, stepping up beside me.

"Miss Delaney," Walz said, smoothing his silk tie. "I hope I'm not interrupting. I've come to ask for your help in a very delicate matter." He was a handsome man, flawed only by his diminutive size and his nattiness.

"How could I possibly help you?" I asked. It was an honest question with a tiny stinger of sarcasm on the end.

"Your friend, Ms. McBride—I'd like to help her out, but she won't even give me a chance to talk to her."

"Lee isn't exactly in a position to entertain guests," I pointed out to him.

The ringing of the telephone halted the conversation. I started to step back inside, but Tinkie touched my shoulder.

"I'll get it," she volunteered. She ran up the steps and into the house, with Sweetie Pie right behind her.

"My desire to speak with Ms. McBride isn't social," Walz said. "It's business." Even as he spoke his gaze swept over Dahlia House and the land around it. In his eyes I could see asphalt and strip malls rising out of the earth, multiplying, followed by subdivisions. There were different visions of the future, and though I didn't have a firm grasp on my personal vista, I knew what I wanted for my home. Nathaniel Walz was the antithesis of it.

"It would be better if you waited until Lee's out of jail. She's having a rough time right now." I took a step toward the front door. As far as I was concerned, the discussion was at an end.

"I was at the ball. What a terrible loss. Her horse and her daughter, all in the same fire." He sighed. "I could see the hard work and love she put into Swift Level. It is a magnificent place."

"Yes, it is." I knew where Walz was heading, and even the thought was offensive. Before I could put a halt to his developing advance, Tinkie came down the steps, a puzzled expression on her face.

"It was some prankster with a funny name.

He said he was leaving the Memphis airport and to 'hold the wedding,' that he was on his way to Dahlia House to help you save the cats."

"What?" I was stumped. "Wedding? Cats?"

"That's what he said. He said you'd know what it meant."

I didn't. But I knew what Walz meant to do, and he was the immediate concern. "Why do you want to see Lee?" I asked.

"I'd like to buy Swift Level." He held up both hands as if he expected us to try and hit him. "I'm making the offer now. I could wait until it all goes to hell around her, and then get the place for a song."

Before I could even think of a response, Tinkie jumped at him. On her high heels she was just his height, and she leaned into his face. "You, sir, are a cad and a profiteer. Do you really think Sarah Booth or I would help you convince Lee to sell her home to you?"

Walz remained calm. "She'll sell to me or someone else, but she'll sell. And then I'll buy it. Swift Level is perfect for my development. I've searched all over the state, and it is exactly the piece of real estate I want."

"Lee won't sell," Tinkie insisted.

"Ladies, she has no choice. That horse was her future, and he's dead. Her kid is dead. She's going to prison. I know for a fact the note on Swift Level is a backbreaker. Ms. McBride simply can't afford a five-thousand-dollar-a-month mortgage. The renovations, the repairs, the maintenance, the livestock—it's a very expensive way of life."

He raised his hand, but before he could say anything, Sweetie bounded down the steps, a low growl issuing from her throat, and her tail, which normally wagged like a metronome, dangerously rigid.

"I'm afraid I'm going to have to ask you to leave," I said. I put a restraining hand on Tinkie's arm. Like Chablis, she was small but fierce. She was ready to leap on Nathaniel Walz and gnaw him to shreds. Sweetie would go for the big chunks.

Still unruffled, Walz reached into the jacket of his coat and handed me a sealed envelope. "Speak to your friend. Give her this. It's my offer in writing, and I assure you it's a generous one. Far more generous than anyone else will make. But I need an answer by tonight. I have investors, and they're growing restless."

He got back in his car and drove away.

"The nerve of that man," Tinkie fumed.

"How did he know how much Lee's note is?" I pondered. "Not even Cece would know that."

"Even if she did, she wouldn't tell him," Tinkie said, but there was a frown on her face. "Would she?"

"Pillow talk can be deadly," I said. "Tinkie, we need to get busy. See what you can find on that insurance. I'm going to pay a call on Cece."

"Tell her if she's joined Nathaniel Walz's camp, we're going to cancel our subscription to the newspaper."

"Will do," I said, as I got my car keys and headed for *The Zinnia Dispatch* and Cece's store of information, printable and not.

27

Cece eyed my empty hands as I slipped into her office and took the only available seat—a perch on the edge of a chair that was stacked with yellowed copy paper and magazine clippings.

"Tinkie just called. She said to remind you she's got Sweetie Pie and is taking her to her appointment. If you'd enter the twenty-first century and use a cell phone, I wouldn't have to play secretary for you. So where is Sweetie going?"

Cece was curious about my dog's social agenda, but I ignored her. There were other issues to be explored, but a frontal attack was never wise. I had devised a bush-beating assault. "If I used a cell phone, you'd have nothing to complain about. I'm not the slave of technology that you are."

"Your hairdo could use an update, too."

I ignored her jabs. "The night of the fire, did you see anything unusual at the ball?"

She leaned back in her chair and templed her fingers. Her nails were a shimmering shade of orange that looked suspiciously like the hard-to-find Mango Magic. She had the matching lipstick, too. Cece's sources—for news and cosmetics—were tightly guarded secrets.

"Didn't Kip set the fire? Since we both know she's alive, I just assumed she'd concocted the plan to get Avenger out of town before Carol Beth could snatch him."

"I'm not so sure." I was having second thoughts. "Avenger could have died in that fire. So could Bud. And it could have spread to all the other barns. Would Kip have risked all of that, if her intention was to save Avenger and her mother?"

Cece tilted her head, considering. A beautiful diamond earring glinted from beneath her hair. "I see your point. But who else would burn the barn?"

"Tell me what you remember from that evening."

"The entire thing happened so fast. I'd only arrived at the ball an hour before. I just missed that incredible scene with Carol Beth and her husband, which I'm still trying to get details on. Then someone rushed into the ballroom and yelled that the barn was on fire. Everyone went streaming out into the night, and there was the awful sight of the flames coming out of the hayloft. From there it was simply pandemonium, as everyone ran around in the dark trying to think of something to do."

"Do you remember seeing Bud or Kip before the fire?"

"Before I saw them framed in the burning doorway, right before the hayloft collapsed on them? No. Well, Bud was at the ball, of course. No one with a quivering hormone in her body could have failed to see him." Her fingers moved in and out like a bellows as she concentrated. "I really can't say the last time I saw him." One eyebrow lifted. "Then again, I don't know when or why you and Coleman left. Together."

I ignored the implication. "Was there anyone at the ball you didn't recognize?"

She shook her head. "I've thought of that already. It was all the usual suspects and their dates."

"And what about your date?" I left it wide open.

"What about Nathaniel?" she asked.

"Was he with you at all times before the fire?"

She didn't bat an eye. "He wasn't at my side like a trained dog, if that's what you're asking.

He was talking with Mike and Krystal about their new home, and he was also talking with Carol Beth."

"What do you know about Walz?" I asked her.

"Not enough. Not nearly enough. But I smell a really big story." There was a glint in her eye that took me by surprise.

"What are you up to, Cece?"

"Don't you find it strange that a developer with a fat bankroll should appear in town just at the same time that Tony LaCoco does? Nathaniel Walz dragged me all over the Delta looking at property, but he knew what he wanted when he came here. He wants Swift Level, and I'm wondering what he and his friends will do to get it."

"He just made a formal offer." I slipped the unopened envelope from my purse and handed it to Cece. She slid a lacquered nail beneath the flap. In a moment she had the document out and her face told the story. Outrage.

"He's only offering a tenth of what Swift Level is worth. We should string him up."

"Surprise, surprise," I said.

"What else did you find out about Walz?" I asked. I felt only a twinge of guilt that I'd ever doubted Cece. I should have known that her taste in men was as impeccable as her taste in clothes and wine.

"He's very smart. Very. And he has plenty of money behind him. I think it's LaCoco's money, but I can't prove it."

"J.B. told me that Walz had somehow pissed Kip off. Did he ever say anything about that?"

Cece shuffled the papers around her desk until she pulled up a white napkin, and began to snack on a piece of cookie. "You should have brought some fresh Danish," she admonished. "One can't talk this intensely without sustenance."

"Cece! Don't toy with me."

She rolled her eyes. "The night of the fire, Nathaniel talked to Kip about buying Swift Level. He said she showed up at the Holiday Breeze and he 'seized the opportunity.' That's why we were late getting to the ball. Nathaniel said Kip was very angry with him. He said she threatened him."

I didn't doubt that for an instant. The idea of someone trying to buy her home wouldn't exactly endear him to Kip. "Do you think Walz might have set the barn fire?"

Cece shook her head. "I don't think so. He really was with me most of the time." She arched one well-drawn eyebrow. "In fact, he made it a point to stay close. Almost as if he wanted to be sure he had an alibi. Even when he was talking with someone else, he'd wave across the room at me."

Epiphanies are seldom wrought with fireworks and marching bands. Cece's last statements unlocked a door, a tiny click of a latch. "Does it seem strange to you that Kemper is killed and an attempt is made to burn down a barn and kill a prize stallion, all at the same place and all within a week's time?" I was leaning forward.

"If Lee hadn't confessed—"

"And if Kip hadn't been the perfect suspect—"

"We would have been looking for someone who would gain financially from all of this," Cece finished.

"Someone like Nathaniel Walz," I said. "And Carol Beth would get the horses she wanted."

Cece picked up the phone and began to dial. "Nathaniel closed the deal for Krystal and Mike on their house. Maybe they can tell us more about Mr. Walz." Cece continued to talk as she waited for someone to answer the phone. "The place used to be called Putnam Hall. Krystal said she needed some privacy. She's due to cut her first album, and she wants to write some original songs." Cece's eyebrows were arched with pride. "Imagine, our own music star. Krystal's going to put Zinnia on the map."

"Putnam Hall is south of here, isn't it?" I vaguely remembered the property as an old plantation that had gone through several hands and cash crops, the latest of which was catfish ponds, a labor-intensive harvest that often catches investors by surprise. As I recalled, the owners had changed the name to Gumbo Lane and developed the property as a hatchery, pond, restaurant, and inn. Somebody had taken a soaking when it went belly-up.

"It was a great restaurant. Too bad they couldn't make a go of it. Krystal says it's intimidating to go in the kitchen to make coffee because of all the professional equipment."

"I seriously doubt Krystal spends enough time in the kitchen to do her self-image any damage." I wasn't being mean. Krystal just wasn't the domestic type. She liked to have a staff of servants to do her bidding, including making coffee.

Cece held up a hand. "Hello, Mike, dahling. Cece Dee Falcon here. Are you busy?" She laughed. "How sweet. You sure know how to flatter a girl. Sarah Booth is here with me and I wanted to send her out to do some photos of your place. Along with her other talents, she's a fabulous photographer, and she's agreed to take this assignment. I'm thinking about a full-page society spread on the renovations you're going to make to the house and grounds. You know, a before-and-after kind of thing."

I picked up the camera on Cece's desk and checked to make sure it had film. The photographs were a brilliant idea.

"No, I promise Sarah Booth won't disturb Krystal. I'm sorry she isn't feeling well, and I appreciate your helping me out with this, Mike." She winked at me and nodded. "Lovely. She won't be there long, but I think a photo spread showing how much a part of the community Krystal is becoming will be the perfect way to keep her name in front of the public. Yes, ta-ta, dahling. Sarah Booth will be there in a shake." She replaced the phone. "I thought it would be better if you had a cover. Now you can just talk to him and see what he says about Nathaniel."

"Thanks, Cece."

"Is there anything I can do from here?"

"Check out a Mitchell Raybon for me. He was Kemper's partner in a resort development near Lafayette, Louisiana."

"Will do, dahling. Anything else?"

"Could you put it at the top of your list?"

"For you, Sarah Booth, I'll reorganize my schedule."

I drove through town, on the lookout for Tinkie's Caddy. I found it parked at Canine Curls, and I wondered if she was actually taking Sweetie for a consultation. Before she went too far, I'd have to put my foot down. Instead of stopping there, I went to Dahlia House to check my phone messages on the off chance that something helpful had come in. No such luck.

I made a quick call to the hospital to check on J.B. He was still in intensive care, and still in a coma. His mother was with him, and the nurse assured me that everything possible was being done in his behalf.

Before I left Dahlia House, I wrote a note and taped it on the door telling Tinkie where I'd gone. When she brought Sweetie home, she'd find the note. I asked her to call me with any new developments.

It was another beautiful afternoon, and I drove south. The sign from the catfish restaurant/inn was still standing, though the first tendrils of kudzu had crept up the posts, and the green leaves had begun to claim more of the sign. In another month, it would be a strangely shaped clump of vines, perhaps resembling a giant dog or a small camel.

The lane, too, bordered on either side by impressive live oaks that had once been hand nurtured by slaves, showed signs of neglect. I had mixed feelings about seeing the old homes turned into commercial ventures such as bed-and-breakfasts, restaurants, and gift shops. But commercialization was often the only solution a hard-pressed landowner could find.

Driving slowly, I noted the details of decay all around the plantation. Out in the field, a couple of mules grazed. I remembered that last Halloween the Jaycees had held their annual hayride here. Putnam Hall was perfect for the house of horrors they'd established, to the delight of young and old.

As I caught the first glimpse of the house through the trees, my heart gave a feeble protest. Vines covered a lot of the windows, and the house had a shuttered and closed look, as if it had accumulated a horde of guilty secrets and didn't want to share with anyone.

Once I shook off the creepies, I could see the loveliness of the Greek Revival architecture beneath the neglect. Maybe Krystal and Mike would bring it back to its former glory.

Gravel scrunched beneath my feet as I

walked to the steps and knocked on the front door. It must have been six inches thick. Though I used my fist until my knuckles were sore, I wasn't certain anyone could hear me.

After ten minutes, I grew tired of waiting. Pushing at the door, I found it was unlocked, so I opened it and stepped into the cool, dark foyer.

"Krystal! Mike!" The house was eerily silent.

"Krystal!" I stepped past the staircase and continued down a dark hallway. Opening another door, I stepped onto a screened porch that was tucked around a fireplace in an arc like a capital C. Glass-topped tables with white chairs were set up with tablecloths, china, crystal, and matching napkins. It looked as if a party had been scheduled and then canceled—several months before. The plates had a thin film of dirt.

"Mike!" I felt the finger of dread tickle my gut. "Krystal!" I called, this time with a lot less force. I wasn't really certain at this point that I wanted Krystal to actually come out and talk to me. The house had that eerie quality of a really haunted place. I was afraid that whoever walked out in Krystal's body wouldn't be the same person who'd formerly been Simpson Fielding. The sense that something was very wrong in the house grew stronger with each second I was there.

From the porch, I had two routes. To the left was a door that led to what was probably some type of game room or private dining area. To the right was the kitchen. I chose right, and found myself tiptoeing along the painted boards of the porch.

My skin prickled and goosed as I eased forward. Even though I kept checking over my shoulder and seeing nothing, I had the sense that I was being watched.

Cece had talked to Mike only an hour or so before. What could have happened to him?

At the door, I pushed easy, then hard. "Mike!" The door was jammed, or possibly locked from the inside. A lacy curtain was thick enough to effectively prevent peeking inside.

There was a screened door to the outside, so I exited and walked around to steps that led up to the back door and another entry to the kitchen.

This door, too, was locked. I made a circuit of the house and reentered the front door, stopping in the foyer. I could go upstairs from here, or left or right. Again I went right, hoping for an interior route to the kitchen.

The minute I left the foyer, I felt as if something cold had begun to breathe on my neck.

Whirling, I found only emptiness behind me. I turned back and almost cried out at the stuffed bobcat perched on a limb sticking directly out of the wall. The room was dim, but I picked out a buffalo head, several deer, an elk, a red fox, also on a limb, and a big, coiled rattler. This room was devoid of all furniture, except for the stuffed creature collection.

I kept a wary eye on the dead animals as I walked through the room. I didn't want any of them to spring to life without enough warning for me to get a good, running start.

"Krystal." I said her name. Well, whispered it. Where in the world could she be? Two cars, including the gold Lexus, were in the drive. Zinnia was a good ten miles away, and there wasn't even a U-Tote-Em closer than six miles.

I made my way across another room, this one for formal dining. The furniture was heavy, old, and beautiful, no doubt part of the original Putnam Hall. The built-in glass china cabinets even held some of the highly collectible red-leaded crystal. It was odd what people left behind when they moved from a place.

I came to a swinging door, and I knew that I had at last gained access to the kitchen. Easing it open a crack, I stopped. There was the strangest sound, an angry, droning noise that sounded like hornets.

It took a few seconds for the smell to register. Gas. Without thinking, I pushed the door open and rushed into the room.

Krystal's legs extended from one of the big, commercial ovens. She was sprawled across the door, most of her upper body inside the maw of the oven. The angry hissing came from the gas jets.

"Krystal!" Fear gave me the strength to pull her out of the oven and drag her, none too gently, onto the floor. I turned the gas off, but the room was saturated with it. Grabbing both of her feet, I dragged her across the kitchen and through the swinging door. I had built up quite a head of steam, so I just kept going until I was out on the front steps and in the pale yellow of a late spring afternoon.

In the sunlight, Krystal looked like she was dead. I knelt beside her, feeling her throat for a pulse that was so weak it took me a while to find it. Against the paleness of her skin, her red hair was garish and her lips a translucent blue.

"Don't die," I ordered her. "Damn you, Krystal, you cannot die." I didn't wait for her response. I ran inside and picked up the phone to call 911. There was no dial tone. I punched the phone on and off several times, to no avail.

The phone was off the hook somewhere in the house, or the line was dead.

Krystal was on her back on the narrow porch, her chest barely rising and falling. I had no way of knowing how seriously she was hurt. I knelt beside her, chafing her hands and rubbing her cheeks and doing everything I'd ever read in a book or seen in a movie to get her to come around. Nothing worked.

"Mike! Mike!" I yelled his name. He'd been at the house only an hour before I arrived, and he was expecting me. Where had he gone?

I needed cold water. The only thing to do was go back into the house and get it. It took every ounce of courage I had to walk back in the front door. The dead animal room was as scary as before, but I ran through it and the formal dining room. Back in the kitchen, I unlocked both outside doors, opened them and all the windows, and got a clean, wet dishcloth and filled it with ice.

When I got back to Krystal, I sat down beside her and pulled her into my lap. Her breathing was shallow and labored. I was terrified she was going to die.

"You are going to live, and you are going to tell me why you did this." I talked to her with righteous fury. I almost wept with relief when she shifted her face away from me.

"Stop," she said, gagging on the fresh air.

"You'd better breathe," I warned her. I listened for the sound of traffic on the road, but there was nothing except the low coo of a dove.

"In the house. Be careful." She groaned out the words.

"What?" I demanded. My sympathies were lagging way behind my fear and anger. "Where's Mike?"

"In the house. Kemper signed them. Avenger." She mumbled the words as her head moved back and forth.

"What? Signed what?"

"He planned all of it." She started crying. "All along." Her eyes opened wide. She searched my features as if she didn't know who I was. Then the flat, dead look gave way to fear. Before I could move, her hands rose and clutched the lapels of my blouse in a grip so tight I felt like she was choking me.

"Krystal." I tried to break her grip. She was looking beyond me into some unknown abyss where terror ruled supreme. "Krystal, it's me, Sarah Booth."

"You're a dead woman," she said, and violently pushed me away from her.

The force knocked her off my lap and down the steps. She rolled toward my car in bone-bruising jolts without making a sound.

"Krystal." I started after her, scrabbling on my hands and knees. It took me a few seconds to realize that something held me in place. I swung around to face Mike Rich. He was staring at Krystal as if she were some awful aberration.

"She tried to kill herself," I said, trying to shake free of the grip he had on my blouse. "We have to help her."

"Do we?" he asked.

Krystal had reached the gravel parking lot, and she crawled on her hands and knees, oblivious to the sharp stones. She fell onto her stomach, splitting her chin. Blood dripped onto the gray stones, while Mike held me like a rag doll.

"Let me go." I twisted with all of my strength.

"Be still," he said, his focus on Krystal as she clawed at the door of my car.

"Turn me loose!" I swung at him, catching him full in the cheek with my fist.

Without a second's thought, he brought his free hand around and slapped me. The pain was instant, a blinding wall of light. Blood spurted from my split lip and inside my mouth, where my teeth had cut my cheek.

"Run, Sarah Booth. Run!" Krystal had gained her feet, and she managed to open my car door and crawl in.

"Get back here." Mike tossed me to the steps with a knee-capping thrust. He was at the car in three strides, but Krystal had managed to slam the door and lock it. Her hands fumbled at the keys while her face registered mindless fear.

The pain in my crushed knees kept me facedown on the steps as I watched them. Mike pulled a knife from his pocket, and with a swift, clean gesture, he sliced open the convertible top of my car. His hand went in, clutching Krystal's throat. I saw her eyes widen as her fingers clutched at the keys.

At last the motor caught. Somehow she managed to slam the car into gear and began to drive up the steps. Mike, his hand still at her throat, ran beside the car.

She came straight at me, the car climbing the steps in an awkward bumping lurch. My legs were not mine to control. My brain screamed at them to move, but they lay flaccid and useless on the cement. It wasn't until the car was only feet away that I threw myself to the left, tripping Mike as he came up the steps, arm still clutching Krystal in the car.

He tumbled down beside me as Krystal managed to throw the Mercedes into reverse and back onto the driveway. Spinning gravel, she was gone.

Gasping for breath, I lay on the cement. Before I could attempt an escape, Mike began to stir. I knew I would surely die.

"Get up," he ordered as he climbed to his feet.

I tried rolling to my hands and knees, but he grabbed my arm and tugged me up to stand beside him. "You'll pay for this," he warned me.

I looked down the driveway in time to see my Mercedes turn right onto the highway. Krystal had escaped.

28

In my earlier examination of the dead animal room, I'd missed the one piece of furniture that I now found myself sitting on, a straight-backed chair. Mike had tied me to it with enough knots to keep a seaman busy for an Atlantic voyage. I clearly did not have that long to live.

"I'm going to ask you one more time. Where're the insurance papers on that horse?" The barrel of his gun was cold against my cheek.

"Was he insured?" I wasn't certain if Mike knew that Avenger was still alive. The best I could do was hedge my answers, hoping he would give me a clue to what he knew.

"Answer me now," he demanded. His clean-cut looks were still intact, but he'd dropped all pretense of good manners. He leaned so close that I could feel his breath on my neck. "You're going to tell me, one way or the other."

"I don't know," I said for the tenth time. "I

never saw any papers. I've been looking for them, too."

He spun away from me and paced the room. He checked his watch. "Simpson's been gone about ten minutes. It'll take her another ten to get into town. I don't have time for games."

I clearly saw the sand in the hourglass slipping away. And I did want to go home.

"The night Kemper died, he was trying to kill Avenger, wasn't he?" I asked, hoping to divert Mike.

"Kemper, that idiot, couldn't even kill a horse properly. He couldn't execute a simple plan without botching it. He was all big talk."

"Quit whining," I snapped, surprised that in the midst of my agony I would revert to the behavior of a Daddy's Girl. It was one of the first lessons Aunt LouLane had taught me: When outnumbered, assume authority and give an order. I'd seen it work in more than one ugly situation. Unfortunately, Mike didn't know the rules.

"You're just like Simpson, aren't you?" He glared at me. "She's got her country-girl act down to a T, but scratch the surface and there's Delta-bred bitch. She's not as smart as she thinks, though. She got careless and made it clear that she intended to dump me as soon as she made it to the big time. Right about then, she became more valuable dead than alive. All you Delta girls think the world can't exist without you. But you're wrong. Dead wrong."

My brain had finally started to work, and I added up the details of what he said. Krystal and Avenger shared one thing in common—to Mike, they were worth more dead than alive. "Insurance doesn't always pay on suicide," I pointed out to him.

"That's where you're wrong. You just have to know how to write the policy, and I'm an expert at it."

I understood it all, then. "You wrote the policy on Avenger, and you filed it in . . ." I had to think. To avoid suspicion that as owner of the horse he would benefit from Avenger's death, he couldn't use his own name, so it had to be—"Krystal's name."

"Aren't you the teacher's pet? Except you're wrong. I wrote the policy under my real name. Mitchell Raybon. It was easy to change my name when Simpson changed hers. It was one of those togetherness things that women are so fond of."

I recognized the name only because I'd just spoken it to Cece. "You and Kemper were going to split the insurance money. You'd done it before, with LaCoco, when you torched a resort."

"You got the right answers, but I'd say your timing's a little off."

"I managed to get here in time to save Krystal, and she *will* get help. If you're going to escape, you'd better get moving right now." I could only hope he'd be content to leave me tied in a chair.

"You don't understand. I owe Tony a lot of money. He's been the primary backer of Krystal's career. Tony isn't what I'd call a sentimental man. He wants to be paid, and he wants it yesterday. He would have killed Kemper if someone hadn't gotten there first. If I don't come up with his money, he's going to kill me." The cold barrel of the gun pressed into the back of my neck just at the point that would leave me a quadriplegic. "Where's the policy on that horse?" He grinned wickedly. "And where's the horse and the kid?"

My mouth went dry. He knew Kip and Avenger were alive. "You've already tried to kill the horse twice, once with insulin and then by setting the barn fire. Maybe you should give it up and get out of here before Coleman arrives."

He walked around to face me. "I would have had the money from Krystal if you hadn't come along just a few minutes too soon. My plan was that you'd find her dead, and find me 'knocked out' in the bedroom. You would have been my perfect alibi. Since you screwed that, you're going to help me find the insurance policy."

I had a few cards up my sleeve. "You can't risk trying to collect on Avenger, even if you finally manage to kill him. The sheriff has contacted every insurance company in the nation. They'll never pay off. Take your losses and get out of here while you can."

He checked his watch. "True confessions are over, sweetheart. Tell me where the kid took the horse. I promise I can make you talk. It'll be a lot less painful if you just tell me what I want to know."

He came toward me, and I knew he'd do whatever it took to make me talk. Just his eyes made me want to tell him everything.

"Why are you obsessed with an insurance policy you can't collect on?" I had to either make him leave or keep him talking. I was completely unprepared for the slap.

Tied in the chair, I couldn't even attempt to defend myself. I blinked the tears out of my eyes and felt the blood begin to trickle from my nose. He'd gotten the other side of my face this time.

"Where's the damn policy? It's the only physical evidence that ties me to Kemper in any way, shape, or form. That's the only thing that can cause me trouble."

"What about Krystal? She's not going to look kindly on a man who tried to gas her to death and then strangle her."

Mike laughed. "You don't know how desperate Krystal is for her singing career. Any hint of bad publicity could crash all of her dreams. Right now, the worst I'm looking at is a domestic argument with my wife, a temperamental wannabe star." He shrugged. "At worst, I may be charged with attempted murder." He crouched down so his face was level with mine. "You're the flaw in my plan, Sarah Booth. You've been snooping and poking around in everyone's business, and now it's caught up with you. I know you know where that policy is. Carol Beth said you were out at the farm going through all the files. She said you took the policy."

"I don't have the policy. I never saw it." It didn't matter that I was actually telling the truth. It wasn't what Mike wanted to hear.

The gun barrel swung until it was pointing at my face.

"You won't get away with this." I spoke the television words with as much grit as I could muster.

"Maybe, maybe not, but you're going to

start talking or I'm going to start shooting little bits of you off." I could see his finger slowly beginning to squeeze the trigger. The barrel eased to the right slightly until it was pointed at my ear. I'd never be able to wear matching earrings again.

"Okay, I know where the policy is." I had to come up with something. "The sheriff has it. He's had it all along. You're a dead man if you hurt me. When Coleman gets his hands on you, he'll make you suffer in ways you can't even imagine." Lying in the teeth of death is a peculiarly liberating act.

"I don't believe you." But he lowered the gun even as he spoke.

"It's over, Mike. There's no escaping. You'll only make it a lot worse on yourself if you hurt me." I sat up as tall as the ropes would allow. "I wouldn't want to spend the rest of my life in prison as the sheriff's boy, and Coleman will see to it that every man in there has a shot at you." Tony LaCoco wasn't the only person who could steal lines from the movies.

He swallowed but held the gun steady.

I saw a chink and pressed harder. "Maybe you can make a case that Kemper's death was an accident. You didn't intend for him to fall under the horse." I wasn't going to bring up the tiny details of the insulin and the nippers. "The barn fire could have been an accident, too. J.B. Washington is recovering from the head wound. There's nothing here you can't put behind you."

He looked at me hard. "I didn't kill Kemper."

I didn't believe him, but I wanted to keep him talking. "If you didn't kill Kemper, who did?"

"Lee killed him. She confessed."

"Right." I couldn't help the skepticism.

"She must have. When I left the barn, Kemper was still alive. He'd stolen the insulin from the veterinarian's truck. We'd originally planned to electrocute Avenger. You know, the old wires in the nostrils. The insulin was a better idea. Kemper said he could handle it, so I left. The difference between me and Kemper is that he wanted to watch the horse die. For some reason, he hated that animal. I just wanted the money. Kemper was very much alive when I left him. Either Lee killed him, or the kid did it."

There was a slight noise from the front door, enough that Mike drew back from me and started toward it. He moved sideways, glancing from me to the open door.

"What was that?" he demanded.

I didn't say anything. The wrong word could tease his trigger finger into action, and I was still the target.

The sound came again, like a piece of furniture sliding over the polished floors.

"Who's there?" he yelled.

There was no answer, just the sliding sound again. Closer now, moving toward us.

"Stay away or I'll kill her," he yelled, bringing the gun barrel level with my head. From psychology I remembered that suicidal women who chose guns most often shot themselves in the chest. Vanity. They wanted an open casket. I didn't want a casket at all.

The noise stopped, replaced by the crash of glass.

"Who's out there?" Mike roared. His gaze shifted from me to the door in such rapid motion that I was terrified he'd accidentally squeeze the trigger.

The only answer was another crash of glass. My heart sank at the thought that Krystal had turned around and come back to try to help me. She hadn't had time to get to town, get help, and drive back out here. I rued my hardheadedness in not getting a cell phone and leaving it in the car. I'd been pigheaded and antitechnology, but I would change—if I got a chance.

Mike had slipped along the wall, and when he stuck his head out to see who was in the house, a plate sailed toward him, narrowly missing his head. It hit the wall and shattered.

"Damn you!" he yelled out the door, but his focus swung back to me. "No more time for games." He cocked the gun.

A vase flew through the door and landed right at my feet, shattering into a thousand pieces like a small explosion.

The gunshot that followed was strangely muted, more of a pop. Mike staggered, a frown crossing his face. He lurched forward, and his finger squeezed the trigger. The bullet tore into my arm. It was like being punched, but without any pain. It took a few seconds for the pain to arrive.

Before I could utter a scream, a lithe figure leaped through the doorway. There was the sound of another shot and Mike crumpled over, grabbing his gut. His brow was furrowed as he looked up at Carol Beth. She pointed a gun at him with complete aplomb. Somehow I'd missed the DG lesson on firearms.

"You shot me," he said, amazement evident in his voice.

"No kidding." She pulled the trigger again.

Mike staggered back and fell. He didn't move again.

"Carol Beth." I was astounded. "How did you get here?"

"Don't ask stupid questions, Sarah Booth." She walked over and looked at the gunshot wound in my arm. Blood was running down the length of my shirt, dripping onto the floor in a puddle that was getting much too large. "Too bad. Looks like he nicked an artery."

"Untie me," I said.

"You don't really look like you're in a position to give orders." She smiled, and flicked her mahogany ponytail off her shoulder. She was wearing her riding breeches, a white sleeveless shirt, and black boots with a spit-shined polish. She was awfully well turned out for a cold-blooded killer.

I was suddenly sick to my stomach and dizzy.

"If you bought a cell phone, Sarah Booth, you wouldn't have to go running all over the county. First the newspaper, then the dog groomer, then back to Dahlia House, then here. That's a lot of wasted time for me, waiting to get you alone. But it turned out best this way. Mike will take the blame." She bent closer to my bleeding arm. "I think you're going to bleed out. Too bad, I was looking forward to shooting you again."

She was holding a gun as black and ugly as

the one Mike had been holding. Only I was no longer capable of witty repartee. I was bleeding to death.

"Why?" I had a full question to ask, but that was as much as I could say.

"Even in high school you were a nosy Nellie. I wouldn't exactly classify you as a top-rate investigator, but you know the old saying, even a blind hog finds an acorn every now and then. You were getting too close. Eventually you would have figured out that I killed Kemper."

"Why?" I asked again.

"The horses were mine. The dirty bastard was double-crossing me, and no one gets away with that."

Even though I was weak, I could clearly discern the anger in her voice. I'd never realized how much the word "mine" meant to Carol Beth. It was a fatal mistake on my part.

"Avenger won't ever be yours," I said. "He's beyond your reach." I tried to focus on my surroundings, to fight the sense of spiraling into darkness. "In the end, Kemper was smarter than you."

"Kemper was a fool. I walked in just as he was trying to give the horse a shot of insulin. He'd sold Avenger to me, and then he was going to double-cross me to collect a big insurance policy on the horse. When I realized what he was doing, I picked up a pair of nippers and struck him from behind. He fell on the syringe. Which was it that killed him, the blow to the head or the insulin? I didn't wait around to find out. I heard someone coming. There were some papers on his desk. I thought the registration for Avenger was with them, so I snatched them up. It wasn't until later that I discovered it was the insurance policy Mike's been turning the county upside down to find."

My head was beginning to sink forward. I had other questions, but they were lost in the whirl of images and thoughts that were driven by pain. I never realized bleeding to death would be painful. Cramps shot through my body. I knew it was organs and muscles suddenly aware that they were dying. They were putting up a terrible ruckus.

"Lee . . ." I couldn't remember what I was going to say.

"Lee won't suffer too much. I promise. But she'll stick to the story that she killed Kemper."

"Why should she?" I hung on to her voice.

"That's Lee for you, always so noble. She thinks Kip killed Kemper. It's ironic, isn't it? She's taking the rap for me and thinks she's saving her kid. I love it."

I tried to swallow and couldn't. I couldn't

even hold my head up, much less ask another question, and I still had plenty of them. A P.I. shouldn't have to die with unanswered questions.

"See you at the pearly gates, Sarah Booth. I guess I'd better call Coleman and tell him the tragic news, how Mike shot you and I had to kill him, but it was too late for you. Who would have thought a little flesh wound could bleed so much?"

Somewhere in the darkness that had descended on me, I heard the baying of a hound, and I thought of Sweetie Pie. Who would care for her? Tinkie, I supposed. And Jitty! What would become of her and Dahlia House? All of her pushing and prodding to get me to step into the future had failed. I'd never married, and I'd never produced an heir. There would be no future for Dahlia House. The Delaney womb was at last defeated.

I knew I was dying when I heard the scrabble of toenails. It sounded just like Sweetie when she was in a rush to get into the kitchen and steal a roast. I forced my head up and my eyes open, and knew that I was dead.

A big hound rushed into the room, but it wasn't Sweetie Pie. This hound was wearing a glittery faux-diamond collar, and she was a rich, solid red-brown, not my brindled red tic.

"What in the hell—" Carol Beth asked just before the hound sprang across the room and struck her squarely in the chest.

A man in a big black cowboy hat rushed into the room and kicked the gun out of Carol Beth's hand. A big black boot pinned her wrist to the floor. "Hold the weddin'!" he said as he applied enough pressure to make Carol Beth yelp.

There was a sharp, squealing bark, and a six-inch mop of sun-glitzed hair bounced across the room and joined the hound and the black-hatted stranger in pinning Carol Beth to the floor. The hound fell across her chest, while the smaller dog tried to suffocate her by jumping on her face.

"Hang on, Sarah Booth," Tinkie said as she ran into the room. "You're okay now. I'm here to take care of you."

Her words were action. She was at my side, untying the knots that held me in the chair.

"Good thing we have plenty of rope here," she said. "You need a tourniquet, Sarah Booth. You're bleeding like a stuck pig."

"Thanks, Tinkie," I mumbled.

"No thanks necessary. Coleman's on the way. You gave us all a bad scare." She punched numbers in her cell phone and placed an order for an ambulance. Pronto. "Thank goodness Mr. Friedman was at Dahlia House when I went to take Sweetie Pie home from her grooming appointment." She was talking a mile a minute. "Remember the phone call from the strange man at the Memphis airport? Well, that was Mr. Kinky. Anyway, I read your note, put two and two together, and we came straight out here."

"Ummmm." Once again Tinkie had proven she wasn't a real blonde. She had put the pieces of the puzzle together and brought the cavalry. I wanted to talk, but it was just too hard. I felt something wet and warm on my face and opened my eyes to see a row of sharp, pointed teeth belonging to a rather sweet hound face. The dog tongue slurped my cheek. "Who in the hell is that?" I asked.

"Why, you don't even recognize your own dog?" Tinkie's voice was so bright and perky it verged on hysteria. "I took Sweetie up to Canine Curls and got her a dye job. It's called Ravishing Redbone. Do you like it?"

Even as she talked, she'd applied a tourniquet and was easing me down on the floor.

From my vantage point, I looked up at the man in black. It was indeed Kinky Friedman. I recognized him from his book covers, his record albums, and my dreams.

"Nice decor," he said, looking around the

room at the dead animals. "I'd like the name of the interior exterminator."

Carol Beth began to wiggle on the floor, attempting to extricate herself from dogs and the Kinkster.

"Nice movement, wrong symphony," Kinky said, pressing down a little more firmly on her wrist.

"Carol Beth killed Kemper," I said. "She confessed. I can testify to it."

"If you live that long," Carol Beth snarled.

"Sarah Booth, dear, you just concentrate on not dying," Tinkie babbled. She was about to cry. "I think Sweetie looks a lot better as a redhead, but to be truthful, I'm really not up to rearing a hound. Chablis is enough for me."

Speaking of the furball, she trotted up to my side and gave my other cheek a few delicate little licks.

"Just hold on, Sarah Booth. Coleman's on the way."

I did hear the sound of a siren. It was the low, wailing sound of the blues.

29

When I came to in the emergency room, Coleman was standing over me and Doc Sawyer was bent over a tray by a sink.

"Welcome back, Sarah Booth," Coleman said, and there was such relief in his blue eyes that I had to smile.

I didn't feel a thing, except a strange and wonderful floating sensation. "The drugs here are pretty good. Are they legal? You know, I dreamed that Tinkie dyed Sweetie Pie mahogany, and Kinky Friedman showed up to help rescue me."

Coleman grinned. "Fancy that."

I tried to sit up, but he held me down with one big hand. "Doc has to stitch you up."

Doc turned around and came toward me, his daffodil hair shining like an angel's halo—then I noticed the curved needle that looked like something you could use to land a fifty-pound channel cat. It took about two seconds to figure that it was the needle intended to sew on me.

"I'm fine." I tried again to get up, but Coleman once more pressed me to the table. "Police brutality," I said.

Coleman leaned down. "You can report it to Barney later. Right now you're staying here until Doc gives you the high sign to leave."

Instead of fighting I closed my eyes. Surprisingly, though I felt the tugging of my flesh, I didn't feel pain. It was over in less than ten minutes.

"Lie still awhile," Doc ordered me. "Coleman can take you home in a bit."

"I'm ready now."

"She's still as stubborn as a mule," Doc said. "And about as pretty as Joe Frazier."

"What?"

"Your face," Doc said with a merry grin. "Nothing broken, but it sure as hell looks like you had a fight."

I put my fingers up to feel my face. I withdrew them instantly. That part of my anatomy hadn't been deadened.

"The swelling will go down," Coleman assured me. "Of course, your eyes are probably going to be black." He leaned down and brushed a kiss on my cheek. "Yeah, there's already some color coming in right there."

"I don't know," Doc said, coming to my other side to examine me. "Her eyes aren't going to be black, but she's going to have some beautiful scabs on her knees."

"You are sadists." I was ready to move along.

"Happy sadists," Coleman said. "Happy that you're alive. And you have some friends outside who want to talk to you. It's a small thing, but you owe your life to Tinkie. She figured it out to rush out to Putnam Hall." He motioned with an arm before I could respond. When the door swung open, I heard a babble of voices.

Lee was the first one up to the table. Her red hair was neatly braided down her back, and she grabbed my uninjured arm. "Thank you, Sarah Booth."

"You're out!" I wondered if the drugs were better than I thought.

"I can't thank you enough. If you hadn't kept on and on, relentless as a pit bull, Carol Beth would have gotten away."

"Pit bull" wasn't exactly a description I would want engraved on my tomb. The drugs had mellowed me, though, so I didn't argue.

Tinkie pressed forward and held Chablis out to give me a kiss on the face. "We were worried sick," she said. "I thought Sweetie was going to kill Carol Beth. She just collapsed on her and completely shut off her lungs. I never realized that it might be a benefit to have a fat, ugly dog."

She looked over her shoulder and signaled someone else into the room. The man in the black cowboy hat stepped over to my bedside. "The number one rule of private investigating is always wait for the cavalry. I can see you need a little work with the P.I. handbook."

Tinkie slipped up beside him. "It was Mr. Friedman who convinced Sweetie Pie to get off Carol Beth. Although he's a cat person, I think he's bonded with Sweetie."

I vaguely remembered a visit from Kinky, but I wasn't certain what part of my life was dream and what part reality. "Thanks," I said, holding out my good hand.

"My pleasure," he said. "which is what everyone around here says when they really want to say 'What the hell's going on?' "

Tinkie tapped his arm playfully. She was happily married, but had still retained her DG skills. "Sarah Booth will explain everything, as soon as she's well. I don't have any idea about the cat business, but Sarah Booth's great-aunt Elizabeth was a little . . . eccentric. She had eighty-seven cats."

"Fifty-eight," I corrected her.

"Anyway, Sarah Booth has only the one dog. But if she sent you a message about cats in trouble, then she'll explain it, all in good time," Tinkie assured him, looking up at him with open admiration. She'd been biting down on her bottom lip and it popped out of her mouth. It was a moment that not even the Kinkster could resist.

He leaned down and whispered, sotto voce, "If you're not busy later tonight, we might talk about a little trip. You could send my penis to Venus."

Tinkie blushed and giggled. "I didn't realize you were a poet, too."

I touched Tinkie's arm. "Thanks for coming to the rescue. Hey, I dreamed you dyed Sweetie Pie." My laugh sounded high and funny. "Can you imagine anything more ridiculous?"

Tinkie's eyebrows drew together and she bit her bottom lip again. "Sarah Booth, that wasn't a—"

"I think she's had enough excitement," Doc Sawyer said. "Maybe you folks should go on home."

Lee picked up my hand and squeezed it hard. "I have some really good news for you, Sarah Booth." Her green eyes sparkled. "We'll be at Dahlia House, waiting for you."

I didn't get a chance to ask any more questions. Doc shooed them out of the room, and I was left to drift in the zone between sleep and wakefulness where the subconscious is free to conjure and entertain. There were voices and whispers. Someone stroked my forehead, and I thought for a while I was a young girl again. The chill of an ice pack on my face reminded me of cold winter mornings in New York when I was trying to be an actress. The wind would come blasting down narrow streets and into my face with a force so different from the grand sweep of a Delta wind.

It was dark when I finally woke up. Doc was sitting on a chair, watching me.

"Sweet dreams? You were mumbling up a fog."

"Depends on what you consider sweet."

"You're going to be weak for a couple of days," he said. "Blood loss. And a bit sore. We'll get the stitches out in about ten days. I did what I could, but you'll have a scar."

"I suppose my ambitions to model strapless gowns are over," I said as I swung my feet over the side of the table. I was a little dizzy, but it passed immediately.

"You're a lucky young woman."

"Yes, I suppose I am."

"And you have a lot of people who care about you, including me." He came over and patted my uninjured shoulder. "I'll call

Coleman. He's right down the hall. He wanted to take you home personally."

I realized that I was no longer wearing my jeans. Instead, my bandaged knees hung out of a backless hospital gown, which was a putrid pastel and did little to enhance my figure. I didn't want to ask Doc what had happened to my pants or my bra, or who had removed them. Sometimes details are best left unknown. I slipped to my feet and found I could stand and walk. All in all, things were improving rapidly.

Coleman came into the room with a grin as big as Texas. "You're looking more like yourself. Ready to go home?"

"Dorothy couldn't be any readier." I took his arm and he led me out into the Delta night. The cicadas were singing loud and vibrant in a stand of pines behind the hospital. The air was clean, with the tang of newly turned dirt from the fields all around us. Spring in the Delta is one of the very best times of year, and I took in a deep breath, glad to be alive.

"How's Krystal?" I asked.

"Not exactly a grieving widow. And that friend of yours, J.B. Washington, came out of his coma. He was trying to tell you that Mike was going to kill Krystal. He overheard him on the phone telling LaCoco about the insurance policy."

"Is J.B. going to be okay?"

"Right as rain. No permanent damage done, and I think his mama's flung a net over Doc Sawyer. I caught them out in the parking lot, staring at some pine trees like it was a majestic bit of scenery."

"That's great." I leaned a little heavier on his arm than I really needed to. It was just nice to have an arm to lean on. "Another few minutes and Krystal would have been dead."

"She knows that. She said to tell you that she's dedicating her first album to you." Coleman chuckled. "The irony here is that she'll finance that album with Mike's insurance policy. They had mutual policies—a million dollars each."

"That's what I'd call an ironic twist."

Coleman's laugh was easy as he firmly grasped my elbow and helped me to his car. "By the way, that was terrific detective work. When Cece followed that lead you gave her and discovered that Mitchell Raybon was really Mike Rich, she called me right away. I was afraid you were in trouble, so I headed straight out to Putnam Hall. As it happened, Tinkie had stopped by Dahlia House to take

Sweetie home from Canine Curls, and she found Kinky on the front porch with your note. Lucky for you Tinkie likes to drive that Caddy about a hundred and five. Tinkie and Kinky got there in the nick of time."

"They sound like a bad vaudeville act." I stumbled on a rock, and Coleman's arm went around my waist. "Are you okay?"

"A little tired, but there are other things you need to know. Mike burned the barn."

"I know. Kip saw him. When LaCoco indicated he'd kill Avenger, Kip decided to ride him over to a friend's house and hide him out. She saw Mike in the loft and smelled the gasoline. By the time she got Bud, the barn was in flames, and they decided to stage a dramatic exit." He handed me into the car and then got behind the wheel.

"They did a good job. How is Nathaniel Walz tied up in this?"

"Through LaCoco. I call them the Buzzard Brigade. When Lee confessed to Kemper's death, LaCoco knew Swift Level was in jeopardy. If Lee went to prison, Swift Level would be sold. He called Walz in as the front man to buy the property. They planned on getting it for nothing and developing it as a fancy resort." Coleman eased the car out of the hospital parking lot and into the night.

"Where are Walz and LaCoco?"

"They left town. There was nothing I could actually charge them with, but I made it clear I'd keep looking until I found something. They decided to go where there was less scrutiny of their activities."

It was really over. I leaned back in the car seat. This was a much different ride from the last one I'd taken with Coleman. We were going a lot slower, and my hospital gown was a far cry from the beautiful red dress I'd worn.

"I had a mechanic pick up your car," Coleman said. "They'll repair the rag top for you."

"Thanks, Coleman. Thanks for everything."

He turned on the car radio, and I stared out the window at all of the familiar sights as Willie Nelson's "Stardust" played. The night sky over the dark fields was bejeweled with stars. The land was a part of me, deep inside, like blood and muscle. I'd traveled a good bit and seen beauty in many places, but none of it had the power to move me like the flat, fertile land of my home.

Coleman's voice in the easy comfort of the car was part of my homecoming. "Sarah Booth, you scared the life out of me. When I saw all of that blood . . ."

He reached across the seat and took my

good hand. Holding it lightly, he squeezed my fingers just as we turned down the drive to my home.

Dahlia House was ablaze with lights. Tinkie's Caddy was there, as well as Krystal's car, and several others I didn't recognize. My friends, and Mr. Friedman, were standing on the porch.

Cece, dazzling in a sheer red sundress with spaghetti straps and dancing sandals, held up her glass. "To Sarah Booth!" They all lifted their glasses and someone stuck a flute of champagne in my hand. We toasted as the front door burst open. A big brown dog rushed out to greet me.

"Sweetie Pie?" I almost choked. My gaze shot up to Tinkie.

"It's not permanent," she said in a rush. "It'll wash out in a few weeks."

Lee was laughing, and I thought how young she looked. It was as if she'd left the old woman back in the cell.

"I have a surprise for you." She took my elbow and began to steer me off the porch and around the house. "Sarah Booth, I know I made it hard on you. All of the evidence pointed to Kip as the murderer. The only thing I could do was protect her the only way I knew how. That was to take the blame. Bud was the only one who really believed she was innocent. He never would concede that she might have killed Kemper, even if she had every reason in the world to do it."

"We both owe Kip an apology," I pointed out.

"She owes you one, too. She lured Mr. Friedman here under false pretenses, but that will all be explained soon enough."

She was hustling me along pretty rapidly. Everyone else had fallen into line behind us. There was an expectant silence that both warned and excited me.

We rounded the corner, and I saw that someone had turned on the lights in the old barn that Aunt LouLane had used as a storage shed. Lee let out a whistle, and there was an answering whinny from inside the barn. A magnificent buckskin horse burst out of the barn and ran to the rickety fence.

"His name is Reveler. He's a four-year-old by Avenger, out of a terrific mare, Miss Scrap-Iron. He's yours, Sarah Booth."

"Mine?" I had to be dreaming. I'd always wanted a horse.

Reveler came to the fence and tossed his head, thick black mane flying. With a snort, he spun and galloped across the paddock, his muscles rippling.

"You can keep him here, or bring him back out to Swift Level. Whatever is easiest for you." Lee's hand was on my back, gently rubbing.

"Lee, I can't accept a horse. Especially not one of Avenger's babies." I knew how valuable Reveler's lineage made him.

"Sure you can. You can have the horse, or wait until spring and I'll pay you the money I owe you for handling my case. Now for the rest of the surprise." Lee whistled again. "Come on out!"

I looked to the open doorway and felt a small explosion in my heart. A teenage girl and a tall cowboy came walking out. Kip was leading a big gray stallion.

I stared at them. "I hope Coleman can figure out a charge to put you both in jail for scaring us all half to death." I hadn't realized how mad I was at Bud and Kip.

"Sarah Booth, dahling," Cece called out, "you don't have to act like an ass just because yours is hanging out the back of that devastatingly awful hospital gown."

Cece, as usual, was right on target. Kip, Bud—and Avenger—were safe. That was all that really mattered.

Kip climbed through the fence and wrapped an arm around me. "I'm sorry, Sarah Booth. I let you know as soon as I could."

"I'm glad you're okay." I kissed her cheek.

"I won't stay mad at you for thinking I was a murderer if you won't stay mad at me," she said, her eyes dancing. "Thank you, Sarah Booth. You saved my mother."

"Tinkie actually gets the credit. And Kinky," I said. "They saved me, too. Now, where have you been?" I asked her.

"At Roscoe's place. Over in Leflore County. Not very far away." She turned to Kinky. "I've explained everything to Mr. Friedman, and how you weren't involved in the story I made up." She bit her lip and leaned over to whisper. "He's been really nice about it."

"Should I ever decide to write a book about crazy Mississippians," Kinky said, "I've got more than enough material."

Cece tucked her arm through Kinky's. "We do crazy like nobody else can do it." She waved a hand. "One can't celebrate without food. Millie's on her way with some barbecue and cole slaw," she said. "Harold's bringing some ice. This is going to be the first barbecue of the season. I've got to call Garvel to bring a camera. Imagine the spread I can do—Kinky Friedman as celebrity guest; Lee absolved;

Carol Beth in jail; Bud, Kip, and Avenger risen from the dead. It's a perfect pre-Easter story."

It was the wee hours before I finally made it to my bedroom. Since I was only wearing a hospital gown, the process of undressing was much easier.

I crawled beneath the comforter. My arm throbbed, despite the tender ministrations of my good friend Jack. I had a bit of him beside the bed, which I intended to sip, while I unwound.

"So, you get yourself shot and still end up in bed alone."

I looked up to find Jitty in the rocker. She was heel-toeing it to beat the band. Any minute that old rocker was going to throw her on the floor.

"Getting shot isn't exactly in the romance guide as foreplay." I put my book aside, glad to be alive to argue with Jitty. She was even more stunning than usual in a glittering green unitard. "Where are you headed?"

"I'm lookin' to the future, Sarah Booth."

"I'm glad someone is. I'm pretty happy to be right here." For one night, at least, I had found the perfect balance between past and future.

"You might explain what that mystery writer is doing as your housepest."

I gave her a sharp look. She was beginning to talk like Kinky. "He's here because he helped save my life, and because I invited him to stay. Also because Kip e-mailed him that someone was murdering all the cats in Sunflower County, and that I needed his help on the case. She was playing on his sympathies as a cat lover."

"That girl has a way with computers," Jitty retorted. "Of course, she has a tendency to exaggerate, but maybe that's an indication of a career in writing. If she could devise an E-mail that gets men runnin' after you, she has real talent."

"Aren't you going to congratulate me for solving the case?" I decided to take the high road and ignore her jabs. "Lee is free. All charges have been dropped."

"Congratulations, Sarah Booth. Now that we've taken care of that, I want to point out that you're missin' an opportunity. There's a live one sleepin' in your guest room."

"Tonight, I'm sleeping alone, Jitty. The only thing I'm taking to bed with me is this book." I held up the Kinkster's mystery. I had one chapter to go before I finished.

"Your life is a series of wrong choices," Jitty admonished as she began to fade.

I picked up my book and slipped easily into the world of the Kinkster: his apartment, beneath the loft of the lesbian dance class, where he was deviled by a know-it-all cat and a cluster of friends as ornery and loyal as my own.

ABOUT THE AUTHOR

A native of Mississippi, Carolyn Haines lives in southern Alabama on a farm with her horses, dogs, and cats. She was recently honored with an Alabama State Council on the Arts literary fellowship for her writing. A former photojournalist, she is active in organizations that rescue animals and promote animal rights.